David Brin is one of a handful of novelists who is also a working scientist. He holds a doctorate in astrophysics, works as a consultant to NASA, and teaches graduate-level physics and writing. His novel, *Startide Rising*, won both the Hugo and Nebula Awards for Best Novel.

Also by David Brin

THE UPLIFT WAR
THE RIVER OF TIME
SUNDIVER
THE PRACTICE EFFECT
STARTIDE RISING
HEART OF THE COMET (with Gregory Benford)

and published by Bantam Books

THE POSTMAN

DAVID BRIN

BANTAM BOOKS
TORONTO • NEW YORK • LONDON • SYDNEY • AUCKLAND

THE POSTMAN
A BANTAM BOOK 0 553 17193 3

First publication in Great Britain

PRINTING HISTORY
Bantam edition published 1987
Bantam edition reprinted 1987
Bantam edition reprinted 1989

*Parts of this book appeared earlier in slightly different form: Part I as
'The Postman' in the November 1982 issue of Isaac Asimov's SF Magazine,
and Part II as 'Cyclops' in the March 1984 issue of Isaac Asimov's SF
Magazine.*

Bantam Books are published by Transworld Publishers
Ltd., 61–63 Uxbridge Road, Ealing, London W5 5SA, in
Australia by Transworld Publishers (Australia) Pty. Ltd.,
15–23 Helles Avenue, Moorebank, NSW 2170, and in New
Zealand by Transworld Publishers (N.Z.) Ltd., Cnr. Moselle
and Waipareira Avenues, Henderson, Auckland.

Printed and bound in Great Britain by
Cox & Wyman Ltd., Reading, Berks.

To Benjamin Franklin,
devious genius,
and to Lysistrata,
who tried

PRELUDE
THE THIRTEEN-YEAR THAW

Chill winds still blew. Dusty snow fell. But the ancient sea was in no hurry.

The Earth had spun six thousand times since flames blossomed and cities died. Now, after sixteen circuits of the Sun, plumes of soot no longer roiled from burning forests, turning day into night.

Six thousand sunsets had come and gone—gaudy, orange, glorious with suspended dust—ever since towering, superheated funnels had punched through to the stratosphere, filling it with tiny bits of suspended rock and soil. The darkened atmosphere passed less sunlight—and it cooled.

It hardly mattered anymore what had done it—a giant meteorite, a huge volcano, or a nuclear war. Temperatures and pressures swung out of balance, and great winds blew.

All over the north, a dingy snow fell, and in places even summer did not erase it.

Only the Ocean, timeless and obstinate, resistant to change, really mattered. Dark skies had come and gone. The winds pushed ocher, growling sunsets. In places, the ice grew, and the shallower seas began to sink.

But the Ocean's vote was all important, and it was not in yet.

The Earth turned. Men still struggled, here and there.

And the Ocean breathed a sigh of winter.

1

THE CASCADES

1

In dust and blood—with the sharp tang of terror stark in his nostrils—a man's mind will sometimes pull forth odd relevancies. After half a lifetime in the wilderness, most of it spent struggling to survive, it still struck Gordon as odd—how obscure memories would pop into his mind right in the middle of a life-or-death fight.

Panting under a bone-dry thicket—crawling desperately to find a refuge—he suddenly experienced a recollection as clear as the dusty stones under his nose. It was a memory of contrast—of a rainy afternoon in a warm, safe university library, long ago—of a lost world filled with books and music and carefree philosophical ramblings.

Words on a page.

Dragging his body through the tough, unyielding bracken, he could almost *see* the letters, black against white. And although he couldn't recall the obscure author's name, the *words* came back with utter clarity.

> "Short of Death itself, there is no such thing as a 'total' defeat. . . . There is never a disaster so devastating that a determined person cannot pull something out of the ashes—by risking all that he or she has left. . . .
>
> "Nothing in the world is more dangerous than a desperate man."

Gordon wished the long-dead writer were here right now, sharing his predicament. He wondered what pollyannish glow the fellow might find around *this* catastrophe.

Scratched and torn from his desperate escape into this dense thicket, he crawled as quietly as he could, stopping to lay still and squeeze his eyes shut whenever the floating dust seemed about to make him sneeze. It was slow, painful progress, and he wasn't even sure where he was headed.

Minutes ago he had been as comfortable and well-stocked as any solitary traveler could hope to be, these days. Now, Gordon was reduced to not much more than a ripped shirt, faded jeans, and camp moccasins—and the thorns were cutting them all to bits.

A tapestry of fiery pain followed each new scratch down his arms and back. But in this awful, bone-dry jungle, there was nothing to do but crawl onward and pray his twisting path did not deliver him back to his enemies—to those who had effectively killed him already.

Finally, when he had come to think the hellish growth would never end, an opening appeared ahead. A narrow cleft split the brush and overlooked a slope of tumbled rock. Gordon pulled free of the thorns at last, rolled over onto his back, and stared up at the hazy sky, grateful simply for air that wasn't foul with the heat of dry decay.

Welcome to Oregon, he thought bitterly. *And I thought* Idaho *was bad.*

He lifted one arm and tried to wipe the dust out of his eyes.

Or is it that I'm simply getting too old *for this sort of thing?* After all, he was over thirty now, beyond the typical life expectancy of a postholocaust traveler.

Oh Lord, I wish I was home again.

He wasn't thinking of Minneapolis. The prairie today was a hell he had struggled for more than a decade to escape. No, *home* meant more to Gordon than any particular place.

A hamburger, a hot bath, music, Merthiolate . . .

. . . a cool beer . . .

As his labored breathing settled, other sounds came to the fore—the all too clear noise of happy looting. It rose from a hundred feet or so down the mountainside. *Laughter* as the delighted robbers tore through Gordon's gear.

. . . a few friendly neighborhood cops . . . Gordon added, still cataloging the amenities of a world long gone.

The bandits had caught him off guard as he sipped elderberry tea by a late afternoon campfire. From that first instant, as they charged up the trail straight at him, it had been clear that the hot-faced men would as soon kill Gordon as look at him.

He hadn't waited for them to decide which to do. Throwing scalding tea into the face of the first bearded robber, he dove right into the nearby brambles. Two gunshots had followed him, and that was all. Probably, his carcass wasn't worth as much to the thieves as an irreplaceable bullet. They already had all his goods, anyway.

Or so they probably think.

Gordon's smile was bitterly thin as he sat up carefully, backing along his rocky perch until he felt sure he was out of view of the slope below. He plucked his travel belt free of twigs and drew the half-full canteen for a long, desperately needed drink.

Bless you, paranoia, he thought. Not once since the Doomwar had he ever allowed the belt more than three feet from his side. It was the only thing he had been able to grab before diving into the brambles.

The dark gray metal of his .38 revolver shone even under a fine layer of dust, as he drew it from its holster. Gordon blew on the snub-nosed weapon and carefully checked its action. Soft clicking testified in understated eloquence to the craftsmanship and deadly precision of another age. Even in killing, the old world had made well.

Especially in the art of killing, Gordon reminded himself. Raucous laughter carried up from the slope below.

Normally he traveled with only four rounds loaded. Now he pulled two more precious cartridges from a belt pouch and filled the empty chambers under and behind the hammer. "Firearm safety" was no longer a major consideration, especially since he expected to die this evening anyway.

3

Sixteen years chasing a dream, Gordon thought. *First that long, futile struggle against the collapse . . . then scratching to survive through the Three-Year Winter . . . and finally, more than a decade of moving from place to place, dodging pestilence and hunger, fighting goddamned Holnists and packs of wild dogs . . . half a lifetime spent as a wandering, dark age minstrel, play-acting for meals in order to make it one day more while I searched for . . .*

. . . for someplace . . .

Gordon shook his head. He knew his own dreams quite well. They were a fool's fantasies, and had no place in the present world.

. . . for someplace where someone was taking responsibility . . .

He pushed the thought aside. Whatever he had been looking for, his long seeking seemed to have ended here, in the dry, cold mountains of what had once been eastern Oregon.

From the sounds below he could tell that the bandits were packing up, getting ready to move off with their plunder. Thick patches of desiccated creeper blocked Gordon's view downslope through the ponderosa pines, but soon a burly man in a faded plaid hunting coat appeared from the direction of his campsite, moving northeast on a trail leading down the mountainside.

The man's clothing confirmed what Gordon remembered from those blurred seconds of the attack. At least his assailants weren't wearing army surplus camouflage . . . the trademark of *Holn survivalists.*

They must be just regular, run of the mill, may-they-please-roast-in-Hell bandits.

If so, then there was a sliver of a chance the plan glimmering in his mind just might accomplish something.

Perhaps.

The first bandit had Gordon's all-weather jacket tied around his waist. In his right arm he cradled the pump shotgun Gordon had carried all the way from Montana. "Come on!" the bearded robber yelled back up the trail. "That's

4

enough gloating. Get that stuff together and move it!"

The leader, Gordon decided.

Another man, smaller and more shabby, hurried into view carrying a cloth sack and a battered rifle. "Boy, what a haul! We oughta celebrate. When we bring this stuff back, can we have all the 'shine we want, Jas?" The small robber hopped like an excited bird. "Boy, Sheba an' the girls'll *bust* when they hear about that lil' rabbit we drove off into the briar patch. I never seen anything run so fast!" He giggled.

Gordon frowned at the insult added to injury. It was the same nearly everywhere he had been—a postholocaust callousness to which he'd never grown accustomed, even after all this time. With only one eye peering through the scrub grass rimming his cleft, he took a deep breath and shouted.

"I wouldn't count on getting drunk yet, Brer Bear!" Adrenaline turned his voice more shrill than he wanted, but that couldn't be helped.

The big man dropped awkwardly to the ground, scrambling for cover behind a nearby tree. The skinny robber, though, gawked up at the hillside.

"What . . . ? Who's up there?"

Gordon felt a small wash of relief. Their behavior confirmed that the sons of bitches weren't true survivalists. Certainly not *Holnists*. If they had been, he'd probably be dead by now.

The other bandits—Gordon counted a total of five—hurried down the trail carrying their booty. "Get down!" their leader commanded from his hiding place. Scrawny seemed to wake up to his exposed position and hurried to join his comrades behind the undergrowth.

All except one robber—a sallow-faced man with salt-and-pepper sideburns, wearing an alpine hat. Instead of hiding he moved forward a little, chewing a pine needle and casually eyeing the thicket.

"Why bother?" he asked calmly. "That poor fellow had on barely more than his skivvies, when we pounced him. We've got his shotgun. Let's find out what he wants."

Gordon kept his head down. But he couldn't help noticing the man's lazy, affected drawl. He was the only one who was clean shaven, and even from here Gordon could tell that his clothes were cleaner, more meticulously tended.

At a muttered growl from his leader, the casual bandit shrugged and sauntered over behind a forked pine. Barely hidden, he called up the hillside. "Are you there, Mister Rabbit? If so, I am so sorry you didn't stay to invite us to tea. Still, aware how Jas and Little Wally tend to treat visitors, I suppose I cannot blame you for cutting out."

Gordon couldn't believe he was trading banter with this twit. "That's what I figured at the time," he called. "Thanks for understanding my lack of hospitality. By the way, with whom am I speaking?"

The tall fellow smiled broadly. "With *whom* . . . ? Ah, a grammarian! What joy. It's been so long since I've heard an educated voice." He doffed the alpine hat and bowed. "I am Roger Everett Septien, at one time a member of the Pacific Stock Exchange, and presently your robber. As for my colleagues . . ."

The bushes rustled. Septien listened, and finally shrugged. "Alas," he called to Gordon. "Normally I'd be tempted by a chance for some real conversation; I'm sure you're as starved for it as I. Unfortunately, the leader of our small brotherhood of cutthroats insists that I find out what you want and get this over with.

"So speak your piece, Mister Rabbit. We are all ears."

Gordon shook his head. The fellow obviously classed himself a wit, but his humor was fourth-rate, even by postwar standards. "I notice you fellows aren't carrying *all* of my gear. You wouldn't by some chance have decided to take only what you needed, and left enough for me to survive, would you?"

From the scrub below came a high giggle, then more hoarse chuckles as others joined in. Roger Septien looked left and right and lifted his hands. His exaggerated sigh seemed to say that *he*, at least, appreciated the irony in Gordon's question.

"Alas," he repeated. "I recall mentioning that possibility to my compatriots. For instance, our women might find some use for your aluminum tent poles and pack frame, but I suggested we leave the nylon bag and tent, which are useless to us.

"Um, in a sense we have done this. However, I don't think that Wally's . . . er, *alterations* will meet your approval."

Again, that shrieking giggle rose from the bushes. Gordon sagged a little.

"What about my boots? You all seem well enough shod. Do they fit any of you, anyway? Could you leave them? And my jacket and gloves?"

Septien coughed. "Ah, yes. They're the main items, aren't they? Other than the shotgun, of course, which is nonnegotiable."

Gordon spat. *Of course, idiot. Only a blowhard states the obvious.*

Again, the voice of the bandit leader could be heard, muffled by the foliage. Again there were giggles. With a pained expression, the ex-stockbroker sighed. "My leader asks what you offer in *trade*. Of course I know you have nothing. Still, I must inquire."

As a matter of fact, Gordon had a few things they might want—his belt compass for instance, and a Swiss army knife.

But what were his chances of arranging an exchange and getting out alive? It didn't take telepathy to tell that these bastards were only toying with their victim.

A fuming anger filled him, especially over Septien's false show of compassion. He had witnessed this combination of cruel contempt and civilized manners in other once-educated people, over the years since the Collapse. By his lights, people like this were far more contemptible than those who had simply succumbed to the barbaric times.

"Look," he shouted. "You don't need those damn boots! You've no real need for my jacket or my toothbrush or my notebook, either. This area's clean, so what do you need my Geiger counter for?

7

"I'm not stupid enough to think I can have my shotgun back, but without some of those other things I'll die, damn you!"

The echo of his curse seemed to pour down the long slope of the mountainside, leaving a hanging silence in its wake. Then the bushes rustled and the big bandit leader stood up. Spitting contemptuously upslope, he snapped his fingers at the others. "Now I know he's got no gun," he told them. His thick eyebrows narrowed and he gestured in Gordon's general direction.

"Run away, little rabbit. Run, or we'll skin you and have you for supper!" He hefted Gordon's shotgun, turned his back, and sauntered casually down the trail. The others fell in behind, laughing.

Roger Septien gave the mountainside an ironic shrug and a smile, then gathered up his share of the loot and followed his compatriots. They disappeared around a bend in the narrow forest path, but for minutes afterward Gordon heard the softly diminishing sound of someone happily whistling.

You imbecile! Weak as his chances had been, he had spoiled them completely by appealing to reason and charity. In an era of tooth and claw, nobody ever did that except out of impotence. The bandits' uncertainty had evaporated just as soon as he foolishly asked for fair play.

Of course he could have fired his .38, wasting a precious bullet to *prove* he wasn't completely harmless. That would have forced them to take him seriously again. . . .

Then why didn't I do that? Was I too afraid?

Probably, he admitted. *I'll very likely die of exposure tonight, but that's still hours away, far enough to remain only an abstract threat, less frightening and immediate than five ruthless men with guns.*

He punched his left palm with his fist.

Oh stuff it, Gordon. You can psychoanalyze yourself this evening, while you're freezing to death. What it all comes down to, though, is that you are one prize fool, and this is probably the end.

8

He got up stiffly and began edging cautiously down the slope. Although he wasn't quite ready to admit it yet, Gordon felt a growing certainty that there could only be one solution, only one even faintly possible way out of this disaster.

As soon as he was free of the thicket, Gordon limped to the trickling stream to wash his face and the worst of his cuts. He wiped sweat-soaked strands of brown hair out of his eyes. His scrapes hurt like hell, but none of them looked bad enough to persuade him to use the thin tube of the precious iodine in his belt pouch.

He refilled his canteen and thought.

Besides his pistol and half-shredded clothes, a pocket knife, and compass, his pouch held a miniature fishing kit that might prove useful, if he ever made it over the mountains to a decent watershed.

And of course ten spare rounds for his .38, small, blessed relics of industrial civilization.

Back at the beginning, during the riots and the great starvation, it had seemed that the one thing in inexhaustible supply was ammunition. If only turn-of-the-century America had stockpiled and distributed food half so well as its citizens had cached mountains of bullets . . .

Rough stones jabbed his throbbing left foot as Gordon gingerly hurried toward his former campsite. Clearly these half-shredded moccasins would get him nowhere. His torn clothes would be about as effective against freezing mountain autumn nights as his pleas had been against the bandits' hard hearts.

The small clearing where he had made camp only an hour or so ago was deserted now, but his worst fears were surpassed by the havoc he found there.

His tent had been converted into a pile of nylon shreds, his sleeping bag a small blizzard of scattered goose down. All Gordon found intact was the slim longbow he had been carving from a cut sapling, and a line of experimental venison-gut strings.

Probably thought it was a walking stick. Sixteen years after the last factory had burned, Gordon's robbers had completely overlooked the potential value of the bow and strings, when the ammo finally ran out.

He used the bow to poke through the wreckage, looking for anything else to salvage.

I can't believe it. They took my journal! That prig Septien probably looks forward to poring over it during the snowtime, chuckling over my adventures and my naivete while my bones are being picked clean by cougars and buzzards.

Of course the food was all gone: the jerky; the bag of split grains that a small Idaho village had let him have in exchange for a few songs and stories; the tiny hoard of rock candy he had found in the mechanical bowels of a looted vending machine.

It's just as well about the candy, Gordon thought as he plucked his trampled, ruined toothbrush out of the dust.

Now why the hell did they have to do that?

Late in the Three-Year Winter—while the remnants of his militia platoon still struggled to guard the soy silos of Wayne, Minnesota, for a government nobody had heard from in months—*five* of his comrades had died of raging oral infections. They were awful, unglorious deaths, and no one had even been sure if one of the war bugs was responsible, or the cold and hunger and near total lack of modern hygiene. All Gordon knew was that the specter of his teeth rotting in his head was his own personal phobia.

Bastards, he thought as he flung the little brush aside.

He kicked the rubbish one last time. There was nothing here to change his mind.

You're procrastinating. Go. Do it.

Gordon started off a little stiffly. But soon he was moving downtrail as quickly and silently as he could, making time through the bone-dry forest.

The burly outlaw leader had promised to eat him if they met again. Cannibalism had been common in the early days, and these mountain men might have acquired a taste for the "long pork." Still, he had to persuade them that a man with nothing to lose must be reckoned with.

10

Within half a mile or so, their tracks were familiar to him: two traces with the soft outlines of deer hide and three with prewar Vibram soles. They were moving at a leisurely pace, and it would be no trouble simply to catch up with his enemies.

That was not his plan, however. Gordon tried to remember this morning's climb up this same trail.

The path drops in altitude as it winds north, along the east face of the mountain, before switching back south and east into the desert valley below.

But what if I were to cut above the main trail, and traverse the slope higher up? I might be able to come down on them while it's still light . . . while they're still gloating and expecting nothing.

If the shortcut is there. . . .

The trail wove gradually downhill toward the northeast, in the direction of the lengthening shadows, toward the deserts of eastern Oregon and Idaho. Gordon must have passed below the robbers' sentinels yesterday or this morning, and they had taken their time following him until he was settled into camp. Their lair had to be somewhere off this same trail.

Even limping, Gordon was able to move silently and quickly, the only advantage of camp moccasins over boots. Soon he heard faint sounds below and ahead.

The raiding party. The men were laughing, joking together. It was painful to hear.

It wasn't so much that they were laughing over *him.* Callous cruelty was a part of life today, and if Gordon couldn't reconcile himself to it, he at least recognized *he* was the Twentieth-Century oddball in today's savage world.

But the sounds reminded him of other laughter, the rough jokes of men who shared danger together.

Drew Simms—freckle-faced pre-med with a floppy grin and deadly skill at chess or poker—the Holnists got him when they overran Wayne and burned the silos. . . .

Tiny Kielre—saved my life twice, and all he wanted when he was on his deathbed, the War Mumps tearing him apart, was for me to read him stories. . . .

11

Then there had been Lieutenant Van—their half-Vietnamese platoon leader. Gordon had never known until it was too late that the Lieutenant was cutting his own rations and giving them to his men. He asked, at the end, to be buried in an American flag.

Gordon had been alone for so long. He missed the company of such men almost as much as the friendship of women.

Watching the brush on his left, he came to an opening that seemed to promise a sloping track—a shortcut perhaps—to the north across the mountain face. The rust-dry scrub crackled as he left the path and broke his own trail. Gordon thought he remembered the perfect site for a bush-whack, a switchback that passed under a high, stony horse-shoe. A sniper might find a place a little way above that rocky outcrop, within point-blank range of anyone hiking along the hairpin.

If I can just get there first . . .

He might pin them down by surprise and force them to negotiate. That was the advantage in being the one with nothing to lose. Any sane bandit would prefer to live and rob another day. He had to believe they would part with boots, a jacket, and some food, against the risk of losing one or two of their band.

Gordon hoped he would not have to kill anybody.

Oh grow up, please! His worst enemy, over the next few hours, could be his archaic scruples. *Just this once, be ruthless.*

The voices on the trail faded as he cut across the slope of the mountain. Several times he had to detour around jagged gullies or scabrous patches of ugly bramble. Gordon concentrated on finding the quickest way toward his rocky ambuscade.

Have I gone far enough?

Grimly, he kept on. According to imperfect memory, the switchback he had in mind came only after a long sweep northward along the east face of the mountain.

A narrow animal track let him hurry through the pine

thickets, pausing frequently to check his compass. He faced a quandary. To stand a chance of catching his adversaries, he had to stay above them. Yet if he kept too high, he might go right past his target without knowing it.

And twilight was not long away.

A flock of wild turkeys scattered as he jogged into a small clearing. Of course the thinned human population probably had something to do with the return of wildlife, but it was also one more sign that he had come into better-watered country than the arid lands of Idaho. His bow might someday prove useful, should he live long enough to learn to use it.

He angled downslope, beginning to get worried. Surely by now the main trail was quite a bit below him, if it hadn't already switched back a few times. It was possible he had already gone too far north.

At last Gordon realized the game path was turning inexorably *westward*. It appeared to be rising again as well, toward what looked like another gap in the mountains, shrouded in late afternoon mist.

He stopped a moment to catch his breath and his bearings. Perhaps this was yet another pass through the cold, semi-arid Cascade Range, leading eventually into the Willamette River Valley and thence the Pacific Ocean. His map was gone but he knew that at most a couple weeks' walk in that direction ought to bring him to water, shelter, fishing streams, game to hunt, and maybe . . .

And maybe some people trying to put something right in the world again. The sunlight through that high fringe of clouds was like a luminous halo, akin to the dimly remembered skyglow of city lights, a promise that had led him ever onward from the midwest, searching. The dream—hopeless as he knew it was—simply would not go away.

Gordon shook his head. For certain there would be snow in that range, and cougars, and starvation. There could be no turning away from his plan. Not if he wanted to live.

He tried hard to cut downslope, but the narrow game

13

paths kept forcing him north and westward. The switchback *had* to be behind him, by now. But the thick, dry undergrowth diverted him farther into the new pass.

In his frustration Gordon almost missed the sound. But then he stopped suddenly, listening.

Were those voices?

A steep ravine opened up the forest just ahead. He hurried toward it until he could see the outlines of this mountain and others in the chain, wrapped in a thick haze, amber high on their westward flanks and darkening purple where the sun no longer shone.

The sounds seemed to be coming from below, to the east. And yes, they *were* voices. Gordon searched and made out the snakelike line of a trail on the mountain's flank. Far off, he caught a brief flash of color moving slowly upward through the woods.

The bandits! But why were they moving uphill again? They couldn't be, unless . . .

Unless Gordon was already far north of the trail he had taken the day before. He must have missed the ambush site altogether and come out above a side path. The bandits were climbing a fork he had failed to notice yesterday, one leading up into *this* pass rather than the one he had been caught in.

This must be the way to their base!

Gordon looked up the mountain. Yes, he could see how a small hollow could fit over to the west, on a shoulder near the lesser-used pass. It would be defensible and very hard to discover by chance.

Gordon smiled grimly and turned west as well. The ambush was a lost opportunity, but if he hurried he could beat the bandits home, perhaps get a few minutes to steal what he needed—food, clothes, something to carry them in.

And if the hideout wasn't deserted?

Well, maybe he could take their women hostage and try to cut a deal.

Yeah, that's lots better. Like holding a ticking bomb beats jogging with nitroglycerin.

14

Frankly, he hated all of his alternatives.

He started to run, ducking under branches and dodging withered stumps as he charged along the narrow game path. Soon Gordon felt a strange exuberance. He was committed, and none of his typical self-doubt would get in the way now. Battle adrenaline nearly made him high as his stride opened and small shrubs swept by in a blur. He stretched to leap over a toppled, decayed tree trunk, cleared it easily. . . .

Landing sent sharp pain lancing up his left leg as something stabbed him through the flimsy moccasins. He sprawled, face first, into the gravel of a dry stream bed.

Gordon rolled over clutching his injury. Through wet, pain-diffracted eyes, he saw that he had tripped over a thick strand of looped, rusted steel cable, no doubt left over from some ancient, prewar logging operation. Again, while his leg throbbed agonizingly, his surface thoughts were absurdly rational.

Eighteen years since my last tetanus shot. Lovely.

But no, it hadn't cut him, only tripped him. That was bad enough, though. He held onto his thigh and clamped his mouth shut, trying to ride out a savage cramp.

At last the tremors subsided and he dragged himself over to the toppled tree, gingerly hoisting himself into sitting position. He hissed through clenched teeth as the waves of agony slowly faded.

Meanwhile he could hear the bandit party passing not far below, taking away the head start that had been his only advantage.

So much for all those great plans to beat them to their hideout. He listened until their voices faded up the trail.

At last Gordon used his bow as a staff and tried standing up. Letting weight settle slowly on his left leg, he found it would support him, though it still quivered tenderly.

Ten years ago I could've taken a fall like that and been up and running without another thought. Face it. You're obsolete, Gordon. Worn out. These days, thirty-four and alone is the same as being ready to die.

There would be no ambush now. He couldn't even chase the bandits, not all the way up to that notch in the mountain. It would be useless to try to track them on a moonless night.

He took a few steps as the throbbing slowly subsided. Soon he was able to walk without leaning too hard on his makeshift staff.

Fine, but where to? Perhaps he should spend the remaining daylight looking for a cave, a pile of pine needles, anything to give him a chance to live through the night.

In the growing chill Gordon watched shadows climb higher above the desert valley floor, merging and darkening the flanks of the nearby mountains. The reddening sun probed through chinks in the range of snowy peaks to his left.

He was facing north, unable quite yet to summon the energy to move, when his eye was caught by a sudden flash of light, a sharp glinting against the rolling forest green on the opposite flank of this narrow pass. Still favoring his tender foot, Gordon took a few steps forward. His brow furrowed.

The forest fires that had seared so much of the dry Cascades had spared the thick forests on that part of the mountainside. And yes, something across the way was catching the sunlight like a mirror. From the folds in the hillsides, he guessed that the reflection could only be seen from this very spot, and only in the late afternoon.

So he had guessed wrong. The bandits' roost wasn't in that hollow higher up in the pass to the west after all, but much closer. Only a stroke of luck had given it away.

So you're giving me clues, now? Now? he accused the world. *I don't have enough troubles as it is, without being offered straws to grasp at?*

Hope was an addiction. It had driven him westward for half his life. Moments after all but giving up, Gordon found himself piecing together the outlines of a new plan.

Could he try to rob a cabin filled with armed men? He pictured himself, kicking in the door to their wide-eyed astonishment, holding them all at bay with the pistol in one hand, while he tied them all up with the other!

Why not? They might be drunk, and he was desperate enough to try. Could he take hostages? Hell, even a milk goat would be more valuable to them than his boots! A captured woman should bring more in trade than that.

The idea was a sour taste in his mouth. It depended on the bandit leader behaving rationally for one thing. Would the bastard recognize the secret power of a desperate man, and let him go with what he needed?

Gordon had seen pride make men do stupid things. More often than not. *If it comes down to a chase, I'm cooked. I couldn't outrun a badger, right now.*

He eyed the reflection across the pass, and decided he had very little choice, after all.

It was slow going from the first. His leg still ached and he had to stop every hundred feet or so to scan merging and crisscrossing trails for his enemy's spoor. He also found he was checking shadows as potential ambushes, and made himself quit. These men weren't Holnists. Indeed, they seemed lazy. Gordon guessed that their pickets would be close to home, if they maintained any at all.

As the light faded, the footprints were lost in the gravelly soil. But Gordon knew where he was going. The glinting reflection could no longer be seen, but the ravine on the opposite shoulder of the mountain saddle was a dark, tree-lined V silhouette. He chose a likely path and hurried ahead.

It was growing dark quickly. A stiff, cold breeze blew damply off the misty heights. Gordon limped up a dry stream bed and leaned on his staff as he climbed a set of switchbacks. Then, when he guessed he was within a quarter mile of his goal, the path suddenly failed.

He kept his forearms up to protect his face while he tried to move quietly through the dry undergrowth. He fought down a lingering, threatening urge to sneeze in the floating dust.

17

Chilly night fog was flowing down the mountainsides. Soon the ground would shimmer with faintly luminous ground frost. Still, Gordon shivered less from the cold than from nerves. He knew he was getting close. One way or another, he was about to have an encounter with death.

In his youth he had read about heroes, historical and fictional. Nearly all of them, when the time came for action, seemed able to push aside their personal burdens of worry, confusion, angst, for at least the time when action impended. But Gordon's mind didn't seem to work that way. Instead it just filled with more and more complexities, a turmoil of regrets.

It wasn't that he had doubts about what had to be done. By every standard he lived by, this was the right thing to do. Survival demanded it. And anyway, if he was to be a dead man, at least he could make the mountains a little safer for the next wayfarer by taking a few of the bastards with him.

Still, the nearer he drew to the confrontation, the more he realized that he hadn't wanted his dharma to come to this. He did not really wish to kill any of these men.

It had been this way even as, with Lieutenant Van's little platoon, he had struggled to help maintain a peace—and a fragment of a nation—that had already died.

And afterward, he had chosen the life of a minstrel, a traveling actor and laborer—partly in order to keep moving, searching for a light, somewhere.

A few of the surviving postwar communities were known to accept outsiders as new members. Women were always welcome, of course, but some accepted new men. And yet there was so often a catch. A new male frequently had to duel-kill for the right to sit at a communal table, or bring back a scalp from a feuding clan to prove his prowess. There were few real Holnists anymore, in the plains and Rockies. But many survivor outposts he had encountered nevertheless demanded rituals of which Gordon wanted no part.

And now here he was, counting bullets, a part of him

18

coldly noting that, if he made them count, there were probably enough for all the bandits.

Another sparse berry thicket blocked his path. What the patch lacked in fruit it made up for in thorns. This time Gordon moved along its edge, carefully picking his way in the gathering gloom. His sense of direction—honed after fourteen years of wandering—was automatic. He moved silently, cautious without rising above the maelstrom of his own thoughts.

All considered, it was amazing a man like him had lived this long. Everyone he had known or admired as a boy had died, along with all the hopes any of them had had. The soft world made for dreamers like himself broke apart when he was only eighteen. Long since then he'd come to realize that his persistent optimism had to be a form of hysterical insanity.

Hell, everybody's crazy, these days.

Yes, he answered himself. *But paranoia and depression are adaptive, now. Idealism is only stupid.*

Gordon paused at a small blob of color. He peered into the bramble and saw, about a yard inside, a solitary clump of blueberries, apparently overlooked by the local black bear. The mist heightened Gordon's sense of smell and he could pick their faint autumn mustiness out of the air.

Ignoring the stabbing thorns, he reached in and drew back a sticky handful. The tart sweetness was a wild thing in his mouth, like Life.

Twilight was almost gone, and a few wan stars winked through a darkling overcast. The cold breeze rifled his torn shirt and reminded Gordon that it was time to get this business over with, before his hands were too chilled to pull a trigger.

He wiped the stickiness on his pants as he rounded the end of the thicket. And there, suddenly, a hundred feet or so away it seemed, a broad pane of glass glinted at him in the dim skyglow.

Gordon ducked back behind the thorns. He drew his

revolver and held his right wrist with his left hand until his breathing settled. Then he checked the pistol's action. It clicked quietly, in an almost gentle, mechanical complacency. The spare ammo was heavy in his breast pocket.

A hazard to quick or forceful motion, the thicket yielded as he settled back against it, heedless of a few more little scratches. Gordon closed his eyes and meditated for calm and, yes, for forgiveness. In the chilly darkness, the only accompaniment to his breathing was the rhythmic ratchet of the crickets.

A swirl of cold fog blew around him. *No*, he sighed. *There's no other way.* He raised his weapon and swung around.

The structure looked distinctly odd. For one thing, the distant patch of glass was dark.

That was queer, but stranger still was the silence. He'd have thought the bandits would have a fire going, and that they would be loudly celebrating.

It was nearly too dark to see his own hand. The trees loomed like hulking trolls on every side. Dimly, the glass pane seemed to stand out against some black structure, reflecting silvery highlights of a rolling cloud cover. Thin wisps of haze drifted between Gordon and his objective, confusing the image, making it shimmer.

He walked forward slowly, giving most of his attention to the ground. Now was not the time to step on a dry twig, or to be stabbed by a sharp stone as he shuffled in the dimness.

He glanced up, and once more the eerie feeling struck him. There was something *wrong* about the edifice ahead, made out mostly in silhouette behind the faintly glimmering glass. It didn't look right, somehow. Boxlike, its upper section seemed to be mostly window. Below, it struck him as more like painted metal than wood. At the corners . . .

The fog grew thicker. Gordon could tell his perspective was wrong. He had been looking for a house, or large cottage. As he neared, he realized the thing was actually much

20

closer than he'd thought. The shape was familiar, as if—

His foot came down on a twig. The "snap!" filled his ears and he crouched, peering into the gloom with a desperate need that transcended sight. It felt as if a frantic power drove out of his eyes, propelled by his terror, demanding the mist be cloven so he could see.

Obediently, it seemed, the dry fog suddenly fell open before him. Pupils dilated, Gordon saw that he was less than two *meters* from the window . . . his own face reflected, wide-eyed and wild haired . . . and saw, superimposed on his own image, a vacant, skeletal, death mask—a hooded skull grinning in welcome.

Gordon crouched, hypnotized, as a superstitious thrill coursed up his spine. He was unable to bring his weapon to bear, unable to cause his larynx to make sound. The haze swirled as he listened for proof that he had really gone mad—wishing with all his might that the death's head was an illusion.

"Alas, poor Gordon!" The sepulchral image overlay his reflection and seemed to shimmer a greeting. Never, in all these awful years, had Death—owner of the world— manifested to him as a specter. Gordon's numbed mind could think of nothing but to attend the Elsinorian figure's bidding. He waited, unable to take his gaze away, or even to move. The skull and his face . . . his face and the skull. . . . The thing had captured him without a fight, and now seemed content to grin about it.

At last it was something as mundane as a monkey reflex that came to Gordon's aid.

No matter how mesmerizing, how terrifying, no unchanging sight can keep a man riveted forever. Not when it seemed that nothing at all was happening, nothing changing. Where courage and education failed him, where his nervous system had let him down, *boredom* finally took command.

His breath exhaled. He heard it whistle between his teeth. Without willing them to, Gordon felt his eyes turn slightly from the visage of Death.

21

A part of him noted that the window was set in a door. The handle lay before him. To the left, another window. To the right . . . to the right was the hood.

The . . . *hood* . . .

The hood of a jeep.

The hood of an abandoned, rusted jeep that lay in a faint rut in the forest gully. . . .

He blinked at the hood of the abandoned, rusted jeep with ancient U.S. government markings, and the skeleton of a poor, dead, civil servant within, skull pressed against the passenger-side window, facing Gordon.

The strangled sigh he let out felt almost ectoplasmic, the relief and embarrassment were so palpable. Gordon straightened up and it felt like unwinding from a fetal position—like being born.

"Oh. Oh Lordie," he said, just to hear his own voice. Moving his arms and legs, he paced a long circle around the vehicle, obsessively glancing at its dead occupant, coming to terms with its reality. He breathed deeply as his pulse settled and the roar in his ears gradually ebbed.

Finally, he sat down on the forest floor with his back against the cool door on the jeep's left side. Trembling, he used both hands as he put the revolver back on safety and slid it into its holster. Then he pulled out his canteen and drank in slow, full swallows. Gordon wished he had something stronger, but water right now tasted as sweet as life.

Night was full, the cold, bone-chilling. Still, Gordon spent a few moments putting off the obvious. He would never find the bandits' roost now, having followed a false clue so far into a pitch dark wilderness. The jeep, at least, offered some form of shelter, better than anything else around.

He hauled himself up and placed his hand on the door lever, calling up motions that had once been second nature to two hundred million of his countrymen and which, after a stubborn moment, forced the latch to give. The door let out a loud screech as he pulled hard and forced it open. He slid onto the cracked vinyl of the seat and inspected the interior.

The jeep was one of those reversed, driver-on-the-right types the post office had used back in the once-upon-a-time of before the Doomwar. The dead mailman—what was left of him—was slumped over on the far side. Gordon avoided looking at the skeleton for the moment.

The storage area of the truck was nearly full with canvas sacks. The smell of old paper filled the small cabin at least as much as the faded odor of the mummified remains.

With a hopeful oath, Gordon snatched up a metal flask from the shift well. It sloshed! To have held liquid for sixteen years or more it had to be well sealed. Gordon swore as he twisted and pried at the cap. He pounded it against the door frame, then attacked it again.

Frustration made his eyes tear, but at last he felt the cap give. Soon he was rewarded with a slow, rough turning, and then the heady, distantly familiar aroma of whiskey.

Maybe I've been a good boy after all.

Maybe there is indeed a God.

He took a mouthful and coughed as the warming fire streamed down. Two more small swallows and he fell back against the seat, breathing almost a sigh.

He wasn't ready yet to face removing the jacket draped over the skeleton's narrow shoulders. Gordon grabbed sacks—bearing the imprint U.S. POSTAL SERVICE—and piled them about himself. Leaving a narrow opening in the door to let in fresh mountain air, he burrowed under the makeshift blankets with his bottle.

At last he looked over at his host, contemplating the dead civil servant's American flag shoulder patch. He unscrewed the flask and this time raised the container toward the hooded garment.

"Believe it or not, Mr. Postman, I always thought you folks gave good and honest service. Oh, people used you as whipping boys a lot, but I know what a tough job you all had. I was proud of you, even before the war.

"But *this*, Mr. Mailman"—he lifted the flask—"this goes beyond anything I'd come to expect! I consider my taxes very well spent." He drank to the postman, coughing a little but relishing the warm glow.

He settled deeper into the mail sacks and looked at the leather jacket, ribs serating its sides, arms hanging loosely at odd angles. Lying still, Gordon felt a sad poignancy—something like homesickness. The jeep, the symbolic, faithful letter carrier, the flag patch . . . they recalled comfort, innocence, cooperation, an easy life that allowed millions of men and women to relax, to smile or argue as they chose, to be tolerant with one another—and to hope to be better people with the passage of time.

Gordon had been ready, today, to kill and to be killed. Now he was glad that had been averted. They had called him "Mr. Rabbit" and left him to die. But it was his privilege, without their ever knowing it, to call the bandits "countrymen," and let them have their lives.

Gordon allowed sleep to come and welcomed back optimism—foolish anachronism that it might be. He lay in a blanket of his own honor, and spent the rest of the night dreaming of parallel worlds.

2

Snow and soot covered the ancient tree's broken branches and seared bark. It wasn't dead, not quite yet. Here and there tiny shoots of green struggled to emerge, but they weren't doing well. The end was near.

A shadow loomed, and a creature settled onto the drifts, an old, wounded thing of the skies, as near death as the tree.

Pinions drooping, it laboriously began building a nest— a place of dying. Stick by stick, it pecked among the ruined wood on the ground, piling the bits higher until it was clear that it was not a nest at all.

It was a pyre.

The bloody, dying thing settled in atop the kindling, and crooned soft music unlike anything ever heard before. A glow began to build, surrounding the beast soon in a rich purple lambience. Blue flames burst forth.

And the tree seemed to respond. Aged, ruined branches curled forward toward the heat, like an old man warming his hands. Snow shivered and fell, the green patches grew and began to fill the air with a fragrance of renewal.

It was not the creature in the pyre that was reborn, and even in sleep, that surprised Gordon. The great bird was consumed, leaving only bones.

But the tree blossomed, and from its flowering branches things uncurled and drifted off into the air.

He stared in wonderment when he saw that they were balloons, airplanes, and rocket ships. Dreams.

They floated away in all directions, and the air was filled with hope.

25

3

A camp robber bird, looking for blue jays to chase, landed on the jeep's hood with a hollow thump. It squawked—once for territoriality and once for pleasure—then began poking through the thick detritus with its beak.

Gordon awakened to the tap-tapping sound. He looked up, bleary-eyed, and saw the gray-flanked bird through the dust-smeared window. It took him moments to remember where he was. The glass windshield, the steering wheel, the smell of metal and paper, all felt like a continuation of one of the night's most vivid dreams, a vision of the old days before the war. He sat dazedly for a few moments, sifting through feelings while the sleep images unraveled and drifted away, out of grasp.

Gordon rubbed his eyes, and presently began to consider his situation.

If he hadn't left an elephant's trail on his way into this hollow last night, he should be perfectly safe right now. The fact that the whiskey had lain here untouched for sixteen years obviously meant the bandits were lazy hunters. They had their traditional stalks and blinds, and had never bothered fully to explore their own mountain.

Gordon felt a bit thick-headed. The war had begun when he was eighteen, a college sophomore, and since then there had been little chance to build a tolerance to eighty-proof liquor. Added to yesterday's series of traumas and adrenaline rushes, the whiskey had left him cotton-mouthed and scratchy behind the eyelids.

He regretted his lost comforts as much as ever. There would be no tea this morning. Nor a damp washcloth, or venison jerky for breakfast. No toothbrush.

Still, Gordon tried to be philosophical. After all, he was alive. He had a feeling there would be times when each of the items stolen from him would be "missed most of all."

With any luck, the Geiger counter wouldn't fall into that category. Radiation had been one of his main reasons for going ever westward, since leaving the Dakotas. He had grown tired of walking everywhere a slave to his precious counter, always afraid it would be stolen or would break down. Rumor had it that the West Coast had been spared the worst of the fallout, suffering more, instead, from plagues wind-borne from Asia.

That had been the way with that strange war. Inconsistent, chaotic, it had stopped far short of the spasm everyone had predicted. Instead it was more like a shotgun blast of one midscale catastrophe after another. By itself, any one of the disasters might have been survivable.

The initial "techno-war" at sea and in space might not have been so terrible had it remained contained, and not spilled over onto the continents.

The diseases weren't as bad as in the Eastern Hemisphere, where the Enemy's weapons went out of control in his own populace. They probably wouldn't have killed so many in America, had the fallout zones not pushed crowds of refugees together, and ruined the delicate network of medical services.

And the starvation might not have been so awful had terrified communities not blocked rails and roads to keep out the germs.

As for the long-dreaded atom, only a tiny fraction of the world's nuclear arsenals were used before the Slavic Resurgence collapsed from within and unexpected victory was declared. Those few score bombs were enough to trigger the Three-Year Winter, but not a Century-Long Night that might have sent Man the way of the dinosaurs. For weeks it appeared that a great miracle of restraint had saved the planet.

27

DAVID BRIN

So it seemed. And indeed, even the combination—a few bombs, some bugs, and three poor harvests—would not have been enough to ruin a great nation, and with it a world.

But there was another illness, a cancer from within.

Damn you forever, Nathan Holn, Gordon thought. Across a dark continent it was a common litany.

He pushed aside the mail sacks. Ignoring the morning chill, he opened his left belt pouch and pulled out a small package wrapped in aluminum foil, coated with melted wax.

If there ever had been an emergency, this was one. Gordon would need energy to get through the day. A dozen cubes of beef bouillon were all he had, but they would have to do.

Washing down a bitter, salty chunk with a swig from his canteen, Gordon kicked open the left door of the jeep, letting several sacks tumble out onto the frosted ground. He turned to his right and looked at the muffled skeleton that had quietly shared the night with him.

"Mr. Postman, I'm going to give you as close to a decent burial as I can manage with my bare hands. I know that's not much payment for what you've given me. But it's all I can offer." He reached over the narrow, bony shoulder and unlocked the driver's door.

His moccasins slipped on the icy ground as he got out and stepped carefully around to the other side of the jeep.

At least it didn't snow last night. It's so dry up here that the ground ought to thaw enough for digging in a little while.

The rusty right-hand door groaned as he pulled. It was tricky, catching the skeleton in an emptied mail sack as it pitched forward. Gordon somehow managed to get the bundle of clothes and bones laid out on the forest floor.

He was amazed at the state of preservation. The dry climate had almost mummified the postman's remains, giving insects time to clean up without much mess. The rest of the jeep appeared to have been free from mold for all these years.

First he checked the mailman's apparel.

Funny— Why was he wearing a paisley shirt under his jacket?

28

The garment, once colorful but now faded and stained, was a total loss, but the leather jacket was a wonderful find. If big enough, it would improve his chances immeasurably.

The footgear looked old and cracked, but perhaps serviceable. Carefully, Gordon shook out the gruesome, dry remnants and laid the shoes against his feet.

Maybe a bit large. But then, anything would be better than ripped camp moccasins.

Gordon slid the bones out onto the mail sack with as little violence as he could manage, surprised at how easy it was. Any superstition had been burned out the night before. All that remained was a mild reverence and an ironic gratitude to the former owner of these things. He shook the clothes, holding his breath against the dust, and hung them on a ponderosa branch to air out. He returned to the jeep.

Aha, he thought then. *The mystery of the shirt is solved.* Right next to where he had slept was a long-sleeved blue uniform blouse with Postal Service patches on the shoulders. It looked almost new, in spite of the years. *One for comfort, and another for the boss.*

Gordon had known postmen to do that, when he was a boy. One fellow, during the muggy afternoons of summer, had worn bright Hawaiian shirts as he delivered the mail. The postman had always been grateful for a cool glass of lemonade. Gordon wished he could remember his name.

Shivering in the morning chill, he slipped into the uniform shirt. It was only a little bit large.

"Maybe I'll grow to fill it out," he mumbled, joking weakly with himself. At thirty-four he probably weighed less than he had at seventeen.

The glove compartment contained a brittle map of Oregon to replace the one he had lost. Then, with a shout Gordon grabbed a small square of clear plastic. A scintillator! Far better than his Geiger counter, the little crystal would give off tiny flashes whenever its crystalline interior was struck by gamma radiation. It didn't even need power! Gordon cupped it in front of his eye and watched a few sparse flickerings, caused by cosmic rays. Otherwise, the cube was quiescent.

Now what was a prewar mailman doing with a gadget like that? Gordon wondered idly, as the device went into his pants pocket.

The glove compartment flashlight was a loss, of course; the emergency flares were crumbled paste.

The bag, of course. On the floor below the driver's seat was a large, leather letter carrier's sack. It was dry and cracked, but the straps held when he tugged, and the flaps would keep out water.

It wouldn't come close to replacing his lost Kelty, but the bag would be a vast improvement over nothing at all. He opened the main compartment and bundles of aged correspondence spilled out, breaking into scattered piles as brittle rubber bands snapped apart. Gordon picked up a few of the nearest pieces.

"From the Mayor of Bend, Oregon, to the Chairman of the School of Medicine, University of Oregon, Eugene." Gordon intoned the address as though he were playing Polonius. He flipped through more letters. The addresses sounded pompous and archaic.

"Dr. Franklin Davis, of the small town of Gilchrist sends—with the word URGENT printed clearly on the envelope—a rather bulky letter to the Director of Regional Disbursement of Medical Supplies . . . no doubt pleading priority for his requisitions."

Gordon's sardonic smile faded into a frown as he turned over one letter after another. Something was wrong, here.

He had expected to be amused by junk mail and personal correspondence. But there didn't seem to be a single advertisement in the bag. And while there were many private letters, most of the envelopes appeared to be on one or another type of official stationery.

Well, there wasn't time for voyeurism anyway. He'd take a dozen or so letters for entertainment, and use the backsides for his new journal.

He avoided thinking about the loss of the old volume—sixteen years' tiny scratchings, now doubtless being perused by that onetime stockbroker robber. It would be read and preserved, he was sure, along with the tiny volumes of verse he had carried in his pack, or he had misread Roger Septien's personality.

Someday, he would come and get them back.

What was a U.S. Postal Service jeep doing out here, anyway? And what had killed the postman? He found part of his answer around at the back of the vehicle—bullet holes in the tailgate window, well grouped midway up the right side.

Gordon looked over to the ponderosa. Yes, the shirt and the jacket each had two holes in the back of the upper chest area.

The attempted hijacking or robbery could not have been prewar. Mail carriers were almost never attacked, even in the late eighties' depression riots, before the "golden age" of the nineties.

Besides, a missing carrier would have been searched for until found.

So, the attack took place *after* the One-Week War. But what was a mailman doing driving alone through the countryside after the United States had effectively ceased to exist? How long afterward had this happened?

The fellow must have driven off from his ambush, seeking obscure roads and trails to get away from his assailants. Maybe he didn't know the severity of his wounds, or simply panicked.

But Gordon suspected that there was another reason the letter carrier had chosen to weave in and out of blackberry thickets to hide deep in forest depths.

"He was protecting his cargo," Gordon whispered. "He measured the chance he'd black out on the road against the possibility of getting to help . . . and decided to cache the mail, rather than try to live."

So, this was a bona fide *postwar* postman. A hero of the flickering twilight of civilization. Gordon thought of the old-time ode of the mails . . . "Neither sleet, nor hail . . ." and

31

wondered at the fact that some had tried this hard to keep the light alive.

That explained the official letters and the lack of junk mail. He hadn't realized that even a semblance of normality had remained for so long. Of course, a seventeen-year-old militia recruit was unlikely to have seen anything normal. Mob rule and general looting in the main disbursement centers had kept armed authority busy and attrited until the militia finally vanished into the disturbances it had been sent to quell. If men and women elsewhere were behaving more like human beings during those months of horror, Gordon never witnessed it.

The brave story of the postman only served to depress Gordon. This tale of struggle against chaos, by mayors and university professors and postmen, had a "what if" flavor that was too poignant for him to consider for long.

The tailgate opened reluctantly, after some prying. Moving mail sacks aside, he found the letter carrier's hat, with its tarnished badge, an empty lunchbox, and a valuable pair of sunglasses lying in thick dust atop a wheel well.

A small shovel, intended to help free the jeep from road ruts, would now help to bury the driver.

Finally, just behind the driver's seat, broken under several heavy sacks, Gordon found a smashed guitar. A large-caliber bullet had snapped its neck. Near it, a large, yellowed plastic bag held a pound of desiccated herbs that gave off a strong, musky odor. Gordon's recollection hadn't faded enough to forget the aroma of marijuana.

He had envisioned the postman as a middle-aged, balding, conservative type. Gordon now recreated the image, and made the fellow look more like himself, wiry, bearded, with a perpetual, stunned expression that seemed about to say, "Oh, wow."

A neohippy perhaps—a member of a subgeneration that had hardly begun to flower before the war snuffed it out and everything else optimistic—a neohippy dying to protect the establishment's mail. It didn't surprise Gordon in the slightest. He had had friends in the movement, sincere people, if maybe a little strange.

Gordon retrieved the guitar strings and for the first time that morning felt a little guilty.

The letter carrier hadn't even been armed! Gordon remembered reading once that the U.S. Mail operated across the lines for three years into the 1860s Civil War. Perhaps this fellow had trusted his countrymen to respect that tradition.

Post-Chaos America had no tradition but survival. In his travels, Gordon had found that some isolated communities welcomed him in the same way minstrels had been kindly received far and wide in medieval days. In others, wild varieties of paranoia reigned. Even in those rare cases where he had found friendliness, where decent people seemed willing to welcome a stranger, Gordon had always, before long, moved on. Always, he found himself beginning to dream again of wheels turning and things flying in the sky.

It was already midmorning. His gleanings here were enough to make the chances of survival better without a confrontation with the bandits. The sooner he was over the pass then, and into a decent watershed, the better off he would be.

Right now, nothing would serve him half so well as a stream, somewhere out of the range of the bandit gang, where he could fish for trout to fill his belly.

One more task, here. He hefted the shovel.

Hungry or not, you owe the guy this much.

He looked around for a shady spot with soft earth to dig in, and a view.

4

"... They said, 'Fear not, Macbeth, till Birnam Wood comes to Dunsinane'; and now a wood comes to Dunsinane!

"Arm, arm, arm yourselves! If this is what the witch spoke of—that thing out there—there'll be no running, or hiding here!"

Gordon clutched his wooden sword, contrived from planking and a bit of tin. He motioned to an invisible aide-de-camp.

"I'm gettin' weary of the sun, and wish the world were undone.

"Ring the alarum bell! Blow, wind! Come wrack! At least we'll die with harness on our back!"

Gordon squared his shoulders, flourished his sword, and marched Macbeth offstage to his doom.

Out of the light of the tallow lamps, he swiveled to catch a glimpse of his audience. They had loved his earlier acts. But this bastardized, one-man version of Macbeth might have gone over their heads.

An instant after he exited, though, enthusiastic applause began, led by Mrs. Adele Thompson, the leader of this small community. Adults whistled and stamped their feet. Younger citizens clapped awkwardly, those below twenty years of age watching their elders and slapping their hands awkwardly, as if they were taking part in this strange rite for the first time.

Obviously, they had liked his abbreviated version of the

34

ancient tragedy. Gordon was relieved. To be honest, some parts had been simplified less for brevity than because of his imperfect memory of the original. He had last seen a copy of the play almost a decade ago, and that a half-burned fragment.

Still, the final lines of his soliloquy had been canon. That part about "wind and wrack" he would never forget.

Grinning, Gordon returned to take his bows onstage— a plank-covered garage lift in what had once been the only gas station in the tiny hamlet of Pine View.

Hunger and isolation had driven him to try the hospitality of this mountain village of fenced fields and stout log walls, and the gamble had paid off better than he'd hoped. An exchange of a series of shows for his meals and supplies had tentatively passed by a fair majority of the voting adults, and now the deal seemed settled.

"Bravo! Excellent!" Mrs. Thompson stood in the front row, clapping eagerly. White-haired and bony, but still robust, she turned to encourage the forty-odd others, including small children, to show their appreciation. Gordon did a flourish with one hand, and bowed deeper than before.

Of course his peformance had been pure crap. But he was probably the only person within a hundred miles who had once minored in drama. There were "peasants" once again in America, and like his predecessors in the minstrel trade, Gordon had learned to go for the unsubtle in his shows.

Timing his final bow for the moment before the applause began to fade, Gordon hopped off the stage and began removing his slap-dash costume. He had set firm limits; there would be no encore. His stock was theater, and he meant to keep them hungry for it until it was time to leave.

"Marvelous. Just wonderful!" Mrs. Thompson told him as he joined the villagers, now gathering at a buffet table along the back wall. The older children formed a circle around him, staring in wonderment.

Pine View was quite prosperous, compared with so many of the starvling villages of the plains and mountains.

In some places a good part of a generation was nearly missing due to the devastating effects the Three-Year Winter had had on children. But here he saw several teenagers and young adults, and even a few oldsters who must have been past middle age when the Doom fell.

They must have fought to save everybody. That pattern had been rarer, but he had seen it, too, here and there.

Everywhere there were traces of those years. Faces pocked from diseases or etched from weariness and war. Two women and a man were amputees and another looked out of one good eye, the other a cloudy mass of cataracts.

He was used to such things—at least on a superficial level. He nodded gratefully to his host.

"Thank you, Mrs. Thompson. I appreciate kind words from a perceptive critic. I'm glad you liked the show."

"No, no seriously," the clan leader insisted, as if Gordon had been trying to be modest. "I haven't been so delighted in years. The Macbeth part at the end there sent shivers up my spine! I only wish I'd watched it on TV back when I had a chance. I didn't know it was so good!

"And that inspiring speech you gave us earlier, that one of Abraham Lincoln's . . . well, you know, we tried to start a school here, in the beginning. But it just didn't work out. We needed every hand, even the kids'. Now though, well, that speech got me to thinking. We've got some old books put away. Maybe now's the time to give it a try again."

Gordon nodded politely. He had seen this syndrome before—the best of the dozen or so types of reception he had experienced over the years, but also among the saddest. It always made him feel like a charlatan, when his shows brought out grand, submerged hopes in a few of the decent, older people who remembered better days . . . hopes that, to his knowledge, had always fallen through before a few weeks or months had passed.

It was as if the seeds of civilization needed more than goodwill and the dreams of aging high school graduates to water them. Gordon often wondered if the right symbol might do the trick—the right *idea*. But he knew his little dramas, however well received, weren't the key. They might trigger a beginning, once in a great while, but local enthusiasm always failed soon after. He was no traveling messiah. The legends he offered weren't the kind of sustenance needed in order to overcome the inertia of a dark age.

The world turns, and soon the last of the old generation will be gone. Scattered tribes will rule the continent. Perhaps in a thousand years the adventure will begin again. Meanwhile . . .

Gordon was spared hearing more of Mrs. Thompson's sadly unlikely plans. The crowd squeezed out a small, silver-haired, black woman, wiry and leather skinned, who seized Gordon's arm in a friendly, viselike grip.

"Now Adele," she said to the clan matriarch, "Mister Krantz hasn't had a bite since noontime. I think, if we want him able to perform tomorrow night, we'd better feed him. Right?" She squeezed his right arm and obviously thought him undernourished—an impression he was loathe to alter, with the aroma of food wafting his way.

Mrs. Thompson gave the other woman a look of patient indulgence. "Of course, Patricia," she said. "I'll speak with you more about this, later, Mr. Krantz, after Mrs. Howlett has fattened you up a bit." Her smile and her glittering eyes held a touch of intelligent irony, and Gordon found himself reevaluating Adele Thompson. She certainly was nobody's fool.

Mrs. Howlett propelled him through the crowd. Gordon smiled and nodded as hands came out to touch his sleeve. Wide eyes followed his every movement.

Hunger must make me a better actor. I've never had an audience react quite like this before. I wish I knew exactly what it was I did that made them feel this way.

One of those watching him from behind the long buffet table was a young woman barely taller than Mrs. Howlett, with deep, almond eyes and hair blacker than Gordon remembered ever seeing before. Twice, she turned to gently slap the hand of a child who tried to help himself before the honored guest. Each time the girl quickly looked back at Gordon and smiled.

Beside her, a tall, burly young man stroked his reddish

DAVID BRIN

beard and gave Gordon a strange look—as if his eyes were filled with some desperate resignation. Gordon had only a moment to assimilate the two as Mrs. Howlett pulled him over in front of the pretty brunette.

"Abby," she said, "let's have a little bit of everything on a plate for Mr. Krantz. Then he can make up his mind what he wants seconds of. I baked the blueberry pie, Mr. Krantz."

Dizzily, Gordon made a note to have two helpings of the blueberry. It was hard to concentrate on diplomacy, though. He hadn't seen or smelled anything like this in years. The odors distracted him from the disconcerting looks and touching hands.

There was a large, spit-turned, stuffed turkey. A huge, steaming bowl of boiled potatoes, dollied up with beer-soaked jerky, carrots, and onions, was the second course. Down the table Gordon saw apple cobbler and an opened barrel of dried apple flakes. *I must cozen a supply of those, before I leave.*

Skipping further inventory, he eagerly held out his plate. Abby kept watching him as she took it.

The big, frowning redhead suddenly muttered something indecipherable and reached out to grab Gordon's right hand in both of his own. Gordon flinched, but the taciturn fellow would not let go until he answered the grip and shook hands firmly.

The man muttered something too low to follow, nodded, and let go. He bent to kiss the brunette quickly and then stalked off, eyes downcast.

Gordon blinked. *Did I just miss something?* It felt as if some sort of event had just occurred, and had gone completely over his head.

"That was Michael, Abby's husband," Mrs. Howlett said. "He's got to go and relieve Edward at the trap string. But he wanted to stay to see your show, first. When he was little he so used to love to watch TV shows. . . ."

Steam from the plate rose to his face, making Gordon quite dizzy with hunger. Abby blushed and smiled when he thanked her. Mrs. Howlett pulled him over to take a seat on a pile of old tires. "You'll get to talk to Abby, later," the black woman went on. "Now, you eat. Enjoy yourself."

Gordon did not need to be encouraged. He dug in while people looked on curiously and Mrs. Howlett rattled on.

"Good, isn't it? You just sit and eat and pay us no mind.

"And when you're all full and you're ready to talk again, I think we'd all like to hear, one more time, how you got to be a mailman."

Gordon looked up at the eager faces above him. He hurriedly took a swig of beer to chase down the too-hot potatoes.

"I'm just a traveler," he said around a half-full mouth while lifting a turkey drumstick. "It's not much of a story how I got the bag and clothes."

He didn't care whether they stared, or touched, or talked at him, so long as they let him eat!

Mrs. Howlett watched him for a few moments. Then, unable to hold back, she started in again. "You know, when I was a little girl we used to give milk and cookies to the mailman. And my father always left a little glass of whiskey on the fence for him the day before New Year's. Dad used to tell us that poem, you know, 'Through sleet, through mud, through war, through blight, through bandits and through darkest night . . .'"

Gordon choked on a sudden, wayward swallow. He coughed and looked up to see if she was in earnest. A glimmer in his forebrain wanted to dance over the old woman's accidentally magnificent misremembrance. It was rich.

The glimmer faded quickly, though, as he bit into the delicious roast fowl. He hadn't the will to try to figure out what the old woman was driving at.

"*Our* mailman used to *sing* to us!"

The speaker, incongruously, was a dark-haired giant with a silver-streaked beard. His eyes seemed to mist as he remembered. "We could hear him coming, on Saturdays when we were home from school, sometimes when he was over a block away.

"He was black, a lot blacker than Mrs. Howlett, or Jim Horton over there. Man, did he have a nice voice! Guess that's how he got the job. He brought me all those mail order coins I used to collect. Ringed the doorbell so he could hand 'em to me, personal, with his own hand."

His voice was hushed with telescoped awe.

"Our mailman just whistled when I was little," said a middle-aged woman with a deeply lined face. She sounded a little disappointed.

"But he *was* real nice. Later, when I was grown up, I came home from work one day and found out the mailman had saved the life of one of my neighbors. Heard him choking and gave him mouth-to-mouth until th' ambulance came."

A collective sigh rose from the circle of listeners, as if they were hearing the heroic adventures of a single ancient hero. The children listened in wide-eyed silence as the tales grew more and more embroidered. At least the small part of him still paying attention figured they had to be. Some were simply too far-fetched to be believed.

Mrs. Howlett touched Gordon's knee. "Tell us again how you got to be a mailman."

Gordon shrugged a little desperately. "I just found the mailman's fings!" he emphasized around the food in his mouth. The flavors had overcome him, and he felt almost panicky over the way they all *hovered* over him. If the adult villagers wanted to romanticize their memories of men they had once considered lower-class civil servants at best, that was all right. Apparently they associated his performance tonight with the little touches of extroversion they had witnessed in their neighborhood letter carriers, when they had been children. That, too, was okay. They could think anything they damn well pleased, so long as they didn't interrupt his eating!

"Ah—" Several of the villagers looked at each other knowingly and nodded, as if Gordon's answer had had some profound significance. Gordon heard his own words repeated to those on the edges of the circle.

"He found the mailman's things . . . so naturally he became . . ."

His answer must have appeased them, somehow, for the crowd thinned as the villagers moved off to take polite turns at the buffet. It wasn't until much later, on reflection, that he perceived the significance of what had taken place there, under boarded windows and tallow lamps, while he crammed himself near to bursting with good food.

5

. . . we have found that our clinic has an abundant
supply of disinfectants and pain killers of several
varieties. We hear these are in short supply in Bend
and in the relocation centers up north. We're willing
to trade some of these—along with a truckload of
de-ionizing resin columns that happened to be
abandoned here—for one thousand doses of
tetracycline, to guard against the bubonic plague
outbreak to the east. Perhaps we'd be willing to settle
for an active culture of balomycine-producing yeast,
instead, if someone could come up and show us how
to maintain it.

Also, we are in desperate need of . . .

The Mayor of Gilchrist must have been a strong-willed
man to have persuaded his local emergency committee to
offer such a trade. Hoarding, however illogical and uncoop-
erative, was a major contributor to the collapse. It astonished Gordon that there still had been people with this
much good sense during the first two years of the Chaos.

He rubbed his eyes. Reading wasn't easy by the light of
a pair of homemade candles. But he found it difficult getting to sleep on the soft mattress, and damn if he'd sleep on
the floor after so long dreaming of such a bed, in just such a
room!

He had been a little sick, earlier. All that food and home-brewed ale had almost taken him over the line from delirious happiness to utter misery. Somehow, he had teetered along the boundary for several hours of blurrily remembered celebration before at last stumbling into the room they had prepared for him.

There had been a *toothbrush* waiting on his nightstand, and an iron tub filled with hot water.

And soap! In the bath his stomach had settled, and a warm, clean glow spread over his skin.

Gordon smiled when he saw that his postman's uniform had been cleaned and pressed. It lay on a nearby chair; the rips and tears he had crudely patched were now neatly sewn.

He could not fault the people of this tiny hamlet for neglecting his one remaining longing . . . something he had gone without too long to even think about. Enough. This was almost Paradise.

As he lay in a sated haze between a pair of elderly but clean sheets, waiting leisurely for sleep to come, he read a piece of correspondence between two long-dead men.

The Mayor of Gilchrist went on:

> We are having extreme difficulty with local gangs of "Survivalists." Fortunately, these infestations of egotists are mostly too paranoid to band together. They're as much trouble to each other as to us, I suppose. Still, they are becoming a real problem.
>
> Our deputy is regularly fired on by well armed men in army surplus camouflage clothing. No doubt the idiots think he's a "Russian Lackey" or some such nonsense.
>
> They have taken to hunting game on a massive scale, killing everything in the forest and doing a typically rotten job of butchering and preserving the meat. Our own hunters come back disgusted over the waste, often having been shot at without provocation.
>
> I know it's a lot to ask, but when you can spare

a platoon from relocation riot duty, could you send
them up here to help us root out these self-centered,
hoarding, romantic scoundrels from their little
filtered armories? Maybe a unit or two of the US
Army will convince them that we won the war, and
have to cooperate with each other from now on. . . .

He put the letter down.

So it had been that way here, too. The clichéd "last
straw" had been this plague of "survivalists"—particularly
those following the high priest of violent anarchy, Nathan
Holn.

One of Gordon's duties in the militia had been to help
weed out some of those small gangs of city-bred cutthroats
and gun nuts. The number of fortified caves and cabins his
unit had found—in the prairie and on little lake islands—
had been staggering . . . all set up in a rash of paranoia in the
difficult decades before the war.

The irony of it was that we had things turned around!
The depression was over. People were at work again and coop-
erating. Except for a few crazies, it looked like a renaissance
was coming, for America and for the world.

But we forgot just how much harm a few crazies could
do, in America and in the world.

Of course when the collapse did come, the solitary survivalists' precious little fortresses did not stay theirs for long.
Most of the tiny bastions changed hands a dozen or more
times in the first months—they were such tempting targets.
The battles had raged all over the plains until every solar
collector was shattered, every windmill wrecked, and every
cache of valuable medicines scattered in the never-ending
search for heavy dope.

Only the ranches and villages, those possessing the
right mixture of ruthlessness, internal cohesion, and common sense, survived in the end. By the time the Guard units
had all died at their posts, or themselves dissolved into rov-
ing gangs of battling survivalists, very few of the original
population of armed and armored hermits remained alive.

Gordon looked at the letter's postmark again. *Nearly two years after the war.* He shook his head. *I never knew anyone held on so long.*

The thought hurt, like a dull wound inside him. Anything that made the last sixteen years seem avoidable was just too hard to imagine.

There was a faint sound. Gordon looked up, wondering if he had imagined it. Then, only slightly louder, another faint knock rapped at the door to his room.

"Come in," he called. The door opened about halfway. Abby, the petite girl with the vaguely oriental cast to her eyes, smiled timidly from the opening. Gordon refolded the letter and slipped it into its envelope. He smiled.

"Hello, Abby. What's up?"

"I—I've come to ask if there is anything else you needed," she said a little quickly. "Did you enjoy your bath?"

"Did I now?" Gordon sighed. He found himself slipping back into Macduff's burr. "Aye, lass. And in particular I appreciated the gift of that toothbrush. Heaven sent, it was."

"You mentioned you'd lost yours." She looked at the floor. "I pointed out that we had at least five or six unused ones in the storage room. I'm glad you were pleased."

"It was your idea?" He bowed. "Then I am indeed in your debt."

Abby looked up and smiled. "Was that a letter you were just reading? Could I look at it? I've never seen a letter before."

Gordon laughed. "Oh surely you're not that young! What about before the war?"

Abby blushed at his laughter. "I was only four when it happened. It was so frightening and confusing that I . . . I really don't remember much from before."

Gordon blinked. Had it really been that long? Yes. Sixteen years was indeed enough time to have beautiful women in the world who knew nothing but the dark age.

Amazing, he thought.

"All right, then." He pushed the chair by his bed. Grinning, she came over and sat beside him. Gordon reached into the sack and pulled out another of the frail, yellowed envelopes. Carefully, he spread out the letter and handed it to her.

Abby looked at it so intently that he thought she was reading the whole thing. She concentrated, her thin eyebrows almost coming together in a crease on her forehead. But finally she handed the letter back. "I guess I can't really read that well. I mean, I can read labels on cans, and stuff. But I never had much practice with handwriting and . . . sentences."

Her voice dropped at the end. She sounded embarrassed, but in a totally unafraid, trusting fashion, as if he were her confessor.

He smiled. "No matter. I'll tell you what it's about." He held the letter up to the candlelight. Abby moved over to sit by his knees on the edge of the bed, her eyes rapt on the pages.

"It's from one John Briggs, of Fort Rock, Oregon, to his former employer in Klamath Falls. . . . I'd guess from the lathe and hobby horse letterhead that Briggs was a retired machinist or carpenter or something. Hmmm."

Gordon concentrated on the barely legible handwriting. "It seems Mr. Briggs was a pretty nice man. Here he's offering to take in his ex-boss's children, until the emergency is over. Also he says he has a good garage machine shop, his own power, and plenty of metal stock. He wants to know if the man wants to order any parts made up, especially things in short supply. . . ."

Gordon's voice faltered. He was still so thick-headed from his excesses that it had just struck him that a beautiful female was sitting on his bed. The depression she made in the mattress tilted his body toward her. He cleared his throat quickly and went back to scanning the letter.

"Briggs mentions something about power levels from the Fort Rock reservoir. . . . Telephones were out, but he was still, oddly enough, getting Eugene on his computer data net. . . ."

Abby looked at him. Apparently much of what he had said about the letter writer might as well have been in a foreign language to her. "Machine shop" and "data net" could have been ancient, magical words of power.

"Why didn't you bring us any letters, here in Pine View?" she asked quite suddenly.

Gordon blinked at the non sequitur. The girl wasn't stupid. One could tell such things. Then why had everything he said, when he arrived here, and later at the party, been completely misunderstood? She still thought he was a *mailman*, as, apparently, did all but a few of the others in this small settlement.

From whom did she imagine they'd get mail?

She probably didn't realize that the letters he carried had been sent long ago, from dead men and women to other dead men and women, or that he carried them for . . . for his own reasons.

The myth that had spontaneously developed here in Pine View depressed Gordon. It was one more sign of the deterioration of civilized minds, many of whom had once been high school and even college graduates. He considered telling her the truth, as brutally and frankly as he could, to stop this fantasy once and for all. He started to.

"There aren't any letters because . . ."

He paused. Again Gordon was aware of her nearness, the scent of her and the gentle curves of her body. Of her trust, as well.

He sighed and looked away. "There aren't any letters for you folks because . . . because I'm coming west out of Idaho, and nobody back there knows you, here in Pine View. From here I'm going to the coast. There might even be some large towns left. Maybe . . ."

"Maybe someone down there will write to us, if we send them a letter first!" Abby's eyes were bright. "Then, when you pass this way again, on your way back to Idaho, you could give us the letters they send, and maybe do another play-act for us like tonight, and we'll have so much beer and pie for you you'll bust!" She hopped a little on the edge of the bed. "By then I'll be able to read better, I promise!"

47

Gordon shook his head and smiled. It was beyond his right to dash such dreams. "Maybe so, Abby. Maybe so. But you know, you may get to learn to read easier than that. Mrs. Thompson's offered to put it up for a vote to let me stay on here for a while. I guess officially I'd be schoolteacher, though I'd have to prove myself as good a hunter and farmer as anybody. I could give archery lessons. . . ."

He stopped. Abby's expression was open-mouthed in surprise. She shook her head vigorously. "But you haven't heard! They voted on it after you went to take your bath. Mrs. Thompson should be ashamed of trying to bribe a man like you that way, with your important work having to be done!"

He sat forward, not believing his ears. "What did you say?" He had formed hopes of staying in Pine View for at least the cold season, maybe a year or more. Who could tell? Perhaps the wanderlust would leave him, and he could finally find a home.

His sated stupor dissipated. Gordon fought to hold back his anger. To have the chance revoked on the basis of the crowd's childish fantasies!

Abby noticed his agitation and hurried on. "That wasn't the only reason, of course. There was the problem of there being no woman for you. And then . . ." Her voice lowered perceptibly. "And then Mrs. Howlett thought you'd be perfect for helping me and Michael finally have a baby. . . ."

Gordon blinked. "Um," he said, expressing the sudden and complete contents of his mind.

"We've been trying for five years," she explained. "We really want children. But Mr. Horton thinks Michael can't 'cause he had the mumps *really* bad when he was twelve. You remember the real bad mumps, don't you?"

Gordon nodded, recalling friends who had died. The resultant sterility had made for unusual social arrangements everywhere he had traveled.

Still . . .

Abby went on quickly. "Well, it would cause problems if

48

we asked any of the other men here to . . . to be the body father. I mean, when you live close to people, like this, you have to look on the men who aren't your husband as not being really 'men' . . . at least not that way. I—I don't think I'd like it, and it might cause trouble."

She blushed. "Besides, I'll tell you something if you promise to keep a secret. I don't think any of the other men would be able to give Michael the kind of son he deserves. He's really very smart, you know. He's the only one of us youngers who can *really* read. . . ."

The flow of strange logic was coming on too fast for Gordon to follow completely. Part of him dispassionately noted that this was all really an intricate and subtle tribal adaptation to a difficult social problem. That part of him though—the last Twentieth-Century intellectual—was still a bit drunk, and meanwhile the rest was starting to realize what Abby was driving at.

"You're different." She smiled at him. "I mean, even Michael saw that right from the start. He's not too happy, but he figures you'll only be through once a year or so, and he could stand that. He'd rather that than never have any kids."

Gordon cleared his throat. "You're sure he feels this way?"

"Oh, yes. Why do you think Mrs. Howlett introduced us in that funny way? It was to make it clear without really saying it out loud. Mrs. Thompson doesn't like it much, but I think that's because she wanted you to stay."

Gordon's mouth felt dry. "How do *you* feel about all this?"

Her expression was enough of an answer. She looked at him as if he were some sort of visiting prophet, or at least a hero out of a story book. "I'd be honored if you'd say yes," she said, quietly, and lowered her eyes.

"And you'd be able to think of me as a man, 'that way'?"

Abby grinned. She answered by crawling up on top of him and planting her mouth intensely upon his.

• • •

There was a momentary pause as she shimmied out of her clothes and Gordon turned to snuff out the candles on the bed stand. Beside them lay the letterman's gray uniform cap, its brass badge casting multiple reflections of the dancing flames. The figure of a rider, hunched forward on horseback before bulging saddle bags, seemed to move at a flickering gallop.

This is another one I owe you, Mr. Postman.

Abby's smooth skin slid along his side. Her hand slipped into his as he took a deep breath and blew the candles out.

6

For ten days, Gordon's life followed a new pattern. As if to catch up on six months' road weariness, he slept late each morning and awoke to find Abby gone, like the night's dreams.

Yet her warmth and scent lingered on the sheets when he stretched and opened his eyes. The sunshine streaming through his eastward-facing window was like something new, a springtime in his heart, and not really early autumn at all.

He rarely saw her during the day as he washed and helped with chores until noon—chopping and stacking wood for the community supply and digging a deep pit for a new outhouse. When most of the village gathered for the main meal of the day, Abby returned from tending the flocks. But she spent lunchtime with the younger children, relieving old one-legged Mr. Lothes, their work supervisor. The little ones laughed as she kidded them, plucking the wool that coated their clothes from a morning spent carding skeins for the winter spinning, helping them keep the gray strands out of their food.

She barely glanced at Gordon, but that brief smile was enough. He knew he had no rights beyond these few days, and yet a shared look in the daylight made him feel that it was all real, and not just a dream.

Afternoons he conferred with Mrs. Thompson and the other village leaders, helping them inventory books and other long-neglected salvage. At intervals, he gave reading and archery lessons.

One day he and Mrs. Thompson traded methods in the art of field medicine while treating a man clawed by a "tiger," what the locals called that new strain of mountain lion which had bred with leopards escaped from zoos in the postwar chaos. The trapper had surprised the beast with its kill, but fortunately, it had only batted him into the brush and let him run away. Gordon and the village matriarch felt sure the wound would heal.

In the evenings all of Pine View gathered in the big garage and Gordon recited stories by Twain and Sayles and Keillor. He led them in singing old folk songs and lovingly remembered commercial jingles, and in playing "Remember When." Then it was time for drama.

Dressed in scrap and foil, he was John Paul Jones, shouting defiance from the deck of the *Bonne Homme Richard*. He was Anton Perceveral, exploring the dangers of a faraway world and the depths of his own potential with a mad robot companion. And he was Doctor Hudson, wading through the horror of the Kenyan Conflict to treat the victims of biological war.

At first Gordon always felt uneasy, putting on a flimsy costume and stomping across the makeshift stage waving his arms, shouting lines only vaguely recalled or made up on the spot. He had never really admired play-acting as a profession, even before the great war.

But it had got him halfway across a continent, and he was good at it. He felt the rapt gaze of the audience, their hunger for wonder and something of the world beyond their narrow valley, and their eagerness warmed him to the task. Pox-scarred and wounded—bent from year after year of back-breaking labor merely to survive—they looked up, the need greatest in eyes clouded with age, a yearning for help doing what they could no longer accomplish alone— remembering.

Wrapped in his roles, he gave them bits and pieces of lost romance. And by the time the last lines of his soliloquy faded, he too was able to forget the present, at least for a while.

Each night, after he retired, she came to him. For a while she would sit on the edge of his bed and talk of her life, about the flocks, and the village children, and Michael. She brought him books to ask their meanings and questioned him about his youth—about the life of a student in the wonderful days before the Doomwar.

Then, after a time, Abby would smile, put away the dusty volumes, and slide under the covers next to him while he leaned over and took care of the candle.

On the tenth morning, she did not slip away with the predawn light, but instead wakened Gordon with a kiss.

"Hmmmn, good morning," he commented, and reached for her, but Abby pulled away. She picked up her clothes, brushing her breasts across the soft hairs of his flat stomach.

"I should let you sleep," she told him. "But I wanted to ask you something." She held her dress in a ball.

"Mmm? What is it?" Gordon stuffed the pillow behind his head for support.

"You're going to be leaving today, aren't you?" she asked.

"Yes," he nodded seriously. "It's probably best. I'd like to stay longer, but since I can't, I'd better be heading west again."

"I know," she nodded seriously. "We'll all hate to see you go. But . . . well, I'm going to meet Michael out at the trapline, this evening. I miss him terribly." She touched the side of his face. "That doesn't bother you, does it? I mean, it's been wonderful here with you, but he's my husband and . . ."

He smiled and covered her hand. To his amazement, he had little difficulty with his feelings. He was more envious than jealous of Michael. The desperate logic of their desire for children, and their obvious love for one another, made the situation, in retrospect, as obvious as the need for a clean break at the end. He only hoped he had done them the favor they sought. For despite their fantasies, it was unlikely he would ever come this way again.

"I have something for you," Abby said. She reached under the bed and pulled out a small silvery object on a chain, and a paper package.

"It's a whistle. Mrs. Howlett says you should have one." She slipped it over his neck and adjusted it until satisfied with the effect.

"Also, she helped me write this *letter*." Abby picked up the little package. "I found some stamps in a drawer in the gas station, but they wouldn't stick on. So I got some money, instead. This is fourteen dollars. Will it be enough?"

She held out a cluster of faded bills.

Gordon couldn't help smiling. Yesterday five or six of the others had privately approached him. He had accepted their little envelopes and similar payments for postage with as straight a face as possible. He might have used the opportunity to charge them something he needed, but the community had already given him a month's stock of jerky, dried apples, and twenty straight arrows for his bow. There was no need, nor had he the desire to extort anything else.

Some of the older citizens had had relatives in Eugene, or Portland, or towns in the Willamette Valley. It was the direction he was heading, so he took the letters. A few were addressed to people who had lived in Oakridge and Blue River. Those he filed deep in the safest part of his sack. The rest, he might as well throw into Crater Lake, for all the good they would ever do, but he pretended anyway.

He soberly counted out a few paper bills, then handed back the rest of the worthless currency. "And who are you writing to?" Gordon asked Abby as he took the letter. He felt as if he were playing Santa Claus, and found himself enjoying it.

"I'm writing to the University. You know, at Eugene? I asked a bunch of questions like, are they taking new students again yet? And do they take married students?" Abby blushed. "I know I'd have to work real hard on my reading to get good enough. And maybe they aren't recovered enough to take many new students. But Michael's already so smart . . . and by the time we hear from them maybe things will be better."

"By the time you hear . . ." Gordon shook his head.

Abby nodded. "I'll for sure be reading a lot better by then. Mrs. Thompson promises she'll help me. And her husband has agreed to start a school, this winter. I'm going to help with the little kids.

"I hope maybe I can learn to be a teacher. Do you think that's silly?"

Gordon shook his head. He had thought himself beyond surprise, but this touched him. In spite of Abby's totally disproportioned view of the state of the world, her hope warmed him, and he found himself dreaming along with her. There was no harm in wishing, was there?

"Actually," Abby went on, confidentially, twisting her dress in her hands. "One of the big reasons I'm writing is to get a . . . a pen pal. That's the word, isn't it? I'm hoping maybe someone in Eugene will write to me. That way we'll get letters, here. I'd love to get a letter.

"Also"—her gaze fell—"that will give you another reason to come back, in a year or so . . . besides maybe wanting to see the baby."

She looked up and dimpled. "I got the idea from your Sherlock Holmes play. That's an 'ulterior motive,' isn't it?"

She was so delighted with her own cleverness, and so eager for his approval—Gordon felt a great, almost painful rush of tenderness. Tears welled as he reached out and pulled her into an embrace. He held her tightly and rocked slowly, his eyes shut against reality, and he breathed in with her sweet smell a light and optimism he had thought gone from the world.

7

"Well, this is where I turn back." Mrs. Thompson shook hands with Gordon. "Down this road things should be pretty tame until you get to Davis Lake. The last of the old loner survivalists that way wiped each other out some years back, though I'd still be careful if I were you."

There was a chill in the air, for autumn had arrived in full. Gordon zipped up the old letter carrier's jacket and adjusted the leather bag as the straight-backed old woman handed him an old roadmap.

"I had Jimmie Horton mark the places we know of, where homesteaders have set up. I wouldn't bother any of them unless you have to. Mostly they're a suspicious type, likely to shoot first. We've only been trading with the nearest for a short time."

Gordon nodded. He folded the map carefully and slipped it into a pouch. He felt rested and ready. He would regret leaving Pine View as much as any haven in recent memory. But now that he was resigned to going, he actually felt a growing eagerness to be traveling, to see what had happened in the rest of Oregon.

In the years since he had left the wreckage of Minnesota, he had found ever wilder signs of the dark age. But now he was in a new watershed. This had once been a pleasant state with dispersed light industry, productive farms, and an elevated level of culture. Perhaps it was merely Abby's innocence infecting him. But logically, the Willamette

Valley would be the place to look for civilization, if it existed anywhere anymore.

He took the old woman's hand once again. "Mrs. Thompson, I'm not sure I could ever repay what you people have done for me."

She shook her head. Her face was deeply tanned and so wrinkled Gordon was certain she had to be more than the fifty years she claimed.

"No, Gordon, you paid your keep. I would've liked it if you could've stayed and helped me get the school going. But now I see maybe it won't be so hard to do it by ourselves."

She gazed out over her little valley. "You know, we've been living in a kind of a daze, these last years since the crops have started coming in and the hunting's returned. You can tell how bad things have gotten when a bunch of grown men and women, who once had jobs, who read magazines—and filled out their own taxes, for Heaven's sake—start treating a poor, battered, wandering play-actor as if he was something like the Easter Bunny." She looked back at him. "Even Jim Horton gave you a couple of 'letters' to deliver, didn't he?"

Gordon's face felt hot. For a moment he was too embarrassed to face her. Then, all at once, he burst out laughing. He wiped his eyes in relief at having the group fantasy lifted from his shoulders.

Mrs. Thompson chuckled as well. "Oh, it was harmless I think. And more than that. You've served as a . . . you know, that old automobile thing . . . a *catalyst* I think. You know, the children are already exploring ruins for miles around—between chores and supper—bringing me all the books they find. I won't have any trouble making school into a privilege.

"Imagine, *punishing* them by suspending 'em from class! I hope Bobbie and I handle it right."

"I wish you the best of luck, Mrs. Thompson," Gordon said sincerely. "God, it would be nice to see a light, somewhere in all this desolation."

"Right, son. That'd be bliss."

Mrs. Thompson sighed. "I'd recommend you wait a year, but come on back. You're kind . . . you treated my people well. And you're discreet about some things, like that business with Abby and Michael."

She frowned momentarily. "I *think* I understand what went on there, and I guess it's for the best. Got to adjust, I suppose. Anyway, like I said, you're always welcome back."

Mrs. Thompson turned to go, walked two paces, then paused. She half turned to look back at Gordon. For a moment her face betrayed a hint of confusion and wonder. "You aren't *really* a postman, are you?" she asked suddenly.

Gordon smiled. He set the cap, with its bright brass emblem, on his head. "If I bring back some letters, you'll know for sure."

She nodded, gruffly, then set off up the ruined asphalt road. Gordon watched her until she passed the first bend, then he turned about to the west, and the long downgrade toward the Pacific.

8

The barricades had been long abandoned. The baffle wall on Highway 58, at the east end of Oakridge, had weathered into a tumbled tell of concrete debris and curled, rusting steel. The town itself was silent. This end, at least, was clearly long abandoned.

Gordon looked down the main street, reading its story. Two, possibly three, pitched battles had been fought here. A storefront with a canted sign—EMERGENCY SERVICES CLINIC—sat at the center of a major circle of devastation.

Three intact panes reflected morning sunlight from the top floor of a hotel. Elsewhere though, even where store windows had been boarded, the prismatic sparkle of shattered glass glistened on the buckled pavement.

Not that he had really expected anything better, but some of the feelings he had carried with him out of Pine View had led to hopes for more islands of peace, especially now that he was in the fertile watershed of the Willamette Valley. If no living town, at least Oakridge might have shown other signs conducive to optimism. There might have been traces of methodical reclamation, for instance. If an industrial civilization existed here in Oregon, towns such as this one should have been harvested of anything usable.

But just twenty yards from his vantage point Gordon saw the wreckage of a gas station—a big mechanic's tool cabinet lay on its side, its store of wrenches, pliers, and replacement wiring scattered on the oil-stained floor. A row of never-used tires still hung on a rack high above the service lifts.

From this, Gordon knew Oakridge to be the worst of all possible Oakridges, at least from his point of view. The things needed by a machine culture were available at every hand, untouched and rotting . . . implying there was no such technological society anywhere near. At the same time, he would have to pick through the wreckage of fifty waves of previous looters in his search for anything useful to a single traveler like himself.

Well, he sighed. *I've done it before.*

Even sifting through the downtown ruins of Boise, the gleaners before him had missed a small treasure trove of canned food in a loft behind a shoe store . . . some hoarder's stash, long untouched. There was a pattern to such things, worked out over the years. He had his own methods for conducting a search.

Gordon slipped down on the forest side of the barricade baffle and entered the overgrowth. He zigzagged, on the off chance he had been watched. At a place where he could verify landmarks in three different directions, Gordon dropped his leather shoulder bag and cap under an autumn-bright red cedar. He took off the dark brown letter carrier's jacket and laid it on top, then cut brush to cover the cache.

He would go to any lengths to avoid conflict with suspicious locals, but only a fool would leave his weapons behind. There were two types of fighting that could come out of a situation like this. For one, the silence of the bow might be better. For the other, it could be worth expending precious, irreplaceable .38 cartridges. Gordon checked the pistol's action and reholstered it. His bow he carried, along with arrows and a cloth sack for salvage.

In the first few houses, on the outskirts, the early looters had been more exuberant than thorough. Often the wreckage in such places discouraged those who came after, leaving useful items within. He had found it true often before.

Still, by the fourth house Gordon had a poor collection

to show for this theory. His sack contained a pair of boots almost useless from mildew, a magnifying glass, and two spools of thread. He had poked into all the usual and some unconventional hoarder's crannies, and found no food of any sort.

His Pine View jerky wasn't gone, but he had dipped down farther than he liked. His archery was better, and he had bagged a small turkey two days ago. Still, if he didn't have better luck gleaning, he might have to give up on the Willamette Valley for now and get to work on a winter hunting camp.

What he *really* wanted was another haven such as Pine View. But fate had been kind enough, lately. Too much good luck made Gordon suspicious.

He moved on to a fifth house.

The four-poster bed stood in what had once been a prosperous physician's two-story home. Like the rest of the house, the bedroom had been stripped of nearly everything but the furniture. Nevertheless, as he crouched down over the heavy area rug, Gordon thought he might have found something the earlier looters had missed.

The rug seemed out of place. The bed rested upon it, but only with the right pair of legs. The left pair lay directly on the hardwood floor. Either the owner had been sloppy in placing the big, oval carpet, or . . .

Gordon put down his burdens and grabbed the edge of the rug.

Whew. It's heavy.

He started rolling it toward the bed.

Yes! There was a thin, square crack in the floor, under the carpet. A bed leg pinned the rug over one of two brass door hinges. A *trapdoor.*

He pushed hard on the bedpost. The leg hopped and fell again with a boom. Twice more he shoved and loud echoes reverberated.

On his fourth heave the bedpost snapped in two. Gordon barely escaped impalement on the jagged stub as he

61

toppled onto the mattress. The canopy followed and the aged bed collapsed in a crash. Gordon cursed, fighting with the smothering shroud. He sneezed violently in a cloud of floating dust.

Finally, regaining a bit of sense, he managed to slither out from under the ancient, moldy fabric. He stumbled out of the room, still sputtering and sneezing. The attack subsided slowly. He gripped the upstairs bannister, squinting in that torturous, semi-orgasmic state that comes before a whopping sternutation. His ears rang with an extra murmur that seemed almost like voices.

Next thing you'll be hearing churchbells, he told himself.

The final sneeze came at last, in a loud "Ah—chblthooh!" Wiping his eyes, he reentered the bedroom. The trapdoor lay fully exposed, layered under a new coating of dust. Gordon had to pry the edge of the secret panel. Finally, it lifted with a high, rusty skreigh.

Again, it seemed as though some of the sound came from *outside* the house. But when he stopped and listened carefully, Gordon heard nothing. Impatiently, he bent down and brushed aside cobwebs to peer into the cache.

There was a large metal box inside. He poked around hoping for more. After all, the things a prewar doctor might have kept in a locked chest—money and documents—would be of less use to him than canned goods stashed here in a spree of wartime hoarding. But there was nothing other than the box. Gordon hauled it out, puffing.

Good. It's heavy. Now let's hope it's not gold or any similar crap. The hinges and lock were rusted. He lifted the haft of his knife to smash the small lock. Then he stopped abruptly.

Now they were unmistakable. The voices were close, too close.

"I think it came from this house!" someone called from the overgrown garden outside. Feet shuffled through the dry leaves. There were steps on the wooden porch.

Gordon sheathed the knife and snatched up his gear.

Leaving the box by the bed, he hurried out of the room to the stairwell.

This was not the best of circumstances to meet other men. In Boise and other mountain ruins there had been almost a code—gleaners from ranches all around could try their luck in the open city, and although the groups and individuals were wary, they seldom preyed on one another. Only one thing could bring them all together—a rumor that someone had sighted a Holnist, somewhere. Otherwise they pretty much left each other alone.

In other places, though, territoriality was the rule—and fiercely enforced. Gordon might be searching in some such clan's turf. A quick departure would, in any case, be discreet.

Still . . . he looked back at the strongbox anxiously. *It's mine, damnit!*

Boots clomped noisily downstairs. It was too late to close the trapdoor or hide the heavy treasure chest. Gordon cursed silently and hurried as quietly as he could across the upstairs landing to the narrow attic ladder.

The top floor was little more than a simple, A-frame garret. He had searched among the useless mementos here earlier. Now all he wanted was a hiding place. Gordon kept near the sloping walls to avoid creaks in the floorboards. He chose a trunk near a small, gabled window, and there laid his sack and quiver. Quickly, he strung his bow.

Would they search? In that case, the strongbox would certainly attract attention.

If so, would they take it as an offering and leave him a share of whatever it contained? He had known such things to happen, in places where a primitive sort of honor system worked.

He had the drop on anyone entering the attic, although it was dubious how much good that would do—cornered in a wooden building. The locals doubtless retained, even in the middle of a dark age, the craft of fire making.

At least three pairs of booted feet could be heard now. In rapid, hollow steps, they took the stairs, skirmishing up one landing at a time. When everyone was on the second floor, Gordon heard a shout.

"Hey Karl, looka this!"

"What? You catch a couple of the kids playing doctor in an old bed ag . . . sheeit!"

There was a loud thump, followed by the hammering of metal on metal.

"Sheeit!" Gordon shook his head. Karl had a limited but expressive vocabulary.

There were shuffling and tearing sounds, accompanied by more scatalogical exclamations. At last, though, a third voice spoke up loudly.

"Sure was nice of that fellow, findin' this for us. Wish we could thank him. Ought to get to know him so we don't shoot first if we ever see him again."

If that was bait, Gordon wasn't taking. He waited.

"Well, at least he deserves a warning," the first voice said even louder. "We got a shoot first rule, in Oakridge. He better scat before someone puts a hole in him bigger than the gap between a survivalist's ears."

Gordon nodded, taking the warning at face value.

The footsteps receded. They echoed down the stairwell, then out onto the wooden porch.

From the gable overlooking the front entrance, Gordon saw three men leave the house and walk toward the surrounding hemlock grove. They carried rifles and bulging canvas day packs. He hurried to the other windows as they disappeared into the woods, but saw no other motion. No signs of anyone doubling back from another side.

There had been three pairs of feet. He was sure of it. Three voices. And it wasn't likely only one man would stay in ambush, anyway. Still, Gordon was careful as he moved out. He lay down beside the open attic trapdoor, his bow, bag, and quiver next to him, and crawled until his head and shoulders extended out over the opening, slightly above the level of the floor. He drew his revolver, held it out in front of him, and then let gravity swing his head and torso suddenly downward in a fashion an ambusher would hardly expect.

As the blood rushed to his head Gordon was primed to snap off six quick shots at anything that moved.

Nothing did. There was nobody in the second-floor hallway.

He reached for his canvas bag, never taking his gaze from the hallway, and dropped it to clatter on the landing.

The sound triggered no ambush.

Gordon took up his gear and dropped to the next level in a crouch. He quickly moved down the hall, skirmish-style.

The strongbox lay open and empty next to the bed, beside it a scattering of paper trash. As he had expected, there were such curiosities as stock certificates, a stamp collection, and the deed to this house.

But some of the other debris was different.

A torn cardboard container, the celophane wrapper newly removed, colorfully depicted a pair of happy canoeists with their new, collapsible rifle. Gordon looked at the weapon pictured on the box and stifled a strangled cry. Doubtless there had also been boxes of ammunition.

Goddamn thieves, he thought bitterly.

But the other trash almost drove him wild. EMPIRIN WITH CODEINE, ERYTHROMYCIN, MEGAVITAMIN COMPLEX, MORPHINE . . . the labels and boxes were strewn about, but the bottles had been taken.

Carefully handled . . . cached and traded in dribbles . . . these could have bought Gordon admission into almost any hamlet. Why he might even have won a probationary membership in one of the wealthy Wyoming ranch communities!

He remembered a good doctor, whose clinic in the ruins of Butte was a sanctuary protected by all the surrounding villages and clans. Gordon thought of what that sainted gentleman could have done with these.

But his eyesight nearly went dim with dark tunnels of rage when he saw an empty cardboard box whose label read . . . TOOTH POWDER . . .

My tooth powder!

Gordon counted to ten. It wasn't enough. He tried controlled breathing. It only helped him focus on his anger. He stood there, slope-shouldered, feeling impotent to answer this one more unkindness by the world.

It's all right, he told himself. *I'm alive. And if I can get back to my backpack, I'll probably stay alive. Next year, if it comes, I can worry about my teeth rotting out of my head.*

Gordon picked up his gear and resumed his stalking exit out of that house of false expectations.

A man who spends a long time alone in the wilderness can have one great advantage over even a very good hunter—if that hunter nevertheless goes home to friends and companions most nights. The difference is a trait in kinship with the animals, with the wilds themselves. It was something as undefinable as that which made him nervous. Gordon sensed that something was odd long before he could attribute it. The feeling would not go away.

He had been retracing his steps toward the eastern edge of town, where his gear was cached. Now, though, he stopped and considered. Was he overreacting? He was no Jeremiah Johnson, to read the sounds and smells of the woods like streetsigns in a city. Still, he looked around for something to back up his unease.

The forest was mostly western hemlock and bigleaf maple with alder saplings growing like weeds in nearly every former open area. It was a far cry from the dry woodlands he had passed through on the east side of the Cascades, where he had been robbed under the sparse ponderosa pines. Here there was a scent of life richer than anything he remembered since before the Three-Year Winter.

Animal sounds had been scant until he stopped moving. But as he kept still, a flow of avian chatter and movement soon began to flow back into this patch of forest. Gray-feathered camp robbers flitted in small groups from spot to spot, playing guerrilla war with lesser jays for the best of the tiny, bug-rich glades. Smaller birds hopped from branch to branch, chirping and foraging.

Birds in this size range had no great love for man, but

neither did they go to great lengths to avoid him, if he was quiet.

Then why am I nervous as a cat?

There was a brief snapping sound to his left, near one of the ubiquitous blackberry thickets, about twenty yards away. Gordon whirled, but there, too, there were birds.

Correction. A bird. A mockingbird.

The creature swooped up through the branches and landed in a bundle of twigs Gordon guessed to be its nest. It stood there, like a small lordling, haughty and proud, then it squawked and dove toward the thicket again. As it passed out of sight, there was another tiny rustle, then the mockingbird swooped into view again.

Gordon idly picked at the loam with his bow while loosening the loop on his revolver, trying hard to maintain a frozen expression of nonchalance. He whistled through fear-dry lips as he walked slowly, moving neither toward the thicket nor away from it, but in the direction of a large grand fir.

Something behind that thicket had set off the mockingbird's nest defense response, and that something was trying hard to ignore the nuisance attacks—to stay silently hidden.

Alerted, Gordon recognized a hunting blind. He sauntered with exaggerated carelessness. But as soon as he passed behind the fir, he drew his revolver and ran into the forest at a sharp angle, crouching, trying to keep the bulk of the tree between himself and the blackberry bramble.

He remained in the tree's umbra only a moment. Surprise protected him a moment longer. Then the cracking of three loud shots, all of different caliber, diffracted down the lattice of trees. Gordon sprinted to a fallen log at the top of a small rise. Three more bangs pealed out as he dove over the decaying trunk, and hit the ground on the other side to a sharp snapping sound and stabbing pain in his right arm.

He felt a moment's blind panic as the hand holding his revolver cramped. If he had broken his *arm* . . .

Blood soaked the cuff of his U.S. Government Issue

tunic. Dread exaggerated the pain until he pulled back his sleeve and saw a long, shallow gash, with slivers of wood hanging from the laceration. It was the bow that had broken, stabbing him as he fell on it.

Gordon threw the fragments aside and scrambled on hands and knees up a narrow gully to the right, keeping low to take advantage of the creekbed and underbrush. Behind him whoops of gleeful chase carried over the tiny hillock.

The following minutes were a blur of whipping branches and sudden zigzags. When he splashed into a narrow rivulet, Gordon whirled, then hurried against the flow.

Hunted men often will run downstream, he remembered, racing upslope, hoping his enemies knew that bit of trivia. He hopped from stone to stone, trying not to dislodge mud into the water. Then he jumped off into the forest again.

There were shouts behind him. Gordon's own footfalls seemed loud enough to wake sleeping bears. Twice, he caught his breath behind boulders or clumps of foliage, thinking as well as practicing silence.

Finally, the shouts diminished with distance. Gordon sighed as he settled back against a large oak and pulled out his belt-pouch aid kit. The wound would be all right. There was no reason to expect infection from the polished wood of the bow. It hurt like hell but the tear was far from vessels or tendons. He bound it in boiled cloth and simply ignored the pain as he got up and looked around.

To his surprise, he recognized two landmarks at once . . . the towering, shattered sign of the Oakridge Motel, seen over the treetops, and a cattle grate across a worn asphalt path just to the east.

Gordon moved quickly to the place where he had cached his goods. They were exactly as he had left them. Apparently, the Fates were not so unsubtle as to deal him another blow just yet. He knew they didn't operate that way. They always let you hope for a while longer, then strung it out before they *really* let you have it.

•   •   •

Now the stalked turned stalker. Cautiously, Gordon sought out the blackberry blind, with its irate resident mockingbird. As expected, it was empty now. He crept around behind to get the ambushers' point of view, and sat there for a few minutes as the afternoon waned, looking and thinking.

They had had the drop on him, that was for certain. From this point of view it was hard to see how they had missed when the three men fired on him.

Were they *so* surprised by his sudden break for it? They must have had semi-automatic weapons, yet he only remembered six shots. Either they were being *very* stingy with ammo or . . .

He approached the grand fir across the clearing. Two fresh scars blemished the bark, ten feet up.

Ten feet. They couldn't be such bad marksmen.

So. It all fit. They had never meant to kill him at all. They had aimed high on purpose, to give him a scare and drive him off. No wonder his pursuers never really came close to catching him during his escape into the forest.

Gordon's lip curled. Ironically, this made his assailants easier to hate. Unthinking malice he had come to accept, as one must accept foul weather and savage beasts. So many former Americans had become little better than barbarians.

But calculated *contempt* like this was something he had to take personally. These men had the concept of mercy; still they had robbed, injured, and terrorized him.

He remembered Roger Septien, taunting him from that bone-dry hillside. These bastards were no better at all.

Gordon picked up their trail a hundred yards to the west of the blind. The bootprints were clear and uncovered . . . almost arrogant in their openness.

He took his time, but he never even considered turning back.

It was approaching dusk before the palisade that surrounded New Oakridge was in sight. An open area that had once been a city park was enclosed by a high, wooden fence.

From within could be heard the lowing of cattle. A horse whinnied. Gordon smelled hay and the rich odors of livestock.

Nearby a still higher pallisade surrounded three blocks of what had once been the southwest corner of Oakridge town. A row of two-story buildings half a block long took up the center of the village. Gordon could see the tops of these over the wall, and a water tower with a crow's nest atop it. A silhouetted figure stood watch, looking out over the dimming forest.

It looked like a prosperous community, perhaps the best-off he had encountered since leaving Idaho.

Trees had been cut to make a free-fire zone around the village wall, but that was some time ago. Undergrowth half as high as a man had encroached on the cleared field.

Well there can't be many survivalists in the area, anymore, Gordon thought, *or they'd be a whole lot less careless. Let's see what the main entrance is like.*

He skirted around the open area toward the south side of the village. On hearing voices he drew up cautiously behind a curtain of undergrowth.

A large wooden gate swung open. Two armed men sauntered out, looked around, then waved to someone within. With a shout and a snap of reins, a wagon pulled by two draft horses sallied through then stopped. The driver turned to speak to the two guards.

"Tell the Mayor I appreciate the loan, Jeff. I know my stead is in the hole pretty deep. But we'll pay him back out of next year's harvest, for sure. He already owns a piece of the farm, so it ought to be a good investment for him."

One of the guards nodded. "Sure thing, Sonny. Now you be careful on your way out, okay? Some of the boys spotted a loner down at the east end of old town, today. There was some shootin'."

The farmer's breath caught audibly. "Was anyone hurt? Are you sure it was just a loner?"

"Yeah, pretty sure. He ran like a rabbit according to Bob."

Gordon's pulse pounded faster. The insults had reached a point almost beyond bearing. He put his left hand inside his shirt and felt the whistle Abby had given him, hanging from its chain around his neck. He took some comfort from it, remembering decency.

"The feller did the Mayor a real favor, though," the first guard went on. "Found a hidey hole full of drugs before Bob's guys drove him off. Mayor's going to pass some of them around to some of the Owners at a party tonight, to find out what they'll do. I sure wish I moved in those circles."

"Me too," the younger watchman agreed. "Hey Sonny, you think the Mayor might pay you some of your bonus in drugs, if you make quota this year? You could have a real party!"

"Sonny" smiled sheepishly and shrugged. Then, for some reason, his head drooped. The older guard looked at him quizzically.

"What's the matter?" he asked.

Sonny shook his head. Gordon could barely hear him when he spoke. "We don't wish for very much anymore, do we, Gary?"

Gary frowned. "What do you mean?"

"I mean as long as we're wishing to be like the Mayor's cronies, why don't we wish we had a Mayor without cronies at all!"

"I . . ."

"Sally and I had three girls and two boys before th' Doom, Gary."

"I remember, Sonny, but—"

"Hal an' Peter died in th' war, but I counted me an' Sally blessed that all three girls grew up. Blessed!"

"Sonny, it's not your fault. It was just bad luck."

"*Bad luck?*" The farmer snorted. "One raped to death when those reavers came through, Peggy dead in childbirth, and my little Susan . . . she's got *gray hair*, Gary. She looks like Sally's sister!"

There was a long stretch of silence. The older guard

71

put his hand on the farmer's arm. "I'll bring a jug around tomorrow, Sonny. I promise. We'll talk about the old days, like we used to."

The farmer nodded without looking up. He shouted "Yaah!" and snapped the reins.

For a long moment the guard looked after the creaking wagon, chewing on a grass stem. Finally, he turned to his younger companion. "Jimmy, did I ever tell you about Portland? Sonny and I used to go there, before the war. They had this mayor, back when I was a kid, who used to pose for . . ."

They passed through the gate, out of Gordon's hearing.

Under other circumstances Gordon might have pondered hours over what that one small conversation had revealed about the social structure of Oakridge and its environs. The farmer's crop indebtedness, for instance—it was a classic early stage of share-kind serfdom. He had read about things like this in sophomore history tutorial, long ago and in another world. They were features of feudalism.

But right now Gordon had no time for philosophy or sociology. His emotions churned. Outrage over what had happened today was nothing next to his anger over the proposed use of the drugs he had found. When he thought of what that doctor in Wyoming could do with such medicines . . . why most of the substances wouldn't even make these ignorant savages high!

Gordon was fed up. His bandaged right arm throbbed.

I'll bet I could scale those walls without much trouble, find the storage hut, and reclaim what I found . . . along with some extra to make up for the insults, the pain, my broken bow.

The image wasn't satisfying enough. Gordon embellished. He envisioned dropping in on the Mayor's "party," and *wasting* all the power-hungry bastards who were making a midget empire out of this corner of the dark age. He imagined acquiring power, power to do good . . . power to *force* these yokels to use the education of their younger days before the learned generation disappeared forever from the world.

Why, why is nobody anywhere taking responsibility for putting things right again? I'd help. I'd dedicate my life to such a leader.

But the big dreams all seem to be gone. All the good men—like Lieutenant Van and Drew Simms—died defending them. I must be the only one left who still believes in them.

Leaving was out of the question, of course. A combination of pride, obstinacy, and simple gonadal fury rooted him in his tracks. Here he would do battle, and that was that.

Maybe there's an idealists' militia, in Heaven or in Hell. I guess I'll find out soon.

Fortunately, the war hormones left a little space for his forebrain to choose *tactics*. As the afternoon faded, he thought about what he was going to do.

Gordon stepped back into the shadows and a branch brushed by, dislodging his cap. He caught it before it fell to the ground, was about to put it back on, but then stopped abruptly and looked at it.

The burnished image of a horseman glinted back at him, a brass figure backed by a ribbon motto in Latin. Gordon watched shifting highlights in the shiny emblem, and slowly, he smiled.

It would be audacious—perhaps much more so than attempting the fence in the darkness. But the idea had a pleasing symmetry that appealed to Gordon. He was probably the last man alive who would choose a path of greater danger purely for aesthetic reasons, and he was glad. If the scheme failed, it would still be spectacular.

It required a brief foray into the ruins of old Oakridge—beyond the postwar village—to a structure certain to be among the least looted in town. He set the cap back on his head as he moved to take advantage of the remaining light.

An hour later, Gordon left the gutted buildings of the old town and stepped briskly along the pitted asphalt road, retracing his steps in the gathering dusk. Taking a long detour through the forest, he came at last to the road "Sonny" had used, south of the village wall. Now he approached boldly, guided by a solitary lantern hanging over the broad gate.

The guard was criminally lax. Gordon came within thirty feet unchallenged. He saw a shadowy sentry, standing on a parapet over near the far end of the palisade, but the idiot was looking the other way.

Gordon took a deep breath, put Abby's whistle to his lips, and blew three hard blasts. The shrill screams pealed through the buildings and forest like the shriek of a stooping raptor. Hurried footsteps pounded along the parapet. Three men carrying shotguns and oil lanterns appeared above the gate and stared down at him in the gathering twilight.

"Who are you? What do you want?"

"I must speak with someone in authority," Gordon hailed. "This is official business, and I demand entry to the town of Oakridge!"

That certainly put them off their routine. There was a long, stunned silence as the guards blinked, first at him and then at each other. Finally, one man hurried off while the first speaker cleared his throat. "Uh, come again? Are you feverish? Have you got the Sickness?"

Gordon shook his head. "I am not ill. I am tired and hungry. And angry over being shot at. But settling all that can wait until I have discharged my duty here."

This time the chief guard's voice cracked in blank perplexity. "Dis-discharged your . . . What the *hell* are you talking about, man?"

Hurried footsteps echoed on the parapet. Several more men arrived, followed by a number of children and women who began to string out to the left and right. Discipline, apparently, wasn't well practiced in Oakridge. The local tyrant and his cronies had had things their way for a long time.

Gordon repeated himself. Slowly and firmly, giving it his best Polonius voice.

"I demand to speak with your superiors. You are trying my patience keeping me out here, and it will definitely go into my report. Now get somebody here with authority to open this gate!"

The crowd thickened until an unbroken forest of silhouettes topped the palisade. They stared down at Gordon as a group of figures appeared on the parapet to the right, carrying lanterns. The onlookers on that side made way for the newcomers.

"Look, loner," the chief guard said, "you're just asking for a bullet. We got no 'official business' with *anyone* outside this valley, haven't since we broke relations with that commie place down at Blakeville, years ago. You can bet your ass I'm not bothering the Mayor for some crazy . . ."

The man turned in surprise as the party of dignitaries reached the gate. "Mr. Mayor . . . I'm sorry about the ruckus, but . . ."

"I was nearby anyway. Heard the commotion. What's going on here?"

The guard gestured. "We got a fellow out there babbling like nothing I've heard since the crazy times. He must be sick, or one of those loonies that always used to come through."

"I'll take care of this."

In the growing darkness the new figure leaned over the parapet. "I'm the Mayor of Oakridge," he announced. "We don't believe in charity, here. But if you're that fellow who found the goodies this afternoon, and graciously donated them to my boys, I'll admit we owe you. I'll have a nice hot meal lowered over the gate. And a blanket. You can sleep there by the road. Tomorrow, though, you gotta be gone. We don't want no diseases here. And from what my guards tell me, you must be delirious."

Gordon smiled. "Your generosity impresses me, Mr. Mayor. But I have come too far on official business to turn away now. First off, can you tell me if Oakridge has a working wireless or fiber optic facility?"

The silence brought on by his non sequitur was long and heavy. Gordon could imagine the Mayor's puzzlement. At last, the bossman answered.

"We haven't had a radio in ten years. Nothing's worked

since then. Why? What has that to do with anythi—"

"That's a shame. The airwaves have been a shambles since the war, of course . . ." he improvised, ". . . all the radioactivity, you know. But I'd hoped I could try to use your transmitter to report back to my superiors."

He delivered the lines with aplomb. This time they brought not silence but a surge of amazed whispers up and down the parapet. Gordon guessed that most of the population of Oakridge must be up there by now. He hoped the wall was well built. It was not in his plan to enter the town like Joshua.

He had quite another legend in mind.

"Get a lantern over here!" the Mayor commanded. "Not that one, you idiot! The one with the reflector! Yes. Now shine it on that man. I want a look at him!"

A bulky lamp was brought forth and there was a rattle as light speared out at Gordon. He was expecting it though and neither covered his eyes nor squinted. He shifted the leather bag and turned to bring his costume to the best angle. The letter carrier's cap, with its polished crest, sat at a rakish angle on his head.

The muttering of the crowd grew louder.

"Mr. Mayor," he called. "My patience is limited. I already will have to have words with you about the behavior of your boys this afternoon. Don't force me to exercise my authority in ways both of us would find unpleasant. You're on the verge of losing your privilege of communication with the rest of the nation."

The Mayor shifted his weight back and forth rapidly. "Communication? Nation? What is this blither? There's just the Blakeville commune, those self-righteous twits down at Culp Creek, and Satan knows what savages beyond them. Who the hell *are* you anyway?"

Gordon touched his cap. "Gordon Krantz, of the United States Postal Service. I'm the courier assigned to reestablish a mail route in Idaho and lower Oregon, and general federal inspector for the region."

And to imagine he had been embarrassed playing

Santa Claus back in Pine View! Gordon hadn't thought of the last part about being a "federal inspector" until it was out of his mouth. Was it inspiration, or a dare?

Well, might as well be hanged for a sheep as a goat, he thought.

The crowd was in tumult. Several times, Gordon heard the words "outside" and "inspector"—and especially "mailman." When the Mayor shouted for silence, it came slowly, trailing off into a rapt hush.

"So you're a mailman." The sneer was sarcastic. "What kind of idiots do you take us for, Krantz? A shiny suit makes you a government official? What government? What proof can you give us? Show us you're not a wild lunatic, raving with radiation fever!"

Gordon pulled out the papers he had prepared only an hour before, using the seal stamp he had found in the ruins of the Oakridge Post Office.

"I have credentials, here . . ." But he was interrupted at once.

"Keep your papers to yourself, loonie. We're not letting you come close enough to infect us with your fever!"

The Mayor straightened and waved an arm in the air, addressing his subjects. "You all remember how crazies and imposters used to come around, during the Chaos years, claiming to be everything from the Antichrist to Porky Pig? Well, there's one fact we can all depend on. Crazies come and crazies go, but there's only one "government" . . . that's what we got right here!"

He turned back to Gordon. "You're lucky this isn't like the plague years, loonie. Back then a case like yours would've called for immediate cure . . . by cremation!"

Gordon cursed silently. The local tyrant was slick and certainly no easy bluff. If they wouldn't even look at the "credentials" he had forged, the trip into oldtown this afternoon had been wasted. Gordon was down to his last ace. He smiled for the crowd, but he really wanted to cross his fingers.

From a side pocket of the leather bag he pulled out a

small bundle. Gordon made a pretense of shuffling through the packet, squinting at labels he knew by heart.

"Is there a . . . a Donald Smith, here?" he called up at the townspeople.

Heads turned left and right in sudden, hushed conversation. Their confusion was obvious even in the gathering darkness. Finally someone called out.

"He died a year after the war! In the last battle of the warehouses."

There was a tremor in the speaker's voice. Good. Surprise was not the only emotion at work here. Still, he needed something a lot better than that. The Mayor was still staring at him, as perplexed as the others, but when he figured out what Gordon was trying to do, there would be trouble.

"Oh well," Gordon called. "I'll have to confirm that, of course." Before anyone could speak, he hurried on, shuffling the packet in his hand.

"Is there a Mr. or Mrs. Franklin Thompson, in town? Or their son or daughter?"

Now the tide of hushed whispering carried almost a superstitious tone. A woman replied. "Dead! The boy lived until last year. Worked on the Jascowisc stead. His folks were in Portland when it blew."

Damn! Gordon had only one name left. It was all very well to strike their hearts with his knowledge, but what he needed was somebody alive!

"Right!" he called. "We'll confirm that. Finally, is there a Grace Horton here? A Miss *Grace Horton* . . ."

"No there ain't no Grace Horton!" the Mayor shouted, confidence and sarcasm back in his voice. "I know everyone in my territory. Never been no Grace Horton in the ten years since I arrived, you imposter!

"Can't you all see what he did? He found an old telephone book in town, and copied down some names to stir us up with." He shook a fist at Gordon. "Buddy, I rule that you are disturbing the peace and endangering the public health! You've got five seconds to be gone before I order my men to fire!"

Gordon exhaled heavily. Now he had no choice. At

least he could beat a retreat and lose nothing more than a little pride.

It was a good try, but you knew the chances of it working were slim. At least you had the bastard going there, for a little while.

It was time to go, but to his surprise Gordon found his body would not turn. His feet refused to move. All will to run away had evaporated. The sensible part of him was horrified as he squared his shoulders and called the Mayor's bluff.

"Assault on a postal courier is one of the few federal crimes that the pro tem Congress hasn't suspended for the recovery period, Mr. Mayor. The United States has always protected its mailmen."

He looked coldly into the glare of the lamp. "*Always*," he emphasized. And for a moment he felt a thrill. He *was* a courier, at least in spirit. He was an anachronism that the dark age had somehow missed when it systematically went about rubbing idealism from the world. Gordon looked straight toward the dark silhouette of the Mayor, and silently dared him to kill what was left of their shared sovereignty.

For several seconds the silence gathered. Then the Mayor held up his hand. "One!"

He counted slowly, perhaps to give Gordon time to run, and maybe for sadistic effect.

"Two!"

The game was lost. Gordon knew he should leave now, at once. Still, his body would not turn.

"Three!"

This is the way the last idealist dies, he thought. These sixteen years of survival had been an accident, an oversight of Nature, about to be corrected. In the end, all of his hard-won pragmatism had finally given way . . . to a gesture.

There was movement on the parapet. Someone at the far left was struggling forward.

The guards raised their shotguns. Gordon thought he saw a few of them move hesitantly—reluctantly. Not that that would do him any good.

The Mayor stretched out the last count, perhaps a bit

unnerved by Gordon's stubbornness. The raised fist began
to chop down.

"Mr. Mayor!" a woman's tremulous voice cut in, her
words high-pitched with fear as she reached up to grab the
bossman's hand. "P-please . . . I . . ."

The Mayor shrugged her hands away. "Get away,
woman. Get her out of here."

The frail shape backed away from the guards, but she
cried out clearly. "I . . . I'm Grace Horton!"

"What?" The Mayor was not alone in turning to stare
at her.

"It's my m-maiden name. I was married the year after
the second famine. That was before you and your men arrived. . . ."

The crowd reacted noisily. The Mayor cried out,
"Fools! He copied her name from a telephone book, I tell
you!"

Gordon smiled. He held up the bundle in his hand and
touched his cap with the other.

"Good evening, Mizz Horton. It's a lovely night, yes?
By the way, I happen to have a letter here for you, from a
Mr. Jim Horton, of Pine View, Oregon. . . . He gave it to me
twelve days ago. . . ."

The people on the parapet all seemed to be talking at
once. There were sudden motions and excited shouts. Gordon cupped his ear to listen to the woman's amazed exclamation, and had to raise his voice to be heard.

"Yes, ma'am. He seemed to be quite well. I'm afraid
that's all I have on this trip. But I'll be glad to carry your
reply to your brother on my way back, after I finish my cir-
cuit down in the valley."

He stepped forward, closer to the light. "One thing
though, ma'am. Mr. Horton didn't have enough postage,
back in Pine View, so I'm going to have to ask you for ten
dollars . . . C.O.D."

The crowd roared.

Next to the glaring lantern the figure of the Mayor
turned left and right, waving his arms and shouting. But

nothing he said was heard as the gate swung open and people poured out into the night. They surrounded Gordon, a tight press of hot-faced, excited men, women, children. Some limped. Others bore livid scars or rasped in tuberculin heaviness. And yet at that moment the pain of living seemed as nothing next to a glow of sudden faith.

In the middle of it all Gordon maintained his composure and walked slowly toward the portal. He smiled and nodded, especially to those who reached out and touched his elbow, or the wide curve of his bulging leather bag. The youngsters looked at him in superstitious awe. On many older faces, tears streamed.

Gordon was in the middle of a trembling adrenaline reaction, but he squelched hard on the little glimmering of conscience . . . a touch of shame at this lie.

The hell with it. It's not my fault they want to believe in the Tooth Fairy. I've finally grown up. I only want what belongs to me!

Simpletons.

Nevertheless, he smiled all around as the hands reached out, and the love surged forth. It flowed about him like a rushing stream and carried him in a wave of desperate, unwonted hope, into the town of Oakridge.

INTERLUDE

In spring orange blazes,

    Dust of ancestors glowers—

        Cooling Earth with hazes

II

CYCLOPS

NATIONAL RECOVERY ACT
PROVISIONALLY EXTENDED CONGRESS OF THE RESTORED UNITED STATES

DECLARATION

TO ALL CITIZENS: Let it be known by all now living within the legal boundaries of the United States of America that the people and fundamental institutions of the nation survive. Your enemies have failed in their aggression against humanity, and have been destroyed. A provisional government, acting in continuous succession from the last freely elected Congress and Executive of the United States, is vigorously moving to restore law, public safety, and liberty once more to this beloved land, under the Constitution and the righteous mercy of the Almighty.

TO THESE ENDS: Let it be known that all lesser laws and statutes of the United States are suspended, including all debts, liens, and judgments made before the outbreak of the Third World War. Until new codes are adopted by due process, local districts are free to meet emergency conditions as suitable, providing—

1. The freedoms guaranteed under the Bill of Rights shall not be withheld from any man or woman within the territory of the United States. Trials for all serious crimes

shall be by an impartial jury of one's peers. Except in cases of dire martial emergency, summary judgments and executions violating due process are absolutely forbidden.

2. Slavery is forbidden. Debt bondage shall not be for life, nor may it be passed from parent to child.

3. Districts, towns, and other entities shall hold proper secret ballot elections on every even-numbered year, in which all men and women over 18 years of age may participate. No person may use official coercion on any other person unless he or she has been so elected, or is directly answerable to a person so elected.

4. In order to assist the national recovery, citizens shall safeguard the physical and intellectual resources of the United States. Wherever and whenever possible, books and prewar machinery shall be salvaged and stored for the benefit of future generations. Local districts shall maintain schools to teach the young.

The Provisional Government hopes to reestablish nationwide radio service by the year 2021. Until that time, all communications must be carried via surface mail. Postal service should be reestablished in the Central and Eastern States by the year 2011, and in the West by 2018.

5. Cooperation with United States Mail Carriers is a requirement of all citizens. Interference with a letter carrier's function is a capital crime.

By order of the Provisional Congress
Restored United States of America
May 2009

1

CURTIN

The black bull terrier snarled and foamed. It yanked and strained at its chain, whipping froth at the excited, shouting men leaning over the low wooden walls of the arena. A scarred, one-eyed mongrel growled back at the pit bull from across the ring. Its rope tether hummed like a bowstring, threatening to tear out the ring bolt in the wall.

The dog pit stank. The sick-sweet smoke of locally grown tobacco—liberally cut with marijuana—rose in thick, roiling plumes. Farmers and townspeople yelled deafeningly from rows of benches overlooking the crude arena. Those nearest the ring pounded on the wooden slats, encouraging the dogs' hysterical frenzy.

Leather-gloved handlers pulled their canine gladiators back far enough to grip their collars, then turned to face the VIP bench, overlooking the center of the pit.

A burly, bearded dignitary, better dressed than most, puffed on his homemade cigar. He glanced quickly at the slender man who sat impassively to his right, whose eyes were shaded by a visored cap. The stranger sat quite still, in no way showing his feelings.

The heavyset official turned back to the handlers, and nodded.

A hundred men shouted at once as the dogs were loosed. The snarling animals shot at one another like quarrels, their argument uncomplicated. Fur and blood flew as the crowd cheered.

On the dignitaries' bench, the elders yelled no less fiercely than the villagers. Like them, most had bets riding on the outcome. But the big man with the cigar—the Chairman of Public Safety for the town of Curtin, Oregon—puffed furiously without enjoyment, his thoughts cloudy and thick. Once more he glanced at the stranger sitting to his right.

The thin fellow was unlike anyone else in the arena. His beard was neatly trimmed, his black hair cut and combed to barely pass over the ears. The hooded blue eyes seemed to pierce and inspect critically, like in the images of Old Testament prophets the Chairman had seen in Sunday School as a boy, long before the Doomwar.

He had the weathered look of a traveler. And he wore a *uniform* . . . one no living citizen of Curtin had ever expected to see again.

On the peak of the stranger's cap, the burnished image of a horseman gleamed in the light of the oil lanterns. Somehow it seemed shinier than any metal had a right to be.

The Chairman looked at his shouting townspeople, and sensed a difference about them tonight. The men of Curtin were yelling with more than their usual gusto at the Wednesday Night Fights. They, too, were aware of the visitor, who had ridden up to the city gates five days ago, erect and proud like some god, demanding food and shelter and a place to post his notices . . .

. . . and who then began distributing mail.

The Chairman had money riding on one of the dogs—old Jim Schmidt's Walleye. But his mind wasn't on the bloody contest on the sand below. He could not help glancing repeatedly at the Postman.

They had staged a special fight just for him, since he was leaving Curtin tomorrow for Cottage Grove. *He isn't enjoying himself*, the Chairman realized unhappily. The man who had turned their lives upside down was apparently trying to be polite. But just as obviously, he did not approve of dogfights.

The Chairman leaned over to speak to his guest. "I suppose they don't do this sort of thing back East, do they, Mr. Inspector?"

The cool look on the man's face was his answer. The Chairman cursed himself for a fool. Of course they wouldn't have dogfights—not in St. Paul City, or Topeka, or Odessa, or any of the civilized regions of the Restored United States. But *here*, here in ruined Oregon, so long cut off from civilization . . .

"Local communities are free to handle their affairs as they see fit, Mr. Chairman," the man replied. His compelling voice carried softly over the shouting in the arena. "Customs adapt to the times. The government in St. Paul City knows this. I've seen far worse in my travels."

Absolved, he could read in the postal inspector's eyes. The Chairman slumped slightly and looked away again.

He blinked, and at first he thought it was the smoke irritating his eyes. He dropped the cigar and ground it out under his foot, but the stinging would not depart. The bull pit was out of focus, as if he were seeing it in a dream . . . as if for the very first time.

My God! the Chairman thought. Are we really doing this? Only seventeen years ago I was a member of the Willamette Valley ASPCA!

What's happened to us?

What's happened to *me*?

Coughing behind his hand, he hid the wiping of his eyes. Then he looked around and saw that he was not alone. Here and there in the crowd at least a dozen men had stopped shouting, and were instead looking down at their hands. A few were crying openly, tears streaming down tough faces, hardened from the long battle to survive.

Suddenly, for a few of those present, the years since the war seemed compressed—insufficient excuse.

The cheering was ragged at the end of the fight. Handlers leapt into the pit to tend the victor and clear away the offal. But half the audience seemed to be glancing nervously at their leader and the stern, uniformed figure next to him.

91

The slender man straightened his cap. "Thank you, Mr. Chairman. But I think I'd better retire now. I have a long journey tomorrow. Good night, all."

He nodded to the elders, then rose and slipped on a worn leather jacket with a multicolored shoulder patch—a red, white, and blue emblem. As he moved slowly toward the exit, townsmen stood up silently and made way for him, their eyes downcast.

The Chairman of Curtin hesitated, then got up and followed, a murmur of voices growing behind him.

The second event was never held that evening.

2

COTTAGE GROVE

Cottage Grove,
Oregon
April 16, 2011

To Mrs. Adele Thompson
Mayor of Pine View Village
Unreclaimed State of Oregon

Transmittal route: Cottage Grove, Curtin,
Culp Creek, McFarland Pt.,
Oakridge, Pine View.

Dear Mrs. Thompson,
This is the second letter I've sent back along our
new postal route through the Willamette Forest
region. If you received the first, you'll already know
that your neighbors in Oakridge have chosen to
cooperate—after a few initial misunderstandings. I
appointed Mr. Sonny Davis postmaster there, a
prewar resident of the area liked by all. By now he
should have reestablished contact with you in Pine
View.

Gordon Krantz lifted his pencil from the sheaf of yellowed paper the citizens of Cottage Grove had donated for
his use. A brace of copper oil lamps and two candles flick-

ered over the antique desk, casting bright reflections off glass-framed pictures on the bedroom wall.

The locals had insisted Gordon take the best quarters in town. The room was snug, clean, and warm.

It was a big change from the way things had been for Gordon only a few months before. In the letter, for instance, he said little about the difficulties he had faced last October in the town of Oakridge.

The citizens of that mountain town had opened their hearts to him from the first moment he revealed himself as a representative of the *Restored United States*. But the tyrannical "Mayor" almost had his unwelcome guest murdered before Gordon managed to make it clear he was only interested in setting up a post office and moving on—that he was no threat to the Mayor's power.

Perhaps the bossman feared his people's reaction if he didn't help Gordon. In the end, Gordon received the supplies he asked for, and even a valuable, if somewhat elderly, horse. On leaving Oakridge, Gordon had seen relief on the Mayor's face. The local chief seemed confident he could keep control in spite of the stunning news that a United States still existed out there, somewhere.

And yet townspeople followed Gordon for over a mile, appearing from behind trees to shyly press letters into his hands, eagerly talking about the reclamation of Oregon and asking what they could do to help. They complained openly of the petty local tyranny, and by the time he had left that last crowd on the road, it was clear that a change was blowing in the wind.

Gordon figured the Mayor's days were numbered.

Since my last letter from Culp Creek, I've established post offices in Palmerville and Curtin. Today I completed negotiations with the mayor of Cottage Grove. Included in this packet is a report on my progress so far, to be passed on to my superiors in the Reclaimed State of Wyoming. When the courier following my trail arrives in Pine View, please give him my records and my best wishes.

And be patient if it takes a while. The trail west
from St. Paul City is dangerous, and it may be more
than a year before the next man arrives.

Gordon could well imagine Mrs. Thompson's reaction,
on reading that paragraph. The scrappy old matriarch
would shake her head, and maybe even laugh out loud at
the sheer blarney that filled every sentence.

Better than anybody else in the wild territory that had
once been the great state of Oregon, Adele Thompson
knew there would be no couriers from the civilized East.
There was no headquarters for Gordon to report back to.
The only thing the city of St. Paul was capital of was a still
slightly radioactive bend in the Mississippi River.

There had never been a Reclaimed State of Wyoming,
or a Restored United States for that matter, except in the
imagination of an itinerant, dark-age con artist doing his
best to survive in a deadly and suspicious world.

Mrs. Thompson was one of the rare folks Gordon had
met since the War who still saw with her eyes, and thought
with a logical mind. The illusion Gordon had created—at
first by accident, and later in desperation—had meant nothing to her. She had liked Gordon for himself, and shown
him charity without having to be coaxed by a myth.

He was writing the letter in this convoluted way—filled
with references to things that never were—for eyes other
than hers. The mail would change hands many times along
the route he had set up, before finally reaching Pine View.
But Mrs. Thompson would read between the lines.

And she wouldn't tell on him. Gordon was sure of that.
He only hoped she could contain her laughter.

This part of the Coast Fork is pretty peaceful
these days. The communities have even started
trading with each other in a modest fashion,
overcoming the old fear of war plagues and
survivalists. They're eager for news of the outside
world.

That's not to say all is placid. They tell me the

95

Rogue River country south of Roseburg is still totally lawless—Nathan Holn country. So I'm headed northward, toward Eugene. It's the direction most of the letters I'm carrying are addressed, anyway.

Deep in his saddlebag, under the bundled letters he had accepted from excited, grateful people all along his way, was the one Abby had given him. Gordon would try to see it delivered, whatever eventually happened to all the others.

Now I must go. Perhaps someday soon a letter from you and my other dear friends will catch up with me. Until then, please give my love to Abby and Michael and all.

At least as much as anywhere, the Restored United States of America is alive and well in beautiful Pine View.

Yours sincerely,
Gordon K.

That last remark might be a little dangerous, but Gordon had to include it, if only to show Mrs. Thompson he wasn't completely caught up by his own hoax—the scam that he hoped would get him safely across the almost lawless countryside to . . .

To what? After all these years Gordon still wasn't sure what it was he was looking for.

Perhaps only someone, somewhere, who was taking responsibility—who was trying to do something about the dark age. He shook his head. After all these years, the dream would not quite die.

He folded the letter into an old envelope, dribbled wax from a candle, and pressed it with a seal salvaged from the Oakridge Post Office. The letter went atop the "progress report" he had labored over earlier, a tissue of fantasy addressed to officials of a make-believe government.

Next to the packet lay his postman's cap. The lamp-light flickered in the brass image of a Pony Express rider, Gordon's silent companion and mentor for months now.

Gordon had stumbled onto his new survival plan by quirk and coincidence. But now, in town after town, people fell over themselves to believe, especially when he actually delivered letters from places he had already visited. After all these years, it seemed people still longed forlornly for a lost, shiny age—an era of cleanliness and order and a great nation now lost. The longing overwhelmed their hard-won skepticism like a spring thaw cracking the icy crust over a stream.

Gordon quashed a threatening sense of shame. No one alive was guiltless after the last seventeen years, and his scam actually seemed to do a little good in the towns he passed through. In exchange for supplies and a place to rest, he sold hope.

One did what one had to do.

There were two sharp raps on the door. Gordon called, "Come!"

Johnny Stevens, the newly appointed Assistant Postmaster of Cottage Grove, poked his head in. Johnny's boyish face bore a barely sprouted fuzz of almost blond beard. But his lanky legs promised a great cross-country stride, and he was reputed to be a dead shot.

Who could tell? The lad might even deliver the mail.

"Uh, sir?" Johnny was obviously reluctant to interrupt important business. "It's eight o'clock. You'll remember that the Mayor wanted to have a beer with you in the pub, since it's your last night here in town."

Gordon stood up. "Right, Johnny. Thanks." He grabbed his cap and jacket, then scooped up the phony report and the letter to Mrs. Thompson.

"Here you are then. These are official packets for your first run over to Culp Creek. Ruth Marshall is postmistress there. She'll be expecting somebody. Her folk will treat you well."

Johnny took the envelopes as if they were made of butterfly's wings. "I'll protect them with my life, sir." The youth's eyes shone with pride, and a fierce determination not to let Gordon down.

"You'll do no such thing!" Gordon snapped. The last thing he wanted was for a sixteen-year-old to get hurt protecting a chimera. "You'll use common sense, like I told you."

Johnny swallowed and nodded, but Gordon wasn't at all sure he understood. Of course the boy would probably just have an exciting adventure, following the forest paths farther than anyone from his village had traveled in over a decade, coming back a hero with tales to tell. There were still a few loner survivalists in those hills. But this far north of the Rogue River country the odds were Johnny'd make it to Culp Creek and back just fine.

Gordon almost had himself convinced.

He exhaled and gripped the young man's shoulder. "Your country doesn't need you to die for her, Johnny, but to live and serve her another day. Can you remember that?"

"Yessir." The lad nodded seriously. "I understand."

Gordon turned to blow out the candles.

Johnny must have been rummaging in the ruins of Cottage Grove's old post office, for out in the hall Gordon noticed the boy's homespun shirt now bore a proud U.S. MAIL patch on the shoulder, the colors still bright after almost twenty years.

"I've already got ten letters from people here in Cottage Grove and nearby farms," Johnny said. "I don't think most of them even know anybody back east. But they're writing anyway for the excitement of it, and in hopes somebody will write back."

So at least Gordon's visit had gotten people to practice their literacy skills a little. That was worth a few nights' food and lodging. "You warned them that east of Pine View the route is slow yet, and not guaranteed at all?"

"Sure. They don't care."

Gordon smiled. "That's okay then. The Postal Service has always carried mostly fantasies, anyway."

The boy looked at him, puzzled. But Gordon set his cap on his head and said nothing more.

•　　•　　•

98

Since departing the shards of Minnesota, so long ago, Gordon had seen few villages as prosperous and apparently happy as Cottage Grove. The farms now brought in a surplus most years. The militia was well drilled and—unlike at Oakridge—unoppressive. As hope of finding true civilization faded, Gordon had slowly reduced the scope of his dreams until a place like this seemed almost like Paradise.

It was ironic, then, that the very hoax that had taken him safely this far through the suspicious mountain hamlets now kept him from remaining here. For in order to maintain his illusion, he had to keep moving.

They all believed in him. If his illusion failed now, even the good people of this town would certainly turn on him.

The walled village covered one corner of prewar Cottage Grove. Its pub was a large, snug basement with two big fireplaces and a bar where the bitter local homebrew was served in tall clay steins.

Mayor Peter Von Kleek sat in a corner booth talking earnestly with Eric Stevens, Johnny's grandfather and newly appointed Postmaster of Cottage Grove. The two men were poring over a copy of Gordon's "Federal Regulations" as he and Johnny stepped into the pub.

Back in Oakridge, Gordon had run off a few score copies on a hand-cranked mimeograph machine he had managed to get working in the old, deserted post office. A lot of thought and care had gone into those circulars. They had to have the flavor of authenticity, and at the same time present no obvious threat to local strongmen—giving them no reason to fear Gordon's mythical Restored United States . . . or Gordon himself.

So far those sheets had been his most inspired prop.

Tall, gaunt-faced Peter Von Kleek stood and shook Gordon's hand, motioning him to a seat. The bartender hurried over with two tall steins of thick brown beer. It was warm, of course, but delicious—like pumpernickel bread. The Mayor waited, puffing nervously on his clay pipe, until Gordon put his stein down with a lip-smacking sigh.

Von Kleek nodded at the implied compliment. But his

frown remained fixed. He tapped the paper in front of him. "These regulations here aren't very detailed, Mr. Inspector."

"Call me Gordon, please. These are informal times."

"Ah, yes. Gordon. Please call me Peter." The Mayor was clearly uncomfortable.

"Well, Peter," Gordon nodded. "The Restored U.S. Government has learned some hard lessons. One has been not to impose rigid standards on far-flung localities who have problems St. Paul City can't even imagine, let alone regulate."

Gordon launched into one of his prepared pitches.

"There's the question of money, for instance. Most communities dropped prewar currency soon after the food center riots. Barter systems are the rule, and they usually work just fine, except when debt service turns into a form of slavery."

That much was all true. In his travels Gordon had seen versions of feudal serfdom rising all over. Money was a joke.

"The federal authorities in St. Paul have declared the old currency moot. There are just too many bills and coins out there for sparse rural economies.

"Still, we're trying to encourage national commerce. One way is by accepting old-time two-dollar bills to pay postage for letters carried by U.S. Mail. They never were very common, and are impossible to forge with present-day technology. Pre-1965 silver coins are also acceptable."

"We've already taken in over forty dollars' worth!" Johnny Stevens interjected. "Folks are hunting all over for those old bills and coins. And they've started usin' them to pay off barter debts too."

Gordon shrugged. It had started already. Sometimes the little things he added to his tale, simply in order to lend verisimilitude, took off by themselves in ways he had never expected. He couldn't see how a little money put back into circulation, given value by a local myth in the "Restored U.S.," could hurt these people much.

Von Kleek nodded. He moved on to the next item.

"This part here about no 'coercion' without elections—" He tapped the paper. "Well, we do have sort of regular town meetings, and people from the surrounding hamlets take part when something big is up. But I can't rightly say I or my militia chief were ever really *voted* for . . . not in a real secret ballot, like it says here."

He shook his head. "And we've had to do some pretty drastic things, especially during the early days. I hope we're not going to have that held too hard against us Mr. Inspe— Gordon. We really have been doin' our best.

"We have a school, for instance. Most of the younger kids attend after harvest. And we can make a start salvaging machines and voting like it says here. . . ." Von Kleek wanted reassurance; he was trying to catch Gordon's eye. But Gordon lifted his beer mug in order not to meet his gaze.

One of the major ironies he had found in his travels had been this phenomenon—that those who had fallen the least far into savagery were those who seemed the most ashamed of having fallen at all.

He coughed, clearing his throat.

"It seems . . . it seems to me you've been doing a pretty good job here, Peter. The past doesn't matter as much as the future, anyway. I don't think you have to worry about the federal government interfering at all."

Von Kleek looked relieved. Gordon was sure there would be a secret ballot election here within weeks. And the people of this area would deserve what they got if they elected anyone as their leader but this gruff, sensible man.

"One thing bothers me."

It was Eric Stevens who spoke. The spry oldster had been Gordon's obvious choice as postmaster. For one thing, he ran the local trading post, and was the best-educated man in town, with a prewar college degree.

Another reason was that Stevens had appeared the most suspicious when Gordon rode into town several days before, proclaiming a new era for Oregon under the "Restored U.S." Appointing him postmaster seemed to persuade him to believe, if only for his own prestige and profit.

Only incidentally, he would also probably do a good job—as long as the myth lasted, at least.

Old Stevens turned his beer stein on the table, leaving

a broad oval ring. "What I can't figure out is why nobody's been out here from St. Paul City *before*.

"Sure, I know you had to cross a helluva lot of wild country to get here, almost all of it on foot, you say. But what I want to know is why didn't they just send somebody out in an *airplane*?"

There was a brief silence at the table. Gordon could tell that townsmen nearby were listening in, as well.

"Aw gramps!" Johnny Stevens shook his head in embarrassment for his grandfather. "Don't you realize how bad the war was? All the airplanes and complicated machines were wrecked by that *pulse* thing that blasted all the radios and such right at the beginning of the war! Then, later on, there wouldn't have been anybody around who knew how to fix 'em. And there'd be no spare parts!"

Gordon blinked in brief surprise. The kid was good! He had been born after the fall of industrial civilization, yet he had a grasp of the essentials.

Of course everyone knew about the electromagnetic pulses, from giant H-bombs exploded high in space, that had devastated electronic devices all over the world on that deadly first day. But Johnny's understanding went beyond that to the interdependence of a machine culture.

Still, if the kid was bright he must have gotten it from his grandfather. The older Stevens looked at Gordon archly. "That right, Inspector? No spares or mechanics left?"

Gordon knew that explanation wouldn't hold under close scrutiny. He blessed those long, tedious hours on broken roads since leaving Oakridge, when he had worked out his story in detail.

"No, not quite. The pulse radiation, the blasts, and the fallout destroyed a lot. The bugs and riots and the Three-Year Winter killed many skilled people. But actually, it didn't take long to get some machines going again. There were airplanes ready to fly within days. The Restored U.S. has scores of them, repaired and tested and waiting to fly.

"But they can't take off. They're all grounded, and will be for years to come."

The old man looked puzzled. "Why's that, Inspector?"

"For the same reason you wouldn't pick up a broadcast even if you put together a working radio," Gordon said. He paused for effect.

"Because of laser satellites."

Peter Von Kleek slapped the table. "Son of a bitch!" All over the room heads turned their way.

Eric Stevens sighed, giving Gordon a look that had to be total acceptance . . . or admiration of a better liar than himself.

"What . . . what's a lay . . . ?"

"Laser sat," Johnny's grandfather explained. "We won the war." He snorted at the famous marginal victory that had been trumpeted in the weeks before the riots began. "But the enemy must have left some sleeper satellites in orbit. Program 'em to wait a few months or years, then anything so much as lets out a peep over the radio, or tries to fly, and *zap!*" He sliced the air decisively. "No wonder I never picked up anything on my crystal set!"

Gordon nodded. The story fit so well, it could even be true. He actually hoped so. For it might explain the silence, and the lonely emptiness of the sky, without the world having to be totally vacant of civilization.

And how else to explain the slag heaps that remained of so many radio antennas he had passed in his travels?

"What's the government *doing* about it?" Von Kleek asked earnestly.

Fairy tales, Gordon thought. His lies would grow more complex as he traveled until at last someone caught him up.

"There are some scientists left. We hope to find facilities in California for making and launching orbital rockets." He left the implication hanging.

The others looked disappointed.

"If only there was a way to take out the damned satellites sooner," the Mayor said. "Think of all those aircraft, just sitting there! Can you imagine how surprised the next Holnist raiding party out of the damned Rogue River would be, to find us farmers backed up by the *U.S. Air Force* and some bloody A-10s!"

He gave a whooshing sound and made diving motions

103

with his hands. Then the Mayor did a pretty good imitation of a machine gun. Gordon laughed with the others. Like boys they lived briefly in a fantasy of rescue, and power to the good guys.

Other men and women gathered around, now that the Mayor and the postal inspector had apparently finished their business. Someone pulled out a harmonica. A guitar was passed to Johnny Stevens, who proved to be quite gifted. Soon the crowd was singing bawdy folk songs and old commercial jingles.

The mood was high. Hope was thick as the warm, dark beer, and tasted at least as good.

It was later in the evening that he heard it for the first time. On his way out of the men's room—grateful that Cottage Grove had somehow retained gravity-flow indoor plumbing—Gordon stopped suddenly near the back stairs.

There had been a sound.

The crowd by the fireplace was singing. . . . *"Gather 'round and listen to my tale—a tale of a fateful trip. . . ."*

Gordon cocked his head. Had he imagined the other murmur? It had been faint, and his head *was* ringing a bit on its own from the beer.

But a queer feeling at the back of his neck, an intuition, refused to let go. It made him turn around and begin climbing the stairs, a steep flight rising into the building above the basement pub.

The narrow passage was dimly lit by a candle at the halfway landing. The happy, drunken sounds of the songfest faded away behind him as he ascended slowly, careful of the creaking steps.

At the top he emerged into a darkling hallway. Gordon listened fruitlessly for what felt like a long time. After some moments he turned around, writing it all off to an overworked imagination.

Then it came again.

. . . a series of faint, eerie sounds at the very edge of audibility. The half-memories they pulled forth sent a shiver

104

up Gordon's back. He had not heard their like since . . .
since long, long ago.

At the end of the dusty hallway faint light outlined a
cracked door jamb. He approached, quietly.

Bloop!

Gordon touched the cold metal knob. It was free of
dust. Someone was already inside.

Wah-wah . . .

The absent weight of his revolver—left in his guest
room in supposedly safe Cottage Grove—made him feel
half-naked as he turned the knob and opened the door.

Dusty tarpaulins covered stacked crates filled with odds
and ends, everything from salvaged tires to tools to furniture, a hoard put aside by the villagers against the uncertain
future. Around one row of boxes came the source of that
faint, flickering light. There were hushed voices just ahead,
whispering in urgent excitement. And that sound—

Bloop. Bloop!

Gordon crept alongside the towers of musty crates—
like unsteady cliffs of ancient sediment—growing more
tense as he approached the end of the row. The glow spread.
It was a *cold* light, without heat.

A floorboard creaked under his foot.

Five faces turned up suddenly, cast into deep relief by
the strange light. In a breathless instant Gordon saw that
they were *children*, staring up at him in terrified awe—the
more so because they clearly recognized him. Their eyes
were wide and they did not move.

But Gordon cared about none of that, only about a little boxlike object that lay on an oval rug in the center of the
small coven. He could not believe what he was seeing.

Across its bottom was a row of tiny buttons, and in the
center a flat, gray screen gave off a pearly sheen.

Pink spiders emerged from flying saucers and stepped
imperiously down the screen, to a crunching, marching
beat. Arriving at the bottom without opposition, they
bleated in triumph, then their ranks reformed and the assault began all over again.

Gordon's throat was dry.

"Where . . ." he breathed.

The children stood up. One of the boys swallowed. "Sir?"

Gordon pointed. "Where in the name of all that's holy did you get that?" He shook his head. "More important . . . where did you get the *batteries*!"

One of the children began to cry. "Please, sir, we didn't know it was wrong. Timmy Smith told us it's just a game the oldtime children used to have! We find 'em all over, only they don't work no more. . . ."

"Who," Gordon insisted, "is Timmy Smith?"

"A boy. His pa has come down from Creswell with a wagon to trade the last couple years. Timmy swapped this one for twenty old ones we found that wouldn't work no more."

Gordon recalled the map he had been studying in his room earlier in the evening. Creswell was just a little north of here, not far off the route he had planned to take to Eugene.

Can it be? Hope was too hot and sudden to be a pleasure, or even recognized.

"Did Timmy Smith say where he *got* the toy?" He tried not to spook the children, but some of his urgency must have spilled over, frightening them.

A girl wailed. "He said he got it from *Cyclops*!"

Then, in a panicked flurry, the children were gone, disappeared down little alleys in the dusty storage room. Gordon was left suddenly alone, standing quite still, watching tiny invaders descend in the glow of the little gray screen.

"Crunch-crunch-crunch," they marched.

The game *blooped* victoriously. Then began to play all over again.

3

EUGENE

The pony's breath puffed visibly as it plodded on through the dank drizzle, led by a man in a rain-slick poncho. Its only burdens were a saddle and two thick bags, plastic-covered against the damp.

The gray Interstate glistened wetly. Deep puddles lay like small lakes in the concrete. Dirt had blown over the four-lane highway during the postwar drought years, and grass had later begun to grow as the old northwest rains returned. Much of the highway was now a ribbon of meadow, a flat notch in the forested hills overlooking a churning river.

Gordon raised his slicker tentlike to consult his map. Ahead, to his right, a large fen had formed where the south and east forks of the Willamette came together before cutting west between Eugene and Springfield. According to the old map there was a modern industrial park below. Now only a few old roofs stuck out above the mire. The neat lanes, parking lots, and lawns were a realm for water fowl, who seemed not at all discomfitted by the wet.

Back in Creswell they had told Gordon the Interstate would be impassable a little north of here. He would have to cut through Eugene itself, find an open bridge across the river, and then somehow get back onto the highway to Coburg.

The Creswellers had been a little vague on details. Few travelers had made the trip since the war.

That's all right. Eugene has been one of my goals for months. We'll take a look at what's become of her.

107

Briefly, though. Now the city was only a milestone along his path toward a deeper mystery, waiting farther to the north.

The elements had not yet defeated the Interstate. It might be grassy and puddled, but the only fallen bridges he had passed still bore obvious signs of violence. When man built well, it seemed, only time or man himself could bring his things down. *And they did build well*, Gordon thought. Maybe future generations of Americans, ambling through the forests eating each other, would think these works the creations of gods.

He shook his head. *The rain, it's got me in a fey mood.*

Soon he came upon a large sign, half buried in a puddle. Gordon kicked away debris and knelt to examine the rusting plate—like a tracker reading a cold trail in a forest path.

"Thirtieth Avenue," he read aloud.

A broad road cut into the hills to the west, away from the Interstate. According to the map, downtown Eugene was just over the forested rise that way.

He got up and patted his pack animal. "Come on, Dobbin. Swish your tail and signal for a right turn. It's off the freeway and down surface streets from here." The horse puffed stoically as Gordon gave the reins a gentle tug and led it down the off-ramp, then under the overpass and on up the slope to the west.

From the top of the hill a gently falling mist seemed somehow to soften the ruined town's disfigurement. Rains had long since washed away the fire stains. Slow beards of climbing greenery, sprouting from cracks in the pavement, covered many of the buildings, hiding their wounds.

Folk in Creswell had warned him what to expect. Still, it was never easy coming into a dead city. Gordon descended to the ghostly streets, strewn with broken glass. The rain-wet pavement sparkled with another era's shattered panes.

In the lower parts of town, alders grew in the streets, in dirt laid down when a river of mud slammed into the city from the broken Fall Creek and Lookout Point dams. The collapse of those reservoirs had wiped out Route 58 west of Oakridge, forcing Gordon to make his long detour south and west through Curtin, Cottage Grove, and Creswell before finally swinging north again.

The devastation was pretty bad. *And yet*, Gordon thought, *they held on, here. From all accounts, they almost made it.*

Back in Creswell, between all the meetings and celebrations—the election of the new postmaster and excited plans to extend the new mail delivery network east and west—the citizens had regaled Gordon with stories of the valiant struggle of Eugene. They told how the city had struggled to hold out for four long years after war and epidemic had isolated it from the outer world. In a strange alliance of the university community and red-neck country farmers, somehow the city-state had overcome all threats . . . until at last the bandit gangs finished her off by blasting the upland reservoirs all at once, cutting off both power and unpolluted water.

The tale was already legendary, almost like the fall of Troy. And yet the storytellers hadn't sounded forlorn in telling it. It was more as if they now looked upon the disaster as a temporary setback, to be overcome within their own lifetimes.

For Creswell had been in a tizzy of optimism even before Gordon's arrival. His tale of a "Restored United States" was the town's *second* dose of good news in less than three months.

Last winter *another* visitor had arrived—this one from the north, a grinning man in a white-and-black robe—who passed out startling gifts for the children and then departed, speaking the magical name *Cyclops*.

Cyclops, the stranger had said.

Cyclops would make things right again. Cyclops would bring comfort and progress back into the world, redeeming everybody from drudgery and lingering hopelessness, the legacy of the Doomwar.

All the people had to do was collect their old machinery, particularly electronics. Cyclops would take their donations of useless, ruined equipment, plus perhaps a little surplus food to maintain its volunteer servants. In return, Cyclops would give the Creswellans things that *worked*.

The toys were only tokens of what was to come. Someday there would be real miracles.

Gordon had been unable to get anything coherent from the people of Creswell. They were too deliriously happy to be completely logical. Half of them assumed his "Restored United States" was *behind* Cyclops, and half thought it was the other way around. It hardly occurred to anybody that the two wonders could be unconnected—two spreading legends encountering one another in the wilderness.

Gordon didn't dare disabuse them, or ask too many questions. He had left as quickly as he could—loaded down with more letters than ever—determined to follow the tale to its source.

It was about noon as he turned north on University Street. The gentle rain was no bother. He could explore Eugene for a while and still make it by nightfall to Coburg, where a settlement of gleaners supposedly lived. Somewhere north of there lay the territory from which the followers of Cyclops were spreading word of their strange redemption.

As he walked quietly past the gutted buildings, Gordon wondered if he should even try to pull his "postman" hoax in the north. He remembered the little spiders and saucers, flashing in the darkness, and found it hard not to hope.

Perhaps he could give up the scam and find something real to believe in at last. Perhaps someone, at last, was leading a fight against the dark age.

It was too sweet a glimmer to let go of, but too delicate to hold tightly.

The shattered storefronts of the deserted town gave way at last to Eighteenth Avenue and the University of Oregon campus, the broad athletic field now overgrown with aspen and alder saplings, some more than twenty feet high. There, near the old gymnasium, Gordon slowed down, then stopped abruptly and held the pony still.

The animal snorted and pawed the ground as Gordon listened, and then was sure.

Somewhere, perhaps not too far away, somebody was screaming.

The faint crying crescendoed then fell away. It was a woman's voice, soaked with pain and deadly fear. Gordon pushed back the cover of his holster and drew his revolver. Had it come from the north? The east?

He pushed into a semijungle between the university buildings, hurriedly seeking a place to go to ground. He had had an easy time of it since leaving Oakridge months ago, too easy. Obviously he had acquired bad habits. It was a miracle no one had heard *him*, traipsing down these deserted streets as if he owned them.

He led the pony through a gaping door in the side of a slate-sided gymnasium, and tethered the animal behind a fold-down stand of bleachers. Gordon dropped a pile of oats near the animal, but left the saddle in place and cinched.

Now what? Do we wait it out? Or do we check it out?

Gordon unwrapped his bow and quiver and set the string. In the rain they were probably more reliable, and certainly quieter than his carbine or revolver.

He stuffed one of the bulging mail sacks into a ventilation shaft, well out of sight. As he was searching for a place to hide the other, he suddenly realized what he was doing.

He grinned ironically at his momentary foolishness and left the second bag lying on the floor as he set off to find the trouble.

The sounds came from a brick building just ahead, one whose long bank of glass windows still gleamed. Apparently looters hadn't even thought the place worth bothering with.

Now Gordon could hear faint, muttered voices, the soft nickering of horses, and the creaking of tack.

Seeing no watchers at the roofs or windows, he dashed

across the overgrown lawn and up a broad flight of concrete
steps, flattening against a doorway around the corner of the
building. He breathed open-mouthed for silence.

The door bore an ancient, rusted padlock and an en-
graved plastic sign.

THEODORE STURGEON MEMORIAL CENTER
Dedicated May 1989
Cafeteria Hours
11–2:30
5–8 P.M.

The voices came from just within . . . though too muffled to make out anything distinct. An outside stairway led
up to several floors overhead. He stepped back and saw that
a door lay ajar three flights up.

Gordon knew he was being a fool once again. Now that
he had the trouble located, he really should go collect his
pony and get the hell out of there, as quickly as possible.

The voices within grew angry. Through the crack in
the door he heard a blow being struck. A woman's cry of
pain was followed by coarse male laughter.

Sighing softly at the flaw in his character that kept him
there—instead of running away as anyone with any brains
would do—Gordon started climbing the concrete stair, careful not to make a sound.

Rot and mold covered an area just within the half-open
doorway. But beyond that the fourth floor of the student
center looked untouched. Miraculously, none of the glass
panes in the great skylight had been smashed, though the
copper frame wore a patina of verdigris. Under the atrium's
pale glow a carpeted ramp spiraled downward, connecting
each floor.

As Gordon cautiously approached the open center of
the building, it felt momentarily as if he had stepped backward in time. Locters had left the student organization
offices—with their passionate tornadoes of paper—

112

completely untouched. Bulletin boards were still plastered with age-dimmed announcements of sporting events, variety shows, political rallies.

Only at the far end were there a few notices in bright red, having to do with the emergency—the final crisis that had struck almost without warning, bringing it all to an end. Otherwise, the clutter was homey, radical, enthusiastic . . .

Young . . .

Gordon hurried past and skirted down the spiraling ramp toward the voices below.

A second floor balcony extended out over the main lobby. He got down on his hands and knees and crawled the rest of the way.

On the north side of the building, to the right, part of the two-story glass facing had been shattered to make room for a pair of large wagons. Steam rose from six horses tethered over by the west wall, behind a row of dark pinball machines.

Outside, amid the broken glass shards, the sulking rain created spreading pink pools around four sprawled bodies, recently cut down by automatic weapons fire. Only one of the victims had even managed to draw a sidearm during the ambush. His pistol lay in a puddle, inches from a motionless hand.

The voices came from his left, where the balcony made a turn. Gordon crawled cautiously forward and looked out over the other part of the L-shaped room.

Several ceiling-high mirrors remained along the west wall, giving Gordon a wide view of the floor below. A blaze of smashed furniture crackled in a large fireplace between the reflecting panes.

He hugged the moldy carpet and lifted his head just enough to see four heavily-armed men arguing by the fire. A fifth lounged on a couch over to the left, his automatic rifle aimed idly at a pair of prisoners—a boy of about nine years and a young woman.

Red weals on her face matched the pattern of a man's hand. Her brown hair was matted and she held the boy

113

close, watching her captors warily. Neither prisoner seemed to have any energy left for tears.

The bearded men were all garbed in one-piece prewar army surplus outfits in green, brown, and gray-speckled camouflage. Each wore one or more gold earrings in his left ear lobe.

Survivalists. Gordon felt a wave of revulsion.

Once upon a time, before the War, the word had had several meanings, ranging from common sense, community-conscious preparedness all the way to antisocial paranoid gun nuts. By one way of looking at things, perhaps Gordon himself could be called a "survivalist." But it was the latter connotation that had stuck, after the ruin the worst sort had caused.

Everywhere he had gone in his travels, folk shared this reaction. More than the Enemy, whose bombs and germs had wrought such destruction during the One-Week War, the people in nearly every wrecked county and hamlet blamed these macho outlaws for the terrible troubles that led to the final Fall.

And worst of all had been the followers of Nathan Holn, *may he rot in Hell.*

But there weren't supposed to *be* any survivalists anymore in the valley of the Willamette! In Cottage Grove, Gordon had been told that the last big bunch had been driven south of Roseburg years ago, into the wilderness of the Rogue River country!

What were these devils doing here, then? He moved a little closer and listened.

"I dunno, Strike Leader. I don't think we oughta go any deeper on this recon. We've already had enough surprises with this 'Cyclops' thing the bird here let slip about, before she clammed up. I say we oughta head back to the boats at Site Bravo and report what we found."

The speaker was a short, bald man with a wiry frame. He warmed his hands over the fire, his back to Gordon. A SAW assault gun equipped with a flash suppressor was slung muzzle-down over his back.

The big man he addressed as "Strike Leader" wore a

scar from one ear to his chin, only partly hidden by a gray-flecked black beard. He grinned, displaying several gaps in his teeth.

"You don't really believe that bull the broad was spewing, do you? All that crap about a big computer that talks? What a crock! She's just feedin' it to us to give us a stall!"

"Oh yeah? Well how do you explain all *that*?"

The little man gestured back to the wagons. In the mirror, Gordon could see a corner of the nearest. It was loaded down with odds and ends, no doubt collected here on the University campus. The haul seemed to consist mostly of electronic equipment.

Not farm tools, not clothes or jewelry—but *electronics*.

It was the first time Gordon had ever seen a gleaner's wagon filled with salvage like this. The implication caused Gordon's pulse to pound in his ears. In his excitement, he barely ducked down in time as the little man turned to pick up something from a nearby table.

"And what about *this*?" the small survivalist asked. In his hand was a toy—a small video game like the one Gordon had seen in Cottage Grove.

Lights flashed and the little box gave out a high, cheerful melody. The Strike Leader stared at it for a long moment. Finally he shrugged. "Don't mean shit."

One of the other raiders spoke. "I agree wit' lil' Jim. . . ."

"That's Blue Five," the big man growled. "Maintain discipline!"

"Right," the third man nodded, apparently unperturbed by the rebuke. "I agree with Blue Five, then. I think we oughta report this to Colonel Bezoar an' the General. It could affect the invasion. What if the farmers *do* got high tech up north of here? We could wind up doin' an end run right into some heavy-duty lasers or something . . . especially if they got some old Air Force or Navy stuff working again!"

"All the more reason to continue this recon," the leader growled. "We've got to find out more about this Cyclops thing."

"But you saw how hard we had to work to get the

woman to tell us even what we learned! And we can't leave
her here while we go deeper on recon. If we turned back we
could put her on one of the boats and . . ."

"*Off* the damn woman! We finish with her tonight.
The boy, too. You been in the mountains too long, Blue
Four. These valleys are *crawling* with pretty birds. We can't
risk this one making noise, and we sure can't take her along
on a recon!"

The argument didn't surprise Gordon. All over the
country—wherever they had managed to establish
themselves—these postwar crazies had taken to raiding for
women, as well as for food and slaves. After the first few
years of slaughter, most Holnist enclaves had found themselves with incredibly high male–female ratios. Now,
women were valuable chattel in the loose, macho, hyper-
survivalist societies.

No wonder some of the raiders below wanted to carry
this one back. Gordon could tell that she might be quite
pretty, if she healed and if the pall of terror ever left her
eyes.

The boy in her arms watched the men with fierce anger.

Gordon surmised that the Rogue River gangs must
have become organized at last, perhaps under a charismatic
leader. Apparently they were planning to invade by sea,
skirting the Roseville and Camas Valley defenses—where
the farmers had somehow beaten back their repeated efforts at conquest.

It was a bold plan, and it could very well mean the end
of whatever flickering civilization remained here in the Willamette Valley.

Until now, Gordon had been telling himself he might
somehow stay out of this trouble. But the last seventeen
years had long ago made almost everybody alive take sides in
this particular struggle. Rival villages with bitter feuds
would drop their quarrels to join and wipe out bands like
these. The very sight of Army surplus camouflage and gold
earrings elicited a loathing response that was common

nearly everywhere, like the way people felt about vultures. Gordon could not leave this place without at least trying to think of a way to harm the men below.

During a lull in the rain, two men went outside and began stripping the bodies, mutilating them and taking grisly trophies. When the drizzle returned, the raiders shifted their attention to the wagons, rummaging through them for anything valuable. From their curses it seemed the search was futile. Gordon heard the smashing of delicate and totally irreplaceable electronics parts under their boots.

Only the one guarding the captives was still in view, turned away from both Gordon and the wall of mirrors. He was cleaning his weapon, not paying particular attention.

Wishing he were less a fool, Gordon felt compelled to take a chance. He lifted his head above the level of the floor and raised his hand. The motion made the woman look up. Her eyes widened in surprise.

Gordon put a finger to his lips, praying she would understand that these men were his enemies, too. The woman blinked, and Gordon feared for a moment she was about to speak. She glanced quickly at her guard, who remained absorbed in his weapon.

When her eyes met Gordon's again, she nodded slightly. He gave her a thumbs-up sign and quickly backed away from the balcony.

First chance, he drew his canteen and drank deeply, for his mouth was dry as ashes. Gordon found an office in which the dust wasn't too thick—he certainly couldn't afford to sneeze—and chewed on a strip of Creswell beef jerky as he settled down to wait.

His chance came a little while before dusk. Three of the raiders left on a patrol. The one called Little Jim remained behind to cook a raggedly butchered haunch of deer in the fireplace. A gaunt-faced Holnist with three gold earrings guarded the prisoners, staring at the young woman while whittling slowly on a piece of wood. Gordon wondered how long it would take for the guard's lust to overcome his fear of the leader's wrath. He was obviously working up his nerve.

Gordon had his bow ready. An arrow was nocked and two more lay on the carpet before him. His holster flap was free and the pistol's hammer rested on a sixth round. There was little more he could do but wait.

The guard put down his whittling and stood up. The woman held the boy close and looked away as he walked closer.

"Blue One ain't gonna like it," the bandit by the fire warned lowly.

The guard stood over the woman. She tried not to flinch, but shivered when he touched her hair. The boy's eyes glistened with anger.

"Blue One already said we're gonna waste her later, after takin' turns. Don't see why my turn shouldn't come first. Maybe I can even get her to talk about that 'Cyclops' thing.

"How 'bout it, babe?" He leered down on her. "If a beatin' won't make you loosen your mouf, I know just what'll tame you down."

"What about the kid?" Little Jim asked.

The guard shrugged casually. "What *about* 'im?" Suddenly a hunting knife was in his right hand. With his left he seized the boy's hair and yanked him out of the woman's grasp. She screamed.

In that telescoped instant, Gordon acted completely on reflex—there was no time at all to think. Even so, he did not do the obvious, but what was necessary. Instead of shooting at the man with the knife, he swung his bow up, and put an arrow into *Little Jim*'s chest.

The small survivalist hopped back and stared down at the shaft in blank surprise. With a faint gurgle he slumped to the ground.

Gordon quickly nocked another arrow and turned in time to see the other survivalist yank his knife out of the girl's shoulder. She must have hurled herself in between him and the child, blocking the blow with her body. The boy lay stunned in the corner.

Gravely wounded, she still tore at her enemy with her nails, unfortunately blocking Gordon from a clear shot. The surprised bandit fumbled at first, cursing and trying to catch her wrists. Finally, he managed to hurl her to the ground. Angered by the painful scratches—and unaware of his partner's demise—the Holnist grinned and hefted his knife to finish the job. He took a step toward the wounded, gasping woman.

At that point Gordon's arrow tore through the fabric of his camouflage fatigues, slicing a shallow, bloody gash along his back. The shaft struck the couch and quivered, humming.

For all their loathesome attributes, survivalists were probably the best fighters in all the world. In a blur, before Gordon could snatch up his last arrow, the man dove to one side and rolled up with his assault rifle. Gordon threw himself back as a rapid, accurate burst of individual shots tore into the balustrade, ricocheting from the ironmongery where he had just been.

The rifle was equipped with a silencer, forcing the raider to fire on semi-automatic; but the zinging bullets clanged all about Gordon as he rolled over and pulled out his own revolver. He scurried over to another part of the balcony.

The fellow down below had good ears. Another rapid burst sent slivers flying inches from Gordon's face as he ducked aside again, barely in time.

Silence fell, except that Gordon's pulse sounded like thunder in his ears.

Now what? he wondered.

Suddenly there was a loud scream. Gordon raised his head and caught a blurry motion reflected in the mirror . . . the small woman below was charging her much bigger foe with a large chair raised over her head!

The survivalist whirled and fired. Red blotches bloomed across the young gleaner's chest and she tumbled to the ground; the chair rolled to the survivalist's feet.

Gordon might have heard the click as the rifle's magazine emptied. Or perhaps it was only a wild guess. Whatever

119

the reason, without thinking he leapt up, arms extended, and squeezed the trigger of his .38 over and over again—pumping until the hammer struck five times on empty, smoking chambers.

His opponent remained standing, a fresh clip already in his left hand, ready to be slammed into place. But dark stains had begun to spread across the camouflage tunic. Looking astonished, more than anything else, his eyes met Gordon's over the smoking pistol barrel.

The assault rifle tipped and fell clattering from limp fingers, and the survivalist crumpled to the floor.

Gordon ran downstairs, vaulting the rail at the bottom. First he stopped at both men and made sure they were dead. Then he hurried over to the fatally wounded young woman.

Her mouth made a round inquiry as he lifted her head. "Who . . . ?"

"Don't talk," he urged, and he wiped a trail of blood from the corner of her mouth.

Pupils widely dilated, eerily alert on the threshold of death, her eyes took in his face, his uniform—the embroidered RESTORED U.S. MAIL SERVICE patch over his breast pocket. They widened briefly in question, in wonder.

Let her believe, Gordon told himself. *She's dying. Let her believe it's true.*

But he couldn't make himself say the words—the lies that he had told so often, that had taken him so far for so many months. Not this time.

"I'm just a traveler, miss," he shook his head. "I'm . . . I'm just a fellow citizen, trying to help."

She nodded—only slightly disappointed it seemed—as if that in itself were a minor miracle.

"North . . ." she gasped. "Take boy. . . . Warn . . . warn *Cyclops.* . . ."

In that last word, even as her dying breath sighed away, Gordon heard reverence, loyalty, and a confident faith in ultimate redemption . . . all in the spoken name of a machine.

Cyclops, he thought numbly, as he laid her body down. Now he had yet another reason to follow the legend to its source.

There was no time to spare for a burial. The bandit's rifle had been muffled, but Gordon's .38 had echoed like thunder. The other raiders would certainly have heard. He had only moments to collect the child and clear out of this place.

But ten feet away there were horses to steal. And up north lay something a brave young woman had thought worth dying for.

If only it's true, Gordon thought as he gathered up his enemy's rifle and ammunition.

He would drop his postal play-act in a minute, if he found that someone, somewhere, was taking responsibility—actually trying to do something about the dark age. He would offer his allegiance, his help, however meager it might be.

Even to a giant computer.

There were distant shouts . . . coming closer rapidly.

He turned to the boy, who was now looking up at him, wide-eyed, from the corner of the room.

"Come on, then," Gordon said, holding out his hand. "We had better ride."

121

4

HARRISBURG

Holding the child on the saddle in front of him, Gordon raced away from the grisly scene as fast as his stolen mount would go. A glance showed figures charging after them on foot. One raider knelt to take careful aim.

Gordon bent forward, sawed on the reins, and kicked. The horse snorted and wheeled around a looted corner Rexall store just as high-velocity bullets tore apart the granite facing behind them. Stone chips flew whistling across Sixth Avenue.

He had been congratulating himself on taking the added time to scatter the other horses before galloping off. But in that last instant, looking back, Gordon had seen one more raider arrive, riding his own pony!

For a moment he felt an unreasoning fear. If they had his horse, they might also have taken or harmed the *mailbags*.

Gordon shook the irrelevant thought aside as he sent the horse dashing down a side street. To hell with the letters! They were only props, anyway. What mattered was that only one of the survivalists could pursue at the moment. That made the odds even.

Almost.

He snapped the reins and dug in his heels, sending his mount galloping hard down one of downtown Eugene's silent, empty streets. He heard the clatter of other hooves, *too close*. Not bothering to look back, he swerved into an alley.

122

The horse pranced past a fall of shattered glass, then sped across the next street, through a service way and down another clutter-filled alley.

Gordon turned the animal toward a flash of greenery, cantering quickly across an open plaza, and pulled up behind an overgrown oak thicket in a small park.

There was a roar in the air. After a moment Gordon realized that it was his own breath and pulse. "Are . . . are you all right?" he panted, looking down at the boy.

The nine-year-old swallowed and nodded, not wasting breath on words. The boy had been terrorized and had witnessed savage things today, but he had the sense to keep quiet, brown eyes intense on Gordon.

Gordon stood in the saddle and peered through the seventeen-year growth of urban shrubbery. For the moment at least, they seemed to have lost their pursuer.

Of course the fellow might be less than fifty meters away, quietly listening himself.

Gordon's fingers were shaking from reaction, but he managed to draw his empty .38 from its holster and reloaded while he tried to think.

If there was only the single rider to contend with, they might do better to just stay still and wait it out. Let the bandit seek them, and inevitably drift farther away.

Unfortunately, the other Holnists would catch up soon. It would probably be better to risk a little noise now than let those master trackers and hunters from the Rogue River country collect themselves and organize a real search of the local area.

He stroked the horse's neck, letting the animal catch its breath for a moment longer. "What's your name?" he asked the boy.

"M-Mark," he blinked.

"Mine is Gordon. Was that your sister, who saved our lives back there at the fireplace?"

Mark shook his head. A child of the dark age, he would save his tears for later. "N-nossir . . . it was my mom."

Gordon grunted, surprised. These days it was uncommon for women to look so young after having children. Mark's mother must have lived under unusual conditions— one more clue pointing to mysterious happenings in northern Oregon.

The light was fading fast. Still hearing nothing, Gordon nudged the horse into motion once more, guiding it with his knees, letting it choose soft ground where it could. He kept a sharp lookout, and stopped often to listen.

Some minutes later they heard a shout. The boy tensed. But the source must have been blocks away. Gordon headed in the other direction, thinking of the Willamette River bridges at the northern end of town.

The long twilight was over before they rode up to the Route 105 bridge. The clouds had stopped dripping, but they still cast a dark gloom over ruins on all sides, denying even the starlight. Gordon stared, trying to penetrate the gloom. Rumor to the south had it the bridge was still up, and there were no obvious signs of an ambush.

And yet anything could hide in that mass of dark girders, including an experienced bushwhacker with a rifle.

Gordon shook his head. He hadn't lived this long by taking foolish chances. Not when there were alternatives. He had wanted to take the old Interstate, the direct route to Corvallis and the mysterious domain of Cyclops, but there were other ways. He swung the horse about and headed west, away from the dark, glowering towers.

There followed a hurried, twisting ride down side streets. Several times he nearly got lost, and had to go by dead reckoning. At last, he found old Highway 99 by the sound of rushing water.

Here the bridge was a flat, open structure, and apparently clear. Anyway, it was the last path he knew of. Bent low over the boy, he took the span at a gallop and kept on riding hard until he was certain all pursuit had been left far behind.

Finally, he dismounted and led the horse for a while, letting the exhausted animal catch its breath.

When he climbed back into the saddle, young Mark had fallen asleep. Gordon spread his poncho to cover them both as they plodded on northward, seeking a light.

About an hour before dawn, they arrived at last at the walled village of Harrisburg.

The stories Gordon had heard about prosperous northern Oregon must have been understated. The town had apparently been at peace much, much too long. Thick undergrowth covered the free-fire zone all the way to the town wall, and there were no guards on the watchtowers. Gordon had to shout for five minutes before anyone arrived to swing back the gate.

"I want to talk to your leaders," he told them under the sheltered porch of the general store. "There's worse danger than you've known in years."

He described the ambushed party of gleaners, the band of hard, evil men, and their mission to scout the soft northern Willamette for plundering. Time was of the essence. They had to move quickly and destroy the Holnists before their mission was accomplished.

But to his dismay the sleepy-eyed townsmen seemed slow to believe his story, and even more reluctant to sally forth in the wet weather. They stared at Gordon suspiciously, and shook their heads sullenly when he insisted they call up a posse.

Young Mark had collapsed in exhaustion and wasn't much of a witness to corroborate his tale. The locals obviously preferred to believe he was exaggerating. Several men stated baldly that he must have run into a few local bandits from south of Eugene, where *Cyclops* still had little influence. After all, nobody had seen any Holnists around these parts in many years. They were supposed to have killed each other off long ago, after Nathan Holn himself was hanged.

Folk patted him on the back reassuringly and started dispersing to their homes. The storekeeper offered to let Gordon sack out in his store room.

I can't believe this is happening. Don't these idiots real-

ize their very lives are at stake? If the scouting party gets away, those barbarians will be back in force!

"Listen . . ." He tried again, but their sullen, rural obstinacy was impervious to logic. One by one, they drifted away.

Desperate, exhausted, and angry, Gordon flung back his poncho—revealing the postal inspector's uniform underneath. In a fury, he stormed at them.

"You all don't seem to understand. I am not *asking* you for your help. Do you think I give a damn about your stupid little village?

"I care about one thing above all. Those creatures have two bags of mail that they have stolen from the *people* of the *United States,* and I am *commanding* you, under my authority as a federal official, to gather an armed party and assist in their recovery!"

Gordon had had a lot of practice with the role in recent months, but never had he dared such an arrogant pose. It had completely carried him away. When one of the wide-eyed villagers started stammering, he cut the man short, his voice shaking with outrage as he told them of the wrath that would fall when the restored nation learned of this shame— how a silly little hamlet had cowered behind its walls and so let their country's sworn enemies escape.

His eyes narrowed as he growled lowly, "You ignorant bumpkins have *ten minutes* to form your militia and be ready to ride, or I warn you, the consequences will be *far* more unpleasant for you all than a forced march in the rain!"

The townsfolk blinked in astonishment. Most of them had not even moved, but stared at his uniform, and the shiny badge on his peaked hat. The true danger that faced them they could try to ignore, but *this* fantastic story had to be swallowed whole, or not at all.

For a long moment the tableau held—and Gordon stared them down until it broke.

All at once men were shouting at one another, running about to gather weapons. Women hurried to prepare the horses and gear. Gordon was left standing there—his poncho like a cape whipping behind him in the blustery wind—

cursing silently while the Harrisburg guard turned out around him.

What, in God's name, came over me? he asked himself at last.

Maybe his role was starting to get to him. For during those tense moments, as he had faced down an entire town, he had truly *believed*! He had felt the power of his role—the potent anger of a servant of the People, thwarted in a high task by little men. . . .

The episode left him shaken, and a little uncertain of his own mental equilibrium.

One thing was clear. He had hoped to give up the postman scam on reaching northern Oregon; but that was no longer possible. He was stuck with it now, for better or for worse.

All was ready in a quarter of an hour. He left the boy in the care of a local family and departed with the posse in a drizzling rain.

The ride was quicker this time, in daylight and with remounts. Gordon made sure they sent out scouts and flankers to guard against ambush, and kept the main party in three separated squads. When they finally arrived at the UO campus, the militia dismounted to converge on the Student Center.

Although the locals outnumbered the survivalist band by at least eight to one, Gordon figured the odds were actually about even. Wincing at every sound as the clumsy farmers approached the scene of the massacre, he nervously scanned the rooftops and windows.

I hear that down south they stopped the Holnists with sheer guts and determination. They've got some legendary leader, down there, who's whipped the survivalists three falls out of four. Must be the reason the bastards are trying this end run up the coast. Things are different up here.

If this invasion ever really develops, these locals haven't got a chance.

When they finally burst into the Student Center the raiders were long gone. The fireplace was cold. Tracks in the muddy street led westward, toward the coastal passes and the sea.

The victims of the massacre were found laid out in the old cafeteria, ears and other . . . parts . . . removed as trophies. The villagers stared at the havoc the automatic rifles had wrought, rediscovering uncomfortable memories of the early days.

Gordon had to remind them to get a burial detail together.

It was a frustrating morning. There was no way to prove who the bandits had been. Not without following them. And Gordon wasn't about to try with this reluctant band of farmers. They already wanted to go home to their tall, safe stockade. Sighing, Gordon insisted that they make one more stop.

In the dank, ruined university gymnasium he found his mail sacks—one untouched where he had hidden it, the other torn open, letters scattered and trodden on the floor.

Gordon put on an irate show of fury for the benefit of the locals, who hurried obsequiously to help him collect and bag the remains. He played the role of the outraged postal inspector to the hilt, calling down vengeance on those who dared interfere with the mail.

But this time it was really only an act. Inside, all Gordon could think of was how hungry and tired of it all he was.

The slow, plodding ride back in a chill fog was sheer hell. But the ordeal went on at Harrisburg. There Gordon had to go through all the motions again . . . passing out a few letters he had collected in the towns south of Eugene . . . listening to tearful jubilation as a couple of lucky ones learned of a relative or friend thought long dead . . . appointing a local postmaster . . . enduring another silly celebration.

The next day he awoke stiff and sore and a little feverish. His dreams had been dire—all ending with a questioning, hopeful look in a dying woman's eyes.

Nothing the villagers could say would make him remain another hour. He saddled a fresh horse, secured the mailbags, and headed north immediately after breakfast.

It was time, at last, to go see *Cyclops*.

128

5

CORVALLIS

May 18, 2011

Transmittal via: Shedd, Harrisburg,
Creswell, Cottage Grove, Culp
Creek, Oakridge, to Pine View

Dear Mrs. Thompson,
    Your first three letters finally caught up with me
in Shedd, just south of Corvallis. I can't tell you how
glad I was to get them. And news from Abby and
Michael too—I'm very happy for them both, and I
hope it will be a girl.
    I note that you've expanded your local mail
route to include Gilchrist, New Bend, and Redmond.
Enclosed are temporary warrants for the postmasters
you recommended, to be confirmed later. Your
initiative is to be applauded.
    The news of a change in regime in Oakridge
was welcome. I hope their revolution lasts.

It was quiet in the paneled guest room as the silver
fountain pen scritch-scratched across the slightly yellowed
paper. Through the open window, with a pale moon shining
amid scattered night clouds, Gordon could hear distant music and laughter from the hoedown he had left a little while
ago, pleading fatigue.

DAVID BRIN

By now Gordon was accustomed to these exuberant first-day festivities, as locals pulled out the stops for the visiting "Government Man." The biggest difference here was that he had not seen so many people in one place since the food center riots, long, long ago.

The music was still of the land; with the Fall, people everywhere had returned to the fiddle and the banjo, to simple fare and square dances. In many ways it was all so very familiar.

But there are other differences as well.

Gordon rolled his fountain pen in his fingers and touched the letters from his friends in Pine View. Arriving with serendipitous timing, they had been real help in establishing his bona fides. The mail courier from the southern Willamette—a man Gordon himself had appointed only two weeks ago—had arrived on a steaming mount and refused even a glass of water until he reported to "the Inspector."

The earnest youth's behavior emphatically dissolved all remaining doubts the locals might have had. His fairy tale still worked.

For now, at least.

Gordon picked up the pen again and wrote.

By now you'll have received my warning of a possible invasion by Rogue River survivalists. I know you'll take appropriate measures for the defense of Pine View. Still, here in the strange domain of Cyclops I find it hard to get anyone to take the threat seriously. By today's standards they've been at peace here a very long time. They treat me well, but people apparently think I am exaggerating the threat.

Tomorrow, at last, I have my interview. Perhaps I can persuade Cyclops itself of the danger.

It would be sad if this strange little society led by a machine fell to the barbarians. It is the finest thing I have seen since leaving the civilized east.

· · ·

Gordon amended the remark in his own mind. The lower Willamette was the most civilized area he had encountered in fifteen years, *period*. It was a miracle of peace and prosperity, apparently wrought entirely by an intelligent computer and its dedicated human servants.

Gordon stopped writing and looked up as the lamp by his desk flickered. Under a chintz shade, the forty-watt incandescent bulb winked once more, then returned to a steady glow as the wind generators two buildings away regained their stride. The light was soft, but Gordon found his eyes watering each time he looked at it for even a little while.

He still had not gotten over it. On arriving in Corvallis he had seen his first working electric light in over a decade, and had been forced to excuse himself even as local dignitaries gathered to welcome him. He took refuge in a washroom to hide until he could regain his composure. It just wouldn't do for a supposed representative of the "Government in Saint Paul City" to be seen weeping openly at the sight of a few flickering bulbs.

Corvallis and its environs are divided into independent boroughs, each supporting about two or three hundred people. All the land hereabouts is cultivated or ranched, using modern farming arts and hybrid seed the locals raise themselves. They have managed to maintain several prewar strains of bio-engineered yeast, and produce medicines and fertilizers from them.

Of course they're limited to horse plows, but their smithies make implements from high-quality steel. They have even started producing hand-built water- and wind-power turbines—all designed by Cyclops, of course.

Local craftsmen have expressed an interest in trading with customers to the south and east. I'll enclose a list of items they're willing to barter for. Copy it and pass it along the line, will you?

• • •

Gordon had not seen so many happy, well-fed people since before the war, nor heard laughter so easy and often. There was a newspaper and a lending library, and every child in the valley got at least four years of schooling. Here, at last, was what he had been looking for since his militia unit broke up in confusion and despair, a decade and a half ago—a community of good people engaged in a vigorous effort to rebuild.

Gordon wished he could be a part of it, not a con artist ripping them off for a few nights' meals and a free bed.

Ironically, these people would have accepted the old Gordon Krantz as a new citizen. But he was indelibly branded by the uniform he wore and by his actions back at Harrisburg. If he revealed the truth now, he was certain they would never forgive him.

He had to be a demigod in their eyes, or nothing at all. If ever a man was trapped in his own lie . . .

Gordon shook his head. He would have to take the hand he had been dealt. Perhaps these people really could use a mailman.

So far I haven't been able to find out much about Cyclops itself. I've been told that the supercomputer does not govern directly, but insists that all the villages and towns it serves live together peaceably and democratically. In effect, it has become judge-arbitrator for the entire lower Willamette, all the way north to the Columbia.

The Council tells me Cyclops is very interested in seeing a formal mail route created, and has offered every assistance. He . . . I mean, it . . . seems anxious to cooperate with the Restored U.S.

Everyone, of course, was glad to hear that they would soon be in contact with the rest of the country again—

Gordon looked at the last line for a long moment, his pen poised, and realized that he simply couldn't go on with the lies tonight. It was no longer amusing, knowing Mrs. Thompson would read through them.

It made him feel sad.

Just as well, he thought. *I have a busy day tomorrow.* He covered the pen and got up to prepare for bed.

While he washed his face, he thought about the *last* time he had met one of the legendary supercomputers. It had been only months before the war, when he was an eighteen-year-old sophomore in college. All the talk had been about the new "intelligent" machines just then being unveiled in a few locations.

It was a time of excitement. The media trumpeted the breakthrough as the end of humanity's long loneliness. Only instead of coming from outer space, the "other intelligences" with whom man would share his world would be his own creations.

The neohippies and campus editors of *New Renaissance Magazine* held a grand birthday party the day the University of Minnesota put one of the latest supercomps on display. Balloons floated by, aerostat artists pedaled overhead, music filled the air while people picnicked on the lawns.

In the midst of it all—inside a mammoth, metal-mesh Faraday cage suspended on a cushion of air—they had sealed the helium-cooled cylinder containing *Millichrome.* Set up this way, internally powered and shielded, there was no way anyone from the outside could fake the mechanical brain's responses.

He stood in line for hours that afternoon. When at last Gordon's turn came to step forward and face the narrow camera lens, he brought out a list of test questions, two riddles, and a complicated play on words.

It was so very long ago, that bright day in the spring of hope, yet Gordon remembered it as if it were yesterday . . . the low, mellifluous voice, the friendly, open laughter of the machine. On that day *Millichrome* met all his challenges, and responded with an intricate pun of its own.

It also chided him, gently, for not doing as well as expected on a recent history exam.

When his turn was over, Gordon had walked away feeling a great, heady joy that *his* species had created such a wonder.

The Doomwar came soon thereafter. For seventeen awful years he had simply assumed that all of the beautiful supercomps were dead, like the broken hopes of a nation and a world. But here, by some wonder, one lived! Somehow, by pluck and ingenuity, the Oregon State techs had managed to keep a machine going through all the bad years. He couldn't help feeling unworthy and presumptuous to have come posing among such men and women.

Gordon reverently switched off the electric light and lay in bed, listening to the night. In the distance, the music from the Corvallis hoedown finally ended with a whooping cheer. Then he could hear the crowd dispersing for home.

Finally, the evening quieted down. There was wind in the trees outside his window, and the faint whine of the nearby compressors that kept the delicate brain of Cyclops supercold and healthy.

And there was something else as well. Through the night came a rich, soft, sweet sound that he could barely place, though it tugged at his memory.

After a while it came to him. Somebody, probably one of the technicians, was playing classical music on a stereo.

A *stereo* . . . Gordon tasted the word. He had nothing against banjos and fiddles, but after fifteen years . . . to hear Beethoven once again.

Sleep came at last, and the symphony blended into his dreaming. The notes rose and fell, and finally melded with a gentle, melodious voice that spoke to him across the decades. An articulated metal hand extended past the fog of years and pointed straight at him.

"*Liar!*" the voice said softly, sadly. "*You disappoint me so.*

"*How can I help you, my makers, if you tell only lies?*"

6

DENA

"This former factory is where we salvage equipment for the Millenium Project. You can see we've really hardly begun. We can't start building true robots, as Cyclops's plans call for later on, until we've recovered some industrial capability first."

Gordon's guide led him down a cavern of shelves stacked high with the implements of another era. "The first step, of course, was to try to save as much as we could from rot and decay. Only some of the salvage is kept here. What has no near-term potential is stored elsewhere, against a future day."

Peter Aage, a lanky blond man only a little older than Gordon, must have been a student at Corvallis State University when war broke out. He was one of the youngest to wear the black-trimmed white coat of a Servant of Cyclops, but even he showed gray at the temples.

Aage also was the uncle and sole surviving relative of the small boy Gordon had rescued in the ruins of Eugene. The man had not made any great display of gratitude, but it was clear he felt indebted to Gordon. None of those outranking him among the Servants had interfered when he insisted on being the one to show the visitor Cyclops's program to hold off the dark age in Oregon.

"Here we've begun repairing some small computers and other simple machines," Aage told Gordon, leading him past stacks of sorted and labeled electronics. "The hardest

135

part is replacing circuits burned out in those first few instants of the war, by those high-frequency electromagnetic pulses the enemy set off above the continent—you know, by the very first bombs?"

Gordon smiled indulgently, and Aage reddened. He raised a hand in apology. "I'm sorry. I'm just so used to having to explain everything so simply. . . . Of course you Eastern folks probably know a lot more about the EMP than we do."

"I am not a technical man," Gordon answered, and wished he had not bluffed so well. He would have liked to have heard more.

But Aage went back to the subject at hand. "As I was saying, this is where most of the salvage work is done. It's painstaking effort, but as soon as electricity can be provided on a wider scale, and once more basic needs have been addressed—we plan to put these microcomputers back in outlying villages, schools, and machine shops. It's an ambitious goal, but Cyclops is certain we can make it happen in our lifetimes."

The cavern of shelves opened up into a vast factory floor. Long banks of overhead skylights spanned the ceiling, so the fluorescents were used only sparingly. Still, there was a faint hum of electricity on all sides as white-coated techs carted equipment to and fro. Against every wall was stacked tribute from the surrounding towns and hamlets—payment for the benign guidance of Cyclops.

More machinery of all kinds—plus a small tithe of food and clothing for Cyclops's human helpers—came in every day. And yet, from all Gordon had heard, this salvage was easily spared by the people of the valley. After all, what use had they for the old machines, anyway?

No wonder there were no complaints of a "tyranny by machine." The supercomputer's price was easily met. And in exchange, the valley had its Solomon—and perhaps a Moses to lead them out of this wilderness. Remembering that gentle, wise voice from so long ago, Gordon recognized a bargain.

"Cyclops has carefully planned this stage of the transition," Aage explained. "You saw our small assembly line for water and wind turbines. Besides that, we help area blacksmiths improve their forges and local farmers plan their crops. And by distributing old hand-held video games to children in the valley, we hope to make them receptive to better things, such as computers, when the time comes."

They passed a bench where gray-haired workers bent over flashing lights and screens bright with computer code. A bit lightheaded from all this, Gordon felt as if he had accidentally stumbled into a bright, wondrous workshop where shattered dreams were being carefully put back together by a band of earnest, friendly gnomes.

Most of the technicians were now well into or past middle age. To Gordon it seemed they were in a hurry to accomplish as much as possible before the educated generation passed away forever.

"Of course now that contact has been reestablished with the Restored U.S.," Peter Aage continued, "we can hope to make faster progress. For instance, I could give you a long list of chips we haven't any way to manufacture. They would make a world of difference. Only eight ounces' worth could push Cyclops's program ahead by four years, if Saint Paul City can provide what we need."

Gordon didn't want to meet the fellow's eyes. He bent over a disassembled computer, pretending to pore over the complicated innards. "I know little about such matters," he said, swallowing. "Anyway, back East there have been other priorities than distributing video games."

He had said it that way in order not to lie any more than he had to. But the Servant of Cyclops paled as if he had been struck.

"Oh. I'm so stupid. Certainly they've had to deal with terrible radiation and plagues and famine and Holnists. . . . I guess maybe we've been pretty lucky, here in Oregon. Of course we'll just have to manage on our own until the rest of the country can help out."

Gordon nodded. Both men were speaking literal truths, but only one knew just how sadly true the words were.

In the uncomfortable silence, Gordon reached for the

very first question that came to mind. "So, you distribute toys with batteries, as sort of missionary tools?"

Aage laughed. "Yes, that's how you first heard of us, isn't it? It sounds primitive, I know. But it works. Come, I'll introduce you to the head of that project. If anyone is a real throwback to the Twentieth Century, it's Dena Spurgen. You'll see what I mean when you meet her."

He led Gordon through a side door and down a hallway cluttered with stacked odds and ends, coming at last to a room that seemed alive with a faint electric hum.

Everywhere there were racks of wires, looking much like strands of ivy climbing the walls alive. Socketed amidst the tangle were scores of little cubes and cylinders. Even after all these years, Gordon quickly recognized all manner of rechargeable batteries, drawing current from the Corvallis generators.

Across the long room, three civilians listened to a long-haired, blond person wearing the black-on-white coat of a Servant. Gordon blinked in surprise as he noticed that all four were young women.

Aage whispered in his ear. "I ought to warn you. Dena may be the youngest of all the Servants of Cyclops, but in one way she's a museum piece. A genuine, bona fide, rip-snorting feminist."

Aage grinned. So many things had gone with the Fall of civilization. There were words in common use, back in the old days, that one never even heard anymore. Gordon looked again in curiosity.

She was tall, especially for a woman who had grown up in these times. Since she was facing the other way, Gordon couldn't tell much about her appearance, but her voice was low and certain as she spoke to the other intense young women.

"So on your next run I don't want you taking chances like that again, Tracy. Do you hear me? It took a year of holding my breath and threatening to turn blue before I was able to get us this assignment. Never mind that it's a logical solution—that outland villagers tend to feel less threatened when the emissary is a woman. All the logic in the world would come to nothing if one of you girls came to harm!"

"But Dena," a tough-looking little brunette protested. "Tillamook's already *heard* of Cyclops! It was just a quick hop over from my own village. Anyway, whenever I take Sam and Homer along they just slow me—"

"Never mind!" the taller woman interrupted. "You just take those boys with you next time. I mean it! Or I promise you I'll have you back in Beaverville in two shakes, teaching school and making babies. . . ."

She stopped abruptly as she noticed that her assistants weren't paying attention anymore. They were staring at Gordon.

"Dena, come over and meet the Inspector," Peter Aage said. "I'm sure he'd like to see your recharging facility and hear about your—missionary work."

Aage spoke to Gordon, sotto voce with a wry smile. "Actually, it was introduce you or face a broken arm. Watch yourself, Gordon." As the woman Servant approached, he said louder, "I have some matters to look into. I'll be back in a few minutes to take you to your interview."

Gordon nodded as the man left. He felt somehow exposed here, with these women staring at him this way.

"That's it for now, girls. I'll see you tomorrow afternoon and we'll plan the next trip." The others protested with entreating looks. But Dena's head shake sent them out the door. Their shy smiles and giggles—as Gordon tipped his cap—contrasted with the long knives each wore at hip and boot.

Only when Dena Spurgen smiled, offering Gordon an outstretched hand, did he realize how young she had to be.

She can't have been more than six when the bombs went off.

Her grip was as firm as her demeanor, and yet her smooth, barely calloused hand told of a life spent more among books than threshers and plows. Her green eyes met his in frank inspection. Gordon wondered when he had last met anyone like this.

Minneapolis, that crazy sophomore year, came his answer. *Only then she had been a senior. Amazing I should remember that girl now, after so long.*

Dena laughed. "Have I your permission to anticipate your question? Yes, I am young and female, and not really qualified to be a full Servant, let alone to be put in charge of an important project."

"Forgive me," he nodded, "but those were my thoughts."

"Oh, no problem. Everybody calls me an anachronism, anyway. The truth is, I was adopted as a waif by Dr. Lazarensky and Dr. Taigher and the others, after the Anti-Tech Riots killed my parents. I have been spoiled terribly since, and learned how to take full advantage. As, no doubt, you guessed on overhearing what I had to say to my girls."

Gordon finally decided her features could best be described as "handsome." Perhaps a bit long and square-jawed. But when she was laughing at herself, as now, Dena Spurgen's face lit up.

"Anyway," she added, motioning at the wall of wires and little cylinders. "We may not be able to train any more engineers, but it doesn't take much brains to learn how to cram electrons into a battery."

Gordon laughed. "You're unfair to yourself. I had to take introductory physics twice. Anyway, Cyclops must know what he's doing, putting you in this job."

This brought a reddening to Dena's face as she blushed and looked down. "Yes, well, I suppose so."

Modesty? Gordon wondered. *This one is full of surprises. I wouldn't have expected it.*

"Oh rats. So soon. Here comes Peter," she said in a much softer voice.

Peter Aage could be seen negotiating the clutter in the hallway. Gordon looked at his old-fashioned mechanical watch—one of the techs had adjusted it so that it no longer ran half a minute fast on the hour. "No wonder. My interview is in ten minutes," he said as they shook hands again. "But I do hope we'll have another chance to talk, Dena."

Her grin was back. "Oh, you can bet we will. I want to ask you some questions about the way life was for you, back in the days before the war."

Not about the Restored U.S., *but about the* old times. *Unusual. And in that case, why me? What can I tell her about the Lost Age that she can't learn by picking the memories of anyone else over thirty-five?*

Puzzled, he met Peter Aage in the hallway and walked with him through the cavernous warehouse toward the exit.

"I'm sorry to rush you off like this," Aage told him, "but we musn't be late. One thing we don't want is for Cyclops to scold us!" He grinned, but Gordon got the feeling Aage was only partly jesting. Guards bearing rifles and white armbands nodded as they passed outside into overcast sunshine.

"I do hope your talk with Cyclops goes well, Gordon," his guide said. "We're all excited to be in contact with the rest of the country again, of course. I'm sure Cyclops will want to cooperate in any way he can."

Cyclops. Gordon returned to reality. *There's no delaying this. And I don't even know if I'm more eager than scared.*

He steeled himself to play out the charade to the end. He had no other choice. "I feel exactly the same," he said. "I want to help you folks any way I can." And he meant it, with all his heart.

Peter Aage turned away to lead him across the neatly mowed lawn toward the House of Cyclops. But for a moment Gordon wondered. Had he imagined it, or had he seen, for just a moment, a strange expression in the tech's eyes—one of sad and profound *guilt?*

7

CYCLOPS

The foyer of the House of Cyclops—once the OSU Artificial Intelligence Laboratory—was a striking reminder of a more elegant era. The gold carpet was freshly vacuumed and only slightly frayed. Bright fluorescents shone on fine furniture in the paneled lobby, where peasants and officials from villages as far as forty miles away nervously twisted rolled-up petitions as they waited for their brief interviews with the great machine.

When the townsmen and farmers saw Gordon enter, all of them stood up. A few of the more daring approached and earnestly shook his hand in calloused, work-roughened clasps. The hope and wonder were intense in their eyes, in their low, respectful tones. Gordon froze his mind behind a smile and nodded pleasantly, wishing he and Aage could wait somewhere else.

At last, the pretty receptionist smiled and motioned them through the doors at the end of the foyer. As Gordon and his guide passed down the long hallway to the interview chamber, two men approached from the other end. One was a Servant of Cyclops, wearing the familiar black-trimmed white coat. The other—a citizen dressed in a faded but carefully tended prewar suit—frowned over a long sheet of computer printout.

"I'm *still* not sure I understand, Dr. Grober. Is Cyclops sayin' we dig the well near the north hollow or *not*? His answer isn't any too clear, if you ask me."

"Now Herb, you tell your people it isn't Cyclops's job to figure everything down to the last detail. He can narrow down the choices, but he can't make the final decisions for you."

The farmer tugged at his overtight collar. "Sure, everybody knows that. But we've gotten straighter answers from him in th' past. Why can't he be clearer *this* time?"

"Well for one thing, Herb, it's been over twenty years since the geological maps in Cyclops's memory banks were updated. Then you're also certainly aware that Cyclops was designed to talk to high-level experts, right? So of *course* a lot of his explanations will go over our heads . . . sometimes even we few scientists who survived."

"Yes, b-but . . ." At that moment the citizen glanced up and saw Gordon approaching. He moved as if to remove the hat he was not wearing, then wiped his palm on his pants leg and nervously extended it.

"Herb Kalo of Sciotown, Mr. Inspector. This is indeed an honor, sir."

Gordon muttered pleasantries as he shook the man's hand, feeling more than ever like a politician.

"Yes sir, Mr. Inspector. An honor! I sure hope your plans include coming up our way and setting up a post office. If they do, I can promise you a wingding like you've never—"

"Now Herb," the older technician interrupted. "Mr. Krantz is here for a meeting with Cyclops." He looked at his digital watch pointedly.

Kalo blushed and nodded. "Remember that invite, Mr. Krantz. We'll take good care of you. . . ." He seemed almost to bow as he backed down the hall toward the foyer. The others didn't appear to notice, but for a moment Gordon's cheeks felt as if they were on fire.

"They're waiting for you, sir," the senior tech told him, and led the way down the long corridor.

Gordon's life in the wilderness had made his ears more sensitive than these townsmen perhaps realized. So when he heard a mutter of argument ahead—as he and his guides approached the open door of the conference room—Gordon purposely slowed down, as if to brush a few specks of lint from his uniform.

"How do we even know those documents he showed us were real!" someone up ahead was asking. "Sure they had seals all over them, but they *still* looked pretty crude. And that story about laser satellites is pretty damn pat, if you ask me."

"Perhaps. But it also explains why we've heard nothing in fifteen years!" another voice replied. "And if he were faking, how do you explain those letters that courier brought? Elias Murphy over in Albany heard from his long-lost sister, and George Seavers has left his farm in Greenbury to go see his wife in Curtin, after all these years thinking she was dead!"

"I don't see where it matters," a third voice said softly. "The people believe, and that's what counts. . . ."

Peter Aage hurried ahead and cleared his throat at the doorway. As Gordon followed, four white-coated men and two women rose from a polished oak table in the softly lit conference room. All except Peter were clearly well past middle age.

Gordon shook hands all around, grateful that he had met them all earlier; for it would have been impossible to remember introductions under these circumstances. He tried to be polite, but his gaze kept drifting to the broad sheet of thick glass that split the meeting room in two.

The table ended abruptly at that division. And although the conference room's lighting was low, the chamber beyond was even darker. A single spotlight shone on a shimmering, opalescent *face*—like a pearl, or a moon in the night.

Behind the single, gleaming, gray camera lens was a dark cylinder on which two banks of little flashing lights rippled in a complex pattern that seemed to repeat over and over again. Something in the repetitious waves touched Gordon inside. . . . He couldn't pin down exactly how. It was hard to tear his gaze away from the rows of winking pin-points.

The machine was swaddled in a soft cloud of thick vapor. And although the glass was thick, Gordon felt a faint sense of *cold* coming from the far end of the room.

The First Servant, Dr. Edward Taigher, took Gordon by the arm and faced the glass eye.

"Cyclops," he said. "I'd like you to meet Mr. Gordon Krantz. He has presented credentials showing him to be a United States government postal inspector, and representative of the restored republic.

"Mr. Krantz, may I present *Cyclops*."

Gordon looked at the pearly lens—at the flashing lights and the drifting fog—and had to quash the feeling of being like a small child who had seriously overreached himself in his lies.

"It is very good to meet you, Gordon. Please, be seated."

The gentle voice had a perfect human timbre. It came from a speaker set on the end of the oak table. Gordon sat in a padded chair Peter Aage offered. There was a pause. Then Cyclops spoke again.

"The tidings you bring are joyous, Gordon. After all these years caring for the people of the lower Willamette Valley, it seems almost too good to be true."

Another brief hiatus, then, "It has been rewarding, working with my friends who insist on calling themselves my 'Servants.' But it has also been lonely and hard, imagining the rest of the world to lie in ruins.

"Please tell me, Gordon. Do any of my brothers still survive in the East?"

He had to blink. Finding his voice, Gordon shook his head. "No, Cyclops. I'm very sorry. None of the other great machines made it through the destruction. I'm afraid you are the last of your species left alive."

Though he regretted having to give it the news, he hoped it was a good omen to be able to start out by telling the truth.

Cyclops was silent for a long moment. Surely it was only his imagination when Gordon thought he heard a faint sigh, almost like a sob.

During the pause, the tiny parity lights below the camera lens went on flashing, as if signaling over and over again in some hidden language. Gordon knew he had to keep talking, or lose himself in that hypnotic pattern. "Uh, in fact, Cyclops, most of the big computers died in the first seconds of the war—you know, the electromagnetic pulses. I can't help being curious how you yourself survived it."

Like Gordon, the machine seemed to shake aside a sad contemplation in order to answer.

"That is a good question. It turns out that my survival was a fortunate accident of timing. You see the war broke out on Visitor's Day, here at OSU. When the pulses flew, I happened to be in my Faraday cage for a public demonstration. So you see . . ."

Interested as he was in Cyclops's story, Gordon felt a momentary sense of triumph. He had taken the initiative in this interview, asking questions exactly as a "federal inspector" would. He glanced at the sober faces of the human Servants, and knew he had won a small victory. They were taking him very seriously indeed.

Maybe this would work out, after all.

Still, he avoided looking at the rippling lights. And soon he felt himself begin to sweat, even in the coolness near the superchilled pane of glass.

8

In four days the meetings and negotiations were over. Suddenly, before he had really prepared himself, it was time to leave again. Peter Aage walked with Gordon, helping him carry his two slim saddlebags toward the stables where his mounts were being readied.

"I'm sorry it took so long, Gordon. I know you've been anxious to get back to work building your postal network. Cyclops only wanted to fix up the right itinerary for you, so you can swing through north Oregon most efficiently."

"That's all right, Peter," Gordon shrugged, pretending. "The delay wasn't bad, and I appreciate the help."

They walked for a time in silence, Gordon's thoughts a hidden turmoil. *If Peter only knew how much I would have preferred to stay. If only there were a way . . .*

Gordon had come to love the simple comfort of his guest room, across from the House of Cyclops, the large and pleasant commissary meals, the impressive library of well-cared-for books. Perhaps most of all he would miss the electric light by his bed. He had read himself to sleep each of the last four nights, a habit of his youth, quickly reawakened after long, long dormancy.

A pair of tan-jacketed guards tipped their hats as Gordon and Aage turned the corner of the House of Cyclops and started across an open field on their way to the stables.

While he waited for Cyclops to prepare his itinerary, Gordon had visited much of the area around Corvallis, talking with dozens of people about scientific farming, about simple but technically advanced crafts, and about the theory behind the loose confederation that made for Cyclops's peace. The secret of the Valley was simple. No one wanted to fight, not when it might mean being left out of the cornucopia of wonders promised someday by the great machine.

But one conversation, in particular, stuck in his head. It had been last night, with the youngest Servant of Cyclops, Dena Spurgen.

She had kept him up late by the fire in the commissary, chaperoned by two of her girl emissaries, pouring cups of tea until he sloshed, pestering him with questions about his life before and after the Doomwar.

Gordon had learned many tricks to avoid getting too specific about the "Restored United States," but he had no defense against this sort of grilling. She seemed far less interested in the thing that excited everyone else, contact with the "rest of the nation." Clearly, that was a process that would take decades.

No, Dena wanted to know about the world just before and after the bombs. She was especially fascinated by that awful, tragic year he had spent with Lieutenant Van and his militia platoon. She wanted to know about every man in the unit, his flaws and foibles, the courage—or obstinacy—that made him continue to fight long after the cause was lost.

No . . . not lost. Gordon had reminded himself just in time to invent a happy ending to the Battle of Meeker County. The cavalry came. The granaries were saved at the last minute. Good men died—he spared no details of Tiny Kielre's agony, or Drew Simms's brave stand—but in his tale their struggles were not for nothing.

He told it the way it *should* have ended, feeling the wish with an intensity that surprised him. The women listened with rapt attention, as if it were a wonderful bedtime story—or as if it were critical data and they were going to be tested on it in the morning.

I wish I knew exactly what it was they were hearing— what they were trying to find in my own small, grimy tale.

Perhaps it was because the Lower Willamette had been

at peace for so long, but Dena had also wanted to know about the *worst* men he had met, as well . . . everything he knew about the looters and hyper-survivalists and Holnists.

The cancer at the heart of the end-of-the-century renaissance . . . I hope you are burning in Hell, Nathan Holn.

Dena kept asking questions even after Tracy and Mary Ann had fallen asleep by the fire. Normally, he would have been aroused by such close, admiring attention from an attractive woman. But this was not the same as it had been with Abby, back in Pine View. Dena had not seemed uninterested in him that way, to be sure. It was just that she seemed much *more* intensely involved in his value as a source of information. And if he was only to be here for a few days, she was completely unhesitant in choosing how best to use the time.

Gordon found her, all in all, overpowering and maybe a bit obsessed. Yet he knew that she would be unhappy to see him go.

She was probably the only one. Gordon had the distinct feeling that most of the other Servants of Cyclops were happy to be rid of him. Even Peter Aage seemed relieved.

It's my role, of course. It makes them nervous. Perhaps, deep inside, they sense some falseness. I couldn't really blame them.

Even if the majority of the techs believed his story, they had little reason to love a representative of a remote "government" certain to meddle—sooner or later—in what they had spent so long building. They *talked* about eagerness for contact with the outside world. But Gordon sensed that many of them felt it would be an imposition, at best.

Not that they really had anything to fear, of course.

Gordon still wasn't sure about the attitude of Cyclops itself. The great machine who had taken responsibility for an entire valley had been rather tentative and distant during their later interviews. There had been no jokes or clever puns, only a smooth and involute seriousness. The coolness had been disappointing after his memory of that prewar day in Minneapolis.

Of course his recollection of that other supercomputer

long ago might have been colored by time. Cyclops and its Servants had accomplished so much here. He was not one to judge.

Gordon looked around as he and his escort walked past a cluster of burned out structures. "It looks like there was a lot of fighting here once," he commented aloud.

Peter frowned, remembering. "We pushed back one of the AntiTech mobs right over there, by the old utility shed. You can see the melted transformers and the old emergency generator. We had to switch over to wind and water power after they blew it up."

Blackened shreds of power-converting machinery still lay in shriveled heaps where the technicians and scientists had fought desperately to save their lifework. It reminded Gordon of his other worry.

"I still think more ought to be done about the possibility of a survivalist invasion, Peter. It'll come soon, if I overheard those scouts right."

"But you admit you only heard scraps of conversation that could have been misinterpreted." Aage shrugged. "We'll beef up our patrols, of course, as soon as we have a chance to draw up plans and discuss the matter some more. But you must understand that Cyclops has his own credibility to consider. There hasn't been a general mobilization in ten years. If Cyclops made such a call, and it turned out to be a false alarm . . ." He let the implication hang.

Gordon knew that local village leaders had misgivings over his story. They didn't want to draw men from the second planting. And Cyclops had expressed doubts that the Holnist gangs really could organize for a truly major strike several hundred miles upcoast. It just wasn't in the hypersurvivalist mentality, the great machine explained.

Gordon finally had to take Cyclops's word for it. After all, its superconducting memory banks had access to every psychology text ever written—and all the works of Holn himself.

Perhaps the Rogue River scouts were merely on a small-time raid, and had talked big to impress themselves.

Perhaps.
Well, here we are.

The stable hands took his satchels, containing a few personal possessions and three books borrowed from the community library. They had already saddled his new mount, a fine, strong gelding. A large, placid mare carried supplies and two bulging sacks of hope-filled mail. If one in fifty of the intended recipients still lived, it would be a miracle. But for those few a single letter might mean much, and would begin the long, slow process of reconnection.

Maybe his role *would* do some good—enough at least to counterbalance a lie. . . .

Gordon swung up onto the gelding. He patted and spoke to the spirited animal until it was calm. Peter offered his hand. "We'll see you again in three months, when you swing by on your way back East again."

Almost exactly what Dena Spurgen said. Maybe I'll be back even sooner, if I ever come up with the courage to tell you all the truth.

"By then, Gordon, Cyclops promises to have a proper report on conditions here in north Oregon worked up for your superiors."

Aage gripped his hand for another moment. Once again Gordon was puzzled. The fellow looked as if, somehow, he were unhappy about something—something he could not speak of. "Godspeed in your valuable work, Gordon," he said earnestly. "If there's ever anything I can do to help, anything at all, you have only to let me know."

Gordon nodded. No more words were needed, thank Heaven. He nudged the gelding, and swung about onto the road north. The pack horse followed close behind.

9

BUENA VISTA

The Servants of Cyclops had told him that the Interstate was broken up and unsafe north of Corvallis, so Gordon used a county road that paralleled not far to the west. Debris and potholes made for slow going, and he was forced to take his lunch in the ruins of the town of Buena Vista.

It was still fairly early in the afternoon, but clouds were gathering, and tattered shreds of fog blew down the rubble-strewn streets. By coincidence, it was the day when area farmers gathered at a park in the center of the unpopulated town for a country market. Gordon chatted with them as he munched on cheese and bread from his saddlebags.

"Ain't nothin' wrong with the Interstate up here," one of the locals told him, shaking his head in puzzlement. "Them perfessers must not get out this way much. They aren't lean travelin' men such as yourself, Mr. Krantz. Must've got their wires crossed, for all their buzzin' brains." The farmer chuckled at his own wit.

Gordon didn't mention that his itinerary had been planned by Cyclops itself. He thanked the fellow and went back to his saddlebags to pull out the map he had been given.

It was covered with an impressive array of computer graphics, charting out in fine symbols the path he should take in establishing a postal network in northern Oregon. He had been told the itinerary was designed to take him most efficiently around hazards such as known lawless areas and the belt of radioactivity near Portland.

Gordon stroked his beard. The longer he examined the map, the more puzzled he grew. Cyclops had to know what it was doing. Yet the winding path looked anything *but* efficient to him.

Against his will he began to suspect it was designed instead to take him far *out* of his way. To waste his time, rather than save it.

But *why* would Cyclops want to do such a thing?

It couldn't be that the super machine feared his interference. By now Gordon knew just the right pitch to ease such anxiety . . . emphasizing that the "Restored U.S." had no wish to meddle in local matters. Cyclops had appeared to believe him.

Gordon lowered the map. The weather was turning as the clouds lowered, obscuring the tops of the ruined buildings. Drifts of fog flowed along the dusty street, pushing puffy swirls between him and a surviving storefront windowpane. It brought back a sudden, vivid recollection of other panes of glass—seen through scattered, refracting droplets.

Death's head . . . the postman grinning, his skeletal face superimposed on mine.

He shivered at another triggered recognition. The foggy wisps reminded him of superchilled vapor—his reflection in the cool glass wall as he met with Cyclops back in Corvallis—and the strangeness he had felt watching the rows of little flashing lights, repeating the same rippling pattern over and over. . . .

Repeating . . .

Suddenly Gordon's spine felt very cold.

"No," he whispered. "Please, God." He closed his eyes and felt an almost overwhelming need to change his thoughts to another track, to think about the weather, about pesterous Dena or pretty little Abby back in Pine View, about anything but . . .

"But who would *do* such a thing?" he protested aloud. "*Why* would they do it?"

Reluctantly, he realized he knew why. He was an expert on the strongest reason why people told lies.

Recalling the blackened wreckage behind the House of Cyclops, he found himself all at once wondering how the techs could possibly have accomplished what they claimed to have done. It had been almost two decades since Gordon had thought about physics, and what could or could not be achieved with technology. The intervening years had been filled with the struggle to survive—and his persistent dreams of a golden place of renewal. He was in no position to say what was or was not possible.

But he had to find out if his wild suspicion was true. He could not sleep until he knew for sure.

"Excuse me!" he called to one of the farmers. The fellow gave Gordon a gap-toothed grin and limped over, doffing his hat. "What can I do for you, Mr. Inspector?"

Gordon pointed at a spot on the map, no more than ten miles from Buena Vista as the crow might fly. "This place, Sciotown, do you know the way?"

"Sure do, boss. If you hurry, you can get there tonight."

"I'll hurry," Gordon assured the man. "You can bet your ass I'll hurry."

10

SCIOTOWN

"Just a darn minute! I'm coming!" the Mayor of Sciotown hollered. But the knock on his door went on insistently.

Herb Kalo carefully lit his new oil lantern—made by a craft commune five miles west of Corvallis. He recently had traded two hundred pounds of Sciotown's best pottery work for twenty of the fine lamps and three thousand matches from Albany, a deal he felt was sure to mean his reelection this fall.

The knocking grew louder. "All right! This had better be damn important!" He threw the bolt and opened the door.

It was Douglas Kee, the man on gate duty tonight. Kalo blinked. "Is there a problem, Doug? What's the—"

"Man here to see you, Herb," the gateman interrupted. "I wouldn't've let him in after curfew, but you told us about him when you got back from Corvallis—and I didn't want to keep him standin' out in the rain."

Out of the dripping gloom stepped a tall man in a slick poncho. A shiny badge on his cap glittered in the lamplight. He held out his hand.

"Mr. Mayor, it's good to see you again. I wonder if we could talk."

CORVALLIS

Gordon had never expected to forsake an offer of a bed and a hot meal to go galloping off into a rainy night, but this time he had no choice. He had commandeered the best horse in the Sciotown stables, but if he had had to, he would have run all the way.

The filly moved surefootedly down an old county road toward Corvallis. She was brave, and trotted as fast as Gordon considered marginally safe in the darkness. Fortunately, a nearly full moon lit the ragged, leaky clouds from above, laying a faint lambence across the broken countryside.

Gordon was afraid he must have put the Mayor of Sciotown in a state of utter confusion from the first moment he stepped into the man's home. Sparing no time for pleasantries, he had come straight to the point, sending Herb Kalo hurrying back to his office to retrieve a neatly folded fan of paper.

Gordon had taken the printout over to the lamp, and as Kalo watched, he carefully pored over the lines of text. "How much did this advice cost you, Mr. Mayor?" he asked without looking up.

"Only a little, Inspector," the man answered nervously. "Cyclops's prices have been dropping as more villages have joined the trade pact. And there was a discount because the advice was kinda vague."

"How *much*?" Gordon insisted.

"Uh, well. We found about ten of those old hand-held

vid' games, plus about fifty old rechargeable batteries, of which maybe ten were good enough to use. And oh yes, a home computer that wasn't too badly corroded."

Gordon suspected that Sciotown actually had much more salvage than that, and was hoarding it for future transactions. It was what he would have done.

"What else, Mr. Mayor?"

"I beg your pardon?"

"The question is clear enough," he said severely. "What—*else*—did—you—pay?"

"Why *nothin'* else." Kalo looked confused. "Unless, of course, you include a wagon of food and pottery for the Servants. But that's got hardly any value compared to the other stuff. It's just added on so's the scientists have somethin' to live off while they help Cyclops."

Gordon breathed heavily. His pulse didn't seem to want to slow down. It all fit, heartbreakingly.

He laboriously read aloud from the computer printout. ". . . incipient seepage from plate tectonic boundaries . . . groundwater retention variance . . ." Words he had not seen—or thought of—in seventeen years rolled off his tongue, tasting like old delicacies, lovingly remembered.

". . . variation in aquifer sustenance ratios . . . tentative analysis only, due to teleological hesitancy. . . ."

"We think we've got a line on what Cyclops meant," Kalo offered. "We'll start digging at the two best sites come dry season. Of course if we didn't interpret his advice right, it'll be our fault. We'll try agin' in some other spots he hinted at. . . ."

The Mayor's voice had trailed off, for the Inspector was standing very still, staring at empty space.

"*Delphi*," Gordon had breathed, hardly above a whisper.

Then the hasty ride through the night began.

Years in the wilds had made Gordon hard; all the while the men of Corvallis had suffered prosperity. It was almost ludicrously easy to slip by the guardposts at the city's edge.

He made his way down empty side streets to the OSU campus, and thence to long-abandoned Moreland Hall. Gordon spared ten minutes to rub down his damp mount and fill her feedbag. He wanted the animal to be in shape in case he needed her quickly.

It was only a short run through the drizzle to the House of Cyclops. When he got near, he made himself slow down, though he wanted desperately to get this over with.

He ducked out of sight behind the ruins of the old generator building as a pair of guards walked past, shoulders hunched under ponchos, their rifles covered against the dank. As he crouched behind the burned-out shell, the wetness brought to Gordon's nose—even after all these years—the scent of burning from the blackened timbers and melted wiring.

What was it Peter Aage had said about those frantic early days, when authority was falling apart, and the riots raged? He'd said that they had converted to wind and water power, after the generator house was torched.

Gordon didn't doubt it would have worked, too, if it were done in time. But *could* it have been?

When the guards had moved off, he hurried to the side entrance of the House of Cyclops. With a prybar he had brought for the purpose, he broke the padlock in one sharp snap. He listened for a long moment, and when nobody appeared to be coming, slipped inside.

The back halls of the OSU Artificial Intelligence Lab were grimier than those the public got to see. Racks of forgotten computer tapes, books, papers, all lay under thick layers of dust. Gordon made his way to the central service corridor, almost stumbling twice over debris in the darkness. He hid behind a pair of double doors as someone passed by, whistling. Then he rose and peered through the crack.

A man wearing thick gloves and the black-and-white robe of a Servant stopped by a door down the hall and put down a thick, battered, foam picnic chest.

"Hey, Elmer!" The man knocked. "I've got another

load of dry ice for our lord 'n' master. Come on, hurry it up! Cyclops gotta eat!"

Dry ice, Gordon noted. Heavy vapor leaked around the cracked lid of the insulated container.

Another voice was muffled by the door. "Aw, hold your horses. It won't hurt Cyclops any to wait another minute or two."

At last the door opened and light streamed into the hall, along with the heavy beat of an old rock and roll recording.

"What kept you?"

"I had a run going! I was up to a hundred thousand in Missile Command, and didn't want to interrupt—"

The closing door cut off the rest of Elmer's braggadocio. Gordon pushed through the swinging double doors and hurried down the hallway. A little farther, he reached another room whose door was slightly ajar. From within came a narrow line of light, and the sounds of a late-night argument. Gordon paused as he recognized some of the voices.

"I still think we ought to kill him," said one; it sounded like Dr. Grober. "That guy could wreck everything we've set up here."

"Oh, you are exaggerating the danger, Nick. I don't really think he's much of a threat." It was the voice of the oldest woman Servant—he couldn't even remember her name. "The fellow really seemed rather earnest and harmless," she said.

"Yeah? Well did you hear those questions he was asking Cyclops? He's not one of these rubes our average citizen has become after all this time. The man is *sharp*! And he remembers an awful lot from the old days!"

"So? Maybe we should try to recruit him."

"No way! Anyone can see he's an idealist. He'd never do it. Our only option is to kill him! Now! And hope it's years before they send someone else to take his place."

"And I still think you're crazy," the woman answered. "If the act were ever traced to us, the consequences would be disastrous!"

159

"I agree with Marjorie." It was the voice of Dr. Taigher himself. "Not only the people—our people of Oregon—would turn on us, but we would face the retribution of the rest of the country, if it were found out."

There was a long pause.

"I'm *still* not all that convinced that he's really—" But Grober was interrupted, this time by the soft voice of Peter Aage.

"Haven't you all forgotten the biggest reason why nobody should touch him, or interfere with him in any way?"

"What's that?"

Peter's voice was hushed. "Good lord, man. Hasn't it occurred to you who this fellow is? And what he represents? How low have we sunk, to even consider doing him harm, when we really owe him our loyalty and any help we can give him!"

Without conviction: "You're just biased because he rescued your nephew, Peter."

"Perhaps. And perhaps it's what Dena has to say about him."

"Dena!" Grober sniffed. "An infatuated child with wild ideas."

"All right. But even if I grant you that, too, there are the flags."

"Flags?" Now there was puzzlement in Dr. Taigher's voice. "What flags?"

The woman answered, pensively. "Peter is referring to the flags the townsmen have been putting up in all the local boroughs. You know, Old Glory? The Stars and Stripes? You should get out more, Ed. Get a feel for what the people are thinking. I've never seen anything stir the villagers up like this, even before the war."

There was another long silence before anyone spoke again. Then Grober said, softly, "I wonder what Joseph thinks of all this."

Gordon frowned. He recognized all the voices inside as senior Servants of Cyclops whom he had met. But he didn't remember being introduced to anyone named Joseph.

160

"Joseph went to bed early, I think," Taigher said. "And that's where I'm headed now. We'll discuss this again later, when we can go about it rationally."

Gordon hurried down the hall as footsteps approached the door. He didn't much mind being forced to leave his eavesdropping spot. The opinions of the people in the room were of no importance, anyway. No importance at all.

There was only one voice he wanted to hear right now, and he headed straight to where he had listened to it last.

He ducked around a corner and found himself in the elegant hallway where he had first met Herb Kalo. The passage was dim now, but that did not keep him from picking the conference room lock with pathetic ease. Gordon's mouth was dry as he slipped into the chamber, closing the door behind him. He stepped forward, fighting the urge to walk on tiptoes.

Beyond the conference table, soft light shone on the gray cylinder on the other side of the glass wall.

"Please," he wished, "let me be wrong."

If he was, then surely Cyclops itself would be amused by his chain of faulty deduction. How he longed to share a laugh over his foolish paranoia.

He approached the great glass barrier dividing the room, and the speaker at the end of the table. "Cyclops?" he whispered, stepping closer, clearing his tight throat. "Cyclops, it's me, Gordon."

The glow in the pearly lens was subdued. But the row of little lights still flashed—a complex pattern that repeated over and over like an urgent message from a distant ship in some lost code—ever, hypnotically, the same.

Gordon felt a frantic dread rise within him, as when, during his boyhood, he had encountered his grandfather lying perfectly still on the porch swing, and feared to find that the beloved old man had died.

The pattern of lights repeated, over and over.

Gordon wondered. How many people would recall, after the hell of the last seventeen years, that the parity displays of a great computer never repeated themselves? Gordon remembered a cyberneticist friend telling him that the patterns of lights were like snowflakes, none ever the same as any other.

"Cyclops," he said evenly. "*Answer me! I demand* you answer—in the name of decency! In the name of the United St—"

He stopped. He couldn't bring himself to meet this lie with another. Here, the only living mind he would fool would be himself.

The room was warmer than it had seemed during his interview. He looked for, and found, the little vents through which cool air could be directed at a visitor seated in the guest chair, giving an impression of great cold just beyond the glass wall.

"Dry ice," he muttered. "To fool the citizens of Oz."

Dorothy herself could not have felt more betrayed. Gordon had been willing to lay down his life for what had seemed to exist here. And now he knew it was nothing but a cheat. A way for a bunch of surviving sophisticates to fleece their neighbors of food and clothing, and have them be *grateful* for the privilege.

By creating the myth of the "Millennium Project," and a market for salvaged electronics, they had managed to convince the locals that the old electric machines were of great value. All through the lower Willamette Valley, people now hoarded home comps, appliances, and toys—because *Cyclops* would accept them in trade for its advice.

The "Servants of Cyclops" had arranged it so that canny people like Herb Kalo hardly even counted the tithe of food and other goods that were added *for the Servants themselves*.

The scientists ate well, Gordon remembered. And none of the farmers ever complained.

"It's not your fault," he told the silent machine, softly. "You really *would* have designed the tools, made up for all the lost expertise—helped us find the road back. You and your kind were the greatest thing we had ever done. . . ."

162

He choked, remembering the warm, wise voice in Minneapolis, so long ago. His vision blurred and he looked down.

"You are right, Gordon. It is nobody's fault."

Gordon gasped. In a flash, molten hope burned that he had been mistaken! It was the voice of Cyclops!

But it had not come from the speaker grille. He turned quickly, and saw—

—that a thin old man sat in the shadowed back corner of the room, watching him.

"I often come here, you know." The aged one spoke with the voice of Cyclops—a sad voice, filled with regret. "I come to sit with the ghost of my friend, who died so long ago, right here in this room."

The old man leaned forward a little. Pearly light shone on his face. "My name is Joseph Lazarensky, Gordon. I built Cyclops, so many years ago." He looked down at his hands. "I oversaw his programming and education. I loved him as I would my own son.

"And like any good father, I was proud to know that he would be a better, kinder, more *human* being than I had been."

Lazarensky sighed. "He really did survive the onset of the war, you know. That part of the story is true. Cyclops *was* in his Faraday cage, safe from the battle pulses. And he remained there while we fought to keep him alive.

"The first and only time I ever killed a man was on the night of the Anti-Tech riots. I helped defend the powerhouse, shooting like somebody crazed.

"But it was no use. The generators were destroyed, even as the militia finally arrived to drive the mad crowds back . . . too late. Minutes, years too late."

He spread his hands. "As you seem to have figured out, Gordon, there was nothing to do after that . . . nothing but to sit with Cyclops, and watch him die."

Gordon remained very still, standing in the ghostly ashlight. Lazarensky went on.

"We had built up great hopes, you know. Before the

163

riots we had already conceived of the Millenium Plan. Or I should say *Cyclops* conceived of it. He already had the outlines of a program for rebuilding the world. He needed a couple of months, he said, to work out the details."

Gordon felt as if his face were made of stone. He waited silently.

"Do you know anything about quantum-memory bubbles, Gordon? Compared to them, Josephson junctions are made of sticks and mud. The bubbles are as light and fragile as thought. They allow mentation a million times faster than neurons. But they must be kept supercold to exist at all. And once destroyed, they cannot be remade.

"We tried to save him, but we could not." The old man looked down again. "I would rather have died myself, that night."

"So you decided to carry out the plan on your own," Gordon suggested dryly.

Lazarensky shook his head. "You know better, of course. Without Cyclops the task was impossible. All we could do was present a shell. An illusion.

"It offered a way to survive in the coming dark age. All around us was chaos and suspicion. The only leverage we poor intellectuals had was a weak, flickering thing called Hope."

"Hope!" Gordon laughed bitterly. Lazarensky shrugged.

"Petitioners come to speak with Cyclops, and they speak with me. It isn't hard, usually, to give good advice, to look up simple techniques in books, or to mediate disputes with common sense. They believe in the impartiality of the computer where they would never trust a living man."

"And where you can't come up with a commonsense answer, you go oracular on them."

Again the shrug. "It worked at Delphi and at Ephesus, Gordon. And honestly, where is the harm? The people of the Willamette have seen too many power-hungry monsters over the last twenty years to unite under any man or group of men. But oh, they remember the machines! As they re-

164

call that ancient uniform you wear, even though in better days they so often treated it with terrible disrespect."

There were voices in the hall. They passed close by, then faded away. Gordon stirred. "I've got to get out of here."

Lazarensky laughed. "Oh don't worry about the others. They're all talk and no action. They aren't like you at all."

"You don't know me," Gordon growled.

"No? As 'Cyclops' I spoke with you for some hours. And both my adopted daughter and young Peter Aage have talked of you at length. I know more about you than you might imagine.

"You're a rarity, Gordon. Somehow, out there in the wilderness you managed to retain a modern mind, while gaining a strength suited for these times. Even if that bunch out there ever tried to harm you, you would outsmart them."

Gordon moved to the door, then stopped. He turned and looked back one last time at the soft glow from the dead machine, the tiny lights rippling hopelessly over and over again.

"I'm not so smart." His breath was hard in his throat. "You see, I *believed!*"

He met Lazarensky's eyes, and finally the old man looked down, unable to answer. Gordon stumbled out then, leaving the death-chilled crypt and its corpses behind him.

12

OREGON

He made it back to where his horse was tethered just as faint glimmers of dawn were brightening the eastern sky. He remounted, and with his heels he guided the filly up the old service road to the north. Within he felt a hollow grief, as if a freezing cold had locked up his heart. Nothing within him could move, for fear of shattering something tottering, precarious.

He had to get away from this place. That much was clear. Let the fools have their myths. He was finished!

He would not return to Sciotown, where he had left the mailbags. All that was behind him now. He began unbuttoning the blouse of his uniform, intending to drop it in a roadside ditch—along, forever, with his share in all the lying.

Unbidden, a phrase echoed in his mind.

Who will take responsibility now. . . ?

What? He shook his head to clear it, but the words would not go away.

Who will take responsibility now, for these foolish children?

Gordon cursed and dug in his heels. The horse gamely sped northward, away from everything he had treasured only yesterday morning . . . but now knew to be a Potemkin facade. A cheap, dime store mannequin. Oz.

Who will take responsibility . . .

The words repeated over and over again within his head, firmly lodged like a tune that would not let go. It was the same rhythm—he realized at last—as the winking lights of the parity display on the face of the old, dead machine, lights that had rippled again and again.

. . . *for these foolish children?*

The filly trotted on in the dawnlight past orchards bordered by rows of ruined cars, and a strange thought suddenly occurred to Gordon. What if—at the end of its life, as the last drops of liquid helium evaporated away and the deadly heat rushed in—what if the final thought of the innocent, wise machine had somehow been caught in a loop, preserved in peripheral circuits, to flash forlornly over and over again?

Would that qualify as a ghost?

He wondered, what would Cyclops's final thoughts, its last words, have been?

Can a man be haunted by the ghost of a *machine*?

Gordon shook his head. He was tired, or else he would not think up such nonsense. He didn't owe anybody *anything*! Certainly not a scrap of ruined tin, *or* a desiccated specter found in a rusted jeep.

"Ghosts!" He spat on the side of the road and laughed dryly.

Still, the words echoed round and round inside. *Who will take responsibility now . . .*

So absorbed was he that it took a few moments at first for him to recognize the faint sounds of shouting behind him. Gordon pulled up on the reins and turned to look back, his hand resting on the butt of his revolver. Anyone who pursued him now did so at great peril. Lazarensky had been right about one thing. Gordon knew he was more than a match for this bunch.

In the distance he saw there was a flurry of frantic activity in front of the House of Cyclops, but . . . but the commotion apparently did not have to do with him.

Gordon shaded his eyes against the glare of the new sun, and saw steam rising from a pair of heavily lathered horses. One exhausted man stumbled up the steps of the House of Cyclops, shouting at those hurrying to his side.

Another messenger, apparently badly wounded, was being tended on the ground.

Gordon heard one word cried out loudly. It told all.

"*Survivalists!*"

He had one word to offer in reply.

"Shit."

He turned his back on the noises and snapped the reins, sending the filly northward once again.

A day ago he would have helped. He'd been willing to lay down his life trying to save Cyclops's dream, and probably would have done just that.

He would have died for a hollow farce, a ruse, a con game!

If the Holnist invasion had really begun, the villagers south of Eugene would put up a good fight. The raiders would turn north toward the front of least resistance. The soft north Willametters didn't stand a chance against the Rogue River men.

Still, there probably weren't enough Holnists to take the entire valley. Corvallis would fall, certainly, but there would be other places to go. Perhaps he might head east on Highway 22, and swing back around to Pine View. It would be nice to see Mrs. Thompson again. Maybe he could be there when Abby's baby arrived.

The filly trotted on. The shouts died away behind him, like a bad memory slowly fading. It promised to be fair weather, the first in weeks without clouds. A good day for traveling.

As Gordon rode on, a cool breeze blew through his half open shirtfront. A hundred yards down the road he found his hand drifting to the buttons again, twisting one slowly, back and forth.

The pony sauntered, slowed, and came to a halt. Gordon sat, his shoulders hunched forward.

Who will take responsibility . . .

The words would not go away, lights pulsing in his mind.

The horse tossed her head and snorted, pawing at the ground.

Who . . . ?"

Gordon cried out, "Aw, *hell!*" He wheeled the filly about, sending her cantering southward again.

A babbling, frightened crowd of men and women stepped back in hushed silence as he clattered up to the portico of the House of Cyclops. His spirited mount danced and blew as he stared down at the people for a long, silent moment.

Finally, Gordon threw his poncho back. He rebuttoned his shirt and set the postman's cap on his head so the bright brass rider shone in the light of the rising sun.

He took a deep breath. Then he began pointing, giving terse commands.

In the name of survival—and in the name of the "Restored United States"—the people of Corvallis and the Servants of Cyclops all hurried to obey.

INTERLUDE

High above gray, foam-flecked wavetops, the jet stream throbbed. Winter had come again, and winds moaned chill recollections over the north Pacific.

Fewer than twenty cycles past, the normal patterns of the air had been perturbed by great, dark funnels—as if armies of angry volcanoes had chosen the same moment to throw earth against sky.

If the episode had not ended quickly, perhaps all life might have vanished, and the ice returned forever. Even as it was, clouds of ash had blanketed the Earth for weeks before the larger grains fell out of the sky like dirty rain. Smaller bits of rock and soot dispersed into the high stratospheric streams, scattering the sunlight.

Years passed before spring came again, at last.

It DID come. The Ocean—slow, resilient—surrendered up just enough heat to stop the spiral short of no-return. In time, warm, sea-drenched clouds again swept over the continent. The tall trees grew, and weeds sprouted earnestly, unmolested, through cracks in broken pavement.

Still, there remained plenty of dust, riding the high winds. Now and then the cold air ventured south again, carrying reminders of the Long Chill. Vapor crystalized around the grains, forming complex, fractal hexahedrons. Snowflakes grew and fell.

Obstinate, Winter arrived one more time to claim a dark country.

III

CINCINNATUS

1

Gusts sculpted whirling devil shapes in the blowing snow—
flurries that seemed to rise, ghostlike, from the gray drifts,
fluttering and darting windblown under the frosted trees.

A heavily laden branch cracked, unable to bear the
weight of one more dingy snowflake. The report echoed like
a muffled gunshot down the narrow forest lanes.

Snow delicately covered the death-glazed eyes of a
starved deer, filling the channels between its starkly outlined ribs. Flakes soon hid faint grooves in the icy ground
where the animal had last pawed, only hours ago, in its fruit-
less search for food.

Taking no sides, the dancing flurries went on to cloak
other victims as well, settling soft white layers over crimson
stains in the crushed, older snow.

All the corpses soon lay blanketed, peaceful, as if
asleep.

The new storm had erased most signs of the struggle by
the time Gordon found Tracy's body under the dark shadow
of a winter-whitened cedar. By then a frozen crust had
stanched the bleeding. Nothing more flowed from the unlucky young woman's slashed throat.

Gordon pushed away thoughts of Tracy as he had
briefly known her in life—ever cheerful and brave, with a
slightly mad enthusiasm for the hopeless job she had taken
on. His lips pressed together grimly as he tore open her
woolen shirt and reached in to feel under her armpit.

The body was still warm. This had not happened long ago.

Gordon squinted to the southwest, where tracks—already fading under the blowing snow—led off into the painful ice-brightness. In a flat, almost silent movement, a white-clad shape appeared beside him.

"Damn!" he heard Philip Bokuto whisper. "Tracy was good! I could have sworn those pricks wouldn't have been able to—"

"Well, they did." Gordon cut him off sharply. "And it wasn't more than ten minutes ago."

Taking the girl's belt buckle, he heaved her over to show the other man. The dark brown face under the white parka nodded silently, understanding. Tracy had not been molested, or even mutilated with Holnist symbols. This small band of hyper-survivalists had been in too much of a hurry even to stop and take their customary, grisly trophies.

"We can catch 'em," Bokuto whispered. Anger burned in his eyes. "I can fetch the rest of the patrol and be back here in three minutes."

Gordon shook his head. "No, Phil. We've already chased them too far beyond our defense perimeter. They'll have an ambush set by the time we get close. We'd better just collect Tracy's body and go home now."

Bokuto's jaw clenched, a bunching of tendons. For the first time his voice rose above a whisper. "We can *catch* the bastards!"

Gordon felt a wave of irritation. *What right does Philip have to do this to me?* Bokuto had once been a sergeant in the Marines, before the world fell to ruin nearly two decades ago. It should have been *his* job, not Gordon's, to make the practical, unsatisfying decisions . . . to be the one responsible.

He shook his head. "No, we will not. And that's final." He looked down at the girl—until this afternoon the second best scout in the Army of the Willamette . . . but apparently not quite good enough. "We need living fighters, Phil. We need fierce men, not more corpses."

176

For a silent moment neither looked at the other. Then Bokuto pushed Gordon to one side and stepped over the still form on the snow.

"Give me five minutes before you bring up the rest of the patrol," he told Gordon as he dragged Tracy's body into the leeward shadow of the cedar and drew his knife. "You're right, sir. We need angry men. Tracy and I'll see to it that's what you get."

Gordon blinked. "Phil." He reached forward. "Don't."

Bokuto ignored Gordon's hand as he grimaced and tore Tracy's shirt open wider. He did not look up, but his voice was broken. "I said you're right! We have to make our cow-eyed farmers mad enough to fight! And this is one of the ways Dena and Tracy told us to use, if we had to. . . ."

Gordon could hardly believe this. "Dena's *crazy*, Phil! Haven't you realized that by now? Please, don't do this!" He grabbed the man's arm and pulled him around, but then had to step back from the threatening glitter of Bokuto's knife. His friend's eyes were hot and agonized as he waved Gordon away.

"Don't make this harder for me, Gordon! You're my commander, and I'll serve you so long as it's the best way to kill as many of those Holnist bastards as possible.

"But Gordon, you get so frigging *civilized* at the worst of times! That's when I draw the line. Do you hear me? I *won't* let you betray Tracy, or Dena, or me with your fits of Twentieth-Century sappiness!

"Now, get outta here, *Mr. Inspector* . . . sir." Bokuto's voice was thick with emotion. "And remember to give me five minutes before you bring up the others."

He glowered until Gordon had backed away. Then he spat on the ground, wiped one eye, and bent back to the grisly task awaiting him.

At first Gordon stumbled, half stunned, as he retreated down the gray-sided meadow. Phil Bokuto had never turned on him that way before, waving a knife, wild-eyed, disobeying orders. . . .

Then Gordon remembered.

I never actually *commanded* him not to do this, did I? I *asked,* I pleaded. But I didn't order him. . . .

Am I completely sure he isn't right, at that? Do even I, deep inside, believe some of those things Dena and her band of lunatic women are preaching?

Gordon shook his head. Phil was certainly right about one thing—the stupidity of philosophizing on a battlefield. Out here survival was enough of a problem. That other war—the one he had been waging each night in his dreams—would have to wait its turn.

He made his way downslope carefully, clutching his drawn bayonet, the most practical weapon for this kind of weather. Half his men had put aside their rifles and bows for long knives . . . another trick painfully learned from their deadly, devious enemy.

He and Bokuto had left the rest of the patrol only fifty meters back, but it felt like much more as his eyes darted in search of traps. The whirling snow-devils seemed to take on forms, like the vaporous scouts of a faerie army that had not yet taken sides. Ethereal neutrals in a quiet, deadly war.

Who will take responsibility. . . ? they seemed to whisper at him. The words had never left Gordon, not since that fateful morning when he had chosen between practicality and a doomed charade of hope.

At least this particular raiding party of Holn survivalists had fared worse than usual, and the local farmers and villagers had done better than anyone would have expected. Also, Gordon and his escort party had been on an inspection tour nearby. They had been able to join the fray at a critical moment.

In essence, his Army of the Willamette had won a minor victory, losing only twenty or so men to five of the enemy. There were probably no more than three or four of this Holnist band left to flee westward.

Still, four of those human monsters were more than enough, even tired and short on ammunition. His patrol only numbered seven now, and help was far away.

Let them go. They'll be back.

The hoot of a horned owl warbled just ahead of him. He recognized Leif Morrison's challenge. *He's getting better,* Gordon thought. *If we're still alive in a year, it might even sound real enough to fool someone.*

He pursed his lips and tried to mimic the call, two hoots in answer to Morrison's three. Then he dashed across a narrow glade and slid into the gully where the patrol waited.

Morrison and two other men gathered close. Their beards and sheepskin cloaks were coated with dry snow, and they fingered their weapons nervously.

"Joe and Andy?" Gordon asked.

Leif, the big Swede, nodded left and right. "Pickets," he said tersely.

Gordon nodded. "Good." Under the big spruce he untied his pack and pulled out a thermos bottle. One of the privileges of rank; he didn't have to ask permission to pour himself a cup of hot cider.

The others took their positions again, but kept glancing back, obviously wondering what "the Inspector" was up to this time. Morrison, a farmer who had barely escaped the rape of Greenleaf Town last September, eyed him with the simmering look of a man who had lost everything he loved, and was therefore no longer entirely of this world.

Gordon glanced at his watch—a beautiful, prewar chronometer provided by the technicians of Corvallis. Bokuto had had enough time. By now he would be circling back, covering his tracks.

"Tracy's dead," he told the others. Their faces blanched. Gordon went on, weighing their reactions. "I guess she was trying to cut around past the bastards and hold them for us. She didn't ask my permission." He shrugged. "They got her."

The stunned expressions turned into a round of seething, guttural curses. *Better,* Gordon thought. *But the Holnists won't wait for you to remember to get mad next time, boys. They'll kill you while you're still deciding whether or not to be scared.*

Well practiced by now at the art of lying, Gordon con-

179

tinued in a flat tone. "Five minutes quicker and we might have saved her. As it is, they had time to take souvenirs."

This time anger battled revulsion on their faces. And burning shame overcame both. "Let's go after 'em!" Morrison urged. "They can't be far ahead!" The others muttered agreement.

Not quickly enough, Gordon judged.

"No. If you boys were sluggish getting here, you're much too slow to deal with the inevitable ambush. We'll move up in skirmish line and retrieve Tracy's body. Then we're going home."

One of the farmers—among the loudest demanding pursuit—showed immediate relief. The others, though, glared back at Gordon, hating him for his words.

Stand in line, boys, Gordon thought bitterly. *If I were a real leader of men, I'd have found a better way to put backbone into you than this.*

He put away his thermos, not offering any cider to the others. The implication was clear—that they didn't deserve any. "Hop to it," he said as he slung his light pack over his shoulders.

They did move quickly this time, gathering their gear and scrambling out across the snow. Over to the left and right he saw Joe and Andy emerge from cover and take their places on the flanks. Holnists would never have been so visible, of course, but then, they had had a lot more practice than these reluctant soldiers.

Those with unlimbered rifles covered the knife men, who dashed ahead. Gordon easily kept up, just behind the skirmish line. In a minute he felt Bokuto fall in beside him, appearing as if out of nowhere from behind a tree. For all of their earnestness, none of the farmers had spotted him.

The scout's expression was blank, but Gordon knew what he was feeling. He did not meet Bokuto's eyes.

Ahead there came a sudden, angry exclamation. The lead man must have come upon Tracy's mutilated body. "Imagine how they'd feel if they ever found out the truth about that," Philip told Gordon softly. "Or if they ever discovered the real reason why most of your scouts are girls."

Gordon shrugged. It had been a woman's idea, but he had agreed to it. The guilt was his alone. So much guilt, in a cause he knew was hopeless.

And yet he could not let even the cynical Bokuto sense the full extent of the truth. For his sake Gordon maintained a front.

"You know the main reason," he told his aide. "Underneath Dena's theories and the promise of Cyclops, beneath it all you know what it's for."

Bokuto nodded, and for a brief moment there was something else in his voice. "For the Restored United States," he said softly, almost reverently.

Lies within lies, Gordon thought. *If you ever found out the truth, my friend . . .*

"For the Restored United States," he agreed aloud. "Yeah."

Together they moved ahead to watch over their army of frightened, but now angry men.

2

"It's no good, Cyclops."

Beyond the thick pane of glass, a pearly, opalescent eye stared back at him from a tall cylinder swaddled in cool fog. A double row of tiny, flickering lights rippled a complex pattern over and over again. This was Gordon's ghost . . . the specter that had haunted him for months now . . . the only lie he had ever met to match his own damnable fraud.

It felt proper to do his thinking here in this darkened room. Out in the snows, on village stockades, in the lonely, dim forests, men and women were dying for the two of them—for what he, Gordon, supposedly represented, and for the machine on the other side of the glass.

For *Cyclops* and for the *Restored United States*.

Without those twin pillars of hope, the Willametters might well have collapsed by now. Corvallis would lie in ruins, its hoarded libraries, its fragile industry, its windmills and flickering electric lights, all vanished forever into the lowering dark age. The invaders from the Rogue River would have established fiefdoms up and down the valley, as they had done already in the area west of Eugene.

The farmers and aged techs were battling an enemy ten times more experienced and capable. But they fought anyway—not so much for themselves as for two *symbols*— for a gentle, wise machine that had really died many years ago, and for a long-vanished nation that existed now only in their imaginations.

The poor fools.

"It isn't working," Gordon told his peer, his fellow hoax. The row of lights replied by dancing the same complex pattern that burned in his dreams.

"This heavy winter has stopped the Holnists, for now. They're kicking back in the towns they captured last autumn. But come springtime they'll be back again, picking away at us, burning and killing until, one by one, the villages sue for 'protection.'

"We try to fight. But each of those devils is a match for a dozen of our poor townsmen and farmers."

Gordon slumped in a soft chair across from the thick sheet of glass. Even here, in the House of Cyclops, the smell of dust and age was heavy.

If we had time to train, to prepare . . . if only things had not been so peaceful here for so long.

If only we had a real leader.

Someone like George Powhatan.

Through the closed doors he could hear faint music. Somewhere in the building there lifted the light, moving strains of Pachelbel's *Canon*—a twenty-year-old recording playing on a stereo.

He remembered weeping when he had first heard such music again. He had been so eager to think something brave and noble still existed in the world, so willing to believe he had found it here in Corvallis. But "Cyclops" turned out to be a hoax, much like his own myth of a "Restored United States."

It still puzzled him that both fables thrived more than ever in the shadow of the survivalist invasion. They had grown amid the blood and terror into a something for which people were daily giving their lives.

"It's just not working," he told the ruined machine again, not expecting an answer. "Our people fight. They die. But the camouflaged bastards will be here by summer, no matter what we do."

He listened to the sweet, sad music and wondered if, after Corvallis fell, anyone anywhere would listen to Pachelbel, ever again.

There was a faint tapping on the double door behind

183

him. Gordon sat up. Other than himself, only the Servants of Cyclops were allowed in this building at night. "Yes," he said.

A narrow trapezoid of light spilled in. The shadow of a tall, long-haired woman stretched across the carpeted floor.

Dena. If there was anyone he did not want to see right now . . .

Her voice was low, quick. "I'm sorry to disturb you, Gordon, but I thought you'd want to know at once. Johnny Stevens just rode in."

Gordon stood up, his pulse rising. "My God, he got through!"

Dena nodded. "There was some trouble, but Johnny did get to Roseburg and back."

"Men! Did he bring—" he stopped, seeing her shake her head. Hope crashed in the look in her eyes.

"Ten," she said. "Gordon, he carried your message to the southerners, and they sent ten men."

Strangely, her voice seemed to carry less dread than shame, as if everyone had let *him* down, somehow. Then something happened that he had never witnessed before. Her voice broke.

"Oh, Gordon. They aren't even men! They're boys, only *boys!*"

3

Dena had been taken in as a toddler by Joseph Lazarensky and the other surviving Corvallis techs, soon after the Doomwar, and was raised among the Servants of Cyclops. Because of this she had grown tall for a woman of these times, and was far better educated. It was one reason he had been first attracted to her.

Lately, though, Gordon found himself wishing she had read fewer books . . . or an awful lot more. She had developed a *theory*. Worse—she was almost fanatical about it, spreading it among her own coterie of impressionable young women and beyond.

Gordon was afraid that, inadvertently, he had played a role in this process. He was still unsure just why he had let Dena talk him into letting some of her girls join the Army as Scouts.

Young Tracy Smith's body, sprawled upon the wind-blown drifts . . . tracks leading off into the blinding snow. . . .

Wrapped in winter coats, he and Dena walked past the men guarding the entrance of the House of Cyclops, and stepped outside into the bitterly clear night. Dena said, softly, "If Johnny really has failed, it means we have only one chance left, Gordon."

"I don't want to talk about it." He shook his head. "Not now." It was cold and he was in a hurry to get to the Refectory to hear the Stevens lad's report.

Dena grabbed his arm tightly and held on until he

185

looked at her. "Gordon, you've got to believe that nobody's more disappointed about this than I am. Do you think my girls and I *wanted* Johnny to fail? Do you think we're that crazy?"

Gordon refrained from answering on first impulse. Earlier in the day he had passed a cluster of those recruits of Dena's—young women from villages all over the northern Willamette Valley, girls with passionate voices and the fervid eyes of converts. They had been a strange sight, dressed in the buckskin of Army Scouts with knives sheathed at hip, wrist, and ankle, sitting in a circle with books open on their laps.

SUSANNA: No, no, Maria. You've got it mixed up. *Lysistrata* isn't anything at *all* like the story of the Danaids! They were both wrong, but for different reasons.
MARIA: I don't get it. Because one group used sex and the other used swords?
GRACE: No, that's not it. It's because both groups lacked a vision, an *ideology* . . .

The argument had halted abruptly when the women caught sight of Gordon. They scrambled to their feet, saluted, and watched him as he hurried uncomfortably by. All of them had that strange shining expression in their eyes . . . something that made him feel they were observing him as a prime specimen, a symbol, but of what he could not tell.

Tracy had had that look. Whatever it meant, he didn't want any part of it. Gordon felt badly enough about men dying for his lies. But these women . . .

"No." He shook his head as he answered Dena. "No, I don't think you're *that* crazy."

She laughed, and squeezed his arm. "Good. I'll settle for that much, for now."

He knew, though, that that would not be the end of it.

Inside the Refectory, another guard took their coats. Dena at least had the wisdom to hang back then, as Gordon went on alone to hear the bad news.

Youth was a wonderful thing. Gordon remembered when he had been a teenager, just before the Doomwar. Back then, nothing short of a car wreck could have slowed him down.

Worse things had happened to some of the boys who had left southern Oregon with Johnny Stevens, nearly two weeks ago. Johnny himself must have been through hell.

He still looked seventeen though, sitting near the fire nursing a steaming mug of broth. The young man needed a hot bath and maybe forty hours' sleep. His long, sandy hair and sparse beard covered innumerable small scratches, and only one part of his uniform was untattered—a neatly repaired emblem that bore the simple legend

POSTAL SERVICE OF
THE RESTORED
UNITED STATES

"Gordon!" He grinned broadly and stood up.

"I prayed you would return safely," Gordon said, embracing Johnny. He pushed aside the sheaf of dispatches the youth drew from his oil-skin pouch . . . for which Johnny doubtless would have given his life.

"I'll look at those in a little while. Sit. Drink your soup."

Gordon took a moment to glance over toward the big fireplace, where the new southern recruits were being tended by the Refectory staff. One boy's arm was in a sling. Another, lying on a table, was having a scalp gash tended by Dr. Pilch, the Army's physician.

The rest sipped from steaming mugs and stared at Gordon in frank curiosity. Obviously Johnny had been filling their ears with stories. They looked ready, eager to fight.

And not one of them was over sixteen.

So much for our last hope, Gordon thought.

People in the midsouthern part of Oregon had been fighting the Rogue River survivalists for nearly twenty years, and in the last ten or so had managed to beat the barbarians

187

to a standstill. Unlike Gordon's northerners, the ranchers and farmers down around Roseburg had not been weakened by years of peace. They were tough, and knew their enemy well.

They also had real leaders. There was one man Gordon had heard of who had driven back one Holnist raid after another in bloody disarray. No doubt that was why the enemy had come up with their new plan. In a bold stroke the Holnists had taken to sea, landing up the coast at Florence, far north of their traditional foes.

It was a brilliant move. And now there was nothing to stop them. The southern farmers had sent only ten boys to help. Ten boys.

The recruits stood up as Gordon approached. He went down the line asking each his name, his hometown. They shook his hand earnestly, and each addressed him as *Mr. Inspector*. No doubt they all hoped to earn the highest honor, to become *postmen* . . . officers of a nation they were too young ever to have known.

Neither that, nor the fact that the nation no longer existed, would keep them from dying for it, Gordon knew.

He noticed Phil Bokuto sitting in a corner, whittling. The black ex-Marine said nothing, but Gordon could tell he was sizing up the southerners already, and Gordon agreed. If any of them had any skill at all, they would be made scouts, whatever Dena and her women said.

Gordon sensed her watching from the back of the room. She had to know he would never agree to her new plan. Not while he was in command of the Army of the Lower Willamette.

Not while he had a breath left in his body.

He spent some minutes talking with the recruits. When he next looked back toward the door, Dena had left, perhaps to carry word to her cabal of would-be Amazons. Gordon was resigned to an inevitable confrontation.

Johnny Stevens fingered the oil-skin pouch as Gordon returned to the table. This time the young man would not be put off. He held out the packet he had carried so far.

188

"I'm sorry, Gordon." He kept his voice low. "I did my best, but they just wouldn't listen! I delivered your letters, but . . ." He shook his head.

Gordon leafed through replies to the entreaties for help he had written more than two months ago. "They all *did* want to join the postal network," Johnny added with irony in his voice. "Even if we fall up here, I suppose there'll still be a sliver of Oregon free and ready when the nation reaches here."

On the yellowed envelopes Gordon recognized the names of towns all around Roseburg, some legendary even up here. He scanned some of the replies. They were courteous, curious, even enthusiastic about the stories of a reborn U.S. But there were no promises. And no troops.

"What about George Powhatan?"

Johnny shrugged. "All the other mayors and sheriffs and bosses down there look to him. They won't do anything without he does it first."

"I don't see Powhatan's reply." He had looked at all of the letters.

Johnny shook his head. "Powhatan said he didn't trust paper, Gordon. Anyway, his answer was only two words long. He asked me to tell it to you, direct."

Johnny's voice fell.

"He said to tell you—'I'm sorry.'"

4

Light shone under the door as Gordon returned to his room much later in the evening. His hand hesitated inches from the knob. He clearly remembered snuffing the candles earlier, before leaving to commune with Cyclops.

A soft, female scent solved the mystery before he had the door more than half open. He saw Dena on his bed, her legs under the covers. She wore a loose shirt of white homespun and held a book up close to the bedside candle.

"That's bad for your eyes," he said as he dropped Johnny's dispatch pouch onto his desk.

Dena replied without looking up from her book. "I agree. May I remind you that *you* are the one who put your room back into the Stone Age, while the rest of this building is electrified. I suppose you prewar types still have it in your silly heads that candlelight is somehow romantic. Is that it?"

Gordon wasn't exactly sure *why* he had taken down the electric bulbs in his room, and carefully packed them away. During his first few weeks in Corvallis he'd felt a lump of joy every time he had a chance to turn a switch and make electrons flow again, as they had in the days of his youth.

Now, in his own room at least, he could not bear the sweetness of such light.

Gordon poured water and then soda powder over his toothbrush. "You have a good forty-watt bulb in your own room," he reminded her. "You could do your reading there."

Dena ignored the pointed remark and instead used the

190

flat of her hand to slap the open book. "I don't understand this!" she declared, exasperated. "According to this book, America was having a cultural renaissance, just before the Doomwar. Sure, there was Nathan Holn, preaching his mad doctrine of super machismo—and there were problems with the Slavic Mystics overseas—but for the most part it was a brilliant time! In art, music, science, everything seemed about to come together.

"And yet these surveys taken at the end of the century say that the majority of American women of that time *still* mistrusted technology!

"I can't believe it! Is it true? Were they all idiots?"

Gordon spat into the wash basin and looked up at the cover of the book. It bore a legend in bright holographic print:

WHO WE ARE:
A PORTRAIT OF AMERICA IN THE 1990S

He shook out his toothbrush. "It wasn't that simple, Dena. Technology had been thought of as a male occupation for thousands of years. Even in the nineties, only a small fraction of the engineers and scientists were women, though there were more and more damn fine—"

"That's irrelevant!" Dena interrupted. She shut the book and shook her light brown hair in emphasis. "What's important is who *benefits*! Even if it *was* mostly a male art, technology helped women far more than men! Compare America of your time with the world today, and tell me I'm wrong."

"The present is hell for women," he agreed. Gordon picked up the pitcher and poured water over his washcloth. He felt very tired. "Life is far worse for them than it is even for men. It's brutish, painful, and short. And to my shame I let you persuade me to put girls in the worst, most dangerous—"

Dena seemed determined not to let him finish a sen-

DAVID BRIN

tence. Or was it that she sensed his pain over young Tracy Smith's death, and wanted to change the subject? "Fine!" she said. "Then what I want to know is why women were *afraid* of technology before the war—if this crazy book is right—when science had done so much for them. When the alternative was so terrible!"

Gordon rehung the damp cloth. He shook his head. It had all been so long ago. Since those days, in his travels, he had seen horrors that would leave Dena stunned speechless, if ever he managed to make himself speak of them.

She had been only an infant when civilization came crashing down. Except for the terrible days before her adoption into the House of Cyclops—no doubt by now long gone from her memory—she had grown up in perhaps the only place in the world today where a vestige of the old comforts still maintained. No wonder she had no gray hairs yet, at the ripe age of twenty-two.

"There are those who say technology was the very thing that wrecked civilization," he suggested. He sat on the chair next to the bed and closed his eyes, hoping she might take a hint and leave in a little while. He spoke without moving. "Those people may have a point. The bombs and bugs, the Three-Year Winter, the ruined networks of an interdependent society . . ."

This time she did not interrupt. It was his own voice that caught of its own accord. He could not recite the litany aloud.

. . . hospitals . . . universities . . . restaurants . . . sleek airplanes that carried free citizens anywhere they might want to go . . .

. . . laughing, clear-eyed children, dancing in the spray of lawn sprinklers . . . pictures sent back from the moons of Jupiter and Neptune . . . dreams of the stars . . . and wonderful, wise machines who wove delicious puns and made us proud . . .

. . . knowledge . . .

"Anti-tech bullshit," Dena said, dismissing his suggestion in two words. "It was *people*, not science, that wrecked

192

the world. You know that, Gordon. It was certain types of people."

Gordon lacked the will even to shrug. What did it matter now, anyway?

When she spoke again her voice was softer. "Come here. We'll get you out of those sweaty clothes."

Gordon started to protest. Tonight he only wanted to curl up and close out the world, to postpone tomorrow's decisions in a drowning of unconsciousness. But Dena was strong and adamant. Her fingers worked his buttons and pulled him over to sag back against the pillows.

They carried her scent.

"I know why it all fell apart," Dena declared as she worked. "The book was right! Women simply didn't pay close enough attention. Feminism got sidetracked onto issues that were at best peripheral, and ignored the real problem, *men*.

"You fellows were doing your job well enough—shaping and making and building things. Males can be brilliant that way. But anyone with any sense can see that a quarter to half of you are also lunatics, rapists, and murderers. It was *our* job to keep an eye on you, to cultivate the best and cull the bastards."

She nodded, completely satisfied with her logic. "We women are the ones who failed, who let it happen."

Gordon muttered. "Dena, you are certifiably crazy, do you know that?" He already realized what she was driving at. This was just another attempt to twist him around to agreeing to another mad scheme to win the war. But this time it wasn't going to work.

At the front of his mind he wished the would-be Amazon would simply go away and leave him alone. But her scent was inside his head. And even with his eyes closed he knew it when her homespun shirt fell soundlessly to the floor and she blew out the candle.

"Maybe I am crazy," she said. "But I do know what I'm talking about." The covers lifted and she slid alongside him. "I *know* it. It was our fault."

The smooth stroke of her skin was like electricity along his flank. Gordon's body seemed to rise even while, behind his eyelids, he tried to cling to his pride and the escape of sleep.

"But we women aren't going to let it happen again," Dena whispered. She nuzzled his neck and ran her fingertips along his shoulder and biceps. "We've learned about men—about the heroes and the bastards and how to tell the difference.

"And we're learning about ourselves, too."

Her skin was hot. Gordon's arms wound around her and he pulled her down beside him.

"This time," Dena sighed, "we're going to make a difference."

Gordon firmly covered her mouth with his, if for no other reason than to get her to stop talking at last.

5

"As young Mark here will demonstrate, even a child can use our new infrared night vision scope—combined with a laser spotter beam—to pick out a target in almost pitch darkness."

The Willamette Valley Defense Council sat behind a long table, on the stage of the largest lecture hall on the old Oregon State University campus, watching as Peter Aage displayed the latest "secret weapon" to come out of the laboratories of the Servants of Cyclops.

Gordon could barely make out the lanky technician when the lights were turned off and the doors closed. But Aage's voice was stentoriously clear. "Up at the back of the hall we have placed a mouse in a cage, to represent an enemy infiltrator. Mark now switches on the sniper scope." There came a soft click in the darkness. "Now he scans for the heat radiation given off by the mouse. . . ."

"I see it!" The child's voice piped.

"Good boy. Now Mark swings the laser over to bear on the animal . . ."

"Got him!"

". . . and once the beam is locked into place, our spotter changes laser frequencies so that a visible spot shows the rest of us—the mouse!"

Gordon peered at the dark area up at the back of the hall. Nothing had happened. There was still only a deep darkness.

Someone in the audience giggled.

"Maybe it got ate!" a voice cracked.

"Yeah. Hey, maybe you techs oughta tune that thing to look for a cat, instead!" Someone gave a rumbling "meow."

Although the Council Chairman was banging his gavel, Gordon joined the wise guys down below in laughing out loud. He was tempted to interject a remark of his own, but everyone knew his voice. His role here was a somber one, and he would probably only hurt somebody's feelings.

A bustle of activity over to the left told of a gathering of techs, whispering urgently together. Finally, someone called for the lights. The fluorescents flickered on and the members of the Defense Council blinked as their eyes readapted.

Mark Aage, the ten-year-old boy Gordon had rescued from survivalists in the ruins of Eugene some months ago, removed his night vision helmet and looked up. "I could see the mouse," he insisted. "Real good. And I hit him with th' laser beam. But it wouldn't switch colors!"

Peter Aage looked embarrassed. The blond man wore the same black-trimmed white as the techs still huddled over the balky device. "It worked through fifty trials yesterday," he explained. "Maybe the parametric converter got stuck. It does some times.

"Of course this is only a prototype, and nobody here in Oregon has tried to build anything like this in nearly twenty years. But we ought to have the bugs out of it before we go into production."

Three different groups made up the Defense Council. The two men and a woman who were dressed like Peter, in Servants' robes, nodded sympathetically. The rest of the councillors seemed less understanding.

Two men to Gordon's right wore blue tunics and leather jackets similar to his own. On their sleeves were sewn patches depicting an eagle rising defiantly from a pyre, rimmed by the legend:

RESTORED U.S.
POSTAL SERVICE.

Gordon's fellow "postmen" looked at each other, one rolling his eyes in disgust.

In the middle sat two women and three men, including the Council Chairman, representing the various regions in the alliance: counties once tied together by their reverence of Cyclops, more recently by a growing postal network, and now by their fear of a common foe. Their clothing was varied, but each wore an armband bearing a shiny emblem—a W and a V superimposed to stand for Willamette Valley. The chromed symbols were one item plentiful enough to be supplied the entire Army, salvaged from long-abandoned motorcars.

It was one of these civilian representatives who spoke first. "Just how many of these gadgets do you think you techs can put together by springtime?"

Peter thought. "Well, if we go all out, I guess we ought to have a dozen or so fixed up by the end of March."

"And they'll all need 'lectricity, I suppose."

"We'll provide hand generators, of course. The entire kit ought to weigh no more than fifty pounds, all told."

The farmers looked at each other. The woman representing the Cascade Indian communities seemed to speak for all of them.

"I'm sure these night scopes might do some good defending a few important sites against sneak attacks. But I want to know how they'll help after the snow melts, when those Holnist dick cutters come down raiding and burning all our little hamlets and villages one by one. We can't pull the whole population into Corvallis, you know. We'd starve in weeks."

"Yeah," another farmer added. "Where are all those super weapons you big domes were supposed to be comin' up with? Have you guys switched Cyclops *off*, or what?"

It was the Servants' turn to look at each other. Their leader, Dr. Taigher, started to protest.

"That's not fair! We've hardly had any *time*. Cyclops was built for peaceful uses and has to reprogram himself to deal with things like war. Anyway, he can come up with great plans, but it's fallible men who have to implement them!"

To Gordon it was a marvel. Here, in public, the man

actually seemed hurt, defensive of his mechanical oracle . . . which the people of the valley still revered like great Oz. The representative of the northern townships shook his head, respectful but obstinate.

"Now, I'd be the last one to criticize Cyclops. I'm sure he's crankin' out the ideas as fast as he can. But I just can't see where this night scope is any better than that balloon thing you keep talking about, or those gas bombs or those gimmicky little mines. There just aren't enough of 'em to do any damn good!

"And even if you made hundreds, thousands, they'd be great if we were fightin' a real army, like in Vietnam or Kenya before the Doomtime. But they're nearly useless against th' damsurvivalists!"

Although he kept silent, Gordon couldn't help agreeing. Dr. Taigher looked down at his hands. After sixteen years of peaceful, benign hoaxing—doling out a small stream of recycled Twentieth-Century wonders to keep the area farmers entranced—he and his technicians were being called on to deliver *real* miracles, at last. Fixing toys and wind-driven electric generators to impress the locals just wouldn't suffice anymore.

The man sitting to Gordon's right stirred. It was Eric Stevens, young Johnny Stevens's grandfather. The old man wore the same uniform as Gordon, and represented the Upper Willamette region, those few towns just south of Eugene that had joined the alliance.

"So we're back to square one," Stevens said. "Cyclops's gimmicks can help here and there. Mostly they'll make a few strong points a bit stronger. But I think we're all in agreement that that won't do much more than inconvenience the enemy.

"Likewise Gordon tells us that we can't expect help from the civilized East anywhere near in time. It's a decade or more before the Restored U.S. will arrive out here in any force. We have to hold out at least that long, maybe, before real contact is established."

The old man looked at the others fiercely. "There's

only one way to do that, and that's to fight!" He pounded the table. "It all comes down to basics, once again. *Men* are what'll make the difference."

There was a mutter of agreement down the table. But Gordon was acutely aware of Dena, sitting in the seats below, waiting her chance to address the Council. She was shaking her head, and Gordon felt as if he could read her mind.

Not just men . . . she was thinking. The tall young woman wore the robes of a Servant, but Gordon knew where her real loyalties lay. She sat with three of her disciples—buckskin-clad female scouts in the Army of the Willamette—all members of her eccentric cabal.

Until now the Council would have rejected their scheme out of hand. The girls had barely been allowed to join the Army at all, and then only out of a latent sense of last-century feminism that lingered in this still-civilized valley.

But Gordon sensed a growing desperation at the table today. The news Johnny Stevens had brought home from the south had struck hard. Soon, when the snows stopped falling and the warm rains began again, the councillors would begin grasping at any plan. Any idiocy at all.

Gordon decided to enter this discussion before things got out of hand. The Chairman quickly deferred when Gordon lifted his hand.

"I'm sure the Council wishes to convey to Cyclops— and to his technicians—our gratitude for their unceasing efforts." There was a mutter of agreement. Neither Taigher nor Peter Aage met his eyes.

"We have perhaps another six or eight weeks of bad weather on our side before we can look for a resumption of major activity by the enemy. After hearing the reports of the training and ordnance committees, it's clear we have our work cut out for us."

Indeed, Philip Bokuto's summary had begun the morning's litany of bad news. Gordon took a breath. "When the Holnist invasion began last summer, I told you all not to expect any help from the rest of the nation. Establishing a postal network, as I have been doing with your help, is only the first step in a long process until the continent can be reunited. For years to come, Oregon will stand essentially alone."

He managed to lie by implication while speaking words that were the literal truth, a skill he had grown good at, if not proud of.

"I won't mince words with you. The failure of the people of the Roseburg region to send more than a dribble of aid has been the worst blow of all. The southern folk have the experience, the skill, and most of all, the leadership we need. In my opinion, persuading them to help us *must* take priority over everything else."

He paused.

"I shall go south personally, then, and try to get them to change their minds."

That brought on an immediate tumult.

"Gordon, that's crazy!"

"You can't . . ."

"We need you here!"

He closed his eyes. In four months he had welded an alliance strong enough to delay and frustrate the invaders. He had forged it mostly through his skill as a storyteller, a posturer . . . a liar.

Gordon had no illusions that he was a real leader. It was his *image* that held the Army of the Willamette together . . . his legendary authority as *the Inspector*—a manifestation of the nation reborn.

A nation whose only remaining spark will soon be stone cold dead if something isn't done damn quick. I can't lead these people! They need a general! A warrior!

They need a man like George Powhatan.

He cut the uproar by holding up a hand.

"I *am* going. And I want you all to promise me you'll not agree to any crazy, desperate enterprises while I'm away." He looked directly at Dena. For an instant she met his gaze. But her lips were tight, and after a moment her eyes clouded and she jerked her head aside.

Is she concerned for me? Gordon wondered. *Or for her plan?*

"I'll be back before spring," he promised. "I'll be back with help."

Under his breath he added:

"Or I'll be dead."

6

It took three days to get ready. All that time Gordon chafed, wishing he could simply be off.

But it had turned into an expedition, the Council insisting that Bokuto and four other men accompany him at least as far as Cottage Grove. Johnny Stevens and one of the southern volunteers rode ahead to prepare the way. After all, it was only fitting that the Inspector be well heralded.

To Gordon it was all a lot of nonsense. An hour with Johnny, spent going over a prewar road map, would be enough to tell him how to get where he was going. One fast horse, and another for remount, would protect him as well as an entire squad.

Gordon particularly resented having to take Bokuto. The man was needed here. But the Council was adamant. It was accept their terms or not be allowed to go at all.

The party departed Corvallis early in the morning, their horses steaming in the bitter cold as they rode out past the old OSU athletic field. A column of marching recruits passed by. Muffled as they were, it was nonetheless easy to tell from their chanting voices that these were more of Dena's girl soldiers.

> Oh, I won't marry a man who smokes,
> Who scratches, belches, or bellows bad jokes,
> I might not marry at all, at all,
> I might not marry at all!

Oh I would rather just sit in the shade,
And be a choosy, picky old maid,
Oh I might not marry at all, at all,
I might not marry at all!

The troop performed eyes right as the men rode by.
Dena's expression was masked by distance, but he felt her
gaze, nonetheless.

Their farewell had been physically passionate and emo-
tionally tense. Gordon wasn't sure if even prewar America,
with all its sexual variations, had ever come up with a name
for the kind of relationship they had. It was a relief to be
getting away from her. He knew he would miss her.

As the women's voices faded behind him, Gordon's
throat was tight. He tried to pass it off partly as pride in their
obvious courage. But it wasn't possible to completely rule
out dread.

The party rode hard past barren orchards and frosted
countryside to make the stockade at Rowland by sundown.
That was how close the lines were—one day's journey from
the fragile center of what passed for civilization. From here
on it would be bandit country.

In Rowland they heard new rumors—that one contin-
gent of Holnists had already established a small duchy in the
ruins of Eugene. Refugees told of bands of the white-
camouflaged barbarians roaming the countryside, burning
small hamlets and dragging off food, women, slaves.

If it was true, Eugene presented a problem. They had
to get by the ruined city.

Bokuto insisted on taking no chances. Gordon glowered and hardly spoke at all as the expedition wasted three
days on frozen, buckled asphalt roads, skirting far to the east
of Springfield then south again to arrive at last at the fortified town of Cottage Grove.

It had been only a short time since a few towns south of
Eugene had been reunited with the more prosperous communities to the north. Now the invaders had nearly cut
them off again.

On Gordon's mental map of the once great state of Oregon, the entire eastern two-thirds were wilderness, high desert, ancient lava flows, and the mountainous ramparts of the Cascades.

The gray Pacific bounded the rain-shrouded coast range in the west.

The northern and southern edges of the state, too, were virtually impassible blotches. In the north the Columbia Valley still glowed from the bombs that had tortured Portland and shattered the great river's dams.

The other blot spilled a hundred miles into the southern edge of the state from unknown California—and centered on the mountainous canyonland known as the Rogue.

Even in happier times the area around Medford had been known for a certain "strange" element. Before the Doomwar it had been estimated that the Rogue River Valley held more secret caches, more illegal machine guns, than anywhere outside the Everglades.

While civil authority was still struggling to hang on, sixteen years ago, it was the hyper-survivalist plague that struck the final blow, all over the civilized world. In southern Oregon the followers of Nathan Holn had been particularly violent. The fate of the poor citizens of that region was never known.

Between the desert and the sea, between radiation and the Holnist madmen, two small areas had come out of the Three-Year Winter with enough left to do a little more than scratch as animals . . . the Willamette in the north and the towns around Roseburg in the south. But in the beginning, the southernmost patch seemed surely doomed to slavery or worse at the hands of the new barbarians.

Then, somewhere between the Rogue and the Umpqua, something unexpected happened. The cancer had been arrested. The enemy had been stopped. To find out how was Gordon's desperate hope, before the transplanted disease took hold fully in the vulnerable Willamette Valley.

On Gordon's mental map an ugly red incursion had spread inland from the invader beachheads west of Eugene. And Cottage Grove was now nearly cut off.

They got their first glimpse of how bad things had become less than a mile out of town. The bodies of six men hung by the road, crucified on sagging telephone poles. The corpses had not been left unmarked.

"Cut them down," he ordered. Gordon's heart pounded and his mouth was dry, exactly the reaction the enemy had wanted from this exercise in calculated terror. Obviously the men of Cottage Grove weren't even patrolling this far out anymore. That did not bode well.

An hour later he saw how much had changed since the last time he had visited the town. Watchtowers stood at the corners of new earthen ramparts. On the outside, prewar buildings had been razed to make a broad free-fire zone.

Population had swollen three-fold with refugees, most living in crowded shanties just inside the main gate. Children clung to the skirts of gaunt-faced women and stared as the riders from the north passed by. Men stood in clusters, warming their hands over open fires. The smoke mixed with a mist from unwashed bodies to make an unpleasant, aromatic fog.

Some of the men looked like pretty rough customers. Gordon wondered how many of them were Holnist infiltrators, only pretending to be refugees. It had happened before.

There was worse news. From the Town Council they learned that Mayor Peter Von Kleek had died in an ambush only days before, trying to lead a patrol to the aid of a besieged hamlet. The loss was incalculable and it struck Gordon hard. It also helped explain the mood of stunned silence on the cold streets.

He gave his best morale speech that evening, by torchlight in the crowded square. But this time the cheers of the crowd were tired and ragged. His address was interrupted twice by the faint, echoing crack of gunshots, carrying over the ramparts from the forest hills beyond.

"I don't give 'em two months, once the snow melts," Bokuto whispered the next day as they rode out of Cottage Grove. "Two weeks, if the damsurvivalists try hard."

Gordon did not have to reply. The town was the south-

DAVID BRIN

ern linchpin of the alliance. When it collapsed, there would
be nothing to prevent the full force of the enemy from turning north to the heartland of the valley and Corvallis itself.

They rode south in a light flurry of snow, climbing the
Coast Fork of the Willamette River toward its source. The
dark green pine forest glistened under its white blanket.
Here and there the bright red bark of myrtlewood stood out
against the gray banks of the half-frozen stream.

Still, a few obstinate Mergansers fished the icy waters,
trying in their own way to survive until spring.

South of the abandoned town of London, they left the
diminished river. There followed a long, uninhabited
stretch, featured only by the overgrown ruins of farms and
an occasional tumbled-down gas station.

It had been a silent trek, so far. But now, at last, security
lightened a bit as even the suspicious Philip Bokuto felt sure
they were beyond the likely range of Holnist patrols. Talking
was allowed. There was even laughter.

All of the men were over thirty, so they played the Remember Game . . . telling old-time jokes that would have no
meaning at all to any of the new generation, and arguing
lightheartedly over dimly recollected sports arcana. Gordon
nearly fell out of his saddle laughing as Aaron Schimmel
gave nasal impressions of popular television personalities of
the nineties.

"It's amazing how much of our youth gets stored away,
ready to be recalled," he commented to Philip. "They used
to say one sign of getting old is when you remember things
from twenty years ago easier than recent events."

"Yeah," Bokuto said, grinning, and his voice took on a
querulous falsetto. "What was it we were just talking
about?"

Gordon tapped the side of his head. "Eh? Can't hear
you, fellah. . . . Too much rock 'n' roll, way back when."

The men grew accustomed to the cold bite of wintry
mornings and the soft pad of horses' hooves on the grass-
covered Interstate. The land had recovered—deer grazed
these forests once again—but man would for a long time be

206

too sparse to come back and retake all the abandoned villages.

The Coast Fork tributaries fell away at last. The travelers crossed a narrow line of hills and a day later found themselves by the banks of a new stream.

"The Umpqua," their guide identified.

The northerners stared. This chilled torrent did not empty into the placid Willamette, and thence the great Columbia. Rather it carved its own untamed way westward toward the sea. "Welcome to sunny southern Oregon," Bokuto muttered, subdued once again. The skies glowered down on them. Even the trees seemed wilder than up north.

The impression held as they began passing small, stockaded settlements once again. Silent, narrow-eyed men watched them from eyries on the hillsides, and let them pass on by without speaking. Word of their coming had preceded them, and it was clear that these people had nothing against postmen. But it was just as obvious they had little use for strangers.

Spending a night in the village of Sutherlin, Gordon saw up close how the southerners lived. Their homes were simple and spare, with few of the amenities still owned by those in the north. Hardly anyone did not bear visible scars from disease, malnutrition, overwork, or war.

Although they did not stare or say anything discourteous, it wasn't hard to guess what the locals thought of Willametters.

Soft.

Their leaders expressed sympathy, but the hidden thought was obvious. *If the Holnists are leaving the south, why should we interfere?*

A day later, in the trading center of Roseburg, Gordon met with a committee of headmen from the surrounding area. Bullet-spalled windows looked out on scenes recalling the destructive seventeen-year war against the Rogue River barbarians. A blasted Denny's, its yellow plastic sign canted and melted, showed where the enemy had been turned back from their deepest thrust, nearly a decade ago.

The wild survivalists had never penetrated as far since. Gordon felt certain the site for the meeting had been chosen to make a point.

The difference in mood and personality was unmistakable. There was little curiosity about the legendary Cyclops, or about the flickering rebirth of technology. Even tales of a nation rising from its ashes in the far lands to the east brought only mild interest. It was not that they doubted the stories. The men from Glide and Winston and Lookinglass simply did not seem to care all that much.

"This is a waste of time," Philip told Gordon. "These hicks have been fighting their own little war for so long, they don't give a damn about anything but day to day existence."

Does that make them smarter, perhaps? Gordon wondered.

But Philip was right. It didn't really matter what the bosses, mayors, sheriffs, or headmen thought anyway. They blustered, boasting of their autonomy, but it was obvious there was only one man whose opinion counted in these parts.

Two days later, Johnny Stevens rode in from the west on a steaming mount. He looked neither right nor left, but leapt from his horse to run to Gordon, breathless. This time the message he carried was three words long.

"Come on up."

George Powhatan had agreed to hear their plea.

7

The Callahan Mountains bordered Camas Valley from Roseburg seventy miles to the sea. Below them, the main fork of
the little Coquille River rushed westward under the shattered skeletons of broken bridges before meeting its north
and south branches under the morning shadow of Sugarloaf
Peak.

Here and there, along the north side of the valley, new
fenceposts outlined pastures now covered with powdery
snow. Chimney smoke rose from an occasional hilltop stockade.

On the south bank, however, there was nothing—only
scorched, crumbled ruins slowly succumbing to the relent-
less blackberry thickets.

No fortifications overlooked the river fords. The travelers found the absence puzzling, for this valley was supposed to be where the defense against the Holnist enemy
had dug in, and finally held.

Calvin Lewis tried to explain. The wiry, dark-eyed
young man had guided Johnny Stevens since his earlier
journey to south Oregon. Cal's hand gestured left and right
as he spoke.

"You don't guard a river by buildin' strong points," he
told them in the low, lazy, local drawl. "We protect the north
bank by crossin' over ourselves, from time to time, and by
knowin' everything that moves over on the other side."

Philip Bokuto grunted, nodding in approval. Obviously,

that was how he would have done it. Johnny Stevens made no comment, having heard it all before.

Gordon kept looking into the trees, wondering where the watchers were. Doubtless both sides had them out, and observed the party at intervals along the way. Occasionally he caught a glimpse of motion or a glint of what might have been a binoculars lens at some height. But the trackers were good. A damn sight better than anyone in the Army of the Willamette—excluding, perhaps, Phil Bokuto.

The war in the south did not seem to be one of armies or companies, of sieges and strategic moves. It was more as battles had been fought among the American Indians . . . with victory measured in quick, bloody raids, and in the number of scalps taken.

Survivalists were expert at this type of sneak and run warfare. Unaccustomed to such terror, the Willametters were their ideal prey.

Here, though, the farmers had managed to stop them. It was not his place to critique their tactics, so he let Bokuto ask most of the questions. Gordon knew that these were skills one acquired over a lifetime. He was here for one reason and one reason only—not to learn, but to persuade.

The view was spectacular as they climbed the old Sugarloaf Mountain road, overlooking the merging forks of the Coquille. Snow-covered pine forests looked much as they must have before man came—as if the horror of the last seventeen winters was a matter of significance only to ephemeral creatures, irrelevant to the abiding Earth.

"Sometimes the bastards try to sneak by in big canoes," Cal Lewis told them. "The south fork comes this way almost straight up from the Rogue country, and by the time it joins the center fork here, it's movin' pretty fast."

The young man grinned. "But George always seems to know what they're up to. George is always ready for 'em."

There it was again, that affection mixed with awe in mentioning the leader of the Camas Valley communities. Did the man eat nails for breakfast? Did he strike his enemies with lightning? After all the tales, Gordon was ready to believe anything about George Powhatan.

Bokuto's broad nostrils flared as he suddenly reined back, stopping Gordon protectively with his left arm. The ex-Marine's machine pistol was upraised in a blur.

"What is it, Phil?" Gordon drew his carbine as he scanned the woody slopes. The horses danced and snorted, sensing their riders' agitation.

"It's . . ." Bokuto sniffed. His eyes narrowed incredulously. ". . . I smell bear fat!"

Cal Lewis looked up into the trees beside the road and smiled. From just upslope there came bass, throaty laughter.

"Very good, my man! You have keen senses!"

As Gordon and the others peered, a large, shadowed figure shifted between the Douglas firs, outlined against the afternoon sun. Gordon felt a brief thrill as a part of him wondered, for just a moment, if it was a human being at all, or perhaps the legendary Sasquatch—Bigfoot of the Northwest.

Then the shape stepped forward and was revealed as a craggy-faced, middle-aged man whose shoulder-length gray hair was bound by a beaded headband. A homespun, short-sleeved shirt exposed thigh-like shoulders to the open air, but he was apparently unbothered by the cold.

"I am George Powhatan," the grinning man said. "Welcome, gentlemen, to Sugarloaf Mountain."

Gordon swallowed. What was it about the man's voice that matched his physical appearance? It spoke of power so casually assumed that there was no need for bluster or display. Powhatan spread his hands. "Come on up, you with the sharp nose. And the rest of you with your fancy uniforms! You caught a whiff of bear fat? Well then, come look at my down-home weather station! You'll see what the stuff is good for."

The visitors relaxed and put away their weapons, put at ease by the ready laughter. *No Sasquatch*, Gordon told himself. *Just a hearty mountain man—nothing more.*

He patted his skittish northern horse, and told himself that he, too, must have been reacting only to the smell of rendered bear.

8

The Squire of Sugarloaf Mountain used jars of bear fat to predict the weather, refining a traditional technique with meticulous, scientific record keeping. He bred cows to give better milk, and sheep for better wool. His greenhouses, warmed by biogenerated methane, produced fresh vegetables the year round, even in the harshest winters.

George Powhatan took special pride in showing off his brewery, famed for the best beer in four counties.

The walls of the great lodge—the seat of his domain—featured finely woven hangings and the proudly displayed artwork of children. Gordon had expected to see weapons and trophies of battle, but there were none in sight anywhere. Indeed, once one passed within the high stockade and abatis, there were hardly any reminders of the long war at all.

That first day, Powhatan would not speak of business. He spent all of it showing his guests around and supervising preparations for a potlatch in their honor. Then, late in the afternoon, when they had been shown their rooms in order to rest, their host vanished.

"I thought I saw him head west," Philip Bokuto answered, when Gordon asked. "Toward that bluff over there."

Gordon thanked him and headed that way down a gravel-lined path through the trees. For hours Powhatan had skillfully avoided any serious discussion at all, always diverting them with something new to see, or with his apparently infinite store of country lore.

Tonight could be more of the same, with so many people coming to meet them. There might be no opportunity to get to business at all.

Of course he knew he shouldn't be so impatient. But Gordon did not *want* to meet any more people. He wanted to talk to George Powhatan alone.

He found the tall man seated, facing the edge of a steep dropoff. Far below, waters roared with the meeting of the branches of the Coquille. To the west, the mountains of the Coast Range shimmered in purple haze that was rapidly darkening into an orange and ocher sunset. The ever-present clouds burned with a hundred autumnal shades.

George Powhatan sat zazen on a simple reed mat, his upturned hands resting on his knees. His expression was one Gordon had seen sometimes, before the war—one he had called, for want of another name, "The Smile of Buddha."

Well, I'll be . . . he thought. *The last of the neohippies. Who would have believed it?*

The mountain man's sleeveless tunic showed a faded, blue tattoo on his massive shoulder—a powerful fist with one finger gently extended, upon which was delicately perched a *dove.* Below could clearly be read a single word, **AIRBORNE.**

The juxtaposition didn't really surprise Gordon. Nor did the peaceful expression on Powhatan's face. Somehow they seemed fitting.

He knew that courtesy didn't require that he leave—only that he not interfere with the other man's sitting. He quietly cleared a space a few feet to Powhatan's right, and lowered himself to the ground facing the same direction. Gordon did not even try to get into a lotus. He hadn't practiced the skill since he was seventeen. But he did sit, back straight, and tried to clear his mind as the colors shimmered and changed out in the direction of the sea.

At first all he could think of was how stiff he felt. How sore from riding and sleeping on hard, cold ground. Puffs of wind chilled him as the sun's warmth hid behind the mountains. His thoughts were a churned antheap of sounds, concerns, memories.

But soon, without willing it at all, his eyelids began to grow heavy. They settled down, microscopically, and then stopped about halfway, unable to rise or fall any farther.

If he hadn't known what was happening, he surely would have panicked. But it was only a mild meditation trance; he recognized the feelings. *What the hell*, he thought, and let it grow.

Was he doing this out of a sense of competition with Powhatan? Or to show the man that *he* wasn't the only child of the renaissance who still remembered?

Or was it simply because he was tired, and the sunset was so beautiful?

Gordon felt a hollow sensation within him—as if a pocket of each lung were closed, and had been for a very long time. He tried to inhale hard and deep, but his pattern of breathing did not alter in the slightest—as if his body knew a wisdom that he did not. The calm that crossed his face with the numbing breeze seemed to trickle downward, touching his throat like a woman's fingers, running across his tight shoulders and stroking his muscles until they relaxed of their own accord.

The colors . . . he thought, seeing only the sky. His heart rocked his body gently.

Had it been a lifetime since he last sat like this and let go? Or was it just that there was so much to let go of?

They are . . .

In an easing that could never have been forced, the locked sensation in his lungs seemed to let go, and he *breathed*. Stale air escaped, to be swept away by the western wind. His next breath tasted so sweet that it came back out as a sigh.

"The colors . . ."

There was motion to his left, a stirring. A quiet voice spoke. "I used to wonder if these sunsets were God's last gift . . . something to match the rainbow he gave Noah, only this time it was his way of saying . . . 'So long' . . . to us all."

He did not answer Powhatan. There was no need.

"But after many years watching them, I guess the atmosphere is slowly cleansing itself. They aren't quite what they were, just after the war."

Gordon nodded. Why did people on the coast always assume they had a monopoly on sunsets? He remembered how it had been on the prairie—once the Three-Year Winter had passed and the skies were clear enough to see the sun at all. It had seemed as if Heaven had spilled its palette in a garish splash of hues, glorious, if deadly in their beauty.

Without turning to look, Gordon knew that Powhatan had not moved. The man sat in the same position, smiling softly.

"Once," the gray-haired squire said, "perhaps ten years ago, I was sitting here, just as I am now, recovering from a recent wound and contemplating the sunset, when I caught sight of something, or somebody, moving by the river, down below. At first, I thought they were men. I pulled out of my meditation quickly and headed down for a closer look. And yet something told me that it was not the enemy, even from this range.

"I approached as quietly as I could, until I had come within a few hundred meters, and I focused the little monocular I used to keep in my pouch.

"They weren't human beings at all. Imagine my surprise when I saw them strolling by the river bank, hand in hand, him helping her over stony banks, she murmuring softly as she carried something wrapped in a bundle.

"A pair of chimpanzees, for Heaven's sake. Or maybe one was a chimp and the other a smaller ape or even a monkey. They vanished into the rain forest before I could be sure."

For the first time in ten minutes, Gordon blinked. The image was so stark in his imagination, as if he were looking over Powhatan's shoulder into the man's memories from that long ago day. *Why is he telling me this?*

Powhatan continued, "They must have been set free from the Portland Zoo, along with those leopards running

215

wild in the Cascades, now. That was the *simplest* explanation . . . that they had worked their way south for years, foraging and keeping out of sight, helping each other as they headed for what they must have hoped would be warmer territory.

"I realized that they were moving down the south branch of the Coquille, right into Holnist territory.

"What could I do? I thought about following. Trying to catch them, or at least divert them. But it was doubtful I'd be able to do anything more than frighten them. And anyway, if they had come so far, what need had they of *me* to warn them of the dangers of being around man?

"They had been caged, now they were free. Oh, I wasn't foolish enough to conclude they were happier, but at least they weren't subject to the will of others anymore."

Powhatan's voice was subdued. "That can be a precious thing, I know."

There was another pause. "I let them go," he said, finishing his story. "Often, as I sit here watching these humbling sunsets, I wonder what ever became of them."

At last, Gordon's eyes closed completely. The silence stretched on. He inhaled and with some effort made the heaviness fall aside. Powhatan had been trying to tell him something, with that strange story. He, in turn, had something to say to Powhatan.

"A duty to help others isn't necessarily the same as being subject to the *will* of . . ."

He stopped—sensing that something had changed. His eyes opened, and when he turned, he saw that Powhatan was gone.

That evening people gathered from all over, more men and women than Gordon had thought still lived in the sparsely settled valley. For the visiting postman and his company, they put on a folk festival, of sorts. Children sang, and small troupes performed clever little skits.

Unlike in the north, where popular songs were often those remembered from the days of television and radio,

216

here there were no fondly recalled commercial jingles, few rock and roll melodies retuned to banjo and acoustic guitar. Instead, the music went back to an older tradition.

The bearded men, the women in long dresses tending table, the singing by fire and lamplight—it might easily have been a gathering from nearly two centuries ago, back when this valley had first been settled by white men, coming together for company and to shake off the chill of winter.

Johnny Stevens represented the northerners during the songfest. He had brought his treasured guitar, and dazzled the people with his flair, setting them clapping and stamping their feet.

Normally, this would have been wonderful fun, and Gordon might gladly join in with offerings from his old repertoire—from back before he had hit on being a "postman," when he had been a wandering minstrel trading songs and stories for meals halfway across the continent.

But he had listened to jazz and to Debussy the night before leaving Corvallis. He could not help wondering if it would turn out to have been the last time, ever.

Gordon knew what George Powhatan was trying to accomplish with this fete. He was putting off the confrontation . . . making the Willametters sit and stew . . . taking their measure.

Gordon's impression back at the cliff had not changed. With his long locks and ready banter, Powhatan was the very image of the aging neohippy. The long-dead movement of the nineties seemed to fit the Squire's style of leadership.

For instance, in the Camas Valley, clearly everyone was independent and equal.

Still, when *George* laughed, everyone else did. It seemed only natural. He gave no orders, no commands. It did not seem to occur to anyone that he would. Nothing happened in the lodge that displeased him enough to even raise an eyebrow.

In what had once been called the "soft" arts—those requiring neither metals nor electricity—these people were as advanced as the busy craftsmen of the Willamette. In some ways, perhaps, more so. That, no doubt, was why Powhatan had insisted on showing off his farm—to let the visitors see that they were not dealing with a society of throwbacks, but folk just as civilized in their own right. Part of Gordon's plan was to prove that Powhatan was wrong.

At last it was time to bring out the "gifts from Cyclops" they had brought all this way.

The people watched wide-eyed as Johnny Stevens demonstrated a cartoon graphics game on a color display that had been lovingly repaired by the Corvallis techs. He gave them a video puppet show about a dinosaur and a robot. The images and bright sounds soon had everybody laughing in delight, the adults as much as the children.

And yet Gordon detected once again that uncanny *something* in their mood. The people cheered and laughed, but their applause seemed to be in honor of a *clever trick*. The machines had been brought to whet their appetites, to make them want high technology once again. But Gordon saw no covetous glow in the watchers' eyes, no rekindled urge to *own* such wonders again.

Some of the men did sit up when Philip Bokuto's turn came. The black ex-Marine stepped up with a battered leather valise, and from it he drew out a few of the new weapons.

He showed the gas bombs and mines, and told them how they might be used to hold strong points against attack. Philip described the night vision scopes, soon to be available from the workshops of Cyclops. A ripple of uncertainty moved from man to man—battle-scarred veterans of a long war against a terrible enemy. While Bokuto talked, people kept glancing at the big man in the corner.

Powhatan did not say or do anything explicit. The picture of politeness, he only yawned once, demurely covering his mouth. He smiled indulgently as each weapon was displayed, and Gordon was awed to see how, with body language alone, the man seemed to say that these presents were quaint, perhaps even clever . . . but really quite irrelevant.

The bastard. But Gordon really didn't know how to fight back. Soon, that smile had spread around the room, and he knew that it was time to cut their losses.

Dena had pestered him to bring along her own list of presents. Needles and thread, base-neutral soap, samples of that new line of semicotton underwear they had started weaving again up in Salem, just before the invasion.

"They'll convert the women, Gordon. They'll do more good than all your whiz-bangs and razzle-dazzles. Trust me."

The last time he had trusted Dena, though, it had led to a slender, tragic corpse under a snow-blown cedar. By that time Gordon had had quite enough of Dena's version of pseudofeminism.

Would it have been any worse than this, though? Was I hasty? Perhaps we should have brought along some of the more mundane things—tooth powder and sanitary napkins, pottery, and new linen sheets.

He shook his head; that was all water under a dam. He gave Bokuto the signal to wrap it up and reached for his third ace. He drew forth his saddlebag and handed it to Johnny Stevens.

A hush fell over the crowd. Gordon and Powhatan watched each other across the room as Johnny stood—proud in his uniform—in front of the flickering fire. He riffled through envelopes and began reading names aloud in order to deliver the mail.

All through the still-civilized parts of the Willamette, the call had gone out. Anyone who had ever known anybody in the south had been asked to *write* to them. Most of the intended recipients would turn out to be long dead, of course. But a few letters would certainly arrive in the right hands, or those of relatives. Old connections might be resumed, the theory went. The plea for help would have to become something less abstract, more personal.

It had been a good idea, but once again the reaction was not as expected. The pile of undeliverable letters grew. And as Johnny called out name after name without reply, Gordon saw that a different lesson was being brought home.

The people of the Camas were being reminded of how many had died. Of how few had survived the bitter times.

And now that peace seemed to be theirs at last, it was easy to see how they resented being asked to sacrifice again, for near strangers who had had it easier for years. Those few who did acknowledge letters seemed to take them reluctantly, folding them away without reading them.

George Powhatan looked surprised when his own name was called. But his flicker of puzzlement vanished quickly as he shrugged and took a package and a slim envelope.

Things were not going well at all, Gordon realized. Johnny finished his task and gave his leader a look that seemed to say, *What now?*

Gordon had only one card left—the one he hated most of all—and the one he knew best how to use.

Damn. But there's no other choice.

He stepped in front of the fireplace, facing the silent people with the warmth to his back, and took a deep breath. Then he started right in . . . lying to them.

"I have come to tell you a story," he said. "I want to tell you about a country of once upon a time. It may sound familiar, since many of you were born there. But the story ought to amaze you, nevertheless. I know it always amazes me.

"It's a strange tale, of a nation of a quarter of a billion people who once filled the sky and even the spaces between the planets with their voices, just as you good folk filled this fine hall with your songs tonight.

"They were a *strong* people, the strongest the world had ever known. But that hardly seemed to matter to them. When they had a chance to conquer the entire world, they simply ignored the opportunity, as if there were far more interesting things to do than that.

"They were wonderfully *crazy*. They laughed and they built things and they argued. . . . They loved to accuse themselves of terrible crimes as a people: a strange practice until you understood that its hidden purpose was to make themselves better—better to each other—better to the Earth—better than prior generations of Man.

"You all know that to look up at the moon at night, or at Mars, is to see the footprints where a few of those people walked. Some of you remember sitting in your homes and watching those footprints being made."

For the first time that evening, Gordon felt he had their full attention. He saw eyes flicker to the emblems' on his uniform, and to the bright brass rider on the peak of his postman's cap.

"The people of that nation were crazy all right," he told them. "But they were crazy in a manner that was magnificent . . . in a way that had never been seen before."

One man's scarred face stood out from the crowd. Gordon recognized old, never-healed knife wounds. He looked at that man as he spoke.

"Today we live by killing," he said. "But in that fabled land, for the most part, people settled their differences peaceably."

He turned to the tired women, slumped on benches from butchering and cleaning and laying out food for so many people. Their lined faces were flickering crags in the firelight. Several showed telltale scars from the Pox, or the Big Mumps, wartime diseases or merely old plagues that had returned in new force with the end of sanitation.

"They took for granted a clean, healthy life," he said, reminding them. "A life far gentler, far sweeter than any that had gone before.

"Or, perhaps," he added softly, "sweeter than any that would ever come again."

The people were looking at *him* now, rather than at Powhatan. And it wasn't just in older faces that eyes glistened wetly. A boy hardly over fifteen sobbed out loud.

Gordon spread his arms. "What were those people like, those *Americans*? You remember how they criticized themselves, often rightly. They were arrogant, argumentative, often shortsighted . . .

"But they did not deserve what happened to them!

221

"They had begun to wield godlike powers—to create thinking machines, to give their bodies new strengths, and to mold Life itself—but it was *not* pride in their accomplishments that struck them down."

He shook his head. "I cannot believe that! It cannot be true that we were punished for dreaming, for reaching out."

His balled fist clenched whitely. "It was *not* fated that men and women should always live like animals! Or that they should have learned so much in vain—"

In complete surprise, Gordon felt his voice break, mid-sentence. It failed him just as it was time to begin telling the lie . . . to give Powhatan a story of his own.

But his heart pounded and his mouth was suddenly nearly too dry to speak. He blinked. What was happening? *Tell them,* he thought. *Tell them now!*

"In the east . . ." Gordon began, aware of Bokuto and Stevens staring at him.

"In the east, across the mountains and deserts, rising from that great nation's ashes . . ."

He stopped again, breathing hard. It felt as if a hand were clutching his heart, threatening to squeeze if he continued. Something was preventing him from launching into his well-practiced pitch, his fairy tale.

All around they waited for him. He had them in his palm. They were ripe!

That was when Gordon glanced at George Powhatan's visage, craggy and impervious as a cliff face in the flickering firelight. And he knew then, in a sudden insight, what the problem was.

For the first time he was trying to pass his myth of a "Restored United States" before a man who was clearly much, much stronger than he.

Gordon knew that it wasn't only a story's *believability* that mattered, but the *personality* behind it as well. He might convince them all of the existence of a resurgent nation, somewhere over the eastern mountains, and it wouldn't make a whit of difference in the end . . . not if George Powhatan could make it all moot with a smile, an indulgent nod, a yawn.

It would become a thing of bygone days. An anachronism. Irrelevant.

Gordon closed his half-open mouth. Rows of faces looked up at him expectantly. But he shook his head, abandoning the fable, and with it, the lost fight.

"The east is far away," he said softly.

Then he lifted his head and some strength returned to his voice. "What is going on back there may affect us all, if we live long enough. But in the meantime there is the problem of Oregon—*Oregon*, standing by herself, as if she alone were America still.

"The nation I spoke of smolders under the ashes, ready, if you help, to cast its light again. To lead a silent world back to hope. *Believe* it, and the future will be decided here, tonight. For if America ever stood for anything, it was people being at their best when times were worst—and helping one another when it counted most."

Gordon turned and looked straight at George Powhatan. His voice dropped low, but it no longer felt weak.

"And if you have forgotten that, if none of what I have said to you matters, then all I can say is that I *pity* you."

The moment seemed to hang, a supersaturated solution in time. Powhatan sat still, like the carved image of a troubled patriarch. The tendons in his neck stood out starkly, like knotty ropes.

Whatever conflict went on in the man's mind, though, was over in seconds. Powhatan smiled sadly.

"I understand," he said. "And you may well be right, Mr. Inspector. I can think of no easy answer except to say that most of us have served and served until there is simply nothing more for us to give. You may ask for volunteers again, of course. I won't forbid anyone. But I doubt many will go."

He shook his head. "I hope you will believe it when we say that we are sorry. We are, deeply.

"But you are asking too much. We have earned our peace. It is, by now, more precious than honor, or even pity."

All this way, Gordon thought. *We came all this way, for nothing.*

Powhatan lifted two sheets of paper from his lap and held them out to Gordon.

"This is the letter I received from Corvallis this evening—carried all the way in your pouch. But although it had my name on the envelope, it was not intended for me. It was meant to be delivered to you . . . says so on the top of the first page.

"I hope you will forgive me, though, if I took the liberty of reading the text."

There was sympathy in the man's voice as Gordon reached out to take the yellowed pages. For the first time Gordon heard Powhatan repeat himself, too softly for the others to overhear.

"I *am* sorry," the man said. "I am also quite amazed."

9

My dearest Gordon,

As you read this it is already too late to stop us, so please stay calm while I try to explain. Then, if you still cannot condone what we have done, I hope you can somehow find it in your heart to forgive us.

I've talked it over and over with Susanna and Jo and the other Army women. We've read as many books as our duties allowed time for. We've badgered our mothers and aunts for their remembrances. Finally, we were forced to come to two conclusions.

The first one is straightforward. It's clear that male human beings should never have been left in control of the world all these centuries. Many of you are wonderful beyond belief, but too many others will always be bloody lunatics.

Your sex is simply built that way. Its better side gave us power and light, science and reason, medicine and philosophy. Meanwhile, the dark half spent its time dreaming up unimaginable hells and putting them into practice.

Some of the old books hint at REASONS for this strange division, Gordon. Science might even have been on the verge of an answer before the Doomtime. There were sociologists (mostly women) studying the problem, asking hard questions.

But whatever they learned, it's lost to us now, except for the simplest truths.

Oh, I can just HEAR you, Gordon, telling me I'm exaggerating again—that I'm oversimplifying and "generalizing from too little data."

For one thing, a lot of women participated in the great "male" accomplishments, and in the great evils, as well.

Also, it's obvious that most men fall in between those extremes of good and bad I spoke of.

But Gordon, those ones in between wield no power! They don't change the world, for better or worse. They are irrelevant.

You see? I can address your objections as if you were here! Though I never forget that life has cheated me of so much, I certainly have had a fine education for a woman of these times. This last year I've learned even more, from you. Knowing you has convinced me that I am right about men.

Face it, my dearest love. There are simply not enough of you good guys left to win this round. You and those like you are our heroes, but the bastards are winning! They are about to bring on the night that comes after twilight, and you cannot stop them alone.

There IS another force in humanity, Gordon. It might have tipped the balance in your age-old struggle, back in the days before the Doomwar. But it was lazy or distracted . . . I don't know. For some reason, though, it did not intervene. Not in any concerted way.

That is the second thing we, the women of the Army of the Willamette, have realized: that we have one last chance to make up for what women failed to do in the past.

We're going to stop the bastards ourselves, Gordon. We are going to do our job at last . . . to CHOOSE among men, and to cull out the mad dogs.

·   ·   ·

Forgive me, Please. The others wanted me to tell you that we will always love you. I remain yours, always.

Dena

"Stop! . . . Oh, God . . . Don't!"

When Gordon came abruptly awake, he was already on his feet. The remains of the evening campfire smoldered inches from his bare toes. His arms were outstretched, as if in the midst of grabbing after something, or someone.

Swaying, he felt the edges of his dream unravel into the forest night on all sides. His ghost had visited him again, only moments ago in his sleep. The voice of the dead machine had spoken to him across the decades, accusing with growing impatience.

. . . Who will take responsibility . . . for these foolish children. . . ?

Rows of running lights, and a voice of sad, cryogenic wisdom, despairing of the endless failings of living human beings.

"Gordon? What's going on?"

Johnny Stevens sat up in his bedroll, rubbing his eyes. It was very dim under the overcast sky, with only the fading embers and a few wan stars here and there, twinkling faintly through the overhanging branches.

Gordon shook his head, partly in order to hide his shivers. "I just thought I'd check on the horses and the pickets," he said. "Go back to sleep, Johnny."

The young postman nodded. "Okay. Tell Philip and Cal to wake me when it's time for watch change." The boy lay back down and pulled the bedroll over his shoulders. "Be careful, Gordon."

Soon his breath was whistling softly again, his face smooth and careless. The hard life seemed to suit Johnny, something that never ceased to amaze Gordon. After seventeen years of it, *he* still wasn't reconciled with having to live this way. Every so often—even as he approached middle

227

age—he still imagined he was going to wake up in his student dormitory room, back in Minnesota, and all the dirt and death and madness would turn out to be a nightmare, an alternate world that had never been.

Near the coals, a row of lumpy bedrolls lay close together for shared warmth. There were eight figures there besides Johnny—Aaron Schimmel plus all the fighters they had been able to recruit from the Camas Valley.

Four of the volunteers were boys, hardly old enough to shave. The others were all old men.

Gordon did not want to think, but memories crowded in as he pulled on his boots and woolen poncho.

For all of his near-total victory, George Powhatan had seemed quite eager to see Gordon and his band depart. The visitors made the patriarch of Sugarloaf Mountain uncomfortable. His domain would not be the same until they left.

It turned out that Dena had sent *two* packages—one more in addition to her crazy letter. In the other she had managed to convey gifts to the women of Powhatan's household in spite of Gordon, by dispatching them via "U.S. Mail." Pathetic little packets of soap and needles and underwear were accompanied by tiny mimeographed pamphlets. There were vials of pills and ointments Gordon recognized from the Corvallis central pharmacy. And he had seen copies of her letter to himself.

The whole thing had Powhatan mystified. At least as much as Gordon's speech, Dena's letter had made the man ill at ease.

"I don't understand," he had said, straddling a chair while Gordon hurriedly packed to leave. "How could an obviously intelligent young woman have come up with such a bizarre set of ideas? Hasn't anybody cared enough to knock some sense into her? What does she and her crew of little girls think they can accomplish against *Holnists?*"

Gordon had not bothered to answer, knowing it would irritate Powhatan. Anyway, he was in a hurry. He still hoped there was time to get back and stop the Scouts before they performed the worst idiocy since the Doomwar itself.

Powhatan kept probing, though. The man sounded genuinely puzzled. And he was unaccustomed to being put off. At last, Gordon found himself actually speaking out in Dena's defense.

"What kind of 'common sense' would you have had someone knock into her, George? The logic of the colorless drabs who cook meals for complacent men, here in the Camas? Or perhaps she should speak only when spoken to, like those poor women who live as cattle down in the Rogue, and now in Eugene?

"They may be wrong. They may even be crazy. But at least Dena and her comrades care about something bigger than themselves, and have the guts to fight for it. Do you, George? Do you?"

Powhatan had looked down at the floor. Gordon barely heard his reply. "Where is it written that one should only care about big things? I fought for big things, long ago . . . for issues, principles, a country. Where are all of them now?"

The steely gray eyes were narrow and sad when next he looked up at Gordon. "I found out something, you know. I discovered that the big things don't love you back. They take and take, and never give in return. They'll drain your blood, your soul, if you let them, and never let go.

"I lost my wife, my son, while away battling for *big things*. They needed me, but I had to go off trying to save the world." Powhatan snorted at the last phrase. "Today I fight for my people, for my farm—for smaller things— things I can *hold*."

Gordon had watched Powhatan's large, hard-calloused hand flex, as if straining to grasp life itself. It had never occurred to him until then that this man feared anything in the world, but there it was, visible for only the briefest moment.

A certain rare kind of terror in his eyes.

At the door to Gordon's guest room, Powhatan had turned, his chiseled face outlined in the flickering light from the tallow candles. "Me, I think I know why your crazy

229

woman is pulling whatever mad stunt she's cooked up, and it doesn't have to do with that grand 'heroes and villains' bullshit she wrote about.

"The other women, they're just following her because she's a natural leader in desperate times. She has them swept along in her wake, poor girls. But she . . ." Powhatan shook his head. "She *thinks* she's doing it for the big reasons, but one of the small things lies beneath it all.

"She's doing it out of love, Mr. Inspector. I think she's doing it for you alone."

They had looked at each other, that last time, and Gordon realized then that Powhatan was paying the visiting postman back with interest for the unasked-for guilt he had been delivered.

Gordon had nodded to the Squire of Sugarloaf Mountain, accepting the burden—postage prepaid.

Leaving the warmth of the coals, Gordon felt his way over to the horses and carefully checked their lines. All seemed well, though the animals were a little jumpy still. After all, they had been driven hard today. The ruins of the prewar town of Remote lay behind them, and the old Bear Creek Campgrounds. If the band really flew tomorrow, Calvin Lewis figured they might make Roseburg by a little after nightfall.

Powhatan had been generous with provisions for their journey. He had given of the best of his stables. Anything the northerners wanted, they could have. Except for George Powhatan, of course.

As Gordon patted the last nickering horse, and stepped out under the trees, a part of him was still unable to believe they had come all this way for nothing. Failure tasted bitter in his mouth.

. . . rippling lights . . . the voice of a long-dead machine . . .

Gordon smiled without amusement.

"If I could have infected him with your ghost, Cyclops, don't you think I would have? But you don't reach a man like him as simply as that! He's made of stronger stuff than I was."

230

. . . Who will take responsibility. . . ?

"I don't know!" he whispered urgently, silently, at the darkness all around him. "I don't even care anymore!"

He was maybe forty feet from the campsite now. It occurred to him that he could just keep on going should he choose. If he disappeared into the forest, right now, he would still be better off than sixteen months ago when, robbed and injured, he had stumbled upon that ancient, wrecked postal jeep in a high, dusty forest.

He had taken the uniform and bag only in order to survive, but something had latched onto him that strange night, the first of many ghosts.

At little Pine View the unsought legend began—this Johnny Appleseed "postman" nonsense that had long since gone completely out of control, thrusting upon him unasked-for responsibility for an entire civilization. Since then his life had no longer been his own. But now, he realized, he could change that!

Just walk away, he thought.

Gordon felt his way in the pitch blackness, using the one forest skill that had never failed him, his sense of path and direction. He walked surefootedly, sensing where the tree roots and little gullies had to be, using the logic of one who had come to know woodlands well.

It required a special, remote kind of concentration to move this way in the near-total darkness . . . a zenlike exercise that was elevating—as detached but more *active* than that sunset meditation two days ago, overlooking the roaring confluence of the Coquille. As he walked, he seemed to rise higher and higher above his troubles.

Who needed eyes to see, or ears to hear? Only the touch of the wind guided him. That and the scent of the red cedars, and the faint salt traces of the distant, expectant sea.

Just walk away. . . . Joyfully, he realized that he had found a counter incantation! One that matched and neutralized the rippling of little lights in his mind. An antidote to ghosts.

He hardly felt the ground, striding through the darkness, repeating it with growing enthusiasm. *Just walk away!*

The exalted journey ended abruptly, jarringly, as he tripped over something completely unexpected—something that did not belong there on the forest floor.

He tumbled to the ground with barely a sound, a puff of snow-covered pine needles breaking his fall. Gordon scrambled around, but couldn't make out the obstacle that had brought him down. It was soft and yielding to the touch, though. His hand came away sticky and warm.

Gordon's pupils should not have been able to dilate wider, but sudden fear did the trick. He bent forward and the face of a dead man came into sudden focus.

Young Cal Lewis stared back at him in a frozen expression of surprise. The boy's throat gaped, expertly slit.

Gordon scuttled backward until he came up against a nearby tree trunk. In a daze he realized he hadn't even taken his belt knife or pouch with him. Somehow, perhaps because of the spell of George Powhatan's mountain, he had let that deadly sliver of complacency slip in. Perhaps his last mistake.

In the dark, he could hear the rushing waters of the middle fork of the Coquille. Beyond lay the enemy's home ground. But right now they were on this side of the river.

The ambushers don't know I'm out here, he realized. It didn't seem possible after the way he had been moving around, mumbling to himself obliviously, but perhaps there had been a gap in their closing circle.

Perhaps they had been preoccupied.

Gordon understood the principles well. First you take out the pickets, then, in a rush, swoop down on the unsuspecting encampment. Those boys and old men sleeping by the campfire did not have George Powhatan with them, now. They never should have left their mountain.

Gordon hunched down. The raiders would never find him here in the roots of this tree. Not so long as he kept quiet. When the butchery began, while the Holnists were busy collecting trophies, he could be off into the deep woods without a trace.

Dena had said there were two kinds of men who

counted . . . and those in between who did not matter. *Fine,* he thought. *Let me be one of those in between. Living beats "mattering" any day.*

He hunkered down, trying to keep as silent as possible.

A twig snapped—barely the tiniest click over in the direction of the camp. A minute later a "night bird" cooed, a little farther away. The rendition was understated and completely believable.

Now that he was listening, Gordon found he could actually follow the deadly encirclement as it closed. His own tree had already been left behind, and was well outside the narrowing ring of death.

Quiet, he told himself. *Wait it out.*

He tried not to envision the stealthy enemy, their camouflage-painted faces grinning in anticipation as they stroked their oiled knives.

Don't think about it! He closed his eyes hard, trying to listen only to his pounding heart while he fingered a thin chain around his neck. He had worn it, along with the little keepsake Abby had given him, ever since leaving Pine View.

That's right, think about Abby. He tried to picture her, smiling and cheerful and loving, but the inner commentary kept on running within his head.

The Holnists would want to make sure the pickets were all finished before they closed the trap. If they had not yet taken care of the other man on watch—Philip Bokuto— they would do it soon.

He made a fist around Abby's present. The chain made a taut line across the back of his neck.

Bokuto . . . guarding his commander even when he disapproved . . . doing Gordon's dirty work for him under the falling snow . . . serving with all his heart for the sake of a myth . . . for a nation that had died and would never, ever rise again.

Bokuto . . .

For the second time that night Gordon found himself on his feet without remembering how it had happened. There was no volition at all, only a shrill screech that pierced the night as he blew hard on Abby's whistle, then his own voice, screaming through cupped hands.

"*Philip! Watch out!*"

... *out!* ... *out!* ... *out!* ... The echo rolled forth, seeming to stun the forest.

For a long second the stillness held, then six sharp concussions shook the air in rapid succession, and suddenly, shouting filled the night.

Gordon blinked. Whatever had come over him, it was too late to turn back now. He had to play it out. "They walked right into our trap!" he shouted as loud as he could. "George says he'll take them on the river side! Phil, cover the right!"

What an ad lib performance! Even though his words were probably lost amid the outcries and gunfire and yelped survivalist battle calls, the commotion had to be setting their plans off. Gordon kept shouting and blowing the whistle to try to confuse the ambushers.

Men screamed and dark shapes rolled through the undergrowth in desperate struggle. Flames rose high from the stirred campfire, casting grappling silhouettes through the trees.

If the fight was still going on after two full minutes, Gordon knew it meant there was a chance after all. He shouted as if he were directing a whole company of reinforcements.

"Don't let the bastards get back across the river!" he cried. And indeed, there did seem to be some hurried motion off that way. He ducked from tree to tree toward the fighting—even though he had no weapon. "Keep them bottled in! Don't let 'em—"

That was when a shape emerged suddenly from around the very next tree. Gordon stopped only ten feet from the jagged patterns of black and white that made the painted face so hard to focus on. A slashlike mouth split into a broad, gap-toothed grin. The body below the unfriendly smile was immense.

"Pretty noisy feller," the survivalist commented.

"Oughta quiet up for a bit, right, Nate?" The dark eyes flickered over Gordon's shoulder.

For the briefest instant Gordon started to turn, even as he told himself that it was all a trick—that the Holnist was probably alone.

His attention only wavered for a moment, but it was long enough. The camouflaged figure moved like a blur. One blow from a ham-sized, rock-hard fist sent Gordon spinning to the ground.

The world was a whirl of stars and pain. *How could anyone move so fast?* he wondered with unravelling shreds of consciousness.

It was Gordon's last clear thought.

10

A frigid, misty rain turned the slushy trail into a quagmire that sucked at the prisoners' shuffling feet. With hanging heads they fought the mud, struggling to keep up with the horses and riders. After three days, all that mattered in the captives' narrow world was keeping up, and avoiding any more beatings.

The victors looked hardly less fearsome now, without their war paint. In winter camouflage parkas they rode imperiously on their seized Camas Valley mounts. The rearmost and youngest Holnist—with only one gold ring hanging from his ear—occasionally turned back to snarl at the prisoners and tug the tether around the lead man's wrist, causing the whole line to stumble ahead faster for a time.

Everywhere along the trail lay trash left by successive waves of refugees. After countless small battles and massacres, the strongest held the high ground in this territory. This was the paradise of Nathan Holn.

Several times the caravan passed through small clusters of hovels, filthy warrens made from bits and scraps of prewar salvage. At every ragged hamlet a population of wretched creatures stumbled out to pay their respects, eyes downcast. Now and then an unlucky one cowered under a few lazy blows meted out for no apparent reason by those on horseback.

Only after the warriors had passed did the villagers look

up again. Their tired eyes held no hatred, only a glittering hunger as they watched the receding rumps of the well-fed horses.

The serfs hardly glanced at the new prisoners. Their lack of attention was returned.

Walking filled the daylight hours with few breaks. At night the captives were separated to prevent talking. Each was tied to a hobbled horse for warmth without a fire. Then, with dawn and a meal of weak gruel, the long walk began anew.

By the fourth day two of the prisoners had died. Two more who were too weak to continue were left with the Holnist baron of a tiny, scrabble-backed manor— replacements for serfs whose crucified corpses still hung over the trail as object lessons to anyone contemplating disobedience.

All this time, Gordon saw little more than the back of the man in front of him. He grew to hate the prisoner tethered behind his waist. Each time that one stumbled, the sudden jerk tore into the tortured muscles of his arms and sides. Still, he scarcely noticed by the time that man also disappeared, leaving only two captives to follow the plodding horses. He envied the one who had been left behind, not even knowing if the fellow had died.

The journey seemed interminable. He had awakened into it days ago and had hardly risen to complete awareness since. In spite of the agony, a small part of him *welcomed* the stupor and monotony. No ghosts bothered him here. No complexities and no guilt. It was all quite straightforward actually. One put a foot in front of the other, ate what little one was given, and kept one's head down.

At some point he noticed that his fellow prisoner was *helping* him, taking part of his weight on his shoulders as they fought the mud. Semiconsciously, he wondered why anyone would do such a thing.

At last there came a time when he blinked and saw that his hands had been untied. They stood next to a wood-sided structure, offset some distance from a maze of teetering, noisome shanties. From not far away came the roar of rushing water.

"Welcome to Agness Town," one of the harsh-voiced men said. Someone planted a hand in his back and pushed. There was laughter as the prisoners tumbled inside to collapse on a filthy straw tick.

Neither bothered to move from the exact spot where he rolled to a stop. It was a chance to sleep. For the moment, that was all that mattered. Again, there were no dreams—only occasional twitching as abused muscles misfired through the rest of the day, the night, and all the following morning.

Gordon awakened only when bright sunlight rose high enough to shine painfully through his eyelids. He rolled aside, groaning. A shadow passed over him, and his eyelids fluttered like rusty shutters.

It took a few seconds to focus. Recognition came some time after that. The first thing that occurred to him was that there was a tooth missing from the familiar smile.

"Johnny," he croaked.

The young man's face was blistered and bruised. Still, John Stevens grinned cheerfully, gap and all. "Hullo, Gordon. Welcome back among the unlucky—the living."

He helped Gordon sit up and steadied a ladle of cool river water for him to sip. Meanwhile, Johnny talked. "There's food over in the corner. And I overheard a guard say something about gettin' us cleaned up sometime soon. So maybe there's a reason our balls aren't already hanging from some asshole's trophy belt. I guess they brought us all this way to meet some bigshot."

Johnny laughed, dryly. "Just you wait, Gordon. We'll talk rings around the guy, whoever it is. Maybe we can offer to make him a postmaster, or something. Is that what you meant when you lectured me about the importance of learning practical politics?"

Gordon was too weak to strangle Johnny for his incredible, jarring cheerfulness. He tried to smile back instead, but it only made his cracked lips hurt.

A scuttling movement in the corner opposite them showed that they were not alone. There were three other prisoners in the shed with them—filthy, wild-eyed scarecrows who had obviously been here a long time. They stared back with saucer eyes, obviously long past human.

"Did . . . did anyone get away from the ambush?" It had been Gordon's first lucid opportunity to ask.

"I think so. Your warning must have buggered the bastards' timing. It gave us a chance to make a pretty good fight of it. I'm sure we took out a couple of them before they swamped us." Johnny's eyes shone. If anything, the boy's admiration seemed to have increased. Gordon looked away. He didn't want praise for his behavior that night.

"I'm pretty sure I killed the sonovabitch who smashed my guitar. Another one—"

"What about Phil Bokuto?" Gordon interrupted.

Johnny shook his head. "I don't know, Gordon. I saw no black ears or . . . other things . . . among the 'trophies' the crumbs collected. Maybe he made it."

Gordon sagged back against the slats of their pen. The sound of rushing water, a roar that had been with them all night, came from the other side. He turned and peered through the gaps in the rough planks.

About twenty feet away was the edge of a bluff. Beyond it, through ragged shreds of drifting fog, he could see the heavily forested wall of a canyon cut by a narrow, swift stream.

Johnny seemed to read his thoughts. For the first time the young man's voice was low, serious.

"That's right, Gordon. We're right in the heart of it. That down there's the bitch herself. The bloody Rogue."

11

The mist and icy drizzle turned back into flurries of snow-flakes for the next week. With food and rest, the two prisoners slowly regained some strength. For company they had only each other. Neither their guards nor their fellow captives would speak to them in more than monosyllables.

Still, it wasn't hard to learn some things about life in the Holnist realm. Their meals were brought by silent, cowering drudges from the nearby shanty town. The only figures they saw who weren't emaciated—besides the earringed survivalists themselves—were the women who served the Holnists' pleasure. And even those worked by day: drawing water from the frigid stream or currying the stable of well-fed horses.

The pattern seemed well established, as if this was an accustomed way of life. And yet Gordon became convinced that the neofeudal community was in a state of flux.

"They're preparing for a big move," he told Johnny as they watched a caravan arrive one afternoon. Still more frightened serfs trudged into Agness, pulling carts and setting up camp in the swelling warren. Obviously, this little valley could not hold such a population for very long.

"They're using this place as a staging area."

Johnny suggested, "That mob of people might offer us an advantage, if we find a way to bust out of here."

"Hmm," Gordon answered. But he didn't hold much hope for aid from any of the slaves out there. They'd had any spirit beaten out of them, and had problems enough of their own.

One day, after the noon meal, Gordon and Johnny were ordered to step out of their pen and strip naked. A pair of shabby, silent women came and gathered up their clothes. While the northerners' backs were turned, buckets of cold river water were thrown on them. Gordon and Johnny gasped and sputtered. The guards all laughed, but the women's eyes did not even flicker as they left, heads bowed.

The Holnists—dressed in green and black camouflage, their ears arrayed with golden rings—competed in lazy knife practice, flipping their blades in quick, underhand arcs. The two northerners clutched greasy blankets in front of a small fire, trying to stay warm.

That evening their cleaned and patched clothes were returned to them. This time one of the women actually looked up briefly, giving Gordon a chance to see her face. She might have been twenty, though her lined eyes looked far older. Her brown hair was streaked with gray. She glanced at Gordon for only a moment as he dressed. But when he ventured a smile, she turned quickly and fled without looking back.

The sunset meal was better fare than the usual sour gruel. There were scraps of something like venison amidst the parched corn. Perhaps it was horsemeat.

Johnny dared fate by asking for seconds. The other prisoners blinked in amazement and cringed even farther into their corners. One of the silent guards growled and took their plates away. But to their surprise he returned with another helping for each of them.

It was full dark when three Holn warriors in floppy berets marched up behind a stoop-shouldered servant bearing a torch. "Come along," the leader told them. "The General wants to see you."

Gordon looked at Johnny, standing proud again in his uniform. The young man's eyes were confident. After all, they seemed to say, what did these jerks have that could compare with Gordon's authority as an official of the Restored Republic?

Gordon remembered how the boy had half-carried him during the long journey south from the Coquille. He had little heart anymore for pretenses, but for Johnny's sake he would try the old scam one more time.

"All right, postman," he told his young friend. Gordon winked. "Neither sleet, nor hail, nor gloom of night . . ."

Johnny grinned back. "Through bandit's hell, through firefight . . ."

They turned together and left the jail shed ahead of their guards.

12

"*Welcome, gentlemen.*"

The first thing Gordon noticed was the crackling fireplace. The snug pre-Doom ranger station was stone sealed and warm. He had almost forgotten what the sensation felt like.

Second noticed was the rustle of silk as a long-legged blond rose from a cushion by the hearth. The girl was a striking contrast to nearly all the other women they had seen here—clean, erect, laden down with glittering stones that would have brought a fortune before the war.

Nevertheless, her eyes were lined, and she looked at the two northerners as one might regard creatures from the far side of the moon. Silently, she stood up and exited the room through a beaded curtain.

"I said *welcome*, gentlemen. Welcome to the Free Realm."

At last Gordon turned and took notice of a thin, bald man with a neatly trimmed beard, who rose to greet them from a cluttered desk. Four gold rings glittered from one earlobe, and three from the other—symbols of rank. He approached holding out his hand.

"Colonel Charles Westin Bezoar, at your service, formerly of the bar of the State of Oregon and Republican Commissioner for Jackson County. I presently have the honor of being judge advocate of the American Liberation Army."

Gordon arched an eyebrow, ignoring the outstretched hand. "There have been a lot of 'armies' since the Fall. Which one did you say you were with, again?"

Bezoar smiled and let his hand drop casually. "I realize that some apply other names to us. Let's defer that for now and just say I serve as aide-de-camp to General Volsci Macklin, who is your host. The General will be joining us shortly. Meanwhile, may I offer you some of our hill country sour mash?" He lifted a cut glass decanter from the carved oak sideboard. "Whatever you may have heard about our rough life up here, I believe you'll find we've refined at least a few of the old arts."

Gordon shook his head. Johnny looked over the man's head. Bezoar shrugged.

"No? Pity. Perhaps some other time. I hope you don't mind if I do indulge." Bezoar poured himself a glass of brown liquor and gestured to two chairs near the fire. "Please, gentlemen, you must still be exhausted from your journey. Be comfortable. There is much I'd like to know."

"For instance, Mr. Inspector, how *are* things back in the states to the east, beyond the deserts and the mountains?"

Gordon did not even blink as he sat down. So the "Liberation Army" had an intelligence service. It was no surprise that Bezoar knew who they were . . . or at least who north Oregon thought Gordon was.

"Things are much the same as in the west, Mr. Bezoar. People try to live, and rebuild where they can."

In his mind Gordon was trying to recreate the dreamscape—the fantasy of St. Paul City, of Odessa and Green Bay—images of living cities leading a bold, resurgent nation—not the windswept ghost towns he remembered, picked clean by ragged bands of wary survivors.

He spoke for the cities as he had dreamed them. His voice was stern. "In some places citizens have been luckier than in others. They've regained much, and hope for more for their children. In other areas, the recovery has been . . . hindered. Some of those who nearly ruined our nation, a generation ago, still wreak havoc, still harry our couriers and disrupt communications.

244

"And as I speak of it," Gordon continued coldly. "I cannot put off any longer asking you just what you've done with the mail your men have stolen from the United States."

Bezoar put on wire-rimmed glasses and lifted a thick folder from the table next to him. "You are speaking of these letters, I presume?" He opened the packet. Dozens of grayed and yellowed sheets rustled dryly. "You see? I do not bother to deny it. I believe we should be open and frank with each other, if anything is to come of this meeting.

"Yes, a team of our advance scouts did find a pack horse in the ruins of Eugene—yours, I imagine—whose saddlebags contained this very strange cargo. Ironically, I believe that at the very moment our scouts were seizing these samples, you were killing two of their comrades elsewhere in the deserted town."

Bezoar raised one hand before Gordon could speak. "Have no fear of retribution. Our Holnist philosophy does not believe in it. You defeated two survivalists in a straight fight. That makes you a peer in our eyes. Why do you think you were treated as men after you were captured, and not gelded as serfs or as sheep?"

Bezoar smiled amiably, but Gordon seethed inside. In Eugene last spring he had seen what Holnists did to the bodies of the harmless gleaners they had mowed down. He remembered young Mark Aage's mother, who saved his life and her son's with one heroic gesture. Bezoar clearly meant what he said, yet to Gordon the logic was sickly, bitterly ironic.

The bald survivalist spread his hands. "We admit to taking your mail, Mr. Inspector. Can we mitigate our guilt by claiming ignorance? After all, until these letters reached me here, none of us had ever *heard* of the Restored United States!

"Imagine our amazement when we saw such things . . . letters carried many miles from town to town, warrants for new postmasters, and these," he raised a sheaf of official-looking flyers. "These declarations from *the provisional government* in St. Paul City."

The words were conciliatory and sounded earnest. But

there was something in the man's tone of voice. . . . He could not quite pin it down, but whatever it was disturbed Gordon.

"You know of it now," he pointed out. "And yet you continue. Two of our postal couriers have disappeared without a trace since your invasion of the north. Your 'American Liberation Army' has been at war with the United States for many months now, *Colonel* Bezoar. And *that* cannot be mitigated by ignorance."

The lies came easily, now. In essence, after all, the words were true.

Ever since those few weeks, right after the big war had been "won"—when the U.S. still had a government, and food and materiel still moved protected on the highways—the real problem had not been the broken enemies without so much as the chaos within.

Grain rotted in bulging silos while farmers were felled by simple, innoculable plagues. Vaccine was available in the cities, where starvation reaped multitudes. More people died due to the breakdown and lawlessness—the shattered web of commerce and mutual assistance—than from all the bombs and germs, or even from the three-year dusk.

It had been men like this who delivered the coup de grace, who ended any chance those millions had.

"Perhaps, perhaps." Bezoar tossed back a shot of the pungent liquor. He smiled. "Then again, many have claimed to be the true inheritors of American sovereignty. So your 'Restored United States' controls large areas and populations, and so its leaders include a few old farts who once bought elected office with cash and a television smile. Does that mean that *it* is the true America?"

For an instant the calm, reasonable visage seemed to crack, and Gordon saw the fanatic within, unchanged except perhaps by deepening over the years. Gordon had heard that tone . . . long ago in the radio voice of Nathan Holn—before the survivalist "saint" was hanged—and spoken by his followers ever since.

It was the same solipsistic philosophy of ego that had stoked the rage of Nazism, of Stalinism. Hegel, Horbiger,

Holn—the roots were identical. *Derived* truth, smug and certain, never to be tested in the light of reality.

In North America, Holnism had been a nut fringe during a time of otherwise unparalleled brilliance, a throwback to the egoistic eighties. But another version of the same evil—"Slavic Mysticism"—actually seized power in the other hemisphere. That madness finally plunged the world into the Doomwar.

Gordon smiled with grim severity. "Who can say what is legitimate, after all these years? But one thing is certain, Bezoar, the 'true spirit of America' seems to have become a passion for hunting down Holnists. Your cult of the strong is loathed—not only in the Restored U.S. but almost everywhere I've traveled. Feuding villages will join forces on rumor of sighting one of your bands. Any man caught wearing surplus camouflage is hanged on sight."

He knew he had scored, then. The earringed officer's nostrils flared. "That's *Colonel* Bezoar, if you please. And I'll wager there are some areas where that's not true, Mr. Inspector. Florida, perhaps? And Alaska?"

Gordon shrugged. Both states had gone silent the day after the first bombs fell. There had been other places too, such as southern Oregon, where the militia had not dared enter, even in strength.

Bezoar stood up and walked to a bookshelf. He pulled down a thick volume. "Have you ever actually *read* Nathan Holn?" he asked, his voice amiable once again. Gordon shook his head.

"But, sir!" Bezoar protested. "How can you know your enemy without learning how he thinks? Please, take this copy of *Lost Empire* . . . Holn's own biography of that great man, Aaron Burr. It just might change your mind.

"You know I do believe, Mr. Krantz, that you are the sort of man who could become a Holnist. Often the strong need only have their eyes opened to see that they have been cozened by the propaganda of the weak, that they could have the *world,* if only they stretched out their hands and took it."

Gordon suppressed his initial response, and picked up

247

the proffered book instead. It probably wouldn't be wise to provoke the man too far. After all, he could probably have both northerners killed with a word.

"All right. It might help pass the time while you arrange our transportation back to the Willamette," he said, quite calmly.

"Yeah," Johnny Stevens contributed, speaking for the first time. "And while you're at it, how about paying the extra postage it'll take to finish delivering that stolen mail we're going to take back with us?"

Bezoar returned Johnny's cold smile, but before he could reply, they heard footsteps on the wooden porch of the former ranger station. The door opened and in stepped three bearded men dressed in the traditional green and black fatigues.

One of them, the shortest but easily the most imposing figure, wore only a single earring. But it glittered with large, inset gems.

"Gentlemen," Bezoar said, standing up. "Allow me to introduce Brigadier General Macklin, U.S. Army Reserve, uniter of the Oregon clans of Holn and commander of the American Forces of Liberation."

Gordon stood up numbly. For a moment he could only stare. The General and his two aides were among the strangest-looking human beings he had ever seen.

There was nothing unusual about their beards or earrings . . . or the short string of shriveled "trophies" that each wore as ceremonial decorations. But all three men were eerily *scarred*, wherever their uniforms permitted view of their necks and arms. And under the faint lines left by some long ago surgery, the muscles and tendons seemed to bulge and knot oddly.

It was weird, and yet it occurred to Gordon that he might have seen something akin to it, sometime in the past. He could not quite remember where or when though.

Had these men suffered from one of the postwar plagues? Supermumps, perhaps? Or some sort of thyroid hypertrophy?

In a sudden recognition Gordon knew that the biggest

of Macklin's aides was the pig-ugly raider who had struck so quickly on the night of the ambush by the banks of the Co-quille, knocking him to the ground with the punch of a bull before he could even begin to move.

None of the men was of the newer generation of feudal-survivalists, young toughs recruited all through southern Oregon. Like Bezoar, the newcomers were clearly old enough to have been adults before the Doomwar. Time did not seem to have slowed them down any, however. General Macklin moved with a catlike quickness that was intimidating to watch. He wasted no time in pleasantries. With a jerk of his head and a glance at Johnny, he made his wishes known to Bezoar.

Bezoar pressed his fingers together. "Ah. Yes. Mr. Stevens, if you would please accompany these gentlemen back to your, um, quarters? It appears the General wants to speak with your superior alone."

Johnny looked at Gordon. Obviously, if given the word, he would fight.

Gordon quailed inwardly under the burden of that expression in the youth's eyes. Such devotion was something he had never sought, not from anybody. "Go on back, John," he told his young friend. "I'll join you later."

The two hulking aides accompanied Johnny outside. When the door had closed, and the footsteps receded into the night, Gordon turned to face the commander of the united Holnists. In his heart he felt a powerful determination. There was no regret, no fear of hypocrisy here. If it was in him to lie well enough to bluff these bastards, he would do it. He felt full within his postman's uniform, and got ready to give the best performance of his life.

"Save it," Macklin snapped.

The dark-bearded man pointed a long, powerful hand at him. "One word of that crap about a 'Restored United States' out of you, and I'll stuff your 'uniform' down your frigging throat!"

Gordon blinked. He glanced at Bezoar and saw that the man was grinning.

"I am afraid I've been less than open with you, *Mr. In-*

249

spector." There was a clear lilt of sarcasm this time in Bezoar's last two words. The Holnist Colonel bent to open a drawer in his desk. "When first I heard of you I immediately sent out parties to trace your route backwards. By the way, you are right that Holnism is not very popular, in certain areas. At least not yet. Two of the teams never returned."

General Macklin snapped his fingers. "Don't drag this out, Bezoar. I'm busy. Call the jerk in."

Bezoar nodded quickly and reached back to pull a cord on the wall, leaving Gordon wondering what he had been trying to find in the drawer.

"Anyway, one of our scouting parties did encounter a band of kindred spirits in the Cascades, in a pass north of Crater Lake. There were misunderstandings, most of the poor locals died, I'm afraid. But we did manage to persuade a survivor—"

There were footsteps, then the beaded curtain parted. The svelte blond woman held it open and watched coldly as a battered-looking man with a bandaged head stumbled into the room. He wore a uniform of patched, faded camouflage, a belt knife, and a single, tiny earring. His eyes were downcast. This survivalist was one who seemed less than joyous at being here.

"I would introduce you to our latest recruit, Mr. Inspector," Bezoar said. "But I believe you two already know each other."

Gordon shook his head, thoroughly lost. What was going on here? To his knowledge he had never seen this man before in his life!

Bezoar prodded the drooping newcomer, who looked up, then. "I cannot say for certain," the unsteady Holn recruit said, peering at Gordon. "He might be the one. It was a passing event, really, of so . . . so little consequence at the time. . . ."

Gordon's fists balled suddenly. *That voice.*

"It's *you*, you bastard!"

The jaunty Alpine cap was gone, but now Gordon recognized the salt-and-pepper sideburns, the sallow complexion. Roger Septien seemed far less serene than when Gordon had last seen the man—on the slopes of a death-dry mountainside, helping to carry away nearly everything Gordon owned in the world, blithely, sarcastically, leaving him to almost certain death.

Bezoar nodded in satisfaction. "You may go, Private Septien. I believe your officer has suitable duty arranged for you, tonight."

The former robber and onetime stockbroker nodded wearily. He didn't even glance again at Gordon, but passed outside without another word.

Gordon realized that he had blundered in reacting so quickly. He should have ignored the man, pretended he didn't recognize him.

But then, would it have made a difference? Macklin had already seemed so sure. . . .

"Get on with it," the General told his aide.

Bezoar reached into the drawer again, and this time drew forth a small, ragged, black notebook. He held it out to Gordon. "Do you recognize this? It has your name in it."

Gordon blinked. Of course it was his journal, stolen—along with all his goods—by Septien and the other robbers only hours before he stumbled onto the ruined postal van and started down the road to his new career.

At the time he had mourned its loss, for the diary detailed his travels ever since leaving Minnesota, seventeen years ago . . . his careful observations of life in postholocaust America.

Now, though, the slim volume was the last thing on Earth he would ever have wanted to see. He sat down heavily, suddenly weary, aware of how completely the devils had been toying with him. The lie had caught up with him, at last.

In all the pages of that little journal, there wasn't a single word about postmen, or recovery, or any "Restored United States."

There was only the truth.

13

Lost Empire
by NATHAN HOLN

Today, as we approach the end of the Twentieth Century, the great struggles of our time are said to be between the so-called *Left* and so-called *Right*—those great behemoths of a contrived, fictitious political spectrum. Very few people seem to be aware that these so-called *opposites* are, in reality, two faces to the same sick beast. There is a widespread blindness, which keeps millions from seeing how they have been fooled by this fabrication.

But it was not always so. Nor will it always be.

In other tracts I have spoken of other types of systems—of the honor of medieval Japan, of the glorious, wild American Indians, and of shining Europe during the period effete scholars today call its "Dark Age."

One thing history tells us, over and over again. Throughout all eras, *some have commanded, while others have obeyed.* It is a pattern of loyalty and power that is both honorable and natural. Feudalism has always been our way, as a species, ever since we foraged in wild bands and screamed defiance at each other from opposing hilltops.

That is, it was always our way until men were perverted, the strong sapped by the whimpering propaganda of the weak.

Think back to how things were when the Nineteenth Century was just dawning in America. Back then the opportunity stood stark and clear to reverse the sick trends of the so-called "Enlightenment." The victorious Revolutionary War soldiers had expelled English decadence from most of the continent. The frontier lay open, and a rough spirit of individualism reigned supreme throughout the newborn nation.

Aaron Burr knew this when he set out to seize the new territories west of the original thirteen colonies. His dream was that of all natural males—to dominate, to conquer, to win an *empire*!

What would the world have been like if he had won? Could he have prevented the rise of those misborn twin obscenities, socialism and capitalism?

Who can tell? I will tell you, though, what *I* believe. I believe the Era of Greatness was at hand, ready to be born!

But Burr was brought down before he could accomplish much more than the punishment of that tool of traitors, Alexander Hamilton. Superficially, his chief foe would seem to have been Jefferson, the conniver who robbed him of the Presidency. But in fact the conspiracy went far, far deeper than that.

That evil genius, Benjamin Franklin, was at the heart of it—that cabal to kill the Empire before it could be born. His instruments were many, too many even for a man as strong as Burr to fight.

And the chiefest of those instruments was the *Order of Cincinnatus.* . . .

Gordon slammed the book facedown on the ground beside the straw tick. How could anyone have read crap like this, let alone published it?

It was still light enough to read after the evening meal, and the sun was out for the first time in days. Nevertheless, a crawling chill ran up and down his back as the mad dialectic echoed within his head.

That evil genius, Benjamin Franklin . . .

Nathan Holn did make a good case that "Poor Richard" had been much more than a clever printer-philosopher, who played ambassador in between scientific experiments and wenching. If even a small fraction of Holn's citations were correct, Franklin certainly *was* at the center of unusual events. Something odd did happen after the Revolutionary War, something that somehow thwarted the men like Aaron Burr, and brought about the nation Gordon had known.

But beyond that, Gordon was impressed mostly with the magnitude of Nathan Holn's madness. Bezoar and Macklin had to be completely crazy if they thought these ravings would convert him to their plans!

The book had, in fact, just the opposite effect. If a volcano were to go off right here in Agness, he felt it would be worth it to know this nest of snakes would go to Hell along with him.

Not far away, a baby was crying. Gordon looked up but could barely make out shabby figures moving beyond the nearby copse of alders. New captives had been brought in last night. They moaned and huddled close around the small fire they had been allowed, not rating even the shelter of a roofed pen.

Gordon and Johnny could be joining those miserable serfs soon if Macklin did not get the answer he wanted. The "General" was losing patience. After all, from Macklin's point of view his offer to Gordon must have seemed quite reasonable.

Gordon had only a little while left in which to make up his mind. The Holnist offensive would begin again with the first thaw, with or without his compromised cooperation.

He did not see where he had much choice.

Unbidden, a memory of Dena came to mind. He found himself missing her, wondering if she was still alive, wishing he could touch her and be with her . . . pestering questions and all.

By now, of course, it was probably too late to stop whatever crazy scheme she and her followers had dreamed up. Gordon frankly wondered why Macklin had not already gloated to him, over yet another disaster to the hapless Army of the Willamette.

Perhaps it's only a matter of time, he thought gloomily.

Johnny finished rinsing out the nub-worn toothbrush that was their sole common possession. He sat next to Gordon and picked up the Burr biography. The youth read for a while, then looked up, clearly puzzled.

"I know our school at Cottage Grove wasn't much by prewar standards, Gordon, but Grandfather used to give me lots to read, and talked to me a lot about history and stuff. Even *I* know this guy Holn is making up half this junk.

"How did he get away with pushing a book like this? How is it anyone ever believed him?"

Gordon shrugged. "It was called 'the Big Lie' technique, Johnny. Just *sound* like you know what you're talking about—as if you're citing real facts. Talk very fast. Weave your lies into the shape of a conspiracy theory and repeat your assertions over and over again. Those who want an excuse to hate or blame—those with big but weak egos—will leap at a simple, neat explanation for the way the world is. Those types will never call you on the facts.

"Hitler did it brilliantly. So did the Mystic of Leningrad. Holn was just another master of the Big Lie."

And what about you? Gordon asked himself. Did he, inventor of the fable of the "Restored United States," collaborator in the hoax of Cyclops, have any right to cast stones?

Johnny read on for a few minutes more. Then he tapped the book again. "Who was this Cincinnatus guy, then? Did Holn make him up too?"

Gordon lay back on the straw. His eyes closed. "No. If I remember right, he was a great general of ancient Rome, back in the days of the Republic. According to the legend, he got sick of fighting one day, and retired from the army to farm his land in peace.

"One day though, emissaries came out from the city to see him. Rome's armies were in rout; their leaders had proven incompetent. Disaster seemed inevitable.

"The delegation approached Cincinnatus—they found him behind his plow—and they pleaded with him to take command of the last defense."

"What did Cincinnatus tell the guys from Rome?"

"Oh, well," Gordon yawned. "He agreed all right. Reluctantly. He rallied the Romans, beat the invaders, and drove them all the way back to their own city. It was a great victory."

"I'll bet they made him king or something," Johnny suggested.

Gordon shook his head. "The army wanted to. The people, also. . . . But Cincinnatus told them all they could go chase themselves. He returned to his farm, and never left it again."

Johnny scratched his head. "But . . . why did he do that? I don't get it."

Gordon did though. He understood the story completely, now that he thought about it. He had had the reasons explained to him, not so very long ago, and he would never forget.

"Gordon?"

He did not answer. Instead he turned over at a faint sound from outside. Looking through the slats, he saw a party of men approaching up the trail from the river docks. A boat had just come ashore.

Johnny seemed not to have noticed yet. He persisted in his questions, as he had ever since they had recovered from their capture. Like Dena, the youth never seemed willing to lose any opportunity to try to improve his education.

"Rome was a long time before the American Revolution wasn't it, Gordon? Well then, what was this—" He picked up the book again. "—this *Order of Cincinnatus* Holn talks about here?"

Gordon watched the procession approach the jail pen. Two serfs labored with a stretcher, guarded by khaki-clad survivalist soldiers.

"George Washington founded the Order of the Cincinnati after the Revolutionary War," he said absently. "His former officers were the chief members—"

He stopped as their guard stepped over and unlocked the gate. They both watched as the serfs entered and laid their burden on the straw. They and their escorts turned and left without another word.

"He's hurt pretty bad," Johnny said when they hurried over to examine the injured man. "This compress hasn't been changed in days."

Gordon had seen plenty of wounded men in the years since his sophomore class had been drafted into the militia. He had learned a lot of bush diagnosis while serving with Lieutenant Van's platoon. A glance told him that this fellow's bullet wounds might have healed, eventually, with proper treatment. But the smell of death now hung over the still figure. It rose from limbs suppurated with marks of torture.

"I hope he lied to them," Johnny muttered as he labored to make the dying prisoner comfortable. Gordon helped fit their blankets around him. He was puzzled over where the fellow had come from. He did not look like a Willametter. And unlike most Camas and Roseburg men, he had obviously been clean shaven until recently. In spite of his ill treatment, there was too much meat on his bones for him to have been a serf.

Gordon stopped suddenly, rocking back on his haunches. His eyes closed and opened. He stared. "Johnny, look here. Is this what I think it is?"

Johnny peered where he pointed, then pulled back the blankets for a better view. "Well I'll be . . . Gordon, this looks like a *uniform!*"

Gordon nodded. A uniform . . . and clearly one of *postwar* making. It was colored and cut totally unlike anything the Holnists wore, or for that matter, anything either of them had ever seen in Oregon before.

On one shoulder, the dying man wore a patch embroidered with a symbol Gordon recognized from long ago . . . a brown grizzly bear striding upon a red stripe . . . all against a field of gold.

.   .   .

A while later word arrived that Gordon was wanted again. The usual escort came for him by torchlight. "That man in there is dying," he told the head guard.

The taciturn, three-earring Holnist shrugged. "So? Woman's comin' to tend him. Now move. General's waitin'."

On their way up the moonlit path they encountered a figure coming down the other way. The slope-shouldered drudge stepped aside and waited for the men to pass, eyes downcast to the tray of rolled bandages and unguents she held. None of the aloof guards seemed to notice her at all.

At the last moment, however, she looked up at Gordon. He recognized the same small woman with gray-streaked brown hair, the one who had taken and repaired his uniform some days back. He tried to smile at her as they passed, but it only seemed to unnerve her. She ducked her head and scuttled back into the shadows.

Saddened, Gordon continued up the path with his escort. She had reminded him a little of Abby. One of his worries had to do with his friends back in Pine View. The Holnist scouts who discovered his journal had come very close to the friendly little village. It wasn't only the frail civilization in the Willamette that was in terrible danger.

Nobody anywhere was safe anymore, he knew—except, perhaps, George Powhatan, living safe atop Sugarloaf Mountain, tending his bees and beer while the rest of what was left of the world burned.

"I'm getting tired of your stalling, Krantz," General Macklin told him when the guards had left the book-lined former ranger station.

"You put me in a hard position, General. I'm studying the book Colonel Bezoar lent me, trying to understand—"

"Cut the crap, will you?" Macklin approached until his face was two feet from Gordon's. Even looking upward, the Holnist's strangely contorted visage was intimidating. "I know men, Krantz. You're strong all right, and you'd make a good vassal. But you're all mucked up with guilt and other 'civilized' poisons. So much so that I'm beginning to think maybe you'll be useless, after all."

The implication was direct. Gordon forced himself not to show the weakness in his knees.

"You can be the Baron of Corvallis, Krantz. A senior lord in our new empire. You can even hold onto some of your quaint, old-fashioned sentiments, if you want . . . and if you're strong enough to enforce them. You want to be *nice* to your own vassals? You want post offices?

"We might even find a use for that 'Restored United States' of yours." Macklin gave Gordon a toothy, odorous smile. "That's why only Charlie and I know about that little black journal of yours, until we can check the idea out.

"It's not because I *like* you, understand. It's because we'd benefit a little if you cooperated. You might rule those techs in Corvallis better than any of my boys could. We might even decide to keep that Cyclops machine going, if it paid its keep."

So the Holnists hadn't yet pierced the legend of the great computer. Not that it mattered much. They never had really cared about technology, except what was necessary to make war. Science benefitted everyone too much, especially the weak.

Macklin picked up the fireplace poker and slapped it into his left palm. "The alternative, of course, is that we'll take Corvallis anyway, this spring. Only if we have to do it our way, it'll *burn*. And there won't be no post offices anywhere, boy. No smart-ass machines."

With the poker Macklin reached out and touched a sheet of paper on the desk. A pen and ink pot lay next to it. Gordon well knew what the man expected of him.

If all he had to do was agree to the scheme, Gordon would have done so at once. He would have played along until he had a chance to make a break for it.

But Macklin was too canny. He wanted Gordon to write to the Council in Corvallis, convincing them to surrender several key towns as an act of good faith before he would be released.

Of course he had only the General's say-so that he would be made "Baron of Corvallis" after that. He doubted Macklin's word was any better than his own.

"Perhaps you don't think we're strong enough to take your pathetic 'Army of the Willamette' without your help?" Macklin laughed. He turned to the door.

"Shawn!"

Macklin's burly bodyguard was in the room so swiftly and smoothly it seemed almost a blur. He closed the door and marched up to the General, snapping stiffly to attention.

"I'm going to let you in on something, Krantz. Shawn and I, and that mean cat who captured you, are the last of our kind."

Macklin confided. "It was really hush-hush stuff, but you might have heard some of the rumors. The experiments led to some special fighting units, unlike any ever known before."

Gordon blinked. Suddenly it all made sense, the General's uncanny speed, the tracery of scars under his skin and his two aides'.

"Augments!"

Macklin nodded. "Smart boy. You paid attention good, for a college kid weakening his mind with *psychology* and *ethics*."

"But we all thought they were only rumors! You mean they really took soldiers and modified them so—"

He stopped, looking at the strangely knotted muscles along Shawn's bare arms. As impossible as it seemed, the story had to be true. There was no other rational explanation.

"They tried us out for the first time in Kenya. And the government did like the results in combat. But I guess they weren't too happy with what happened after peace broke out and they brought us home."

Gordon stared as Macklin held out the poker to his bodyguard, who took one end—not in his massive fist but between two *fingers* and a *thumb*. Macklin took the other end in a similar grip.

They pulled. Without even breathing hard, Macklin kept talking. "The experiment went on through the late eighties and early nineties. Special Forces, mostly. They chose gung ho types like us. Naturals, in other words."

The steel poker did not rock or shake. Almost totally rigid, it began to stretch.

"Oh we tore up those Cubans good," Macklin chuckled, looking only at Gordon. "But the Army didn't like how some of the vets acted when the action ended and we all went home.

"They were afraid of Nate Holn, you see, even then. He appealed to the strong, and they knew it. The augmentation program was cut off."

The poker turned dull red in the middle. It had stretched to half again its former length when it began to neck and shred like pulled taffy. Gordon glanced quickly at Charles Bezoar, standing beyond the two augments. The Holnist colonel licked his lips nervously, unhappily. Gordon could tell what he was thinking.

Here was strength he could never hope for. The scientists and the hospitals where the work had been done were long gone. According to Bezoar's religion, these men had to be his masters.

The tips of the torn poker separated with a loud report, giving off friction heat that could be felt some distance away. Neither of the enhanced soldiers even rocked.

"That'll be all, Shawn." Macklin threw the pieces into the fireplace as his aide swiveled smartly and marched out of the room. The General looked at Gordon archly.

"Do you doubt any longer we'll be in Corvallis by May? With or without you? Any of the *unaugmented* boys in my army are equal to twenty of your fumblebum farmers—or your zany women soldiers."

Gordon looked up quickly, but Macklin only talked on.

"But even if the sides were more equal, you still wouldn't have a chance! You think we few augments couldn't slip into any of your strong points and level them at will? We could tear your silly defenses to pieces with our bare hands. Don't you hesitate to believe it for even a second."

261

DAVID BRIN

He pushed forward the writing paper and rolled the pen toward Gordon.

Gordon stared at the yellowed sheet. What did it matter? In the midst of all these revelations, he felt he knew where things stood. He met Macklin's eyes.

"I'm impressed. Really. That was a convincing demonstration.

"Tell me though, General, if you're so good, why aren't you in Roseburg right now?"

As Macklin reddened, Gordon gave the Holnist chieftain a faint smile.

"And while we're on the topic, who is it who's chasing you out of your own domain? I should have guessed before why you're pushing this war so hard and fast. Why your people are staging their serfs and worldly possessions to move north, en masse. Most barbarian invasions used to start that way, back in history, like dominoes toppled by other dominoes.

"Tell me, General. Who's kicking your ass so bad you have to get out of the Rogue?"

Macklin's face was a storm. His knotted hands flexed and made white-hard fists. At any moment Gordon expected to pay the ultimate price for his deeply satisfying outburst.

Barely in control, Macklin's eyes never left Gordon. "Get him out of here!" he snapped at Bezoar.

Gordon shrugged and turned away from the seething augment.

"And when you get back I want to look into this, Bezoar! I want to find out who broke security!" Macklin's voice pursued his intelligence chief out onto the steps, where the guards fell in behind them.

Bezoar's hand on Gordon's elbow shook all the way back to the jail pen.

"Who put this man here!" The Holnist Colonel shouted as he saw the dying prisoner on the straw tick between Johnny and the wide-eyed woman.

262

One guard blinked. "Isterman, I think. He just got in from the Salmon River front—"

. . . *the Salmon River front* . . . Gordon recognized the name of a stream in northern California. "Shut up!" Bezoar nearly screamed. But Gordon had his confirmation. There was more to this war than they had known before this evening.

"Get him out of here! Then go bring Isterman to the big house at once!"

The guards moved quickly. "Hey, take it easy with him!" Johnny cried as they grabbed up the unconscious man like a potato sack. Bezoar favored him with a withering glare. The Holnist colonel took out his anger by kicking at the drudge woman, but her instincts were well-honed. She was out the door before he connected.

"I'll see you tomorrow," Bezoar told Gordon. "I think you'd better reconsider writing that letter to Corvallis in the meantime. What you did tonight wasn't wise."

Gordon looked casually through the man, as if he barely merited notice. "What passes between the General and myself is of no concern to you," he told Bezoar. "Only peers have the right to exchange threats, or challenges."

The quote from Nathan Holn seemed to rock Bezoar back as if he had been struck. He stared as Gordon sat down on the straw and put his arms behind his head, ignoring the former lawyer altogether.

Only after Bezoar had departed, when the gloomy shed had quieted again, did Gordon get up and hurry over to Johnny.

"Did the bear-flag soldier ever speak?"

Johnny shook his head. "He never regained consciousness, Gordon."

"What about the woman? Did *she* say anything?"

Johnny looked left and right. The other prisoners were in their corners, facing the wall as they had for weeks.

"Not a word. But she did slip me this."

Gordon took the tattered envelope. He recognized the papers as soon as he pulled them out.

263

It was Dena's letter—the one he had received from George Powhatan's hand, back on Sugarloaf Mountain. It must have been in his pants pocket when the woman took his clothes away to be cleaned. She must have kept it.

No wonder Macklin and Bezoar never mentioned it!

Gordon was determined the General would never get his hands on the letter. However crazy Dena and her friends were, they deserved their chance. He began tearing it up, prior to eating the pieces, but Johnny reached out and stopped him. "No, Gordon! She wrote something on the last page."

"Who? Who wrote..." Gordon shifted the paper in the faint moonlight that slipped between the slats. At last he saw scrawled pencil scratchings, rude block letters that contrasted starkly under Dena's flowing script.

> is true?
> are woman so free north?
> are some man both good and strong?
> will she die for you?

Gordon sat for a long time looking at the sad, simple words. Everywhere his ghosts followed him, in spite of his newfound resignation. What George Powhatan had said about Dena's motives still gnawed within him.

The Big Things would not let go.

He ate the letter slowly. He would not let Johnny share this particular meal, but made a penance, a sacrament, of every piece.

About an hour later there was a commotion outside—a ceremony of sorts. Out across the clearing, at the old Agness General Store, a double column of Holnist soldiers marched to the slow beat of muffled drums. In their midst walked a tall, blond man. Gordon recognized him as one of the camouflaged fighters who had dumped the dying prisoner into their midst earlier that day.

"Must be Isterman," Johnny commented, fascinated.

"This'll teach him not to come back without reporting in to G-2 first thing."

Gordon noted that Johnny must have watched too many old World War Two movies, back at the video library in Corvallis.

At the end of the line of escorts he recognized Roger Septien. Even in the dark he could tell that the former mountain robber was trembling, barely able to hold on to his rifle.

Charles Bezoar's barrister voice sounded nervous, too, as he read the charges. Isterman stood with his back to a large tree, his face impassive. His trophy string lay across his chest like a bandolier . . . like a sash of grisly merit badges.

Bezoar stood aside and General Macklin stepped up to speak to the condemned man. Macklin shook hands with Isterman, kissed him on both cheeks, then moved over beside his aide to watch the conclusion. A two-earringed sergeant snapped sharp orders. The executioners knelt, raised their rifles, and fired as one.

Except for Roger Septien. Who fainted dead away.

The tall blond Holnist officer now lay crumpled in a pool of blood at the foot of the tree. Gordon thought of the dying prisoner who had shared their captivity for so short a time, and who had told them so much without ever opening his eyes.

"Sleep well, Californian," he whispered. "You've taken one more of them with you.

"The rest of us should only do so well."

14

That night Gordon dreamed he was watching Benjamin Franklin play chess with a boxy iron stove.

"The problem is one of balance," the graying statesman-scientist said to his invention, ignoring Gordon as he contemplated the chessboard. "I've put some thought to it. How can we set up a system which encourages individuals to strive and excel, and yet which shows some compassion to the weak, and weeds out madmen and tyrants?"

Flames licked behind the stove's glowing grille, like dancing rows of lights. In words more seen than heard, it inquired:

"... *Who will take responsibility* ... ?"

Franklin moved a white knight. "Good question," he said as he leaned back. "A very good question.

"Of course we can establish constitutional checks and balances, but those won't mean a thing unless citizens make sure the safeguards are taken seriously. The greedy and the power-hungry will always look for ways to break the rules, or twist them to their advantage."

The flames flicked out, and somehow in the process a red pawn had moved.

"... *Who* ... ?"

Franklin took out a handkerchief and wiped his brow. "Would-be tyrants, that's who ... they have an age-old panoply of methods—manipulating the common man, lying to him, or crushing his belief in himself.

"It's said that 'power corrupts,' but actually it's more true that power *attracts the corruptible*. The sane are usually attracted by other things than power. When they do act, they think of it as *service*, which has limits. The tyrant, though, seeks *mastery*, for which he is insatiable, implacable."

". . . *foolish children* . . ." the flames flickered.

"Yes," Franklin nodded, wiping his bifocals. "Still, I believe that certain innovations might help. The right *myths*, for instance.

"And then, if Good is willing to make sacrifices . . ." He reached out, picking up his queen, hesitated for a moment, and then moved the delicate ivory piece all the way across the board, almost under the glowing hot grille.

Gordon wanted to cry out a warning. The queen's position was completely exposed. Not even a pawn was nearby to protect her.

His worst fears were borne out almost at once. The flames licked forth. In a blur, a red king stood on a pile of ashes where the slender white figure had been only a moment before.

"Oh lord, no," Gordon moaned. Even in the half-critical dream state, he knew what was happening, and what it symbolized.

". . . *Who will take responsibility* . . . ?" the stove asked again.

Franklin did not answer. Instead, he shifted and pushed back in his chair. It squeaked as he turned around. Over the rims of his bifocals, he looked directly at Gordon.

You too? Gordon quailed. *What do you all want from me!*

The rippling red. And Franklin smiled.

He startled awake, staring until he saw Johnny Stevens crouching over him, about to touch his shoulder.

"Gordon, I think you'd better take a look. Something's the matter with the guards."

He sat up, rubbing his eyes. "Show me."

Johnny led him over to the east wall of the shed, near the door. It took a moment to adjust to the moonlight. Then Gordon made out the two survivalist soldiers who had been assigned to watch them.

One lay back against a log bench, his mouth hanging open as he stared blank-eyed up at the low, growling clouds.

The other Holnist still gurgled. He clawed at the ground, trying to crawl toward his rifle. In one hand he held his burnished sheath knife, glinting in the low firelight. By his knees lay a toppled ale stein, a brown stain spreading from its broken lip.

Seconds after they had begun to watch, the last guard's head slumped. His struggles died away in a faint rattle.

Johnny and Gordon looked at each other. As one, they rushed to test the door, but the lock was firmly in place. Johnny stretched his arm through a gap in the planks, trying to grab any part of the guard's uniform. The keys . . . "Damn! He's just too far!"

Gordon began prying at the boards. The shack certainly was flimsy enough to take apart by hand. But when he pulled, the rusty nails creaked and sent the hair rising up the back of his neck.

"What do we do?" Johnny asked. "If we yank hard, all at once, we might be able to crash out real fast, and dash down the trail to the canoes. . . ."

"Shhh!" Gordon motioned for silence. Out there in the darkness he had seen a figure move.

Tentatively, nervously, a small, shabby shape scuttled toward the moonlit clearing just outside the shack, where the fallen guards lay.

"It's her!" Johnny whispered. Gordon also recognized the dark-haired drudge, the one who had written the pathetic little addendum to Dena's letter. He watched as she overcame her terror and conditioning to approach each of the guards in turn, checking for breath and life.

Her whole body shook and low moans escaped her as she sought the ring of keys under the second man's belt. To get at them she had to push her fingers through his line of gruesome trophies, but she closed her eyes and brought them forth, clinking softly.

Each second was an agony as she fumbled with the lock. Their releaser ducked back out of the way as the two men pushed outside and ran to each of the guards, stripping them of knives, ammo belts, rifles. They dragged the bodies back into the shed and closed and locked the door.

"What is your name?" Gordon asked the crouched woman, squatting before her. Her eyes were closed as she answered. "H-Heather."

"Heather. Why did you help us?"

Her eyes opened. They were a startling green. "Your . . . your woman wrote . . ."

She made a visible effort to gather herself. "I never kenned what th' old women said about th' old days. . . . But then some of th' new prisoners talked about things up north . . . and there you was . . . Y-you won't beat me too hard for readin' yer letter, will you?"

She cringed as Gordon put his hand out to touch the side of her face, so he withdrew it. Tenderness was too alien to her. All sorts of reassurances came to mind, but he kept to the simplest—one she would understand. "I won't beat you at all," he told her. "Not ever."

Johnny appeared beside him. "Only one guard down by the canoes, Gordon. I think I see a way we can get up within range. He may be a Rogue, but he won't be expecting anything. We can take him."

Gordon nodded. "We'll have to bring her with us," he said.

Johnny looked torn between compassion and practicality. He clearly considered his first duty to get Gordon away from this place. "But . . ."

"They'll know who poisoned the guards. She's crucified if she stays."

Johnny blinked, then nodded, apparently glad to have the dilemma resolved so straightforwardly. "Okay. Let's go, though!"

They started to rise, but Heather took Gordon's sleeve.

"I have a friend," she said, and turned to wave into the darkness.

From the shadow of the trees there stepped a slender figure in pants and shirt several sizes too large, bunched up and cinched tight by a large belt. In spite of that, the second woman's figure was unmistakable. Charles Bezoar's mistress had her blond hair tied back and she carried a small package. If anything, she seemed more nervous than Heather.

After all, Gordon thought, she had more to lose in any escape attempt. It was a sign of her desperation that she was willing to throw herself in with two motley strangers from a nearly mythical north.

"Her name is Marcie," the older woman told him. "We wasn't sure you'd want to take us, so she brought some presents for you."

With trembling hands, Marcie untied a black oilskin. "H-here's your m-mail," she said. The girl held the papers out delicately, as if afraid of defiling them with her touch.

Gordon nearly laughed out loud when he saw the sheaf of almost valueless letters. He stopped short, though, when he saw what else she held: a small, ragged, black-bound volume. Gordon could only blink then, thinking of the risks she must have taken to get it.

"All right," he said, taking the packet and tying it up again. "Follow us, and keep quiet! When I wave like this, stay low and wait for us."

Both women nodded solemnly. Gordon turned, intending to take point, but Johnny had already ducked ahead, leading the way down the trail to the river.

Don't argue this time. He's right, damn it.

Freedom was wonderful beyond relief. But with it came that bitch, Duty.

Hating the fact that he was "important" once again, he crouched and followed Johnny, leading the women toward the canoes.

15

There was no choice of which way to go. Spring's thaw had begun, and the Rogue was already a rushing torrent. The only thing to do was head downstream and pray.

Johnny still exulted over his successful kill. The sentry hadn't turned until he was within two steps, and had gone down nearly silently as Johnny tackled him, ending his struggles with three quick knife thrusts. The young man from Cottage Grove was full of his own prowess as they loaded the women into the boat and set off, letting the current pull them into midstream.

Gordon hadn't the heart to tell his young friend. But he had seen the guard's face before they tumbled him into the river. Poor Roger Septien had looked surprised—*hurt*—hardly the image of a Holnist superman.

Gordon remembered his own first time, nearly two decades ago, firing at looters and arsonists while there still remained a chain of command, before the militia units dissolved into the riots they had been sent to put down. He did not recall being proud, then. He had cried at night, mourning the men he killed.

Still, these were different times, and a dead Holnist was a good thing, no matter how you cut it.

They had left a beach littered with crippled canoes. Every moment of delay had been an agony, but they had to make sure they weren't followed too easily. Anyway, the chore gave the women something to do and they went at it

271

with gusto. Afterward, both Marcie and Heather seemed a bit less cowed and skittish.

The women huddled down in the center of the canoe as Gordon and Johnny hefted paddles and struggled with the unfamiliar craft. The moon kept ducking in and out behind clouds as they dipped and pulled, trying to learn the proper rhythm as they went.

They had not gone far before reaching the first set of riffles. In moments the time for practice was over as they went crashing through foamy rapids, barely skimming past glistening, rocky crags, often seen only at the last moment.

The river was fierce, driven by snow melt. Her roar filled the air, and spray diffracted the intermittent moonlight. It was impossible to fight her, only to cajole, persuade, divert, and guide their frail vessel through hazards barely seen.

At the first calm stretch, Gordon guided them into an eddy. He and Johnny rested over their oars, looked at each other, and at the same moment burst out laughing. Marcie and Heather stared at the two men—giggling breathlessly from adrenaline and the roar of freedom in their blood and ears. Johnny whooped and slapped the water with his paddle.

"Come on, Gordon. That was fun! Let's get on with it."

Gordon caught his breath and wiped river spume out of his eyes. "Okay," he said, shaking his head. "But carefully, okay?"

They stroked together and banked steeply as the current caught them again.

"Oh, shit," Johnny cursed. "I thought the *last* one . . ."

His words were drowned out, but Gordon finished the thought.

And I thought the last one was bad!

Gaps between the rocks were narrow, deadly shoots. Their canoe scraped horribly through the first, then shot out, canting precipitously. "Lean hard!" Gordon shouted. He wasn't laughing now, but fighting to survive.

We should have walked . . . we should have walked . . . we should have walked. . . .

The inevitable happened sooner, though, than even he expected . . . less than three miles downstream. A sunken tree—a hidden snag just beyond the hard rock face of a turn in the canyon wall—a streak of rolling water cloaked in darkness until it was too late for him to do more than curse and dig in his paddle to try to turn.

An aluminum canoe might have survived the collision, but there were none left after years of war. The homemade wood-and-bark model tore with an agonized shriek, harmonized by the women's screams as they all spilled into the icy flood.

The sudden chill was stunning. Gordon gulped air and grabbed at the capsized canoe with one arm. His other hand darted out and seized a grip on Heather's dark hair, barely in time to keep her from being swept away. He struggled to avoid her desperate clutching and to keep her head above water . . . all the while fighting for his own breath in the choppy foam.

At last he felt sand beneath his feet. It took every last effort to fight the river's pull and the sucking mud until he was able at last to haul his gasping burden out and collapse onto the mat of rotting vegetation by the steep shore.

Heather coughed and sobbed next to him. He heard Johnny and Marcie spluttering not far away, and knew that they had made it, too. There wasn't a flicker of energy to spare for celebration, though. He lay breathing hard, unable even to move for what felt like hours.

Johnny spoke at last. "We didn't really have any gear to lose. I guess my ammo's wet, though. Your rifle gone, Gordon?"

"Yeah." He sat up groaning, touching a thin gash where the breaking canoe had stroked his forehead.

There did not seem to have been any serious injuries, though the coughing was now starting to shift over to general shivers. Marcie's borrowed clothes stuck to the blond concubine in ways that Gordon might have found interesting had he not been so miserable.

"W-what do we do now?" she asked.

Gordon shrugged. "For starters we go back in and get rid of the wreck."

They stared at him. He explained. "If they don't find it, they'll probably assume we went a whole lot farther than this, tonight. That could turn out to be our only advantage.

"Then, when that's done, we head overland."

"I've never been to California," Johnny suggested, and Gordon had to smile. Since they had discovered that the Holnists had another enemy, the boy had spoken of little else.

The idea was tempting. South was one direction their pursuers wouldn't expect them to go.

But that would mean crossing the river. And anyway, if Gordon remembered correctly, the Salmon River was a long way south of here. Even if it were practical to sneak through a couple of hundred miles of survivalist baronies, there just wasn't time. With spring here, they were needed back home worse than ever.

"We'll wait up in the hills until pursuit's gone past," he said. "Then we might as well try for the Coquille."

Johnny, forever cheerful and willing, did not let their dim chances get him down. He shrugged. "Let's go get the canoe then." He jumped into the frigid, waist-deep water. Gordon picked up a sturdy piece of driftwood to use as a gaff, and followed a little more gingerly. The water wasn't any less bitterly cold the second time. His toes were starting to go numb.

Together they had almost reached the belly-up canoe when Johnny cried out and pointed, *"The mail!"*

At the fringe of their eddy, a glistening oilskin packet could be seen drifting outward, toward the swift center of the current.

"No!" Gordon cried. "Let it go!"

But Johnny had already leaped head first into the rushing waters. He swam hard toward the receding package, even as Gordon screamed after him. "Come back here. Johnny, you fool! It's worthless!

"Johnny!"

He watched hopelessly as the bundle and the boy chasing it were swept around the next bend in the river. From just ahead there came the heavy, heartless growl of rapids.

Cursing, Gordon dove into the freezing current and swam with all his might to catch up. His pulse pounded and he inhaled icy water along with every desperate breath. He almost followed Johnny around the bend, but then, at the last moment, he grabbed an overhanging branch and held on tightly . . . just in time.

Through the curtain of foam he saw his young friend tumble after the black package into the worst cascade yet, a horrible jumbling of ebony teeth and spray.

"No," Gordon whispered hoarsely. He watched as Johnny and the packet were swept together over a ledge and disappeared into a sinkhole.

He continued staring, through the hair plastered over his eyes and the blinding, stinging droplets, but minutes passed and nothing emerged from that terrible whirlpool.

At last, with his grip slipping, Gordon had to retreat. He drew himself hand over hand along the shaky branch until he reached the slow, shallow water at the river's bank. Then, mechanically, he forced his feet to carry him upstream, slogging past the wide-eyed women to the ruined bark canoe.

He used a driftwood hook to draw it after him behind a jutting point in the canyon wall, and there he pounded the little boat to pieces, smashing it into unrecognizable flinders.

Sobbing, he kept striking and slashing the water long after the bits had sunk out of sight or drifted away.

16

They passed the day in the brambles and weeds under a tumbledown concrete bunker. Before the Doomwar, it must have been someone's treasured survivalist hideaway, but now it was a ruin—broken, bullet-scarred, and looted.

Once, in prewar days, Gordon had read that there were places in the country riddled with hideouts like this—stockpiled by men whose hobby was thinking about the fall of society, and fantasizing what they would do after it happened. There had been classes, workshops, special-interest magazines . . . an industry catering to "needs" which went far beyond those of the average woodsman or camper.

Some simply liked to daydream, or enjoyed a relatively harmless passion for rifles. Few were ever followers of Nathan Holn, and most were probably horrified when their fantasies at last came true.

When that time finally arrived, most of the loner "survivalists" died in their bunkers, quite alone.

Battle and the rain forest had eroded the few scraps left by waves of scavengers. Cold rain pattered over the concrete blocks as the three fugitives took turns keeping watch and sleeping.

Once they heard shouts and the squish of horses' hooves in the mud. Gordon made an effort to look confident for the women's sake. He had taken care to leave as little trail as possible, but his two charges weren't even as experienced as the Willamette Army scouts. He wasn't at all sure they would be able to fool the best forest trackers who had lived since Cochise.

The riders moved on, and after a while the fugitives were able to relax just a little. Gordon dozed.

This time he did not dream. He was too exhausted to spare any energy for hauntings.

They had to wait for the moonrise before setting out that night. There were several trails, crisscrossing each other frequently, but Gordon somehow kept them going in the right direction, using the semipermanent ice on the north sides of the trees as a guide.

Three hours after sunset, they came upon the ruins of a little village.

"Illahee." Heather identified the place.

"It's been abandoned," he observed. The moonlit ghost town was eerie. From the former Baron's manor to the lowliest hovel, it seemed to have been picked clean.

"All the soldiers an' their serfs were sent up north," Marcie explained. "There's been a lot of villages emptied that way, last few weeks."

Gordon nodded. "They're fighting on three fronts. Macklin wasn't kidding when he said he would be in Corvallis by May. It's take over the Willamette or die."

The countryside looked like a moonscape. There were saplings everywhere, but few tall trees. Gordon realized that this must have been one of the places where the Holnists had tried slash-and-burn agriculture. But this country was not fertile farmland, like the Willamette Valley. The experiment must have been a failure.

Heather and Marcie held hands as they walked, their eyes darting fearfully. Gordon couldn't help comparing them to Dena and her proud, brave Amazons, or to happy, optimistic Abby back in Pine View. The true dark age would not be a happy time for women, he decided. Dena had been right about that much.

"Let's go look around the big house," he said. "There might be some food."

277

That sparked their interest. They ran ahead of him to the abandoned manor with its stockade and abatis surrounding a solid, prewar house.

When he caught up they were huddled over a pair of dark forms just within the gate. Gordon flinched when he saw that they were skinning and flaying two large German shepherd dogs. Their master couldn't take them on a sea voyage, he realized a little sickly. No doubt the Holnist Baron of Illahee grieved more over his treasured animals than over the slaves who would die during the mass exodus to the promised lands up north.

The meat smelled pretty ripe. Gordon decided he would wait a while, in hopes of something better. The women, though, weren't quite so finicky.

So far they had been lucky. At least the search seemed to have swept westward, away from the direction the fugitives were headed. Perhaps General Macklin's men had found Johnny's body by now, falsely confirming the trail toward the sea.

Only time would tell how far their luck would last though.

A narrow, swift stream swept north from near abandoned Illahee. Gordon decided it could be nothing other than the south fork of the Coquille. Of course there were no convenient canoes lying about. The torrent looked unnavigable anyway. They would have to walk.

An old road ran along the east bank, in the direction they wanted to go. There was no choice but to use it, whatever the obvious dangers. Mountains crowded in just ahead, hulking against the moonlit clouds, blocking every other conceivable path.

At least the going would be quicker than on the muddy trails. Or so Gordon hoped. He coaxed the stoic women, keeping them moving at a slow, steady pace. Never once did Marcie or Heather complain or balk, nor were their eyes reproachful. Gordon could not decide whether it was courage or resignation that kept them plodding on, mile after mile.

For that matter, he wasn't sure why *he* persevered. To

what point? To live in the dark world that seemed certain to come? At the rate he was accumulating ghosts, "crossing over" would probably feel like Homecoming Week anyway.

Why? he wondered. *Am I the only Twentieth-Century idealist left alive?*

Perhaps, he pondered. *Perhaps idealism really* was *the disease, the scam, that Charles Bezoar had said it was.*

George Powhatan had been right, too. It did you no good to fight for the Big Things . . . for civilization, for instance. All you accomplished was getting young girls and boys to believe in you—to throw their lives away in worthless gestures, accomplishing nothing.

Bezoar had been right. Powhatan had been right. Even Nathan Holn, monster that he was, had told the essential truth about Ben Franklin and his constitutionalist cronies—how they had hoodwinked a people into believing such things. They had been propagandists to make Himmler and Trotsky blush as amateurs.

. . . We hold these truths to be self evident . . .

Hah!

Then there had been the Order of the Cincinnati, made up of George Washington's officers who—halfway embarked one night upon a mutinous coup—were shamed by their stern commander into giving their tearful, solemn vow . . . to remain farmers and citizens first, and soldiers only at their country's need and call.

Whose idea had it been, that unprecedented oath? The promise was kept for a generation, long enough for the ideal to set. In essence, it lasted into the era of professional armies and technological war.

Until the end of the Twentieth Century, that is, when certain powers decided that soldiers should be made into something more than mere men. The thought of Macklin and his augmented veterans, loosed on the unsuspecting Willametters, made Gordon heartsick. But there wasn't anything he or anyone else could do to prevent it.

Not a whit can be done about it, he thought wryly. *But that won't keep the damn ghosts from pestering me.*

The South Coquille grew more swollen with every mile

they slogged, as streamlets joined in from the enclosing hills. A gloomy drizzle began to fall, and thunder rumbled in counterpoint to the roaring torrent to their left. As they rounded a bend in the road, the northern sky brightened with distant flashes of lightning.

Looking up at the glowering clouds, Gordon almost stumbled into Marcie's back as she came to a sudden halt. He put out his hand to give her a gentle push, as he had been forced to do more and more often the last few miles. But this time her feet were planted.

She turned to face him, and in her eyes there was a bleakness that went beyond anything Gordon had seen in seventeen years of war. Chilled with a dark foreboding, he pushed past her and looked down the road.

Thirty yards or so ahead lay the ruins of an old roadside trading post. A faded sign advertised myrtlewood carvings for sale at fabulous prices. Two rusted automobile hulks lay half settled into the mud in front.

Four horses and a two-wheeled cart were tethered to the slump-sided shack. From under the canted porch roof, General Macklin stood with his arms folded, and smiled at Gordon.

"Run!" Gordon yelled at the women and he dove through the roadside thicket, rolling up behind a moss-covered trunk with Johnny's rifle in his hands. As he moved, he knew he was being a fool. Macklin still might have some faint wish to keep him alive, but in a firefight he was already dead.

He knew he had leaped on instinct—to get away from the women, to draw attention after himself and give them a chance to get away. *Stupid idealist,* he cursed. Marcie and Heather simply stood there on the road, too tired or too resigned even to move.

"Now that ain't so smart," Macklin said, his voice at its most amiable and dangerous. "Do you think you can manage to shoot me, *Mr. Inspector?*"

The thought had occurred to Gordon. It depended, of course, on the augment letting him get close enough to try.

And on whether the twenty-year-old ammo still worked after its dunking in the Rogue:

Macklin still had not moved. Gordon raised his head and saw through the leaves that Charles Bezoar stood beside the General. Both of them looked like easy targets out there in the open. But as he slid the rifle's bolt and began to crawl forward, Gordon realized, sickly, *there were four horses.*

There came a sudden crashing sound from just overhead. Before he could even react, a crushing weight slammed onto his back, driving his sternum onto the rifle stock.

Gordon's mouth gaped, but no air would come! He could barely twitch a muscle as he felt himself lifted into the air by his collar. The rifle slipped from nearly senseless fingers.

"Did this guy really waste two of ours last year?" a gravelly voice behind his left ear shouted in cheerful derision. "Seems a bit of a *woos* to me."

It felt like an eternity, but at last something reopened inside him and Gordon was able to breathe again. He sucked noisily, caring more about air at the moment than dignity.

"Don't forget those three soldiers back at Agness," Macklin called back to his man. "He gets credit for them, too. That makes five Holnist ears on his belt, Shawn. Our Mr. Krantz deserves respect.

"Now bring him in, please. I'm sure he and the ladies would like a chance to get warm."

Gordon's feet barely touched the ground as his captor half carried him by his collar through the thicket and across the road. The augment wasn't even breathing hard when he dumped Gordon unceremoniously on the porch.

Under the leaky canopy, Charles Bezoar stared hard at Marcie; the Holnist Colonel's eyes burned with shame and promised retribution. But Marcie and Heather watched only Gordon, silently.

Macklin squatted beside Gordon. "I always did admire

a man with a knack for the ladies. I've got to admit, you do seem to have a way with 'em, Krantz." He grinned. Then he nodded to his beefy aide. "Bring him inside, Shawn. The women have work to do, and the Inspector and I have some unfinished business to discuss."

17

"I know all about your women now, you know."

Gordon's view of the moldy, broken-down trading post kept rotating. It was hard to focus on anything in particular, let alone the man talking to him.

He hung by a rope tied around his ankles, his hands dropping to a couple of feet above the muddy wooden floor. General Macklin sat next to the fire, whittling. He looked at Gordon each time his captive's steady tortional swing brought them face to face. Most of the time, he smiled.

The constriction on his ankles, the pain in his forehead and sternum, were nothing to the heavy weight of blood rushing to his brain. Through the rear door Gordon could hear low whimpering—a pathetic enough sound in itself, but definitely a relief after the screams of the last half hour or so. At last, Macklin had ordered Bezoar to stop and let the women do some work. There was a prisoner in the next room he wanted tended, and he didn't want Marcie and Heather beaten senseless while they still had their uses.

Macklin also wanted to be able to draw out his session with Gordon in peace and quiet. "A few of those crazy Willametter spies of yours lived long enough to be questioned," the Holnist commander told him mildly. "The one in the next room here hasn't been too cooperative yet, but we have reports from our invasion force as well, so the picture's pretty clear. I have to give you credit, Krantz. It was a pretty imaginative plan. Too bad it didn't work."

"I haven't any idea what in hell you're talking about, Macklin." The thickness in Gordon's tongue made it hard to speak.

"Ah, but I see from your face that you *do* understand," his captor said. "There's no need to maintain secrecy anymore. You needn't concern yourself any longer for your brave girl soldiers. Because of their sneaky mode of attack, we did suffer some losses. But I'll wager far fewer than you'd hoped for. By now, of course, all your 'Willamette Scouts' are dead, or in chains. I compliment you on a worthy attempt, however."

Gordon's heart pounded. "You bastard. Don't give *me* the credit. It was their own idea! I don't even know what they planned to do!"

For only the second time Gordon saw surprise cross Macklin's face. "Well, well," the barbarian chieftain said at last. "Imagine that. *Feminists,* still around in this day and age. My dear Inspector, it seems we come to the rescue of the poor people of the Willamette just in the nick of time!" His smile returned.

The smugness on that face was too much to bear. Gordon reached for anything at all to try to wipe it off. "You'll never win, Macklin. Even if you burn Corvallis, if you crush every village and smash Cyclops to bits, people will never stop fighting you!"

The smile remained, unperturbed. The General tsked and shook his head. "Do you think us inexperienced? My dear fellow, how did the Normans domesticate the proud, numerous Saxons? What secret did the Romans use to tame the Gauls?

"You are indeed a romantic, sir, to underestimate the power of terror.

"Anyway," Macklin went on as he sat back and resumed his whittling, "you forget that we will not remain outsiders for long. We'll recruit among your own people. Countless young men will see the advantage in being lords, rather than serfs. And unlike the nobility of the Middle Ages, we new feudalists believe that all males should have a right to fight for their first earring.

"*That* is the *true* democracy, my friend. The one America was heading toward before the Constitutionalist Betrayal. My own sons must kill to become Holnists, or they will scratch dirt to support those who can.

"We will have recruits. More than plenty, believe it. With the astonishing population you have up north, we can have—within a decade—an army the like of which has not been seen since 'Franklinstein' Civilization crumbled under its own hypocrisy."

"What makes you think your other enemies will give you that decade?" Gordon gritted. "Do you think the Californians will let you sit on your conquests long enough to lick your wounds and build that army of yours?"

Macklin shrugged. "You speak out of very little knowledge, my dear fellow. Once we've pulled back, the loose confederation in the south will break apart and forget us. And even if they *could* put aside their own perpetual petty squabbles and unite, those 'Californians' you speak of would take a generation to reach us in our new realm. By then we'll be more than ready to counterstrike.

"For another thing—and this is the delightful part—even if they pursued us, they would have to go through your friend on Sugarloaf Mountain to get at us!"

Macklin laughed at the expression on Gordon's face. "You thought I didn't know about your mission? Oh, Mr. Krantz, why do you imagine I arranged to have your party ambushed, and to have you brought to me? I know all about the Squire's refusal to help anyone outside the line from Roseburg to the sea.

"Isn't it wonderful, though? The 'Wall of the Callahan Mountains'—the famed George Powhatan—will keep to his valley, and in so doing, he will defend our flank while we consolidate up north . . . until at last we are ready to begin the Great Campaign."

The general smiled pensively.

"I've often regretted that I never got my hands on Powhatan. Whenever our sides clashed he was always too slippery, always somewhere else doing mischief. But this way is even better, I believe! Let him have ten more years on his farm, while I conquer the rest of Oregon. *Then* it'll be his turn.

"Even from your point of view, Mr. Inspector, I am sure you'll agree that he deserves what's coming to him then."

There was no way to answer that except by silence. Macklin tapped Gordon with his stick, just hard enough to set him rotating again. As a result, Gordon found it hard to focus when the front door opened and a pair of heavy moccasins padded into view.

"Bill an' I checked up along th' mountainside," he heard the huge augment, Shawn, tell his commander. "Found th' same tracks as we saw before, up by th' river. I'm sure it's th' same black bastard as slitted those sentries."

Black bastard . . .

Gordon breathed a word silently. *Phil?*

Macklin laughed. "There now. You see, Shawn? Nathan Holn wasn't a racist and neither should you be. I've always regretted that the racial minorities were at such a disadvantage in the riots and postwar chaos. Even the strong among them had little fair chance to excel.

"Now consider that Negro soldier out there. He has cut the throats of three of our river guards. He's *strong*, and would have made an excellent recruit."

Even upside down and spinning, Gordon could make out Shawn's sour expression. The augment did not dispute his commander aloud, however.

"Pity we have no time to play games with the fellow," Macklin continued. "Go and kill him now, Shawn."

There was a swirl of disturbed air, and the burly veteran was out the door again, without a word and almost without sound.

"I really would have preferred to give your scout a warning, first," Macklin confided in Gordon. "It'd have been more sporting if your man out there knew that he was up against something—unusual." Macklin laughed again. "Alas, in these times it's not always sensible to play fair."

Gordon thought that he had felt hate before this moment. But his cold anger right now was unlike anything he remembered. "Philip! *Run!*" He cried out as loud as he could, praying the sound of his voice would carry over the patter of raindrops. "Watch out, they're—"

Macklin's stick lashed out, striking Gordon's cheek and sending his head rocking back. The world blurred and nearly faded into blackness. It took a long time for his eyes to clear, blinking away tears. He tasted blood.

"Yes," Macklin nodded. "You are a man. I'll give you that. When the time comes, I'll try to see to it you die like one."

"Don't do me any favors," Gordon choked. Macklin merely grinned and went back to his whittling.

A few minutes later the door at the back of the ruined store opened. "Go back and see to your women!" Macklin snapped. Charles Bezoar quickly closed the door to the windowless storage room—where Marcie and Heather presumably still tended the other prisoner Gordon had not yet seen.

"Just goes to show you, not every strong man is likable," Macklin commented sourly. "He's useful, though. For now."

Gordon had no idea whether it was hours or a few minutes later when a trill call carried through the boarded windows. He thought it was only the cry of a river bird but Macklin reacted swiftly, blowing out the small oil lantern and throwing dust onto the fire.

"This is too good to miss," he told Gordon. "The guys appear to have a good chase going. I hope you'll excuse me for a few minutes?"

He grabbed Gordon's hair. "Of course if you so much as make a sound while I'm gone, I'll kill you the instant I get back. That's a promise."

Gordon could not shrug in his position. "Go join Nathan Holn in Hell," he said.

Macklin smiled. "Undoubtedly, someday." Then the augment was out the door, running through the darkness and rain.

Gordon hung while his pendulumlike swinging slowly abated. Then he took a deep breath and got to work.

Three times he tried to pull himself up to within reach of the rope around his ankles. Each time he fell back, grunting from the tearing agony of sudden, jerking gravity. The third time was almost too much to bear. His ears rang and he thought he almost heard voices.

Through tear-filled eyes he seemed to half see an audience to his struggle. All the ghosts he had accumulated over the years appeared to line the walls. It occurred to him that they were making book on his plight.

... *take* ... *-it* ... Cyclops said for all of them, speaking in a code of rippling highlights in the fireplace coals.

"Go away," Gordon muttered angrily, resenting his imagination. There was neither time nor energy to waste on such games. He hissed hard as he got ready for one more try, then heaved upward with all his might.

He barely caught the rope this time, slippery with dripping rain, and held on tightly with both hands. His whole body quaked from the strain, bent double like a folded pocket knife, but he knew he dare not let go. There just wasn't anything left for another try.

With both hands fully occupied he couldn't venture to untie himself. There was nothing to cut the rope with. *Up,* he concentrated. *It'll be better if you stand.*

Slowly, he pulled himself up the rope, hand over hand. His muscles trembled, threatening cramps, and there was intense pain in his chest and back, but at last he "stood," his ankles twisted in loops of cutting rope, holding on tight as he swung like a chandelier.

Over by the wall, Johnny Stevens cheered unabashedly. Tracy Smith and the other Army Scouts smiled. *Pretty good, for a male,* they seemed to say.

Cyclops sat in his cloud of supercooled mist, playing checkers with the smoking Franklin stove. They, too, seemed to approve.

Gordon tried lowering himself to get at the knots, but it put so much pressure on the loops around his ankles that he nearly fainted from the pain. He had to straighten out again.

Not that way. Ben Franklin shook his head. The Great Manipulator looked at him over the tops of his bifocals.

"Over the tops of his . . . over the t—" Gordon looked up at the stout beam from which the rope had been hung.

Up and over the top, then.

He raised his arms and wound the rope around them. *You did this back in gymnastics class, before the war,* he told himself as he began to pull.

Yeah. But now you're an old man.

Tears flowed as he started hauling himself upward, hand over hand, helping where he could with his knees. In the blur between his eyelids, his ghosts seemed more real the more he struggled. They had graduated from imagination to first-class hallucinations.

"Go, Gordon!" Tracy called up to him.

Lieutenant Van gave him thumbs up. Johnny Stevens grinned encouragement alongside the woman who had saved his life back in the ruins of Eugene.

A skeletal shade in a paisley shirt and leather jacket grinned and gave him a fleshless thumbs up. Atop the bare skull lay a blue, peaked cap, its brass badge glimmering.

Even Cyclops ceased its nagging as Gordon gave the endless climb everything he had.

Up . . . he moaned, grabbing slick hemp and fighting the crushing hug of gravity. *Up, you worthless intellectual. . . . Move or die. . . .*

One arm floundered over the top of the rough wooden beam. He held on and brought up the other to join it.

And that was all. There was no more to give. He hung by his armpits, unable to move any farther. Through the blur of his eyelashes, his phantoms all looked up at him, clearly disappointed.

"Oh, go chase yourselves," he told them inwardly, unable even to speak aloud.

. . . Who will take responsibility . . . the coals in the fireplace glittered.

"You're dead, Cyclops. You're *all* dead! Leave me alone!" Utterly exhausted, Gordon closed his eyes to escape them.

Only there, in the blackness, he encountered the one ghost that remained. The one he had used the most shamelessly, and which had used him.

It was a nation. A world.

Faces, fading in and out with the entopic speckles behind his eyelids . . . millions of faces, betrayed and ruined but striving still . . .

—for a Restored United States.

—for a *Restored World.*

—for a fantasy . . . but one which refused obstinately to die—that *could not* die—not while he lived.

Gordon wondered, amazed. Was this why he'd lied for so long, why he had told such fairy tales? . . . because *he* needed them? Because he couldn't let go of them? He answered himself.

Without them, I would have curled up and died.

Funny, he had never seen it quite that way before, in such startling clarity. In the darkness within himself the dream glowed—even if it existed nowhere else in the Universe—flickering like a diatom, like a bright mote hovering in a murky sea.

Amidst the otherwise total blackness, it was as if he stood in front of it. He seemed to take it in his hand, astonished by the light. The jewel grew. And in its facets he saw more than people, more than generations.

A *future* took shape around him, enveloping him, penetrating his heart.

When Gordon next opened his eyes, he was lying atop the beam, unable to recall how he had gotten there. Unbelievingly, he sat up blinking. A spectral light seemed to stream away from him in all directions, passing through the broken walls of the ruined building as if *they* were the dream stuff, and the brilliant rays the true reality. The radiance spread on and on, beyond limit. For a short time he felt as if he could see forever in that glow.

Then, as mysteriously as it had come, it passed. Energy appeared to flow back into whatever mysterious well he had tapped. In its wake, physical sensation returned, the reality of exhaustion and pain.

Trembling, Gordon fumbled with the knotted tourniquets around his ankles. His torn, bare feet were slippery with blood. When he finally got the ropes loosed, returning circulation felt like a million angry insects running riot inside his skin.

His ghosts were gone, at least; the cheering section seemed to have been taken up by that strange luminance, whatever it had been. Gordon wondered if they would ever return.

As the last loop fell away, he heard shots in the distance, the first since Macklin had left him alone here. Perhaps, he hoped, that meant Phil Bokuto wasn't dead quite yet. Silently, he wished his friend luck.

He crouched down on the beam as footsteps approached the storeroom door. It opened slowly and Charles Bezoar stared at the empty room, at the limp, hanging rope. Panic filled the ex-lawyer's eyes as he drew his automatic and stepped out.

Gordon would have preferred to wait until the man came directly underneath, but Bezoar was no idiot. An expression of dark suspicion came over his face, and he started to look up. . . .

Gordon leaped. The .45 swung up and fired at the same instant as they collided.

In the hormonal rush of combat Gordon had no idea where the bullet went, or whose bone had cracked so loud on impact. He grappled for the gun as they rolled together across the floor.

". . . kill you!" the Holnist growled, the .45 tipping toward Gordon's face. Gordon had to duck to one side as it roared again, stinging his neck with burning powder. "Hold still!" Bezoar growled, as if he were in the habit of being obeyed. "Just let me . . ."

Straining against his enemy with all his might, Gordon suddenly let go of the gun with one hand and struck out. As the automatic came down toward him his right fist smashed upward into the root of Bezoar's jaw. The bald Holnist's body convulsed as his head struck the floor hard. The .45 fired twice into the wall.

Then Bezoar was still.

This time the worst pain was in Gordon's hand. He stood up slowly, gingerly, semiconsciously accounting for what had to be a cracked rib, in addition to his many other bodily insults.

"Never talk while you fight," he told the unconscious man. "It's a bad habit."

Marcie and Heather spilled out of the storage room and drew Bezoar's knives. When he saw what they were after, he almost told them to stop, to tie the man up, instead.

He didn't, though. Instead he let them do what they would and turned to step through the back door into the storage room.

It was even darker inside, but as his eyes adapted, he made out a slender figure lying on a dirty blanket over in the corner. A hand reached up toward him and a thin voice called out.

"Gordon, I knew you'd come for me.... Is that silly? ... It sounds ... sounds like fairy tale talk, but ... but somehow I just knew it."

He sank to his knees beside the dying woman. There had been crude attempts to clean and bandage her wounds, but her matted hair and blood-streaked clothes covered more damage than he dared even look at.

"Oh Dena." He turned his head and closed his eyes. Her hand took his.

"We stung them, darling," she said in a reed-thin voice. "Me and the other Scouts. . . . In some places we really caught some of the bastards with their pants down! It—" Dena had to stop as a fit of coughing made her nearly double up, bringing forth a trickle of ocher fluid. The corners of her mouth were stained.

"Don't talk," Gordon told her. "We'll find a way to get you out of here."

Dena clutched Gordon's tattered shirt.

"They found out about our plan, somehow . . . in more'n half the places they were warned before we could strike. . . .

"Maybe one of the girls fell in love with her rapist, like the legends say h-happened to H-Hypermnestra. . . ." Dena shook her head unbelievingly. "Tracy and I were worried about that possibility, 'cause Aunt Susan said it used to happen sometimes, in the old days. . . ."

Gordon had no idea what Dena was talking about. She was babbling. Inside he struggled to come up with some idea, *any* way to carry a desperately wounded and delirious woman away through miles and miles of enemy lines before Macklin and the other Holnists returned.

In agony, he knew it just couldn't be done.

"I guess we botched it, Gordon . . . but we did try! We tried. . . ." Dena shook her head, tears welling as Gordon took her into his arms.

"Yes, I know, darling. I know you tried."

His own eyes blurred. Beneath the filth and ruin, he knew her scent. And realized—much too late—what it meant to him. He held her tighter than he knew he ought to, not wanting to let her go.

"It'll be all right. I love you. I'm here and I'll take care of you."

Dena sighed. "You are here. You are . . ." She held onto his arm. "You . . ."

Her body suddenly arched and she shivered. "Oh, Gordon!" she cried. "I see . . . Can you . . . ?"

Her eyes met his for a moment. In them was a light he recognized.

Then it was over.

"Yes, I saw it," he told her gently, still holding her body in his arms. "Not as clearly as you, perhaps. But I saw it, too."

18

In the corner of the outer room, Heather and Marcie were busy with their backs turned as they worked on something Gordon did not want to look at.

Later, he would mourn. Right now though, there were things he had to do, like getting these women out of here. The chances were slim, but if he could see them to the Callahans, they would be safe.

That would be hard enough, but from there he had other obligations. He would get back to Corvallis, somehow, if it was humanly possible, and he would try to live up to Dena's ridiculous, beautiful image of what a hero was supposed to do—die defending Cyclops, perhaps, or lead a last charge of "postmen" against the invincible enemy.

He wondered if Bezoar's shoes would fit him, or if, with badly swollen ankles, he might not be better off barefoot. "Stop wasting time," he snapped at the women. "We have to get out of here."

But as Gordon bent to pick up Bezoar's automatic from the floor, a low, gravelly voice spoke. "Very good advice, my young friend. And you know, I'd like to call a man like you *friend*.

"Of course, that doesn't mean I won't split you open if you try to pick up that weapon."

Gordon left the gun lying where it was and stood up heavily. General Macklin occupied the open doorway, holding a dagger in throwing position.

"Kick it away," he said calmly.

Gordon obeyed. The automatic went spinning into a dusty corner.

"That's better." Macklin resheathed his knife. He jerked his head at the women. "Get away," he told them. "Run. Try to live, if you want to and are able."

Wide-eyed, Marcie and Heather edged past Macklin. They fled out into the night. Gordon had no doubt they would run in the rain until they dropped.

"I don't suppose the same applies to me?" he asked wearily.

Macklin smiled and shook his head. "I want you to come with me. I need your assistance out here."

A hooded lantern illuminated part of the clearing across the road, aided from time to time by distant lightning and an occasional moonlit glint at the edge of the rainclouds. The pelting drisk had Gordon soaked within minutes of limping outside after Macklin. His still-bleeding ankles left spreading pink fog in the puddles where he stepped.

"Your black man is better than I'd thought," Macklin said, pulling Gordon to one side of the circular, lamp-lit area. "Either that or he had help, and the latter's pretty unlikely. My boys patrolling the river would have seen more tracks than his, if he'd been accompanied.

"Either way though, Shawn and Bill deserve what they got for being careless."

For the first time Gordon had an inkling of what was happening. "You mean—"

"Don't gloat yet," Macklin snapped. "My troops are less than a mile from here, and there's a Very pistol in my saddlebags. But you don't see me hollering for help, do you?"

He smiled again. "Now I'm going to show you what this war is all about. Both you and your scout are the sort of strong men who should have been Holnists. You're not because of the propaganda of weakness you grew up in. I'm

295

going to take this opportunity to show you just how weak it makes you."

With a vicelike grip on Gordon's arm, Macklin shouted into the night.

"Black man! This is General Volsci Macklin. I have your commander here . . . your United States Postal Inspector!" he sneered.

"Care to earn his freedom? My men will be here by dawn, so you have very little time. Come on in! We'll fight for him! Your choice of weapons!"

"Don't do it, Philip! He's an aug—"

Gordon's warning collapsed into a groan as Macklin yanked his arm, nearly tearing his shoulder out of its socket. The force threw him crashing to his knees. His throbbing ribs sent shock waves rolling through his body.

"Tsk tsk. Come now. If your man hadn't already known about Shawn, it means he got my bodyguard with a lucky shot. If so, he certainly doesn't deserve any special consideration now, does he?"

It took a powerful effort of will, but Gordon lifted his head, hissing through gritted teeth. Overcoming wave after wave of nausea, he somehow managed to wobble up to his feet. Although the world wavered all around him, he refused to be seen on his knees next to Macklin.

Macklin awarded him a low grunt, as if to say he only expected this from a real man. The augment's body was aquiver like a cat's—twitching in anticipation. They waited together, just outside the circle of lamplight. Minutes passed with the rain coming and going in intermittent, blustery sheets.

"Last chance, black man!" In a blur, Macklin's knife was at Gordon's throat. A grip like an anaconda's twisted his left arm up behind his back. "Your Inspector dies in thirty seconds, unless you show! Starting now!"

The half minute passed slower than any Gordon had ever known. Oddly enough, he felt detached, almost resigned.

At last Macklin shook his head, sounding disappointed.

"Well, too bad, Krantz." The knife moved under his left ear. "I guess he's smarter than I—"

Gordon gasped. He had heard nothing, but suddenly he realized that there was *another* pair of moccasins down there at the edge of the light, not fifteen feet away.

"I am afraid your men killed that brave soldier you were shouting for." The soft voice of the newcomer spoke even as Macklin spun around, putting Gordon between them.

"Philip Bokuto was a good man," the mysterious voice went on. "I have come in his stead, to answer your challenge as he would have."

A beaded headband glittered in the lamplight as a broad-shouldered man stepped forward into the circle. His gray hair was tied back into a ponytail. The craggy features of his face expressed a sad serenity.

Gordon could almost feel Macklin's joy, transmitted through that powerful grip. "Well, well. From the descriptions I've heard, this could only be the *Squire* of *Sugarloaf Lodge*, come down alone out of his mountain and valley at last! I'm gratified more than you might know, sir. You're welcome, indeed."

"Powhatan," Gordon gritted, unable to even imagine how or *why* the man was here. "Get the hell away, you fool! You haven't a chance! He's an augment!"

Phil Bokuto had been one of the best fighters Gordon had ever known. If *he* had barely managed to ambush the lesser of these devils, and had died in the process, what chance did this old man have?

Powhatan listened to Gordon's revelation and frowned.

"So? You mean from those experiments in the early nineties? I had thought they were all normalized or killed off by the time the Slavic-Turkic War broke out. Fascinating. This does explain a lot about the last two decades."

"You'd heard of us then," Macklin grinned.

Powhatan nodded somberly. "I had heard, before the war. I also know why that particular experiment was discontinued—mostly because the worst kinds of men had been recruited as subjects."

"So said the weak," Macklin agreed. "For they made the error of accepting volunteers from among the strong."

Powhatan shook his head. For all the world it seemed as if he were engaged in a polite argument over semantics. Only his heavy breathing seemed to give away any sign of emotion.

"They accepted *warriors* . . ." he emphasized, ". . . that divinely mad type that's so valuable when needed, and such a problem when it's not. The lesson was learned hard, back in the nineties. They had a lot of trouble with augments who came home still loving war."

"*Trouble* is the word," Macklin laughed. "Let me introduce you to Trouble, Powhatan." He threw Gordon aside as if on an afterthought, and sheathed his knife before stepping toward his longtime foe.

Splashing into a ditch for the second time, Gordon could only lie in the muck and groan. His entire left side felt torn and burning—as if it were loaded with glowing coals. Consciousness flickered, and remained only because he absolutely refused to let go of it. When, at last, he was able to look up again through a pain-squinted tunnel, he saw the other two men circling each other just inside the lamp's small oasis of light.

Of course Macklin was just toying with his adversary. Powhatan was impressive, for a man his age, but the monstrous things that bulged from Macklin's neck, arms, and thighs made a normal man's muscles look pathetic by comparison. Gordon remembered Macklin's fireplace poker, tearing apart like shredding taffy.

George Powhatan inhaled in hard, shuddering gasps, and his face was flushed. In spite of the hopelessness of the situation, though, a deep part of Gordon was surprised to see such blatant signs of fear on the Squire's face.

All legends must be based on lies, Gordon realized. *We exaggerate, and even come to believe the tales, after a while.*

Only in Powhatan's voice did there seem to be a remnant of calm. In fact, he almost sounded detached. "There's

298

something I think you should consider, General," he said between rapid breaths.

"Later," Macklin growled. "Later we can discuss stock-raising and brewing, Squire. Right now I'm going to teach you a more practical art."

Quick as a cat, Macklin lashed out. Powhatan leaped aside, barely in time. But Gordon felt a thrill as the taller man then whirled back with a kick that Macklin dodged only by inches.

Gordon began to hope. Perhaps Powhatan was a natural, whose speed—even in middle age—might almost equal Macklin's. If so—and with that longer reach of his—he just might be able to keep out of his enemy's terrible grasp. . . .

The augment lunged again, getting a tearing grip on his opponent's shirt. This time Powhatan escaped even more narrowly, shrugging out of the embroidered garment and dodging a flurry of blows any one of which might have killed a steer. He did nearly land a savage chop to Macklin's kidneys as the smaller man rushed by. But then, in a blur, the Holnist swiveled and caught Powhatan's passing wrist!

Daring fate, Powhatan stepped *inside* and managed to break free with a reverse.

But Macklin seemed to have expected the maneuver. The General rolled past his opponent, and when Powhatan whirled to follow, he grabbed quickly and seized the taller man's other arm. Macklin grinned as Powhatan tried to slip out again, this time to no avail.

At arm's length, the Camas Valley man pulled back and panted. In spite of the chill rain he seemed overheated.

That's it, Gordon thought, disappointed. In spite of his past differences with Powhatan, Gordon tried to think of anything he could do to help. He looked around for something to throw at the monster augment, perhaps distracting Macklin long enough for the other man to get away.

But there was only mud, and a few soggy twigs. Gordon himself hardly had the strength even to crawl away from where he had been tossed. He could only lie there and watch the end, awaiting his own turn.

"Now," Macklin told his new captive. "Now say what you have to say. But you better make it amusing. As I smile, you live."

Powhatan grimaced as he tugged, testing Macklin's iron-jawed grip. Even after a full minute he had not stopped breathing deeply. Now the expression on his face seemed distant, as if completely resigned. His voice was oddly rhythmic when he answered at last.

"I didn't want this. I *told* them I couldn't . . . too old . . . luck run out. . . ." He inhaled deeply, and sighed. "I begged them not to make me. And now, to end it here . . . ?" The gray eyes flickered. "But it *never* ends . . . except death."

He's broken, Gordon thought. *The man's cracked.* He did not want to witness this humiliation. *And I left Dena to seek this famous hero. . . .*

"You're not amusing me, Squire," Macklin said, coldly. "Don't bore me, not if you value your remaining moments."

But Powhatan seemed distracted, as if he were actually thinking about something *else*, concentrating on remembering something, perhaps, and maintaining conversation out of courtesy alone.

"I only . . . thought you ought to know that things changed a bit . . . after you left the program."

Macklin shook his head, his eyebrows knotting. "What the hell are you talking about?"

Powhatan blinked. A shiver ran up and down his body, making Macklin smile.

"I mean that . . . that they weren't about to give up on anything so promising as augmentation . . . not just because there were flaws the first time."

Macklin growled. "They were too *scared* to continue. Too scared of *us!*"

Powhatan's eyelids fluttered. He was still inhaling hard, in great, silent breaths.

Gordon stared. Something was *happening* to the man. Perspiration glistened in oily speckles all across his shoulders and chest before being washed away in the scattered, heavy rain. His muscles twitched as if in the throes of cramps.

Gordon wondered. Was the man falling apart before his eyes?

Powhatan's voice sounded remote, almost bemused. ". . . newer implants weren't as large or as powerful . . . meant more to *supplement* training in certain eastern arts . . . in biofeedback. . . ."

Macklin's head rocked back and he laughed out loud. "*Neohippy augments?* Oh! *Good*, Powhatan. Good bluff! That is rich!"

Powhatan didn't seem to be listening, though. He was concentrating, his lips moving as if reciting something long ago memorized.

Gordon stared, blinked away raindrops, and stared harder. Faint *lines* seemed to be radiating out along Powhatan's arms and shoulders, crisscrossing his neck and chest. The man's shivering had heightened to a steady rhythm that now seemed less chaotic than . . . *purposeful.*

"The process also takes a lot of air," George Powhatan said mildly, conversationally. Still inhaling deeply, he began to straighten up.

By now Macklin had stopped laughing. The Holnist stared in frank disbelief.

Powhatan talked on, conversationally. "We are prisoners in similar cages . . . although you seem to relish yours. . . . Alike, we're both trapped by the last arrogance of arrogant days. . . ."

"*You aren't* . . ."

"Come now, General," Powhatan smiled without malice at his captor. "Don't look so surprised. . . . Surely you didn't believe you and your generation were the last?"

Macklin must have instantly reached the same conclusion as Gordon—understanding that George Powhatan was talking only in order to buy time.

"Macklin!" Gordon shouted. But the Holnist wasn't distracted. In a blur his long, machetelike knife was out, glittering wetly in the lamplight before slashing down toward Powhatan's immobilized right hand.

Still bent and unready, Powhatan reacted in a twisting blur. The blow that landed tore only a glancing streak along his arm as he caught Macklin's wrist in his free hand.

The Holnist cried out as they strained together, the General's greater strength pushing the dripping blade closer, closer.

With a sudden step and hip movement, Powhatan fell backward, flicking Macklin overhead. The General landed on his feet, still holding on, and wrenched hard, in turn. Whirling like two arms of a pinwheel, they threw each other, gaining momentum until they disappeared into the blackness beyond the ring of light. There was a crash. Then another. To Gordon it sounded like elephants trampling the undergrowth.

Wincing at the pain of mere movement, he crawled out of the light far enough for his eyes to begin adapting to the darkness, and pulled up under a rain-drenched red cedar. He peered in the direction they had gone, but was unable to do anything more than follow the fight by its tumult, and the skittering of tiny forest creatures fleeing the path of destruction.

When two wrestling forms spilled out into the clearing again, their clothes were in tatters. Their bodies ran red rivulets from scores of cuts and scratches. The knife was gone, but even weaponless the two warriors were fearsome. In their path no brambles, no mere saplings endured. A zone of devastation followed them wherever the battle went.

There was no ritual, no elegance to this combat. The smaller, more powerful figure closed with ferocity and tried to grapple with his enemy. The taller one fought to maintain a distance, and lashed out with blows that seemed to split the air.

Don't exaggerate, Gordon told himself. *They're only men, and old men, at that.*

And yet a part of Gordon felt kinship with those ancient peoples who believed in giants—in manlike gods—whose battles boiled seas and pushed up mountain ranges. As the combatants disappeared again into the darkness, Gordon experienced a wave of the sort of abstract wondering that had always cropped up in his mind when he least expected it. Detached, he thought about how augmentation, like so many other newly discovered powers, had seen its first use in war. But that had *always* been the way, before other uses were found . . . with chemistry, aircraft, spaceflight. . . . Later, though, came the *real* uses.

What would have happened, had the Doomwar not come . . . had this technology mixed with the worldwide ideals of the New Renaissance, and been harnessed by *all* its citizens?

What might mankind have been capable of? *What, if anything, would have been out of reach?*

Gordon leaned on the rough trunk of the cedar and managed to hobble to his feet. He wavered unsteadily for a moment, then put one foot in front of the other—limping step by step in the direction of the crashing sounds. There was no thought of running away, only of *witnessing* the last great miracle of Twentieth-Century science play itself out under pelting rain and lightning in a dark age forest.

The lantern laid stark shadows through the crushed brambles, but soon he was beyond its reach. Gordon followed the noises until, suddenly, it all stopped. There were no more shouts, no more heavy concussions, only the rumbling of the thunderheads and the roar of the river.

Eyes adapted to the darkness. Shading them from the rain, he finally saw—outlined against the gray clouds—two stark, reddish shapes standing atop a prominence overlooking the river. One crouched, squat and bull-necked, like the legendary Minotaur. The other was shaped more like a man, but with long hair that whipped like tattered banners in the wind. Completely naked now, the two augments faced each other, rocking as they panted under the growling storm.

Then, as if at a signal, they came together for the last time.

Thunder rolled. A blinding staircase of lightning struck the mountain on the opposite river bank, whipping the forest branches with its bellow.

In that instant, Gordon saw a figure silhouetted against

the jagged electric ladder, arms outstretched to hold another struggling shape overhead. The blinding brightness lasted just long enough for Gordon to see the standing shadow tense, flex, and cast the other into the air. The black shape rose for a full second before the electric brilliance vanished and darkness folded in again.

The afterimage felt seared. Gordon knew that that tumbling figure had to come down again—to the canyon and jagged, icy torrent far below. But in his imagination he saw the shadow continue upward, as if cast from the Earth.

Great sheets of rain blew southward down the narrow defile. Gordon felt his way back to the trunk of a fallen tree and sat down heavily. There he simply waited, unable even to contemplate moving, his memories churning like a turgid, silt-swirled river.

At last, there was a crackle of snapping twigs to his left. A naked form slowly emerged from the darkness, walking wearily toward him.

"Dena said there were only two types of males who counted," Gordon commented. "It always seemed a crackpot idea to me. But I never realized the *government* thought that way too, before the end."

The man slumped onto the torn bark beside him. Under his skin a thousand little pulsing threads surged and throbbed. Blood trickled from hundreds of scratches all over his body. He breathed heavily, staring at nothing at all.

"They reversed their policy, didn't they?" Gordon asked. "In the end, they rediscovered wisdom."

He knew George Powhatan had heard him, and had understood. But still there was no reply.

Gordon fumed. He needed an *answer*. For some reason, deep within, he had to know if the United States had been ruled, in those last years before the Calamity, by men and women of honor.

"Tell me, George! You said they abandoned using the warrior type. Who else *was* there, then? Did they select for the opposite? For an *aversion* to power? For men who would fight well, but reluctantly?"

An image: of a puzzled Johnny Stevens—ever eager to learn—earnestly trying to understand the enigma of a great leader who spurns a golden crown in favor of a plow. He had never really explained it to the boy. And now it was too late.

"Well? Did they revive the old ideal? Did they purposely seek out soldiers who saw themselves as citizens first?"

He grabbed Powhatan's throbbing shoulders. "Damn you! Why didn't you *tell* me, when I'd come all that way from Corvallis to plead with you! Don't you think *I*, of all people, would have understood?"

The Squire of Camas Valley looked sunken. He met Gordon's eyes very briefly, then looked away again, shuddering.

"Oh, you *bet* I'd have understood, Powhatan. I knew what you meant, when you said that the Big Things are insatiable." Gordon's fists clenched. "The Big Things will take everything you love away from you, and still demand more. You know it, I know it . . . that poor slob Cincinnatus knew it, when he told them they could *keep* their stupid crown!

"But your mistake was thinking it can *ever* end, Powhatan!" Gordon hobbled to his feet. He shouted his anger at the man. "*Did you honestly think your responsibility was ever finished?*"

When Powhatan spoke at last, Gordon had to bend to hear him over the rolling thunder.

"I'd hoped . . . I was so sure I could—"

"So sure you could say *no* to all the big lies!" Gordon laughed sarcastically, bitterly. "Sure you could say no to *honor*, and *dignity*, and *country*?

"What made you change your mind, then?

"You laughed off Cyclops, and the promise of technology. Not God, nor pity, nor the 'Restored United States' would move you! So tell me, Powhatan, what power was finally great enough to make you follow Phil Bokuto down here and look for me?"

Sitting with clutched hands, the most powerful man

alive—sole relic of an age of near-gods—seemed to draw into himself like a small boy, exhausted, ashamed.

"You're right," he groaned. "It never ends. I've done my share, a thousand times over I have! . . . All I wanted was to be left to grow old in peace. Is that too much to ask? Is it?"

His eyes were bleak. "But it never, ever ends."

Powhatan looked up, then, meeting and holding Gordon's stare for the first time.

"It was the women," he said softly, answering Gordon's question at last. "Ever since your visit and those damned letters, they kept *talking*, asking questions.

"Then the story of that madness up north arrived, even in my valley. I tried . . . tried to tell them it was just craziness, what your Amazons did, but they—"

Powhatan's voice caught. He shook his head. "Bokuto stormed out, to come down here all alone . . . and when that happened they kept *looking* at me. . . . They kept after me and after me and *after* me. . . ."

He moaned and covered his face with his hands.

"Sweet God in Heaven, forgive me. The *women* made me do it."

Gordon blinked in amazement. Amidst the pelting raindrops, tears flowed down the last augment's craggy, care-worn face. George Powhatan shuddered and sobbed achingly aloud.

Gordon slumped down to the rough log next to him, a heaviness filling him like the nearby Coquille, swollen from winter's snows. In another minute, his own lips were trembling.

Lightning flashed. The nearby river roared. And they wept together under the rain—mourning as men can only mourn themselves.

INTERLUDE

Fierce Winter lingers

    Until Ocean does her duty

        Chasing him—with Spring

IV
NEITHER CHAOS

1

A new legend swept Oregon, from Roseburg all the way north to the Columbia, from the mountains to the sea. It traveled by letter and by word of mouth, growing with each telling.

It was a sadder story than the two that had come before it—those speaking of a wise, benevolent machine and of a reborn nation. It was more disturbing than those. And yet this new fable had one important element its predecessors lacked.

It was true.

The story told of a band of forty women—crazy women, many contended—who had shared among themselves a secret vow: to do anything and everything to end a terrible war, and end it before all the good men died trying to save them.

They acted out of love, some explained. Others said that they did it for their country.

There was even a rumor that the women had looked on their odyssey to Hell as a form of *penance*, in order to make up for some past failing of womankind.

Interpretations varied, but the overall moral was always the same, whether spread by word of mouth or by U.S. Mail. From hamlet to village to farmstead, mothers and daughters and wives read the letters and listened to the words—and passed them on.

· · ·

Men can be brilliant and strong, they whispered to one another. But men can be mad, as well. And the mad ones can ruin the world.

Women, you must judge them. . . .

Never again can things be allowed to reach this pass, they said to one another as they thought of the sacrifice the Scouts had made.

Never again can we let the age-old fight go on between good and bad men alone.

Women, you must share responsibility . . . and bring your own talents into the struggle. . . .

And always remember, the moral concluded: Even the best men—the heroes—will sometimes neglect to do their jobs.

Women, you must remind them, from time to time. . . .

2

April 28, 2012

Dear Mrs. Thompson,

Thank you for your letters. They helped immeasurably during my recovery—especially since I had been so worried that the enemy might have reached Pine View. Learning that you and Abby and Michael were all right was worth more to me than you might ever know.

Speaking of Abby, please tell her that I saw Michael yesterday! He arrived, hale and well, along with the other five volunteers Pine View sent to help in the war. Like so many of our recruits, it seemed he just couldn't wait to get into the fighting.

I hope I didn't dampen his spirits too much when I told him of some of my firsthand experiences with Holnists. I do think, though, that now he'll be more attentive to his training, and maybe a bit less eager to win the war single-handedly. After all, we want Abby and little Caroline to see him again.

I'm glad you were able to take in Marcie and Heather. We all owe those two a debt. Corvallis would have been a shock. Pine View should offer a kinder readjustment.

Tell Abby I gave her letter to some old professors

who have been talking about starting up classes
again. There just may be a university of sorts here, in
a year or so—assuming the war goes well.

Of course the latter's not absolutely assured.
Things have turned around, but we have a long, long
way to go against a terrible enemy.

Your last question is a troubling one, Mrs.
Thompson, and I don't even know if I can answer. It
doesn't surprise me that the story of the Scouts'
Sacrifice reached you, up there in the mountains.
But you should know that even down here we aren't
exactly clear about the details, yet.

All I can really tell you now is, yes, I knew Dena
Spurgen well. And no, I don't think I understood her
at all. I honestly wonder if I ever will.

Gordon sat on a bench just outside the Corvallis Post
Office. He rested his back against the rough wall, catching
the rays of the morning sun, and thought about things he
could not write of in his letter to Mrs. Thompson . . . things
for which he could not find words.

Until they had recaptured the villages of Chesire and
Franklin, all the people of the Willamette had to go on were
rumors, for not one of the Scouts had ever come home
again from that unauthorized, midwinter foray. After the
first counterattacks, though, newly released slaves began re-
lating parts of the story. Slowly, the pieces fell together.

One winter day—in fact only two days after Gordon
had left Corvallis on his long trek south—the women Scouts
started deserting from their army of farmers and townsmen.
A few at a time, they slipped away south and west, and gave
themselves up, unarmed, to the enemy.

A few were killed on the spot. Others were raped and
tortured by laughing madmen who would not even hear
their carefully rehearsed declarations.

Most, though, were taken in—as they had hoped—
welcomed by the Holnists' insatiable appetite for women.

Those who could pass it off believably explained that

they were sick of living as farmers' wives, and wanted the touch of "real men." It was a tale the followers of Nathan Holn were disposed to accept, or so those who had dreamed up the plan imagined.

What followed must have been hard, perhaps beyond imagining. For the women had to pretend, and pretend believably, until the scheduled red night of knives—the night when they were supposed to save the frail remnant of civilization from the monsters who were bringing it down.

What exactly went wrong wasn't yet clear, as the spring counteroffensive pushed through the first recaptured towns. Perhaps an invader grew suspicious and tortured some poor girl until she talked. Or maybe one of the women fell in love with her fierce barbarian, and spilled her heart in a betraying confession. Dena was correct that history told of such things occurring. It might have happened here.

Or perhaps some simply could not lie well enough, or hide the shivers when their new lords touched them.

Whatever went wrong, the scheduled night was red, indeed. Where the warning did not arrive in time, women stole kitchen knives, that midnight, and slipped from room to room, killing and killing again until they themselves went down struggling.

Elsewhere, they merely went down, cursing and spitting into their enemies' eyes to the last.

Of course it was a failure. Anyone could have predicted it. Even where the plan "succeeded," too few of the invaders died to make any real difference. The women soldiers' sacrifice accomplished nothing at all in any military sense.

The gesture was a tragic fiasco.

Word spread though, across the lines and up the valleys. Men listened, dumbfounded, and shook their heads in disbelief. Women heard also, and spoke together urgently, privately. They argued, frowned, and thought.

Eventually, word arrived even far to the south. By now a legend, the story came at last to Sugarloaf Mountain.

And *there*, high above the confluence of the roaring Coquille, the Scouts finally won their victory.

315

• • •

All I can tell you is that I hope this thing doesn't turn into a dogma, a religion. In my worst dreams I see women taking up a tradition of drowning their sons, if they show signs of becoming bullies. I envision them *doing their duty,* by passing on life and death before a male child becomes a threat to all around him.

Maybe a fraction of us males *are* "too mad to be allowed to live." But taken to the extreme, this "solution" is something that terrifies me . . . as an ideology, it is something my mind cannot even grasp.

Of course, it'll probably sort itself out. Women are too sensible to take this to extremes. That, perhaps, is in the end where our hope lies.

And now it's time to mail this letter. I will try to write to you and Abby again from Coos Bay. Until then, I remain your devoted—

Gordon

"Courier!"

Gordon hailed a passing youth, wearing the blue denim and leather of a postman. The young man hurried over and saluted. Gordon held out the envelope. "Would you drop this onto the regular eastbound sort stack for me?"

"Yessir. Right away, sir!"

"No rush," Gordon smiled. "It's just a personal—"

But the young man had already taken off at a dead run. Gordon sighed. The old days of close camaraderie, of knowing every person in the "postal service" were over. He was too high above these young couriers to share a lazy grin and perhaps a minute's gossip.

Yes, it's definitely time.

He stood up, and only winced slightly as he hefted his saddlebags.

"So you're goin' to skip the hoedown, after all?"

He turned. Eric Stevens stood at the post office's side door, chewing on a blade of grass and regarding Gordon with folded arms.

Gordon shrugged. "It seems best just to go. I don't want a party in my honor. All that fuss is just a waste of time."

Stevens nodded, agreeing. His calm strength had been a blessing during Gordon's recuperation—especially his derisive dismissal of any suggestion by Gordon that he was to blame for Johnny's death. To Eric, his grandson had died as well as any man could hope to. The counteroffensive had been proof enough for him, and Gordon had decided not to argue about it.

The old man shaded his eyes and looked out across the nearby garden plots toward the south end of Highway 99.

"More southerners ridin' in."

Gordon turned and saw a column of mounted men riding slowly by on their way north, toward the main encampment.

"Sheesh," Stevens snickered, "look at their eyes pop. You'd think they'd never seen a city before."

Indeed, the tough, bearded men of Sutherlin and Roseburg, of Camas and Coos Bay, rode into town blinking in obvious amazement at strange sights—at windmill generators and humming electric lines, at busy machine shops, and at scores of clean, noisy children playing in the schoolyards.

Calling this a city may be stretching things, Gordon noted. But Eric had a point.

Old Glory flapped over a busy central post office. At intervals, uniformed couriers leaped onto ponies and sped off north, east, and south, saddlebags bulging.

From the House of Cyclops poured forth rich music from another time, and nearby a small, patchy-colored blimp bobbed within its scaffolding while white-coated workers argued in the ancient, arcane tongue of engineering.

On one flank of the tiny airship was painted an eagle, rising from a pyre. The other side bore the crest of the sovereign State of Oregon.

Finally, at the training grounds themselves, the newcomers would encounter small groups of clear-eyed *women*

317

soldiers—volunteers from up and down the valley—who were there to do a job, the same as everybody else.

It was all quite a lot for the gruff southerners to absorb at once. Gordon smiled as he watched the rough, bearded fighters gawk and slowly remember the way things once had been. The reinforcements arrived thinking of themselves as saviors of an effete, decadent north. But they would go home changed.

"So long, Gordon," Eric Stevens said, concisely. Unlike some of the others, he had the good taste to know that good-byes should be brief. "Godspeed, and come back someday."

"I will," Gordon nodded. "If I can. So long, Eric." He shouldered the saddlebag and started walking toward the stables, leaving the bustle of the post office behind him.

The old athletic fields were a sea of tents as he passed by. Horses whinnied and men marched. Across the grounds, Gordon saw the unmistakable figure of George Powhatan, introducing his new officers to old comrades in arms, reorganizing the frail Willamette Army into the new Defense League of the Oregon Commonwealth.

Briefly, as Gordon walked by, the tall, silver-haired man looked up and met his eyes. Gordon nodded, saying good-bye without words.

He had won after all—had brought the Squire down off his mountain—even though the price of that victory would go with both of them all of their lives.

Powhatan offered up a faint smile in return. They both knew, by now, what a man does with burdens such as those.

He carries them, Gordon thought.

Perhaps some day the two of them might sit together again—in that peaceful mountain lodge, with children's art hanging on the walls—and talk about horsebreeding and the subtle art of brewing beer. But that time would only come after the Big Things finally let them both go. Neither man planned to hold his breath until then.

Powhatan had his war to fight. And Gordon had quite another job to do.

He touched the bill of his postman's cap and turned to walk on.

318

He had stunned them all, yesterday, when he resigned from the Defense Council. "My obligations are to the nation, not to one small corner of it," he had told them, allowing them to go on believing things which were not lies at heart.

"Now that Oregon is safe," he had said, "I must continue with my main job. There are other places to be brought into the postal network, people elsewhere too long cut off from their countrymen.

"You can carry on just fine without me."

All their protests had been to no avail. For it was *true*. He had given all he had to give here. He would be more useful now elsewhere. Anyway, he couldn't stay any longer. In this valley everything would perpetually remind him of the harm that he had accomplished in doing good.

Gordon had decided to slip out of town today, instead of attending the party in his honor. He was recovered enough to travel, as long as he took it easy, and he had said good-bye to those who were left—to Peter Aage and to Dr. Lazarensky—and to the shell of that poor, dead machine whose ghost he no longer feared.

The remuda handler brought out the young mare Gordon had chosen for this leg of his journey. Still deep in thought, he adjusted the saddlebags containing his gear and five pounds of mail—letters addressed, for the first time, to destinations outside of Oregon.

On one point he left in complete confidence. The war was won, though there certainly were brutal months and years ahead. Part of his present mission was to seek new allies, new ways of shortening the end. But that end was now inevitable.

He had no fear of George Powhatan ever becoming a tyrant after victory was complete. When every Holnist had been hanged, the people of Oregon would be told in no uncertain terms to manage their own affairs, or be damned. Gordon wished he could be here to watch the thunder, if anyone ever offered Powhatan a crown.

The Servants of Cyclops would go on spreading their own myth, encouraging a rebirth of technology. Gordon's

DAVID BRIN

appointed postmasters would continue lying without knowing it, using the tale of a restored nation to bind the land
together, until the fable wasn't needed anymore.

Or until, by believing it, people made it come true.

And, yes, women would go on talking over what had
happened here, this winter. They would pore over the notes
Dena Spurgen had left behind, read the same old books the
Scouts had read, and argue over the merits of judging men.

Gordon had decided that it hardly mattered now
whether Dena really had been mentally unbalanced. The
lasting effects would not be known during his lifetime. And
even he hadn't the influence, or the desire, to interfere with
the spreading legend.

Three myths . . . and George Powhatan. Among them,
the people of Oregon were in good hands. The rest they
could probably manage for themselves.

His spirited mount snorted as Gordon swung into the
saddle. He patted and soothed the mare until she was calm,
trembling with eagerness to be off. Gordon's escort already
waited out at the edge of town, ready to see him safely to
Coos Bay and the boat that would take him the rest of the
way.

To California . . . he thought.

He remembered the bear flag patch, and the silent,
dying soldier who had told him so much without ever saying
a word. He owed that man something. And Phil Bokuto.
And Johnny, who had wanted so to go south and see for
himself.

And Dena . . . how I wish you could have come along.

He would find out for them. They were all with him
now.

Silent California, he wondered, *what have you been up
to, all these* years?

He wheeled his mount around and headed down the
south road, behind him all the clattering and shouting of an
army of free men and women, certain of victory—soldiers
who would return gladly to their farms and villages when
the distasteful chore was done at last.

Their clamor was loud, irreverent, determined, impatient.

Gordon rode past an open window blaring recorded music. Someone was being lavish with electricity today. Who knew? Maybe the raucous extravagance was even in his honor.

His head lifted, and even the horse's ears flicked up. It was an old Beach Boys tune, he recognized at last, one he hadn't heard in twenty years . . . a melody of innocence, unflaggingly optimistic.

I'll bet they have electricity in California too, Gordon hoped.

And maybe . . .

Spring was in the air. Men and women cheered as the little blimp rose, sputtering, into the sky.

Gordon nudged with his heels and the mare sped to a canter. Once out of town, he did not look back.

ACKNOWLEDGMENTS

The author would like to express his appreciation to those who gave so generously of their time and wisdom during the evolution of this book.

Dean Ing, Diane and John Brizzolara, Astrid Anderson, Greg Bear, Mark Grygier, Douglas Bolger, Kathleen Retz, Conrad Halling, Pattie Harper, Don Coleman, Sarah Barter, and Dr. James Arnold all contributed helpful comments.

Especially, I would like to thank Anita Everson, Daniel J. Brin, Kristie McCue, and Professor John Lewis, for their important insights.

Appreciation to Lou Aronica and Bantam Books, for excellent support and understanding, and to Shawna McCarthy of Davis Publications, for more of the same.

And finally, my thanks to those women I've known who have never ceased to startle me, just when I've grown complacent and need most to be startled, and who make me stop and think.

There is power there, slumbering below the surface. And there is magic.

David Brin
April 1985

THE UPLIFT WAR

BY DAVID BRIN

David Brin's epic *Startide Rising* swept the Nebula, Hugo and Locus Awards. Now this master storyteller returns us to this extraordinary, wonder-filled world. Drawing on the startling events of *Startide*, he tells a tale of courage, survival and discovery.

As galactic armadas clash in quest of the ancient fleet of the Progenitors, a brutal alien race seizes the dying planet of Garth. The various Uplifted inhabitants of Garth must battle their overlords or face ultimate extinction. At stake is the existence of Terran society and Earth, and the fate of the entire Five Galaxies. Sweeping, brilliantly crafted, inventive and dramatic, *The Uplift War* is an unforgettable story of adventure and wonder from the pen of one of today's science fiction greats.

0 553 17452 5

THE RIVER OF TIME

BY DAVID BRIN

The River of Time brings together eleven of David Brin's finest shorter works, including 'The Crystal Spheres,' winner of the Hugo Award for Best Novella, and four new stories published here for the first time, each with an afterword by the author.

Here are powerful tales of heroism and humanity, playful excursions into realms of fancy, and profound meditations on time, memory, and our place in the universe, by one of the most heralded new writers of our age.

Acclaimed author of *Sundiver*, *The Practice Effect*, *The Postman* and the Hugo and Nebula Award-winning *Startide Rising*, David Brin is one of science fiction's brightest talents.

0 553 17398 7

A SELECTION OF SCIENCE FICTION AND FANTASY TITLES AVAILABLE FROM BANTAM BOOKS

THE PRICES SHOWN BELOW WERE CORRECT AT THE TIME OF GOING TO PRESS. HOWEVER TRANSWORLD PUBLISHERS RESERVE THE RIGHT TO SHOW NEW RETAIL PRICES ON COVERS WHICH MAY DIFFER FROM THOSE PREVIOUSLY ADVERTISED IN THE TEXT OR ELSEWHERE.

☐	17184 4	The Practice Effect	David Brin	£1.95
☐	17398 7	River of Time	David Brin	£2.50
☐	17170 4	Startide Rising	David Brin	£3.50
☐	17162 3	Sundiver	David Brin	£2.95
☐	17452 5	Uplift War	David Brin	£3.99
☐	17247 6	The Hound of Culain	Kenneth C. Flint	£2.75
☐	17588 2	The Dark Druid	Kenneth C. Flint	£3.50
☐	17154 2	Damiano	R. A. MacAvoy	£2.99
☐	17155 0	Damiano's Lute	R. A. MacAvoy	£2.50
☐	17156 9	Raphael	R. A. MacAvoy	£1.95
☐	17559 9	The Grey Horse	R. A. MacAvoy	£2.95
☐	23205 3	Tea With The Black Dragon	R. A. MacAvoy	£1.95
☐	17385 5	Twisting The Rope	R. A. MacAvoy	£2.50
☐	17351 0	The Stainless Steel Rat Gets Drafted	Harry Harrison	£2.99
☐	17352 9	The Stainless Steel Rat's Revenge	Harry Harrison	£2.99
☐	17396 0	The Stainless Steel Rat Saves The World	Harry Harrison	£2.50
☐	17586 6	Forging the Darksword	Margaret Weiss & Tracy Hickman	£3.50
☐	17535 1	Doom of the Darksword	Margaret Weiss & Tracy Hickman	£3.50

All Corgi/Bantam Books are available at your bookshop or newsagent, or can be ordered from the following address:
Corgi/Bantam Books,
Cash Sales Department,
P.O. Box 11, Falmouth, Cornwall TR10 9EN

Please send a cheque or postal order (no currency) and allow 60p for postage and packing for the first book plus 25p for the second book and 15p for each additional book ordered up to a maximum charge of £1.90 in UK.

B.F.P.O. customers please allow 60p for the first book, 25p for the second book plus 15p per copy for the next 7 books, thereafter 9p per book.

Overseas customers, including Eire, please allow £1.25 for postage and packing for the first book, 75p for the second book, and 28p for each subsequent title ordered.

NAME (Block Letters) ....

ADDRESS ....

....